Rabiah

Book 2

POWER

Lisa Lagaly

LL Publishing

Published in the United States of America

First Printing, 2017

ISBN 9780998548227

LL Publishing
Lisa1.author@gmail.com

Dedicated to my wonderful family,

Especially my husband for being so supportive,

and to the Lord,

Who has given us so much.

Pronunciation guide

Symbol	Sound	Symbol	Sound
ă	a in cat	ĭ	i in sit
ā	a in cape	ī	i in ice
ʌ	first a in away	ŏ	o in got
ą	a in car	ō	oa in goat
α	a in father	ő	oo in too
ě	e in get	ŭ	u in cup
ē	e in we	ū	u in mute
ə	e as in her		

Name	Pronunciation
Rabiah	rʌ - bī' - ʌ
Hadassah	hʌ - dă' - sʌ
Tahirah	tʌ - hē' - rʌ
Mame	mā' - mē
Tarja	tąr' - yʌ
Dacia	dā' - cēʌ
Ibirann	ĭb' - ər - ʌn
Ibirannian	ĭb' - ər - ʌn - nē - ăn
Niyaf	nē' - yăf
Kaawa	kʌ' - wʌ
Ice	īs
Yusri	ū' - srē
Chanthou	shăn' - tő
Lagaly	lʌ - gα' - lē

Prologue

"Your cousin has found her mate," the old woman said as she stirred a pot next to the fire. The flames flickered as the wind howled outside.

"Shall I go now?" asked a tall, slim young woman with straight, mostly white hair that hung to her waist. She stood as if to leave immediately into the whirling snowstorm outside.

"No. Not yet. The coming winter will be long and hard. Even you would have trouble surviving."

"When then?"

"When the first flowers bloom."

The girl paced across the small room, "I won't have enough time."

Her grandmother looked at her in a manner that told her she had spoken foolishly. "You will make it."

"But my cousin hasn't been trained."

"She will learn. The Spirit will guide her. Besides, you must stay hidden."

"Why."

"The evil one must not know there are three of you. It will put her in even more danger."

"Three? Am I to take someone with me?"

"No. The spirited one will be there when it is time."

"Who is she?"

"You'll see."

"Why can't you just tell me?"

"Many things could happen before then. The future is not set in stone."

"But if there aren't three…"

"Then the battle may be lost, but that doesn't mean it shouldn't be fought. The Spirit knows what he is doing. We must follow his guidance and have faith."

The girl sighed and sat back down at the table where several open scrolls lay, "Yes, Grandmother."

Chapter 1

Rabiah woke late again. Tristan was already gone. She still felt weak and tired. Healer Marion had said it might take weeks for her to feel like herself again after losing so much blood. Blood loss was harder to heal than other injuries, Marion had explained. With other injuries such as a broken bone, you could pull bone from other bone and mend the break well enough that a person could walk on it. With blood, once it was lost, there was nowhere to pull it from. The blood healer had given her a potion to drink morning and night. It tasted of metal. It made her stomach ache too. She was not looking forward to drinking it again. Maybe she would just go back to sleep.

"Good morning, Your Highness."

Too late. The former queen's maid had seen that her eyes were open.

"Good morning Esmerelda." Rabiah pushed herself into a sitting position. Esmerelda rushed to place some pillows behind her.

"Drink your potion and this cup of water, then I'll serve you breakfast."

"Esmerelda, you don't have to serve me. I can get up."

"Are you sure? Healer Marion said you were to rest as much as you can."

"I'll still be resting while I'm sitting at the table."

"But there is a lot to do today." Esmerelda's voice hitched a little. "You should save your strength."

"All right, but I have to get up for a little anyway."

Esmerelda understood her need and stood by in case Rabiah needed help climbing out of the tall bed and walking to the washroom. She did not. She was, however, disturbingly happy to climb back into bed after the short trip. She drank the nasty potion and ate the food that Esmerelda sat on a tray in front of her. It was strange having a servant. Rabiah felt uncomfortable having Esmerelda wait on her.

"Esmerelda, how long did you serve Queen Naomi?"

"I was a gift to her from her father when she was married."

"A gift?"

"Yes. My parents were poor and I had many younger brothers and sisters. They sold me to Queen Naomi's father when I was twelve. I was trained to be a lady's maid. When the Queen married I went with her."

"So you are a slave?"

"Yes."

"Then I shall free you."

"Do you not like my service?"

"I think you are a wonderful maid, but no one should be a slave. My people don't have slaves."

"What do you do with your captives?"

"They join the Clan that captured them or they are traded back to their own Clans."

"I don't mind being a slave. I guess I'm one of the lucky ones. I have a nice place to live, beautiful clothes, and the work is not hard."

"But you are not free."

"Free to do what? Get married? Have ten children and worry about keeping them all clothed and fed? By selling me, my parents gave me a much better life than I would have had anywhere else."

"What if you were no longer a slave but still the queen's maid?"

"I'd probably ask for more time off," Esmerelda smiled.

"Tell me then, how do I free you?"

"You just have to have a blacksmith remove my bracelets." Esmerelda held up her wrists to show copper bands encircling each one. There were symbols etched along the bands.

"What do they say?" Rabiah asked.

"They say I am the property of the royal family of Arles."

"Let's go find a blacksmith then," Rabiah said, putting the now-empty tray to the side and throwing back her covers. "There's one here at the castle isn't there?"

Esmerelda shook her head and stepped forward to help Rabiah in case she needed it. "It can wait another day. We need to get you ready. Would you like a bath first?"

Rabiah had just had a bath two days ago and she'd been in bed since, but she still caught a whiff of fish occasionally when she turned her head. Also, she really liked warm baths.

"Yes, please," she said.

An hour later, Rabiah joined Tristan where he awaited her at the family entrance to the Great Hall. As had been happening lately, her stomach gave a little lurch when she saw him. He looked so handsome: tall and slim with wavy, light brown hair and gray-blue eyes, a determined jaw and beautiful lips. He gave her a little smile, but she could tell the events to come were weighing on him. She squeezed his hand.

'How are you feeling?' he sent.

'Stronger,' she replied.

'Good. Let's get this over with.'

They entered the Great Hall hand-in-hand. The room was packed with a mix of nobles, merchants, soldiers, and servants. The bodies of Tristan's parents were lying head-to-head on rectangular platforms in the center of the dais at the head of the room. Their crowns sat beside them. Tristan led Rabiah to stand behind the bodies. At Tristan's nod, six soldiers surrounded each body and reverently lifted the platforms. Owen, Tristan's cousin, best friend, advisor, and sometimes body-guard, was one of the King's bearers. The low rumble of voices ceased. A path materialized between the dais and the front entrance to the Great Hall as the pall bearers carried first Tristan's father, then his mother down the dais steps. Tristan and Rabiah followed. Tristan's eyes were dry but he held tightly onto Rabiah's hand. Rabiah heard several people sobbing in the crowd. She was having trouble keeping her own eyes dry.

9

The soldiers placed the bodies on a low cart that was painted a shiny black. They arranged themselves evenly down each side and behind the cart. Tristan led Rabiah to the a carriage waiting behind the cart.

"Are you riding?" Rabiah turned to ask Tristan.

"No."

"Then I won't either. I will stay with you."

Tristan squeezed her hand. "I knew you would say that. The walk is too long and it is too cold. Uncle will walk with me. I'll feel better knowing you are warm and resting in here."

She nodded. He helped her inside. Esmerelda and Marion were waiting for her.

"Sit here," the healer said, patting the cushioned seat beside her. As soon as Rabiah had obeyed, the healer threw a blanket over Rabiah's lap and tucked it in.

Rabiah glared at her, "I'm not an invalid."

"You pretty much are," the healer said, "at least for a few more days."

As the carriage followed the slow procession, Rabiah had to admit she was thankful for the blanket. She seemed much more sensitive to the cold than she usually was.

After about a half-hour, the slow procession stopped in front of a small but grand-looking building of white stone. It stood in prominence on a small hill above the other small buildings around it. Tristan helped Rabiah and the other women down and the carriage drove away. The soldiers placed the bodies before the entrance and waited for all the people to arrive. Rabiah noticed several men in long black robes standing in a row in front of the tomb.

Who are they? Rabiah asked Tristan.

'Priests of the Bull.'

'Your parents worshipped the Bull?'

'My mother did. The priests insisted on honoring her by performing the burial ceremony.'

One of the priests wore a larger black stone around his neck than the rest. It reminded Rabiah of the black walls of the temple. She shivered.

It seemed to take an extraordinary long time for all those attending to complete their trek up the hill to the burial grounds. Rabiah was dressed warmly in her new cape with a hood and two wool tunics, but she soon began to shiver. Tristan noticed and put his arm around her so that she was under his cloak too. Esmerelda stepped closer on the other side. A few snowflakes began to fall. Finally, the black-robed priest with the large stone stepped forward.

He began, "We are here today to celebrate the lives of King Stephen and his Queen, Naomi." His toneless voice droned on and on. Rabiah's mind wandered and she almost fell asleep on her feet. It was good Tristan was there to lean on. After the priest's long speech was finally over, several people stepped forward to talk about the lives of the King and Queen. Even Esmerelda took a turn praising her former mistress. Rabiah was surprised Esmerelda was allowed to speak since she was a slave, but she had been with Queen Naomi a long time. As she listened, Rabiah began to see the Queen, who had not seemed to like her much, in a new light. Tristan's mother had also come from a distant country and had to leave her family behind. She had worked to make sure all the children in the city, whether orphans or just poor, had a place to sleep and food to eat. Perhaps that was where Tristan had acquired his caring nature.

After everyone had finished talking, Tristan's uncle walked to his dead brother's side and said something Rabiah couldn't decipher over the body. He then picked up the crown by his brother's head and carried it to Tristan. Tristan knelt.

The General's eyes were moist as he raised the crown in the air. "I, General Ormond, brother of King Stephen of Arles do hereby crown you Tristan, son of King Stephen and Queen Naomi, King of Arles."

His hands trembled as he lowered the crown onto Tristan's head. Tristan did not immediately stand. He bowed his head for a few moments, then rubbed his hands over his face before standing. The General and his nephew shared a long hug. After they parted, the head priest stepped away from the wall of the mausoleum, removed the crown near Queen Naomi's head, and carried it to Tristan.

Tristan turned with a sad face to Rabiah, the crown held out in front of him.

"Rabiah, daughter of Chief Qadir of the Eagle Clan and my beloved wife, I crown you Queen of Arles."

He raised the crown above her head. The ring around Rabiah's neck pulsed with heat.

'Tristan, wait!' Rabiah held up her hand to stop him. An odd, disconnected feeling washed over her. The world telescoped to a single point then everything went dark. She crumpled.

Tristan saw Rabiah's face go pale but he did not have time to catch her. Marion managed to grab her and lowered her to the ground slowly. Panicked, Tristan was so focused on Rabiah he paid no attention to where he laid the royal crown as he dropped down beside her.

"She's alive. She just fainted," Marion said matter-of-factly. "Too long on her feet. Signal for the carriage and finish the ceremony. Esmerelda and I will care for her," Marion said.

"Are you sure she's all right?" Tristan asked.

Marion pulled a little bottle from her ever-present satchel. "I never go to a funeral without it," she said as she opened the little bottle and waved it under Rabiah's nose.

Tristan could smell the pungent odor from where he knelt. Rabiah got a good whiff, made a face, and turned her head to get away from the smell. She opened her eyes and blinked a few times.

"Are you all right?" Tristan asked, holding her cold hand.

"What happened?" Rabiah asked.

"You fainted," Marion said.

Rabiah frowned. "My ring got warm and I don't remember anything else."

"You didn't miss anything," Marion said.

"Your hands are like ice," Tristan said in concern. He closed his eyes and concentrated on sending her some of his own energy. He'd been practicing sending Rabiah energy some way other than kissing, although that was by far the most enjoyable way.

"Enough of that," Marion said after a few seconds. "You are going to need some for the rest of the day. I'll take care of her. Go. Do what you need to do so we can get out of the cold."

Tristan nodded and squeezed Rabiah's hand once more before standing. The people were muttering and moving about trying to see what had happened. Tristan put his hands out to calm them.

"The Queen is all right. She is still recovering from the events two nights past and has been too long on her feet. We will now lay King Stephen and Queen Naomi in their final resting places."

A few people looked relieved but others frowned and muttered. Tristan ignored them and signaled to the soldiers to carry the bodies into the tomb. The General and Tristan followed them. Rabiah remained sitting on the steps with Esmerelda propping her up from behind.

"He forgot to signal for the carriage," Marion said.

"No. I have already done it," Esmerelda replied.

Tristan and his uncle emerged from the tomb after a few minutes and posted themselves with some of the pall bearers next to the entrance to shake hands and receive condolences. The nobles had to pass Rabiah to enter the tomb. Many glanced curiously at her, then quickly looked away as if hoping not to get caught. She thought a few frowned at her but she wasn't sure.

"What happens next?" Rabiah asked.

"After all the nobles pay their respects, everyone else will be invited to enter. The soldiers will remain at their posts until everyone is done, then they will seal the coffins with stone lids and depart," Marion explained.

"I want to pay my last respects," Rabiah said.

Marion nodded, "As do I and Esmerelda, I'm sure. Here." she placed her hands on Rabiah's shoulders. Rabiah felt energy stream into her body and immediately felt stronger. "That should get you to the carriage at least."

"Thank you."

The women helped Rabiah up. The nobles in line made space for them to squeeze in right next to where Tristan stood.

Tristan took her hands.

"You feel warmer."

"Marion helped me."

Rabiah leaned her cheek against Tristan's shoulder for a second.

I love you,' she sent, simply.

He kissed her on the top of the head, *I love you too.*'

He released her hands and she took a step to greet Tristan's uncle.

"General, I'm sorry you lost your brother. I liked him very much."

"Call me Uncle, Rabiah. Thank you for saving his son."

The General's eyes were shiny with tears. On impulse, Rabiah did something she never imagined she'd do. She hugged him and he, surprisingly, hugged her back. Some of his tears fell on her shoulder. She imagined some of her inner light swirling around his depressed soul. Was this what Tristan felt when he was with her? No wonder the boy was so attached, the General thought as the love and caring she shared almost overwhelmed his fragile control. She was a witch, he thought, but after witnessing her selfless defense of Tristan against the demon, he didn't care what she was. He raised his head and planted a kiss somewhere near her ear, "Thank you, little Queen," he whispered, then let her go.

Esmerelda and Marion each held tightly onto one of Rabiah's arms as they descended into the Mausoleum. It seemed even chillier inside than out. Torches flickered in the built-in sconces around the room. Six soldiers stood at attention around the bodies. They had left room for people to stop at the foot of each body to say goodbye. Owen stood stony-faced on the right side of the King. Rabiah said a prayer over each of the bodies, a tear sliding down her nose and onto the kind King's foot. She nodded to Owen as she passed. He did not respond. Rabiah and Marion waited for Esmerelda to make a tearful final goodbye before they all climbed slowly up the steps again.

The carriage was waiting when they emerged. The driver helped the women up the high step, then quickly returned to his seat to get the carriage out of the way. Rabiah sat down and leaned on Marion's shoulder. She fell asleep almost as soon as she closed her eyes. The trip was much faster on the way back. Marion woke her as soon as they stopped and insisted she lay on a stretcher to be carried back up the stairs to her room. There, Marion tucked her into bed and had the servants build a huge fire in the fireplace. She also made her drink a large mug of hot water flavored with some herbs and then set a platter full of rich foods in front of her.

"I can't eat all this," Rabiah protested.

"Just do your best. There will be no more fainting."

"Yes, Marion." Rabiah bowed her head in acquiescence. It was nice to have a friend who cared so much.

Rabiah ate as much as she could, then fell asleep stuffed and finally warm.

It was starting to snow in earnest now. Although he had gloves on, Tristan's hands were freezing. He tried to focus on each person that stopped to say something but the image of Rabiah crumpling before him kept playing through his mind. The last of the nobles passed by. Most of the locals and non-nobles had viewed the bodies as they lay in state the previous day. It was so cold that many of them had left after the funeral ceremony was finished. Tristan and his uncle went down into the mausoleum one more time to watch as the soldiers put the stone lids on the caskets. As his parents' faces disappeared under the stones, the finality of their deaths hit him. Tristan stood silently as the soldiers passed, avoiding eye contact with Owen. His uncle turned to go as well, indicating the exit with his arm. Tristan shook his head. His uncle patted him on the shoulder and left, leaving Tristan alone. Tristan waited until his uncle was completely up the stairs before throwing himself across his father's coffin. Memories of riding on his father's foot and the first time his father had showed him how to shoot an arrow flooded his mind. A few tears fell on the cold stone. Wiping his cheek, Tristan moved over to his mother's coffin. He laid across the top of her stone to give her a last hug goodbye. She had been a good mother. He couldn't remember specific things, but perhaps that was because she was always there. The one thing he did remember clearly was viewing a pink, crumpled looking thing wrapped tightly in a small blanket. His mother, pale and with her hair uncharacteristically messed, had held

15

the pink thing proudly so he could see. The pink thing had opened its mouth and a loud wail had come out. Tristan had been shooed out of the room by his nanny. That had been a baby brother he knew now. He didn't remember much about him. His brother had been found dead in his crib just a week later.

"Goodbye Mother, Goodbye Father. Until we meet again." He patted his mother's coffin and departed, leaving the torches lit behind him.

His uncle was waiting with the carriage just outside the mausoleum. Tristan climbed in. He leaned back on the seat and closed his eyes. He missed his parents. He was lucky he still had Rabiah. He followed the link to his wife. Her light shone brightly.

Rabiah?

She didn't answer. She must be sleeping. Healer Marion wasn't there to stop him now. He sent some of his energy along their link. Instead of being absorbed as he'd thought it would be, it spiraled up and down around her light. A stream of light from her joined his, then flowed back to him. He felt a surge of peace and love as her light reached his body.

Hello Tristan.'

Did I wake you?'

Yes. It was a very nice way to wake up though.'

'How are you?'

Much better. Marion made me eat enough for a horse and had a huge fire built in the fireplace. It's very warm in here if you are cold.'

I am. We are in the carriage coming back. Everyone will be waiting to eat so I probably won't make it up there for a while.'

Here, then.' Tristan felt warmth seeping into him. His numb fingers began to tingle.

Not too much Rabiah. I don't want you to get cold again.'

I was too warm anyway.'

'Send me a little more to warm Uncle's hands then. Wait so I can grab them.'

The General had been watching Tristan's face. Based on the smile and the almost glow, he surmised Tristan was talking to Rabiah. He teased Tristan about it, but really, it was a beautiful thing to see

16

two people so connected. Tristan opened his eyes and caught him looking.

"Uncle, take off your gloves," Tristan demanded, sounding excited. "I want to try something." Tristan had already pulled off his own gloves.

"Why? They are frozen as it is."

"I know. Take them off and let me hold them."

"Tristan…"

Tristan would not be deterred. He lurched forward, grabbed his uncle's hands, and ripped off the gloves. His uncle's hands were ice-cold.

'All right Rabiah. Just enough to warm his hands. I'm holding them in mine.'

Rabiah sent heat. She'd never tried to focus it before, but she concentrated on just Tristan's hands.

'That's enough Rabiah. I don't want to burn him.'

Tristan's warm hands got even hotter. The General finally had to pull his away.

"Was that you or Rabiah?"

"Rabiah."

"She's feeling better then?"

"Yes, Marion has her roasting in bed."

"It's too bad she fainted right before you officially crowned her. I imagine there will be some who see that as a bad omen."

'Tristan, did it work?'

"Just a minute, Uncle."

General Ormond watched Tristan's face and waited impatiently for him to finish his conversation with Rabiah. He supposed he'd have to excuse Rabiah for rudely interrupting since she couldn't know Tristan had been in another conversation.

'Yes. It worked very well. Go back to sleep. We are almost at the castle. I'll come up when I can get away.'

'Should I come down?'

'Not right away. Rest a while longer.'

'All right.'

17

"Sorry Uncle. Rabiah wanted to know if your hands were warm."

"As I was saying, bad omen?"

"I guess I'll just have to do it tonight. I'll make sure she's sitting this time and I'll use Mother's other crown, the one Father had made for her. It's much lighter. Mother always said the other one gave her a headache."

"What did you do with the other crown after Rabiah fell?"

"I don't know. I forgot all about it. I think I set it down beside her. Do you know where it went?"

"No."

"Perhaps one of the soldiers or the priests picked it up."

"Let's hope so."

The carriage stopped right in front of the castle entrance. Tristan stepped down ahead of his Uncle. Together they walked inside the entrance, through the screening room and into the Great Hall. Somehow an extra table had been squeezed into the lower part of the room and the one on the dais had been returned to its normal place and made longer. Nobles, servants, soldiers, and everyone else associated with the castle were there to celebrate the lives of Tristan's parents. The former King and Queen's seats were left empty. Tristan sat where he always had, to the right of his father's chair. His uncle sat next to the Queen's chair. Tristan stood again. Everyone became quiet.

"Thank you all for coming. I know my parents would have been touched. I also know my father hated long speeches, so in his honor, let's begin our feast."

The cook had outdone herself again. She'd made every one of Tristan's favorites. Tristan couldn't enjoy any of it. The food lacked all taste. He was finished well before anyone else. Taking off the crown, he set it on the table as a placeholder to signify that he would be back. Then he stood and quietly slipped out the family entrance at the back of the dais. Finally free from watching eyes, Tristan ran up the stairs to his rooms. Rabiah was asleep in their large bed. Esmerelda was sitting near the window sewing.

"How is she?" Tristan asked Esmerelda.

18

"Just fine Your Highness. As soon as she got warm and ate a little food the color came back to her cheeks. Take a look."

Tristan walked over to the side of the bed where Rabiah lay with her hands tucked under the pillow beneath her cheek. She still looked pale around her eyes but her cheeks were nice and rosy, probably because it was so warm in the room. He turned to Esmerelda. "Do you know where my Mother kept her other crown, the one my Father had made for her?"

"Yes, Your Highness."

"Could you bring it here please? Quickly?"

"Yes, Your Highness."

Tristan turned back to Rabiah. "Time to wake up my Princess." He kissed her brow. She didn't stir. He kissed her nose. She gave a little smile.

"So you're going to play that game are you?"

He kissed her lips. The energy flowed freely from him as she began to respond. He felt himself getting weaker. Her eyes sprang open. They were a beautiful bright green. The energy flowed back into him as they returned to their normal silver-blue. He pulled away, smiling at her drowsy look.

"Hello my love."

"Hello my husband."

"Are you ready to be crowned Queen?"

"You're going to try again?"

"I can't let people leave thinking that there was some supernatural reason you were not crowned. If we do it now, they will hopefully dismiss what happened earlier as a consequence of your injury."

"I don't think it was due to my injury. Not completely."

"What do you mean?"

"When you put the crown near my head my ring heated. I don't know if I fainted on my own or the ring made me faint to protect me."

"Was it the crown or something else?"

"I don't know."

19

Esmerelda returned with an ornate wooden box. She held it as Tristan opened the lid. The inside of the box was lined with a soft red fabric and held a sturdy yet delicate gold crown decorated with several different precious stones. Tristan reverently lifted the crown with both hands and turned to Rabiah.

"Let's try it now and see what happens. Can you sit up?"

Rabiah did so, unaided by either of them.

"Rabiah of the Clan, I hearby crown you Queen of Arles."

Tristan held the crown over Rabiah's head and began to lower it slowly. Rabiah's ring started to heat.

"Wait. It's happening again."

"Do you feel faint?"

"No, the ring is heating."

"I don't understand." Tristan shook his head, disappointed. "How can it be any more dangerous for you to be Queen than whatever danger you are in now?"

"You think I am in danger?"

"You never know when you are royalty."

"Perhaps it's something on the crown," Rabiah suggested. "Hold it close to the ring and turn it and I'll see if it heats."

Tristan did as she asked. He had only turned the crown a quarter of a turn when the ring not only heated but jumped. A small black stone seemed to be the cause. As soon as she realized it was there, Rabiah identified the icky feeling she'd had since the crown came close as the same one she got when she was near the temple of the bull.

"Esmerelda, has this stone always been in the crown?"

"No. It was a gift from the temple priests. They said it would protect Queen Naomi from losing any more children. She never conceived again after we lost your brother so I don't know if it works."

"Did they give her one for the other crown too?" Tristan asked.

"The other crown doesn't have any stones."

"Do you know where it went?"

Esmerelda gave him a look that clearly said he should take better care of precious things that belonged to the kingdom but verbally said only, "Yes. After you sat it down, one of the guards picked it up. He sent it back with the carriage. I put it in your mother's room."

"Can you bring it here please?"

"Yes, Your Highness."

Esmerelda left to go back down the stairs. Tristan inspected the crown. "If I had something small and sharp I could probably pry the stone out."

"Is there something in Esmerelda's sewing basket you could use?" Rabiah asked.

Tristan went to look and came back with a small pair of scissors. He poked at the stone from the back. It popped out and skittered across the floor.

"Now let's try it."

He held the crown over her head. "I crown you, Rabiah of the Clan, Queen of Arles."

He slowly lowered the crown. The ring stayed cool. He set the crown firmly on Rabiah's head. She did not faint. Tristan let out the breath he had been holding.

"How do you feel?"

"Fine Tristan. Putting a crown on my head is not going to make me faint."

"So you say."

Rabiah took the crown off and looked at it.

"You can tell there's a stone missing."

"I'll get a new one for it."

"Will a stone from one of my Mother's earrings fit?"

Tristan retrieved the box he'd given Rabiah to store them in. The stone did fit, almost perfectly. They just had to pinch the metal in a little at the sides.

Esmerelda came in carrying a second box containing the heavier crown. Tristan took it from her.

"Thank you, Esmerelda. How fast can you have Rabiah ready to go downstairs? I'm sure our guests are wondering where I am. Of course, they can't leave until the crown does so they will still be there no matter how long it takes."

"I'll just need a few minutes."

21

"You get her ready. I'll go put this somewhere safe." He went into the dressing room and stashed the crown far behind everything so they could inspect it later. Belatedly, he remembered the stone still on the floor in the bedroom. He was loathe to touch it since the ring had indicated it was dangerous. He decided it could wait until later. He waited in the sitting room until Esmerelda opened the door to the bedroom again. Rabiah emerged fully dressed with the whip-belt he had bought her around her waist.

Esmerelda held out the lighter crown now back in its box. "Is this the one you will use?"

"Yes. I think we figured out the problem."

"You removed the stone?" she asked, inspecting it.

"Yes."

"It is strange that the stone would be the problem. Many people wear them."

"I'll look into it more later. We've got to hurry now." To Rabiah he asked, "Are you able to make it down the stairs?"

"Yes. I feel much better than I did earlier."

"Are you sure? I could carry you." He was only half teasing.

"The last time you tried to carry me you fell on your rear. I think I'll walk."

Tristan chuckled at the memory then turned to Esmerelda, "Follow behind us with the crown please," Tristan said.

"Yes, Your Highness."

They made it down the stairs without incident. Based on the loud rumble of voices coming from the Great Hall, people were finished eating and were wondering where he was. The talk hushed as people noticed Tristan and Rabiah had entered the room. Tristan left Rabiah standing near the end of the table while he retrieved his crown from the table and asked a servant to bring a chair. With the crown back on his head, and the servant following them, he led Rabiah to the center of the dais in front of the main table. The servant placed the chair so that it faced the rest of the Great Hall. Tristan bade Rabiah to sit. He could tell she was finding his caution amusing. The raw grief he felt at his parents' death and the guilt he still felt for

22

stabbing the woman before him warred with the joy he felt at her smile. It was hard to keep from smiling broadly back at her.

With her safely seated, he turned to address his people now waiting silently to see what he planned to do.

"Citizens of Arles, you see before you my wife, Rabiah, daughter of the Chieftain of the Eagle Clan. Three nights passed, she and Sir Owen not only saved the castle and Auroria from a powerful demon, but she also saved me for the fourth time. In the process she was stabbed and lost almost all the blood in her body. She stopped breathing. I prayed and many of you prayed to the Great Spirit for a miracle. The miracle was granted. Her wounds were healed and she came back to me, to us. She is, however, still recovering from the loss of all that blood. She stood too long in the cold this morning and that is why she does not yet wear the crown. I will now remedy that."

Tristan turned and signaled to Esmerelda. She came forward and held the box for him just as she had upstairs. Just to be doubly sure, Tristan turned the crown as he lifted it and looked to verify that no black stones were there. Rabiah's blue stone seemed to wink at him when he spied it. He turned and lifted it over Rabiah's head.

"Rabiah, daughter of Chief Qadir of the Eagle Clan, and my beloved wife, I now crown you Queen of Arles."

He slowly lowered the crown, holding his breath.

'Anything?'

'No, just put it on my head!'

He did, a little hard. She glared at him and he almost laughed.

"My people, your Queen." Tristan stepped back.

Rabiah had not expected such loud applause. It wasn't from the visiting nobles. They only clapped politely a few times. It was from the soldiers and the servants and the other people of the castle who had felt the effects of the purple fog the demon had spread. She stood slowly, a shy smile on her face. The young soldiers she had beaten soundly just the week before clapped even harder. Tristan took her hand. She turned her head to look at him. He looked so proud but sad at the same time. She turned completely to him and took his other hand. He put his forehead against hers. Their crowns clanked but no one heard.

23

'*I miss them,*' he sent.

'*I know.*'

The applause began to taper off. Tristan led Rabiah back around the table. The servant retrieved the chair. Tristan had Rabiah sit down in his place and told her to eat, then signaled the waiting servants to bring out the mead. In celebration of the former King and Queen, everyone enjoyed a drink in their memory. Marion came by before Rabiah had taken more than three sips and took the cup from her hand.

"Your blood is thin enough already, Your Highness."

It was snowing heavily outside. No one was in a hurry to leave. As the drinks flowed, people began to get up and visit other tables. Tristan stayed in his seat near Rabiah. Several soldiers, including the Master at Arms, Roland, came up to visit. Roland began to tell stories about Tristan's father as a young man. Tristan's uncle and Owen joined them. Owen sat right across the table from Rabiah. He listened for a few minutes to the men, then turned to her.

"How are you feeling?"

"Much better than I was a few days ago. How are you?"

"Still a bit sore from climbing that rope."

"Did you tell Tristan how we got into the castle?"

"Yes and he nearly had me flogged. He's a protective old bat."

"He knows about…," she couldn't bring herself to say it. Instead she gave a quick glance toward her belly.

"I know. I think that's part of the reason he was so mad. I hear you gave him quite a scare today. I never thought you'd be one to faint."

She would have told him about the ring, but an older Lord she didn't know was leaning in to listen. She shrugged and switched the subject. "What happened to Lydia?"

"She's confined to her rooms. We are still investigating. We've found a few things. We can discuss it tomorrow if you are interested."

"Please. My body might be tired but my mind is not."

"Queen Naomi never interfered with an investigation," the old man next to them interrupted.

24

'*Who is he?*' Rabiah sent to Owen. She had discovered during the demon attack that she could link to people other than Tristan, although Owen, at least, could not talk back.

Owen looked startled, but quickly recovered.

"Queen Rabiah, this is Lord Wardley. Lord Wardley, Queen Rabiah."

"Your Highness," the man said somewhat flowerly and rather tipsily. He searched for her hand but she had it in her lap. He decided to bow, nearly banging his head on the table.

"Lord Wardley was one of King Stephen's Advisors."

"Yes, I was. I'm looking forward to working with King Tristan as well. This will be my third king you know."

"No, I didn't."

Lord Wardley continued on. "Since I have been here so long, I thought I'd offer my services to you as well, seeing as you are new to governance and the ruling class, in general"

"That's very nice of you," was all Rabiah could think to say.

"Now, the Queen's role in Arles is …"

"Father, there you are." A middle-aged woman put her hand on the shoulder of the old man.

Lord Wardley patted the hand on his shoulder. "Your Highness, this is my daughter, Lady Arabella."

"It is nice to meet you," Rabiah said politely.

"The pleasure is mine, Your Highness," the Lady said. "I was hoping I'd get a chance to speak to you so I could thank you for saving the castle and the people in it from the demon. My daughter and my son-in-law were both under the spell of the gas. How did you get past it?" The lady took a seat next to her father.

Rabiah glanced at Owen. He gave a little nod, so Rabiah began the tale. "First we tried staying above the gas by leaping between the roofs of the houses until we got to the castle wall, but the demon found out. Thankfully, Sir Owen thought of another way in."

"You were leaping between roofs?" the old man asked, aghast.

"Indeed, the Queen is like a squirrel," Owen spoke up. He sent a sly wink to Rabiah.

"How did you finally get in?" Lady Arabella asked.

25

"That must be kept secret lest our enemies discover it. It was not easy, but we finally got into the castle without being seen," Owen explained. "However, we were on the opposite side of the castle from the demon and we were afraid we'd get caught."

"Luckily, the rope the King and I slid down to escape the gas was still in place," Rabiah said.

"You slid down a rope?" Lord Wardley said weakly. Rabiah nodded.

Owen continued, "So we climbed it, from the first floor on one side of the courtyard to the second floor on the other. Queen Rabiah went first," he made sure to point out to the lord.

"When we got there, we realized the demon was on the floor above us," Rabiah said.

"So Queen Rabiah climbed up the chimney and down to the window to see what was going on," Owen continued.

The old man opened his mouth but nothing came out.

"My son-in-law was there. He said a girl all in black freed him and told him to smear a fishy-smelling rag on everyone," Lady Arabella said.

"That was me. I asked him to do that in case we didn't succeed," Rabiah confirmed.

"But you did."

"No, we didn't, not completely. Sir Owen tried to trap the demon in a bottle by saying its name but it didn't work."

"Queen Rabiah thought the demon had attacked me so she charged through the window to help me," Owen cut in.

"But Owen wasn't there. He had stepped back into the hallway," Rabiah continued.

"I tried to get back in but there were too many people flying out the door," Owen said. "You see, the demon had at least ten people in there with him under his control. He set them against the Queen."

"And I pushed them out the door because I knew Sir Owen had smeared fish oil around the door frame. The fish oil broke the demon's control."

"You didn't tell me about that part," Tristan said sternly to Owen. He and the other soldiers were listening to the story now.

"I didn't think it was worth mentioning," Owen shrugged, giving Rabiah a knowing look.

"You should have seen Sir Owen when he finally came into the room. Tunic-less, with muscles gleaming from all the fish oil," Rabiah said with a grin.

Lady Arabella glanced at Owen appreciatively. The soldiers hooted. Tristan frowned at Rabiah. She winked at him.

"So what happened next?" Lord Wardley asked.

"The room was filling with purple gas. We were both covered in fish oil so we were protected but we couldn't see anything. Sir Owen poured some oil around us and we saw the demon, or at least we saw the man the demon was in, down on his hands and knees, reaching for us."

"What did you do?"

"Queen Rabiah found a belt and tied him up, then we covered the man in fish oil to keep him from releasing any more gas."

"So he's still in the castle?" Lord Wardley asked.

"No," Owen answered. "We thought it would be safer to house him elsewhere. He is under constant guard and surrounded by fish oil."

"But how did you get injured?" Lady Arabella asked Rabiah.

"There was a second demon," Owen said. "He possessed the King on a signal from the first demon. The Queen found out and ran to save him."

"But what could you do?" Lord Wardley asked.

"I guessed the demon's name and exiled him," Rabiah said.

"But right before he left me, he forced me to stab her. The blade pierced her heart." Tristan entered the story, his voice breaking on the last word. He reached for Rabiah's hand.

Lady Arabella put her hand to her mouth, then asked, "And your god healed you?"

"Yes."

"Who is your god?"

"He is the Great Spirit. He made everything and is everywhere and loves his creations. We are his children."

"Do you have a temple and prayer days?" the Lady asked.

The other listeners started to go back to their own discussions.

"The world is his temple and we pray all the time; before we eat, when we wake, and before we sleep."

"Does he heal everyone?"

"No. I think there's something I must do yet before I die. That's why I was sent back."

"Sent back?"

"Yes. I went somewhere. I could still see everyone below, but my mother was there. She died when I was very young."

"Does your god have talismans?"

"Talismans?"

Lady Arabella pulled a necklace from beneath her neckline. It consisted of a black stone wrapped neatly in wire and attached to a chain. Rabiah was too far away to tell if it had the same effect on her as the stone in the crown, but it looked like the same stone. "This is a piece of the stone which makes up our temple. It is said that if you die with this stone on, your soul will join the other worshipers of the Bull in his paradise. It also provides protection and if you are worthy, you are given a miracle. The Bull god could have healed you too."

"So all the followers wear one?"

"Oh no, only the True Believers who have offered the appropriate sacrifice."

"What is an appropriate sacrifice?" Rabiah asked, curiously.

"Either a large sum of money or a child."

"A child!"

"Yes, but it doesn't have to be your own. It can be an orphan or a slave child."

"What becomes of them?"

"The boys are trained to become priests."

"Do they get a lot of children as sacrifices?"

"A few each week."

"They must have a lot of priests."

"Not really. They send many of them away to build new temples and some of the boys just aren't meant to be priests."

"What happens to them?"

"They are given an education and sold as indentured servants to pay for their training."

Lord Wardley cut in, "It's a good system. The children are kept off the streets, taught the proper way to live, and given a means to support themselves."

"What about female children?" Rabiah asked

"They are trained and sold as indentured servants as well."

The evening wore on. Many people came up to speak to Tristan and they all drank to his health. Tristan became quite inebriated. He would occasionally touch Rabiah's arm or leg even while looking and speaking with someone else as if to make sure she was still there. Owen was still sitting across from her. She noticed he wasn't drinking like everyone else.

"Why aren't you enjoying the mead?" she said.

"I thought someone should stay sober." He nodded to the people around him. Half of them had already fallen out of their chairs. Tristan was still upright but he looked very bleary eyed.

"Could you help me get him up to our rooms?" she asked Owen.

"Gladly."

Owen waded around the table through the other people and half-lifted, half-pulled Tristan to a standing position. He had to put Tristan's arm around his shoulder to keep him upright. Rabiah slipped under Tristan's other arm.

"Rabiah, I love you." Tristan planted a wet kiss on her temple just under her crown.

"Don't forget Owen," she said mischievously.

"I love you too, Owen." Owen got a wet kiss on his cheek.

"Thanks Rabiah," Owen said grumpily, wiping his cheek on his shoulder.

"My Lady, let me help him," Esmerelda said at Rabiah's elbow, clearly concerned for Rabiah's strength.

"I'm fine Esmerelda. I'll let you help him on the stairs."

They had only gone a few steps when Captain Bernard, who had traveled with Tristan and Rabiah from the Clanlands, approached.

"Allow me, Your Highness."

Rabiah stepped aside, not to slight Esmerelda, but because she understood the Captain would see it as an honor to be able to help his king.

The men helped Tristan up the stairs and into the washroom to relieve himself, then lay him into the bed with his crown and boots removed.

"Thank you Owen. You'll see to the General?" Rabiah asked.

"As soon as I get back downstairs."

Captain Bernard had already stepped out of the room. Rabiah took the opportunity to say, "I was sorry to hear about Lydia."

"It's all right. It was a spur-of-the-moment thing. It gave her something to think about while I was gone. I would have been shocked if she had said yes."

Rabiah raised her eyebrow at him.

"Pleasantly shocked," he amended.

"You're a good man. A little moody, but the right woman wouldn't mind."

"Me, moody?" Owen threw his hands up in mock disgust and left.

Esmerelda stepped forward, "Would you like me to help you prepare for bed, Your Highness?"

"I can do it. I really am feeling much better. Do you have the box for the crown?"

"It's here."

Rabiah reverently took the off crown and set it in the box. Her mother's blue stone seemed to shine and twinkle more brightly than all the other stones.

"Esmerelda, are you a follower of the bull god?"

"I respect Buchis, but I am just a slave. I have no money or children to give so I cannot become a full member."

"Would you if you could?"

"Maybe. It's nice to think that there's a god who cares and is watching over everyone."

"What does the bull god want?"

"What do you mean?"

"What does he ask of his people? How does he tell them to live?"

"He just wants them to worship him and to get along with one another I guess. I've been to a few services. All the True Believers flock together like one big, happy family."

"Thank you Esmerelda. It's still a bit early in the evening. I noticed you didn't drink anything downstairs. If you want to go back down and visit, go ahead. I'm going to bed."

"I'll stay in the sitting room, Your Highness."

"I meant what I said earlier, Esmerelda. You are free. We just have to get those bracelets off. You can have a drink if you like."

Esmerelda dropped her head. "I would like one, in memory, but I have no one to drink it with."

"I'll drink it with you. Let's go back down."

"No. Healer Marion said you were not to have any more."

"I'll just have some water with a little wine added. I'll be fine. Besides, I'll need something to help me sleep now that sir snores-a-lot is here."

Tristan gave a huge snort behind her. Rolling her eyes, Rabiah turned and pushed him on his side.

"His father was the same way whenever he drank a little too much," Esmerelda smiled sadly.

"Let's go. You can tell me more about the Queen and King and Tristan as a boy."

Chapter 2

It was still snowing in the morning. The snow was over a foot and a half deep and rising. Tristan woke late in the morning feeling very unwell. When Marion came to check on her, Rabiah asked if she had something that could help. Marion reluctantly gave him a potion. It was clear she thought people who over-imbibed deserved to suffer, but since it was his parents' funeral, she would be lenient. The potion helped, but Tristan still didn't feel well, so they spent much of the cold day cuddled together in bed. It was nice. It was the first time they had ever spent so much time together not doing anything. Since Tristan was with her, Rabiah talked Esmerelda into taking the day off. Esmerelda reluctantly agreed.

Late in the afternoon Tristan finally rolled out of bed. The hangover was gone but if he thought about things too much, the anger and sadness he felt made him feel even worse. He needed a distraction. He saw the little black stone still laying on the floor near the fire and remembered the other crown. He retrieved it from the dressing room and inspected the outside. Esmerelda was right. There were no stones on the crown. It was solid gold. He took the crown back into the bedroom. Rabiah watched him from the bed.

"Rabiah, hold your ring up to the crown while I turn it."

She sat up in bed and did as he asked. He turned it almost completely around before her ring began to heat. The room was dim, lit only by a single candle and a small fire in the fireplace. Snow was still falling heavily outside. He took the crown closer to the candle and inspected it more closely. Something was stuck to the inner rim. He poked at it with one of Rabiah's throwing knives. It popped off onto the table. It was a thin black stone like the one on the floor. There was a sticky residue left on the inside of the crown where it had been.

"Who put that there?" Rabiah wondered.

"And why?" Tristan asked.

"When could they have done it?"

"Yesterday or perhaps it's been there for a long time. Maybe that was why the crown gave my mother a headache."

"Surely she would have realized there was a rock stuck to the edge."

"Maybe. I never saw her wear this crown."

Tristan put the crown away and scooped up both rocks with a small towel. He put them in the box with the crown and told Rabiah where they were so she wouldn't come across them unexpectedly. He wanted to toss them in the necessary box in the washroom, but something told him to hang on to them.

It snowed for another day. Esmerelda said they'd never had so much snow. Since many of the Lords or their representatives were trapped in the castle due to the snow, Tristan took the opportunity to keep his mind busy by going over all the affairs of the Kingdom. He began holding meeting after meeting with his advisors and the Lords. Rabiah sat through many of them with him although Esmerelda tried to talk her out of it. Based on their frowns and whispers, several of the advisors and Lords, Lord Wardsley included, were not happy when she joined them. She ignored them and pulled up a chair close to the window so she could look out while she listened. Rabiah wanted to learn about her new country. She had often listened in when her own father held Clan meetings. She found that some of the issues they discussed in Arles weren't all that different from the ones her own Clan had faced.

From the meetings Rabiah learned that Arles did a lot of shipping and had pirate problems. The country had relatively friendly relations with their close neighbors and was so large it stretched across the bay.

Each Lord, Baron, or representative gave a report on the property under their control. Rabiah noticed that one representative who hadn't yet spoken kept frowning in her direction. Tristan finally called upon him to report. Rabiah pretended not to notice as he stood. She looked out the window as if she were very interested in something outside.

"Your Highness," the representative said, addressing Tristan, "Perhaps the Queen would like to take a break."

"Rabiah, is that your desire?" Tristan asked politely.

Rabiah turned and looked at the representative. "No. I'd like to hear what everyone has to say, including the man standing. Why is it he wishes me to leave?"

"He is from the northern-most territory, the one that borders the Clanlands," Tristan explained.

Rabiah sat up straighter, "I'd really like to hear what he has to say then."

"Your Highness, I must protest," the man said. "She is of the Clan. She should not be here. What if she tells them what we discuss here today."

"She is also the Queen of Arles. What is it you wish to discuss that the Queen should not hear?"

"Our plans for the spring campaign."

Rabiah opened her mouth to say something in protest but Tristan spoke up first.

"There won't be a spring campaign."

Several people tried to speak at once. The Northern representative protested the hardest. "But the Clanspeople will be even more troublesome since there wasn't a definitive victory this fall. According to the General's report our losses far exceeded theirs and most of the Clans he attacked got away. He only came back with a few dozen slaves. They will attack us in force if we don't attack them first."

"The slaves will be freed," Tristan said calmly, "and I will send an ambassador to speak with the Clanspeople."

"That has already been tried! It was a complete failure. We need more men along the border to prevent any incursions. We need to push them back and clean them out so they can't attack anymore."

"Our attempts to speak with them failed the first time because we didn't know how to communicate properly. Now we do. Queen

Rabiah is the daughter of a Chieftan and a Clan Champion. The Clans know her. It was her presence that gave us safe passage through the Clanlands and into Arles. The Clanspeople will talk to her. The Clanspeople I met were not barbarians. They tried to save my life. I cannot ignore that. We must try again."

"So you are proposing to send your wife as our ambassador?"

"No, I'm proposing that she pick and train an ambassador and then introduce him to the Clans so we can begin to make peace."

"And what will we say? Please stop stealing our animals? They won't listen."

"Apparently people from Arles have been stealing not only animals, but people from the Clanlands. We need to get both sides to respect the border."

"It won't work."

Rabiah stood, "Tristan, may I speak."

"Yes. Please."

The room became very quiet as she stepped forward to stand at Tristan's side. "People fear what is unknown and fear can lead to hate of the unknown. You were my enemy, but I have met you. You are not bad people. Some of you have become my friends. I think if your people could meet more of my people on a friendly basis, the fear and distrust might lessen."

"And how do you propose we make this happen?" The representative asked in a frustrated tone.

"My people hold tournaments between the tribes. There's food and trade. People get to know one another and share enjoyment instead of fighting. Perhaps the same would work between your people and mine. It won't be easy at first because there is so much mistrust, but if those few on both sides who are causing the problems can be stopped, I imagine the Clanspeople would enjoy a yearly tournament with your people."

The representative was shaking his head. "I've lived along the border all my life. The Clanspeople won't speak with us."

"Why do you say that?" Rabiah asked, "Have you tried to speak with them?"

"I have. Every time they shoot first."

"Have you ever been hit?"

"Well, no, but they are notoriously bad shots."

Tristan snorted, "You wouldn't say that if you'd ever been on the archery range with the Queen."

"They were testing you to see what you'd do. If you want to talk with them, you just need to let the arrow lie and wait for them to show themselves," Rabiah explained patiently.

"What kind of an idiot would stand there while someone is shooting arrows at him?" the representative exploded.

"A non-violent one," Rabiah said calmly, "I can see how the customary greeting of the Clan could be misunderstood, but for them it works." The representative frowned at her, but he appeared to be thinking as well. She returned to her seat.

"So, if this ambassador goes into the Clanlands and just waits while arrows fall around him, the Clanspeople will talk to him?"

"As long as he doesn't fire back, yes. It is our law. The Clan does not attack unless you attack first."

"But we have already fought."

"Yes. But a few men, unarmed, in the presence of a Clansperson should be safe."

"If we are to do this, we must send someone before any incursions are made into Arles in the spring. I fear the conflict will be much worse than in prior years due to the campaign this past season."

"You are likely correct," Rabiah conceded.

"We must send someone as soon as it's warm enough to travel," another man said.

"I don't know when that will be. Winter got a very early start this year. I've already received word of two blizzards. Normally they don't start for another month," the Northern representative said

"Where do the first attacks usually occur?" Rabiah asked.

"Near the point where the Great River meets the Lesser."

"Then the ambassador should start there. We will travel as soon as possible after the second moon cycle past midwinter. You will need someone to speak with your people too. Make them understand that they cannot steal from the Clanspeople if they want peace."

"I will send someone," the Northern representative said.

"Good, we have a plan. We can discuss this in more detail later. It's getting late." Tristan pushed back from the long table. "Let's adjourn for the evening meal."

Tristan stood and walked back to where Rabiah was sitting. The rest of the men started to filter out of the room.

'Do you have someone in mind?' he sent.

'Mitch,' she answered without hesitation.

'You don't think he is too young?'

'No. I think he will get along well with the Clanspeople. He reminds me of my brothers. He was respectful to my people's customs and he has a quick mind.'

'You must teach him your language.'

'We have many. I will teach him the common one first.'

'Will you be able to travel then, do you think?'

'I come from a Clan of travelers. Many women have traveled far into their pregnancies without a problem.'

Tristan sighed. Everyone had left. Aloud he said, "I'd rather not send you but I want to make sure we succeed this time."

"Will you come too?"

"I'd like to."

"But you are the King now and have a lot of responsibilities." She stood and leaned her head on his chest. "Did your father ever get away?"

"Occasionally, but not often." He wrapped his arms around her.

"You still need to take me to see all your lands," Rabiah said.

"I do, don't I?"

"Maybe when I get back?"

"Or maybe a bit after that?" he suggested, smiling.

"Maybe."

Rabiah had not been able to free Esmerelda due to the snow, but as soon as they were able to make it outside to the blacksmith, she took Esmerelda as promised and had the bracelets removed. Esmerelda's skin was pale and smooth where the bands had been. Esmerelda rubbed her wrists and a tear or two flowed down her cheek. She fell to her knees and bowed before Rabiah.

"Thank you, Your Highness."

Rabiah pulled her up. You are welcome, Esmerelda. And, in honor of your long service to his mother, Tristan asked me to give you this." Rabiah handed her a large bag of coins. "He said not to spend it all in one place," she smiled.

Esmerelda hugged the bag close to her chest. "I won't"

"So do you want to take some time off? Is there anywhere you'd like to go?"

"In this weather? No."

"I think you deserve at least a week after your long service. I would give you more but I don't know much about being a queen and I really need your guidance."

"A week? To myself? I wouldn't know what to do with all that time. May I have one day off now and more later? I need to plan how I will spend my time."

"Of course. You can take the rest of today and all day tomorrow if you wish."

"Just tomorrow will be fine. I want to enjoy looking forward to it. Today I will begin your lessons on how to run a castle."

Esmerelda gave Rabiah a very different tour than the one Tristan had given her shortly after she arrived. She met stewards and record-keepers, saw all the places where food and other supplies were stored, and met all of the various wait staff. Her head was spinning with names by the time they were through.

"After lunch Queen Naomi used to take a walk, then she would work on correspondence in the afternoon. I know how to read and write if you ever want to send anything."

"Can you teach me to read? Tristan was going to, but now that he is King I fear he will not have time."

"I would be honored."

"Since I don't have any correspondence, we can start this afternoon," Rabiah said, excited at the thought.

"But you do have correspondence. You have all the letters that came for Queen Naomi and you have some of your own."

"But who would write to me?"

"You are the queen now. People ask the queen for favors. Some are writing to congratulate Tristan on his marriage and others have sent letters of condolence, although there aren't many of those yet, due to the weather."

"What do I have to do?"

"Queen Naomi used to read all the mail addressed to her. She responded to as many as she could and had a couple of scribes who would help her when there was too much. She signed everything."

"Sign?"

"You just write your name or your symbol so they know it passed through your hands."

"I guess you'd better teach me how to do that first."

"Of course, Your Highness."

By the end of the afternoon, after going through what seemed like hundreds of letters, Rabiah wondered why anyone would actually want to be queen. She was not in the best mood during the evening meal. Tristan pleasantly asked her how her day had been. He almost heard the growl in her look.

"What were you doing?" he asked curiously.

"Correspondence."

"That's not bad."

Rabiah gave him a disgruntled look and sent, *Do you know how many letters were waiting for me? Esmerelda insisted I listen to every one of them so I get to know people's names and where they are from. She taught me to sign my name, but then wouldn't let me do it because she said I needed to practice. So she signed everything and I just put an X.*

'Sounds like she did most of the work.'

Rabiah sent him a growl through their link.

Tristan laughed silently back at her. *'I know just what you need. Eat quickly.'*

Rabiah finished before everyone else and waited impatiently for Tristan.

"I didn't mean that quickly," he said, amused.

She raised her eyebrows and looked pointedly at his food.

"You're very tired of sitting around, aren't you."

She tapped her finger on the table in front of her.

"All right, all right." Tristan ate the rest of his food in three big bites, took a large gulp from his mug, and pushed his chair back. Everyone around them looked up.

"Continue please." He offered his arm to Rabiah who had pushed out her own chair as soon as he did his.

'You are supposed to wait for me to pull your chair out for you.'

'Why?'

'I don't know. I guess it's so I can show how much I care for you.'

'I already know.'

She really did need to get out for a while, Tristan thought. First though, he took her up to their rooms and pulled out a package he had hidden earlier. The shorter tunic and pants he had ordered for her before the events of last week had been delivered that morning. Rabiah went into the dressing room to try them on. She came out smiling. The clothiers had outdone themselves. Tristan had ordered tunics with decoration and a leather one to go over the top. Not only had they embroidered the wool ones with silver and gold thread in intricate designs, but they'd also decorated the leather one with etchings of whorls and vines all along the edges. It was striking.

"How did they get this done so fast?" Rabiah asked. "It's beautiful." She ran her hand over the leather tunic.

"I don't know but it fits you. You look every bit the Warrior Princess, or I guess Warrior Queen now. If I weren't married to you I'd be afraid."

"Would you? Perhaps you still should be." She approached him with a wicked gleam in her eye.

Tristan raised his hands and took a step back. "If you hurt me, I won't be able to show you the rest of my surprise."

Her demeanor changed instantly, "There's more?"

Tristan pulled out two practice swords and tossed Rabiah her cape.

"We've got to try out your new clothes haven't we?"

"But there's too much snow."

"All cleared off the training ground. I asked Roland to leave a couple of torches for us."

Rabiah grabbed the front of Tristan's tunic and pulled him close for a good, hard, long kiss. She pushed him back after a minute.

"Let's go."

"After that?" He protested, but he grinned as he chased after her.

He caught up with her at the end of the hall leading to the back stair. Everyone was still eating, so no one but the two guards who had been assigned to Tristan saw them run through the castle and out the back door. There were four torches lying by the door to the weapons building. Tristan lit them all and stuck them in the snowbanks around the field. It was not a hard practice. Rabiah had become winded just running to the field, but she enjoyed practicing the motions. Tristan did too, and if they added a few of their own moves, there was no one around to watch except the guards who kept their backs to them.

Tristan called a halt after half-an-hour. He could tell Rabiah was tiring and he was sure she was getting cold. He was, or at least his ears were. The rest of him was warm. He wrapped her cloak around her and then his arm for extra warmth.

"Thank you, Tristan."

"You're welcome, my love. I was getting tired of being indoors so I was sure you were too."

They walked in silence for a minute or so. Then Rabiah asked, "Tristan, where are my people, the ones your uncle captured?"

"I had Uncle find a place for them to stay until they can go home."

"I must speak to them so they understand what is going on."

"Of course."

"Can I see them tonight? Are they near?"

"They are housed in one of the dormitories at the other barracks. It is getting colder and it is already dark. Let's go in the morning. The road has been cleared. We can take the carriage."

"Or we can walk."

"Or we can walk. Let's see how you feel in the morning."

Chapter 3

She was tired in the morning but she didn't tell Tristan. Instead she ate and drank heartily and prayed for strength to come. She didn't want to arrive in a carriage to visit her people. She was afraid that would make them think she had taken on all the ways of Arles. Tristan wasn't fooled.

"I asked for the carriage."

"But Tristan, aren't we going to walk?"

"It's freezing outside. I've never seen it so cold and you are tired, admit it."

"Only a little."

"We can walk the last bit from the gate if you wish."

"I do."

"Come then, my Queen. Your carriage awaits. Oh, and I thought these might be useful." He pulled out the warm fur cloaks Rabiah's sister-in-law had made for them.

Rabiah beamed at him, "You think of everything."

"Not always, I just didn't want to be cold."

There were already a few people milling about when Rabiah and Tristan walked through the Great Hall to the carriage waiting outside. Furs in the style they were wearing were not often seen in Auroria. People watched and whispered as they passed. They both ignored them. It was much warmer in the fur cape than the wool one. Rabiah had also chosen to wear a new shorter tunic and pants with the leather tunic over the top. The Clanspeople knew her as a champion, not as a woman.

As promised, Tristan had the carriage stop at the gate so they could walk in. The main army was housed inside the compound. Several soldiers came out to see who the visitors were. The soldiers quickly came to attention and saluted when they realized it was their new King and Queen.

The commander in charge walked out to greet them as well. After Tristan had explained their mission, the commander turned and led them to one of the smaller buildings on the edge of the compound.

There were guards posted outside. Without bothering to knock, the commander pushed open the door. The smell of unwashed bodies greeted them. In the dim light from a small fire, the whites of several dozen eyes turn toward them. Her people were skinny, dirty, and under-clothed. They did have mats and blankets, but the blankets were thin and the room was cold.

She looked at her husband with a little frown and sent, *'Tristan, this isn't good enough. You can't make peace if you treat them this way.'*

'I didn't know it was like this. We will fix it.'

Rabiah turned to the commander who had led them there, "Have they been seen by the healers?"

He shrugged, "None of them are sick."

"No, but they are cold and underfed and probably have sores and other complaints from their travels."

She turned back to Tristan, *'Tristan, is there a large hot tub here like in the other barracks?'*

'Yes.'

'May I?'

'Yes, by all means.'

She turned back to the commander, "Commander, get your hot tub ready and let the women and children bathe first. Tristan, can you get healers here with warm clothes of all sizes and some food? I will stay and speak with them."

Tristan turned to the commander, "Please see that the Queen's orders are carried out and send a soldier to fetch the healers and supplies. I will stay here with the Queen."

"One advantage of being king is that you can make other people do what your wife tells you," he said to Rabiah with a grin.

She gave him that look with one eyebrow raised that he was coming to know so well, then turned to the Clanspeople. Some were frowning, but most wore the blank expressions of people who had seen bad and didn't expect anything to get better soon. She knew they were all from the region near the border so she spoke in the most common language there.

"People of the Clan, I am Rabiah. I am also of the Clan, but through marriage I have become the Queen of Arles. My husband has freed you. It is too cold for you to travel home now, but you will be cared for until it is possible to travel. I have ordered hot baths and warm clothes and healers to see to your needs."

A man a little older than her spoke up, "I know who you are. You came to see us when we were still in our lands. Why didn't you free us then? Why now?"

"I was not the queen then. Did you not see the soldiers with me? I was a prisoner myself."

"Tell us then, how a Clanswoman came to be queen in the land of our enemy."

"Gladly." Rabiah sat gracefully on the floor and pulled Tristan down next to her. With a wave of her hand, she invited her people to sit around her. After they were all seated, she began. It took her over a half-hour to tell the whole story. She was a little hoarse by the time she had finished. Tristan signaled the guards to bring her a drink. Meanwhile, the commander came in to say the baths were ready.

The Clanspeople were quiet for a few minutes, then a middle-aged woman asked, "This is your husband, the King?"

"Yes"

"He cares for you?"

"Yes."

"And he freed us for you?"

"No. He freed you because our people tried to save him. These people don't understand our ways. They didn't know the proper way to speak to us. He wants to try again to make peace. I will help him."

"You trust him?"

"With my life."

"With our lives."

"You were slaves. He freed you."

"We were free before they captured us."

"And now he has made you free again."

"Are we? How will we get back home?"

"In the spring, as soon as it is possible, I will take you back to the Clanlands. My husband is sending an ambassador to talk with our people. I will make sure he is welcome."

"And if he is not?"

"I will make sure he is. In fact, I will bring him so you can meet him. He doesn't know yet that I have chosen him."

She waited for more questions, but the people were silent again.

"The commander says the bath is ready. The women and children can go first. I will go with you to make sure it is acceptable."

She stood, a little too quickly. Tristan offered his arm to steady her.

"Where are we off to?" he asked.

"The baths."

"I like the way your language sounds. You will have to teach me."

She said something in her language.

"What does that mean?"

"'Lead on' or 'show me the way'."

He looked at her in confusion.

"To the baths."

"Ah. They are this way."

There were not many children, Rabiah was glad to see. The Clanspeople's clothes were completely inadequate for the cold. Most didn't have shoes. She picked up the little girl who came to walk beside her and tucked her under her fur cloak. The little girl clung to her, enjoying the warmth.

Stepping inside the bathing house was like entering a whole different season. Warm air and steam embraced them. Rabiah made sure there was plenty of soap and towels. She knew the women would also want to wash the clothes they were wearing so she told them more clothes were coming. She'd make the soldiers give them some of theirs if she had to. She needn't have worried. Healer Marion responded quickly to her summons and came with a wagon-load of supplies and four other healers.

"Malnourished and cold, but no major problems," Marion said after she had assessed everyone. "There is one woman who is expecting a child. I'd guess in about two months."

"Thank you, Marion."

"And how are you, my most stubborn of patients?"

"I am not stubborn."

"Who was out sparring in the middle of the night after I expressly told her to take it easy for a few weeks?"

"I *was* taking it easy and how did you know?"

"When the King and Queen leave the table so eagerly together people will try to determine why."

"What if we'd been...you know."

"Then they would know."

Rabiah gave a little sigh.

"At least you weren't, you know. Sparring in the snow is much more interesting, at least to some gossips. Of course, I hear some of your moves were not, shall we say, traditional."

"There was no one else there, well, except the guards, and they were looking the other way."

"Apparently you are wrong."

"What is she wrong about?" Tristan asked, joining them outside the bath.

"Midnight sparring." Marion said cryptically.

"Oh, so people are talking, are they?"

"You expected it?" Rabiah asked.

Tristan shrugged, "I didn't see how we could prevent it. A lack of privacy is one of the downsides to royal life."

"There are a lot of them it seems," Rabiah grumbled.

"On the other hand, you have the power to help people when they need it." Tristan indicated the barracks behind him. "Is everyone all right Marion?"

"Nothing I can't fix, but I fear they are going to get bored and restless staying in that little building all winter long."

"Do you have a suggestion?" Rabiah asked.

"Not yet."

They watched as the women went back to the dormitory wearing their new, warmer clothes and carrying the old, cleaned, wet ones. It was now the men's turn to use the baths. Rabiah noticed there seemed to be many armed guards around watching over the Clanspeople's movements.

"Tristan, we cannot treat them as prisoners. We must treat them as guests. The Clanspeople must be allowed to eat in the Great Hall and mingle with the people."

"That's going to be difficult. There is much mistrust on both sides."

"I know. You have made me queen yet there are many who question your judgement."

"I think he made a very good decision for once in his life," Marion commented.

Rabiah turned to her and smiled, an idea forming. "We need more people like you," she told Marion, "Who will visit them, maybe share some knowledge. If someone was interested in learning more about healing, would you teach them?"

"Possibly," Marion said slowly.

"These people are from different Clans. Some are farmers, some live on the water, and some are hunters. They all have different skills and interests. Their knowledge may be different from those who live here. Perhaps the people can learn from one another and form friendships."

"We must find people willing and without prejudice," Tristan thought aloud.

"I am willing," Marion said.

"And without prejudice," Rabiah nodded. "Let me speak to a few people and see what they think."

"Wait. I need to think on this a little," Marion said.

"I'm just going to see if they are interested," Rabiah called back to her as she headed for the dormitory.

She entered the building and walked up to the woman closest to the door. "I am concerned that you will become very bored staying here all winter. Would you be interested in learning from people of Arles while you are here and maybe teaching them some things that you know?"

The woman spat on the ground. "What could they teach me than how not to treat animals? You may have become corrupted by living among them but I have not."

"Why do you call me corrupted?"

"Look at you! You have been warm and well-cared for while we have been freezing and starving. Where have you been? Why didn't you come sooner?"

Rabiah hung her head. "You are correct. I should have seen to you sooner. I am sorry. I would have come sooner if I had known the conditions were so bad."

The first woman opened her mouth to say something else, but a second woman touched her arm, silencing her.

"Dacia, she couldn't have come much sooner. She was injured, there was a funeral, and much snow. Queen Rabiah, I am Tarja, what is it you are asking of us?"

"The Healer, the one in the darker red, she cared for me when I had a broken leg. She treated me as a person and not as the enemy. She offered to teach me to be a healer. I fear I will not have time now, but if a few of you are interested, she could teach you of medicines the people of Arles know, and if there are some you know of that they don't, I'm sure she would be happy to learn from you."

The woman nodded. "I am interested. My mother was our Clan medicine woman."

"I will introduce you. Do you know their tongue?"

"A little."

"Would anyone else be interested?"

"Perhaps."

"What about the rest? Would they like to learn something?" Rabiah looked around.

"Rabiah," the woman said, gaining Rabiah's full attention, "Let them recover. Take them around and show them the city. Treat

48

them like people again. That is what they need. If they see something they'd like to know more about, you can encourage something then."

Rabiah looked around again then nodded. "You are wise. I am impatient. I want them to see that there is good here too."

"Is there?"

"Yes. I have found several good friends."

"And some who are not?"

Rabiah nodded.

"It is the same whenever two peoples mix. I will remind our people of this so they will look for the golden nuggets among the clods of dirt."

"And I will have my husband speak with his people. I will not let you be treated so poorly again."

After making sure the guards and the soldiers understood they were to treat the Clanspeople with hospitality, allow them daily access to the baths, and feed them the same rations as the soldiers, Tristan and Rabiah left. She told Tristan that she planned to come back the next day and every day to see that everyone was well cared for.

"Good. Maybe some of the women would like to go shopping."

"They don't have any money."

"But you do."

"I do?"

"Of course. As queen you get an allowance to spend on clothes and other personal needs. Since I just bought you some new clothes, there should be plenty to share with the Clanswomen. This carriage is yours too, by the way. Also, if you want, you can pick out a horse when we get back."

"Any horse I want?"

"Well, any horse that's not already been claimed by someone else."

"Will you ride with me?"

"Gladly, if I can get away. It seems like everyone wants a favor or has a dispute to settle. They remind me of a bunch of children."

"Was it like this for your father?"

"I think they're testing me."

"It will get better when everyone can go home."

49

"It already is. That long-winded southern Lord is leaving this morning."

"Can we spar again tonight?"

"I don't want to wear you out."

"You won't. I'm feeling stronger every day."

"Tomorrow is a rest day. We could take a ride then."

"I would love to."

They sat in silence for a minute, then Tristan said, "I'm sorry your people were treated so meanly."

"I wonder if your uncle knew."

"Perhaps, but he is not accustomed to thinking of his captives as people."

"That is not a good excuse."

"No, it is not. I will speak to him."

"What about the other people?"

"What people?"

"The other people you have captured over the years. What did you do with them?"

"Usually captives are sold at the slave markets as soon as they come in."

"I do not like that your people have slaves."

"I know."

"We are all children of the Great Spirit. How can one child own another?"

"Slavery is ingrained into our society. It would not be easy to end it."

"Can we try?"

Tristan looked at her, thinking. He'd always taken slaves for granted, never thinking about their feelings or wants or needs. They were captives. It was just their bad luck that they'd become slaves. But here he sat, next to his amazing wife who could have become a slave herself. He could not imagine her as such. She would probably have been killed trying to escape. How many lives had been stifled or extinguished so that others could live easier lives themselves? Most of the slaves ended up doing jobs that no one else wanted. Their lives were expendable. Thinking on it now, he knew in his heart that it was wrong. He could free them. He *would* free them, somehow.

"Yes, we can try, but it will take time and I must think of the least painful way to do it. There are many businesses that rely on slave labor."

"Thank you, Tristan," she squeezed his hand, "You are a good king."

"We'll see."

The carriage pulled up to the castle. Tristan stepped out, then turned to help Rabiah down. A page ran up to speak to Tristan before Rabiah's foot hit the ground. Tristan listened to the page's message then turned to Rabiah with a little sigh.

"Looks like you'll have to go to the stables yourself."

"We can go later. May I come with you?"

"Of course, although you should probably go change first. You look a bit scary in that attire."

Rabiah smiled and stepped toward him, "Do I?"

Trisan stepped back playfully, "Yes. I don't know if I should draw a sword or kiss you into submission."

"Can you do both?"

He laughed, then leaned forward and whispered, "I will and shall. Later."

They entered the Great Hall together and were immediately approached by a cluster of men who had obviously been waiting for the King. There were several women present who seemed as if they were waiting too, but they stayed back, talking amongst themselves. Tristan bade Rabiah to go ahead. She took his fur cloak and quickly traversed the Great Hall alone. She moved too fast for the two women who took a step forward to catch up with her. The guards who had gone to visit the Clanspeople with them stayed with Tristan.

Rabiah changed into what had become her favorite long tunic and went back downstairs to find her husband. The guards let her into the meeting. She sat near the window with a slate so she could practice her signature while she listened. The argument two lords were having over the rights to a strip of forest was going nowhere.

'*I'm going to go speak to Owen about the investigation,*' she sent to Tristan.

'*I'm sure it will be more interesting than this.*'

Rabiah felt sorry for him. '*Just tell them that if they can't share than neither one gets to play.*'

'*I wish it were that easy.*'

She ran her hand discretely across his back as she left, sending him a jolt of energy and the equivalent of a strong hug.

'*See you later,*' he sent, wishing he could leave with her.

Chapter 4

Rabiah looked everywhere she thought Owen might be. She thought of calling him through their link but didn't want to disturb him if he was doing something important. She finally gave up and went to the stables to look at the horses. After spending some time getting to know a beautiful honey-colored mare, she went back into the castle for the noon meal.

As soon as she entered the Great Hall, an older woman swooped down on her and introduced herself. Almost immediately, a second lady joined them. The first lady frowned at the second. From their names Rabiah realized they must be the wives of the lords who had been arguing over the land this morning. They were both treating her with utmost politeness but each other with mild distain. She gathered that they were only speaking to her so she could sway Tristan's decision. She saw Tristan enter the Great Hall through the family door and quickly excused herself. Several other women started her way as she crossed the Hall. She avoided making eye contact and sat down next to Tristan as quickly as she could.

"Did you find Owen?" he asked.

"No. Did you settle that argument?"

"No. I called in the lawyers to look over the records."

"Their wives just introduced themselves to me."

He raised an eyebrow, "Are you going to suggest I choose one over the other?"

"I say take the land away from both of them and give it to me," she said lightly.

"I might just do that."

'*There seem to be a lot of women who want to speak with me,*' Rabiah sent a little later as they were eating.

'*They probably want to ask you for favors.*'

'*What do I do?*'

'*Listen politely and don't show favorites. My mother used to make herself available once a week in the Great Hall for anyone to approach her. Other times, usually in the afternoon after she had finished any correspondence, she would sew or work on some other project. If the ladies wanted to speak with her, they would sew with her.*'

'*Should I meet with them today?*'

'*You should probably wait until Esmerelda is with you. Some of the ladies can be a little, well, cruel. Some of them are worse than the men.*'

'*I'm sure.*' Rabiah said, thinking of her own experiences with some Clanswomen throughout her life.

"I have another disagreement to listen to this afternoon," Tristan said aloud, in part so the people around them wouldn't think he and Rabiah sat in silence all the time.

"Shall I come?"

"It will be much like this morning," he said aloud, '*Only worse,*' he sent silently. '*These two Lords have been bickering since before I was born.*'

"I suppose I'll go work on correspondence again. I think my signature is looking better."

"Careful what you say in a letter. The wrong phrase can cause all kinds of problems."

Rabiah sighed, "I'll wait for Esmerelda to get back then."

"Why don't you go visit Marion? You said she was going to train you to be a healer."

Rabiah liked the thought. "Maybe I will."

They finished eating. Tristan went back to his meetings and Rabiah slipped through the family door to avoid all the women looking her way. She went up the stairs to the third floor, then around to the back stairs so she could go out by the kitchens without meeting anyone. She was running down the stairs from the third floor when she nearly ran into Owen who was coming up the stairs.

"Oh, sorry Owen," she said, stopping short just before she knocked him backwards.

"Your Highness."

Lydia was standing beside him, her hand delicately placed on Owen's arm.

"Good afternoon Lydia."

Lydia didn't say anything but bowed her head in acknowledgement of Rabiah's greeting.

"Has Lydia been released then?" Rabiah asked Owen.

"No. I'm just taking her for a walk. It's tedious being shut in one room all the time."

"Will I see you at the evening meal?"

Owen looked at Lydia who smiled demurely, "Perhaps."

Rabiah frowned at Owen. Something wasn't right. She looked at his soul. Bright but slightly pink? She looked at Lydia's. A pink mist floated around her soul and extended towards Owen. Another demon or was it something else? A love potion? She didn't remember Tristan's soul having any color when he was under the spell of Lydia's last love potion.

"What have you done to him Lydia? He's not acting right."

"I haven't done anything," Lydia said haughtily. "He's acting the way a gentleman should around a lady."

"Owen, are you feeling all right?"

"Yes, Your Highness."

"I hope you can make it tonight. I need to speak to you about something."

"Yes, Your Highness."

Rabiah nodded to them both and continued down the stairs. Should she tell Tristan? He was so busy that she hated to give him more to worry about. She didn't sense a demon and Owen wasn't acting uncontrollable like Tristan had been under the influence of the love potion. She wondered if Owen would come to the evening meal. She'd seek him out again if he didn't.

Owen came to the evening meal but he was even more quiet than usual. There was still a faint pink color around his soul. Tristan

55

was quiet too. He was tired. His smile didn't quite reach his eyes and when no one was looking his face quickly relaxed into a blank mask. She sent a spiral of light around his and got a tired little smile in return.

"Would you like to go view the stars tonight?" she asked.

"I think I'm too tired even for that."

'Sorry I wore you out so much last night. I'll try and go easy on you next time.'

He raised an eyebrow at her, *'To what are you referring?'*

'Sparring, of course.'

'It wasn't you. It was all the meetings and messengers and accountants I talked to today. The snow is causing all kinds of problems. Roofs are collapsing, waterways are frozen, and people are cold because the coal and the wood aren't arriving fast enough.'

He was using both hands to eat so she reached down to rub his thigh discretely under the table.

'Then there's King Abbus whom we are supposed to have a trade agreement with. I received word today that he has doubled the tare we pay to travel through his waters.'

'Is he the one your father was going to send us to talk to?'

'Yes. I suppose I'll still need to go, and soon.'

"There's no one who could go in your place?"

'Not to meet with King Abbus. He has made it clear it must be me and no one else.'

'How long does it take to get there?'

'About a week.'

Someone kicked Rabiah under the table. She looked up to find Owen glaring at her.

"Why did you do that?" Rabiah asked in surprise.

'What did he do?' Tristan asked.

'He kicked me.'

"Stop," Owen hissed.

"Stop what?" Rabiah asked.

Owen waved his hand from Rabiah to Tristan and back.

"No one's paying any attention," Rabiah said.

"I am."

"What's he so upset about?" Tristan asked.

"Lydia has done something to him."

"She hasn't done anything!" Owen growled.

Tristan's uncle was sitting on the other side of Rabiah, talking with the lady next to him. He turned at the mention of Lydia's name. "Did I hear you mention Lydia?"

"Yes," Rabiah said. "I saw her walking with Owen. She's done something to him."

"She has not," Owen insisted.

"He's not acting like he's under the spell of a love potion," the General said.

"No. It's something else." She leaned over so she could speak quietly in the General's ear. "I can see pink on his soul. Lydia has it too, but it's darker on hers. It doesn't feel like another demon. What could it be?"

The General looked thoughtfully at Owen. "How is Lydia?"

Owen smiled. "She's well, although she's very tired of staying in her room. I'm hoping to conclude the investigation soon so she can be free."

"Good to hear." The General nodded to Owen, then leaned over and spoke quietly to Rabiah, "I think Lydia's talent has finally manifested."

"What is it?"

"I would guess, based on the fond way Owen is talking about her and knowing Lydia, that she is an enchantress. If so, she can make men and even women bend to her will if she wants. She may not have realized her power yet, but if not, I bet she will soon."

"How do you free someone from her influence?"

"There are several ways. One, you could kill her."

"I don't think Owen would like that."

"Well then, you either have to convince her to release her hold on him or block it."

"How do we block it?"

"You'd have to put copper bracelets on both her wrists. It will block the flow of energy between her and everyone else. She won't wear copper though. That's what the slaves wear."

"Will it help to keep her away from him?"

"Perhaps. It depends on how far her power extends."

Tristan, who had been listening, shook his head. "It's like the love potion all over again."

"Not quite. You two were senseless to the world."

"Owen," Tristan said, turning to him and speaking loud enough that he could hear them across the table. "What are your plans for the evening?"

"I thought I'd keep Lydia company for a while."

"How is the investigation coming?"

"Inconclusive."

"How could it be inconclusive? Lord Sauerbury let a demon into the castle," Rabiah said.

"Yes, but there's no proof he had anything to do with the King and Queen's deaths."

"What about the records you talked about?" Rabiah didn't want to be too specific since the people on either side of Owen were showing an interest in their conversation.

"What records?"

Tristan looked at Owen in disbelief, then said in a stern voice, "Sir Owen, you are officially removed from the investigation as of this second. The General will be taking over. Please share anything you have uncovered with him after the meal is through. Furthermore, you are confined to your quarters until further notice."

Tristan, it's not his fault.' Rabiah sent.

I know, but how else will we keep them separated?'

Owen's face turned red, then white. "You cannot...Tristan, there's nothing to find."

"It's for your own good Owen."

"Tristan, I thought we were friends."

"Always. More than friends. Brothers."

Owen shook his head and looked down at his food. He pushed his chair back. "I guess I'll go to my quarters then."

"You may finish your meal," Tristan said, not unkindly.

"Yes, Your Highness," Owen said, punctuating the title rudely. Tristan let it pass.

After the meal was through, Tristan, his uncle, Rabiah, and Tristan's ever-present guards followed Owen to his quarters in the officers' barracks. He had a room of his own. Owen handed the General two pages of notes.

"This is it? This is all you've collected?" the General asked.

"There was more but it didn't make sense. It was fabricated to make Lydia and her father look bad."

"Do you still have it?"

"Yes." Owen's eyes wondered to a pile of paper stacked near the fireplace, "but it really will be a waste of your time to look at it."

"I'll be the judge of that." The General walked over and picked up the papers near the fire. Rabiah looked around. She had never been inside Owen's quarters. After traveling with him for a month, she knew he was very meticulous about packing his things properly. She was surprised to see how messy his quarters were. There were papers everywhere. Only his bed was neatly made. She started picking up the papers around his bed in case the General needed them too.

"Don't touch those," Owen growled.

"What are they?" she asked, turning one upside down and then back the other way. She couldn't read, so they were just small markings on a page to her.

"Mine." Owen tried to grab the paper from her. Rabiah was quicker than Owen. She jerked it out of his reach and quickly handed it to Tristan.

Tristan looked over the paper, then smiled and handed it to Owen.

"Poetry," he explained.

"What is poetry?" Rabiah asked.

"It's hard to explain. Owen read her some."

"I will not," Owen said. "This is for someone else's ears only."

"Lydia's?" Tristan asked, "Have you read any to her yet?"

"No. I was going to tonight," he said pitifully.

"Good thing we stopped you then."

They found more papers under the bed and in the drawers as if Owen was trying to hide them. Rabiah piled all she found on the bed and let the men sort through them. Owen paced back and forth, clearly angry but perhaps not completely willing to stop them. Rabiah couldn't stand seeing him so unlike himself. She walked up to him and gently touched his arm.

"Owen, this is not you. I can see something is affecting you. I know the real you is in there somewhere. Fight it. Come back to us." Owen jerked his arm away. Rabiah didn't give up. She dove at his chest and wrapped her arms tightly around him. He tried to push her off but she only squeezed him tighter. She could see his soul. It was still pink. The link she had forged to him when they were fighting the demon was still there. It went right through the pink. She followed it. There he was, her strong, sensitive friend. The link grew bright. Was it pushing the pink apart? Owen stopped trying to fight her. She pressed her forehead against his chest and sent in more power. It wasn't enough.

Tristan, can you see it? If you follow the link to me can you link to Owen and help me push the mist away?

Tristan came up behind her and put his hand on Rabiah's shoulder, then on Owen's. Rabiah shared what she was seeing with Tristan.

"Yes, I see it. Pink is an odd color on you Owen."

"Can you link to him too?"

"I will try." Tristan followed Rabiah's link to Owen. At first it just made her link brighter, but then it split off so that it went just to Owen. Their links now formed a triangle.

'Let's try to break it,' Rabiah sent.

They tried. The both forced power down the links. The pink swirled away from the bright links, but concentrated where they did not reach. Rabiah turned her head. The crown she still wore for the evening meal was knocked sideways. The pink suddenly disappeared.

Tristan opened his eyes and looked at Rabiah, "What happened?"

"I don't know. Maybe Lydia decided to release him. Owen, how do you feel?" She let go of Owen and took a step back.

He couldn't meet her eye. "Foolish."

She punched him in the shoulder. "Don't. How were you to know what she was?"

Owen rubbed his shoulder as he spoke. "I saw the pink. I saw it coming from her but I didn't move. I didn't care."

"How long ago?" Tristan asked.

"A couple of days."

"Did you destroy any evidence?" the General asked.

"No. I buried some, but I couldn't quite bring myself to destroy it."

"All is not lost then. Go unbury it so we can see what you have."

Chapter 5

It was very early in the morning when they finally left Owen's quarters. Not only had they reassembled all the evidence against Lord Sauerbury, but they had also come up with a way to deal with Lydia. The General was going to try and acquire some copper bracelets disguised as something a lady would wear and Tristan would present them as a gift from the king so she would put them on. Owen didn't think she would wear anything he gave her.

When they finally got back to their rooms, Tristan fell asleep as soon as his head hit the pillow. Rabiah was just about to sleep when she realized there was something they had all overlooked. She rolled tiredly out of bed and put her over-tunic and belt back on. The guards posted outside the door were surprised to see her and asked if she needed something. She shook her head and explained she was going to check on Lydia. One of them followed her.

Rabiah climbed the stairs to the third floor and walked down the dim hall to the side of the castle which faced the lake. There was a guard standing near one of the doors in the middle. She assumed that was Lydia's room.

The guard by the door had a slightly pink tint to his soul. As Rabiah approached him she realized there was someone coming from the other direction. It was dark, but she thought she recognized the shape of the other person. She reached the guard first. He had been leaning against the wall but sprang to attention when he realized he wasn't alone.

"You are relieved. Go to your quarters and stay there until further notice," she told the guard.

"Your Highness, I can't. I have my orders. May I ask why you wish to relieve me?"

Owen approached from the other side. "Do as she says."

"Yes Sir." The guard saluted.

"And leave the key," Owen said.

"Here it is, Sir."

"It wasn't just you," Rabiah said to Owen as the guard walked away.

"No. I can't believe I didn't think of it sooner," Owen said.

"Don't be so hard on yourself. It was late and you were not yourself for several days."

"You can go back to bed. I'll stand guard."

Rabiah peered at his soul just in case. It looked white, but she didn't like the idea of his being alone with Lydia.

"Do you think she's still in there?" she asked.

"I don't know. I don't know where she would go. I guess we had better check."

He reached for the door. Rabiah stopped him. He seemed too eager to see Lydia again, or maybe that was her imagination.

"I'll do it. She might not like a man barging into her room in the middle of the night."

"But what if she wakes? She might try to influence you too. I can see it coming."

"So can I, and I have some protection." Rabiah touched the ring beneath her tunic.

Owen hesitated but finally nodded and unlocked the door. "Call out if you need me."

Rabiah stepped inside. The room was dark and had a faint floral scent. The smell was nice but it made her feel like she needed to sneeze. She was afraid she'd run into something or knock something over if she walked very far into the room, so she stood still and looked for Lydia's soul. It was there, across the room. She recognized the pink tint. She turned to go.

"Who is there?" Lydia's voice was firm but Rabiah detected a note of fear.

63

"Rabiah. I just came to make sure you were here. I will leave now."

"The Queen? Why are you here in the middle of the night? You are the queen. You are supposed to be in bed."

"I am helping Sir Owen."

"Sir Owen? Sir Owen is a soldier. There are many soldiers. Why would he need you?"

"He is my friend."

Rabiah turned to go. Lydia's plaintive voice stopped her.

"What's it like?"

"What?"

"Being queen?"

"What do you think it's like?"

"It must be nice to have people respect you and listen to you, to ask your opinion and to have a husband who cares about you."

"The husband part is nice. I don't think many people respect me, I don't like giving people advice, and I don't like everyone watching everything I do."

"I should have been queen," Lydia sighed.

"Who says you can't be? There are many other countries and you are beautiful. I'm sure there is a king or prince somewhere who would gladly marry you."

"This is my country."

"Don't queens usually come from other countries?"

"But King Tristan is all I ever wanted in a husband."

"King Tristan, for whatever reason, was not attracted to you as a wife."

"But he was to you. Why?"

"I don't know. He didn't even see my full face before he claimed me. I thought he was going to kill me and he kissed me instead. I'm surprised he knew I was a girl."

Lydia was silent. Rabiah turned to go again, then Lydia spoke, "Will you help me?"

"Help you with what?"

"Find someone like Tristan."

"You already have, but you turned him down."

"Who?"

"Sir Owen."

"He's just a soldier."

"He is the King's best friend."

"But he is not king."

"No, he is only one of the most loyal, bravest, and kindest men I've met. He would love you deeply if you let him, but you have pushed him away."

"Not so. We've become quite close the last few days."

"Have you? What if he tried to kiss you?"

"That would not be proper, although I've thought about it a little."

"What you've done to him is not love. You don't respect him. You think he is beneath you. Sir Owen is greater than you'll ever be, even if you became queen of the world."

"You don't know what greatness is," Lydia scoffed.

"Or perhaps we define it differently." Rabiah was very tired and just wanted to go to bed. "Goodnight Lydia." Rabiah turned to leave again.

"Will you come back to see me?"

Rabiah stopped in surprise and turned to look at Lydia in the dark. "Why?"

"No reason. Just wondering."

"I don't know." Rabiah pulled open the door and slipped out. Owen was standing one-legged, leaning against the wall. He pushed himself away when he saw her.

"I'll stand guard. Go to bed, Your Highness.

"Give me the key, Owen."

He dropped it into her hand and she locked the door. "Now go wake two soldiers who have never been near Lydia and are not likely to succumb to her charms. I'll stand guard with James here," she indicated the guard who had followed her upstairs.

"Your Highness, that is not necessary."

"It is. Now hurry so I can get to bed."

"Yes, Your Highness."

"And stop calling me that, at least when it's just in front of the guard or else I'm going to throttle you."

Owen snorted and crossed his arms. "You and what army, Your Highness?" he asked, with extra emphasis on the last two words.

He was not prepared for her quick response. He ended up on his back with her arm across his throat.

"I yield, my Queen," he said, laughing a little.

She shook her head in exasperation. Someone opened a door down the hallway and lifted a candle high to see what the commotion was about. Rabiah removed her arm from Owen's neck and stood with her hand extended. He took it, pulled himself up, then bowed deeply. I'll be back shortly, my Queen."

She growled at him. He gave her a cocky look before quickly departing. She heard whoever held the candle ask if everything was all right as he went by. Owen replied that they were just changing the guard. When she could no longer see him, she posted herself on the opposite side of the door from the guard, James. James, she noticed, was eyeing her with respect or wariness. She wasn't sure which. He quickly looked away when she caught him staring.

It was late the next morning when Rabiah awoke to find Tristan still sleeping beside her. He had said this was a rest day. Did that mean even the servants rested? She rang the bell for breakfast just to see what would happen. A few minutes later a breathless servant appeared with a full tray of food.

"You don't get to rest today?" Rabiah asked.

"No, Your Highness. We take turns working on the rest days. I'll be off on the next rest day."

"Thank you for your service."

The girl bowed and was about to exit the room when Rabiah suddenly realized there was another issue they hadn't considered last night.

"Before you leave, have you taken food to Lydia on the third floor?"

"Yes, Your Highness."

"Did you serve it to her?"

66

"Oh, no. The guards are the only ones allowed in the room."

"No one cleans or does other services?"

"Only in the presence of the guards Your Highness."

"Thank you. You may go."

Rabiah left the food on the table and went to see if Tristan wanted to eat. He looked so adorable to her in the morning light, sprawled across the middle of the bed that she couldn't resist climbing back onto the bed and kissing his forehead. He opened his eyes, startled, then grabbed her. The food was cold before they sat down to eat it.

They went riding after Rabiah had personally made sure new, untainted guards were outside Lydia's room.

Chapter 6

Esmerelda came back after the rest day her usual, stoic self but with an insatiable desire to mold Rabiah into a queen, or at least it seemed to Rabiah. When she wasn't interacting with the staff or working on her handwriting, Esmerelda insisted she interact with the female visitors in the castle and work on the dreaded correspondence. Rabiah couldn't wait to escape for her 'walk' after the midday meal. There'd been another huge snowfall, making any distance challenging. Esmerelda and the other ladies didn't wish to go outside in the cold. Rabiah relished it now that it no longer affected her as much. She had the time all to herself except for the two guards Uncle had insisted accompany her whenever she went outside of the castle.

She didn't see Mitch around the castle for several days, so she mentally asked Owen to have Mitch meet her after the midday meal one day. Owen was with him.

"Are you coming with us Owen?"

"No, my Queen," he grumbled. "Just on my way to see His Royal Highness. With you two in my head I'm lucky to have room for myself in there."

"I'm sorry Owen. I didn't realize it bothered you so much. I wasn't sure where to find Mitch."

"Just don't make it a habit." Owen stomped into the castle, knocking the snow off his boots as he went.

Mitch bowed to her, "My Queen, I hear you have a request for me?"

"Perhaps, but I want you to meet some people first. Come with me." She started walking. Mitch fell into step beside her.

"I hear it was you and Sir Owen who defeated the demon. It was terrible being under his control. I've been wanting to thank you."

"You're welcome Mitch. I'm just glad we figured out how to do it."

"How did you?"

Rabiah told him as they walked, leaving out certain parts. The guards following walked closer than normal so they could hear too. She had just finished the tale when they arrived at the barracks. Rabiah led Mitch to the building where the Clanspeople were housed and knocked. It took longer than usual for someone to answer the door. Dacia opened it. Rabiah could immediately tell something was wrong.

"What has happened?" she asked.

"It's Hadassah. She's having contractions. It's too early. The baby won't make it."

"Have you asked for the healers yet?"

"What could they do?"

"I don't know, but their knowledge is different from ours." Rabiah turned to Mitch. "Can you find Healer Marion and tell her what's going on?"

"Of course my Queen." He gave her a quick bow and ran off through the snow.

"May I come in?"

"Yes."

Hadassah was sitting on a mat with a couple of other women around her, her hand on her swollen belly. Her face was streaked with tears. Rabiah looked at her with her other sight. She could see the baby's soul. It was still alive.

"She has lost so much," Dacia went on, "First her husband, then her daughter, and now this."

"Did she lose them both during the fighting?"

"No, just her husband. Her daughter became very ill and weak on the way here. The soldiers took her away. We never saw her again."

Rabiah knelt down by Hadassah and said in a low voice, "Your baby is still alive. I've sent for the healers. They might be able to help."

Hadassah was doubtful. "How do you know the baby is alive?"

"It is my gift."

Hadassah closed her eyes and grabbed the edge of the mat as a contraction hit. One of the women nearby laid her hands on either side of Hadassah's belly and closed her eyes. Hadassah relaxed a little.

"Her gift is to remove pain from others," Tarja explained.

"I hope she's around if I ever have children," Rabiah said.

The contractions were not close together although Hadassah had two more before Mitch returned with Healer Marion and another woman Rabiah didn't recognize.

"Your Highness, This is Mame, the most experienced midwife in Auroria," Marion said, introducing her.

Mame curtsied, "So we meet again Your Highness. I'm glad to see you are feeling better."

Rabiah frowned, "I don't remember our meeting."

The woman smiled good-naturedly. "You wouldn't. You were unconscious at the time. I spoke with your husband."

"When was this?"

"On the temple steps."

Realization dawned on Rabiah, "Were you the one who told the King about…" She stopped. She wasn't ready to announce anything yet. Luckily no one noticed.

Mame gave a little nod.

"The baby is still alive," Rabiah said as Mame turned to attend to Hadassah.

Mame looked back at her and nodded, "You can sense it?"

"Yes. It is my gift."

"Did you know before I talked to the King?"

"Yes."

"That's rare to see them so early. Come, kneel here with me. Let's see if we can help her."

Rabiah did as she was told. Mame had Hadassah lay back so she could feel her belly.

"The baby appears to be in good health and is already low. It is small but not as small as it could be. Place your hands here Your Highness. What do you feel?"

"Something hard. Wait, is that a foot?"

The woman laughed. "Yes, the baby is eager to leave. He or she is in position. I think the baby is older than everyone realizes. Have you ever attended a birth, Your Highness?"

"Yes, those of my niece and nephew."

"Would you like to attend another?"

Rabiah removed her hands from Hadassah's belly.

"Among my people it is an honor to be asked to attend a birth. I am sure there are others whom Hadassah would rather be present."

Hadassah put her hand on Rabiah's arm. "Queen Rabiah, I would be honored if you would stay."

"And I am honored to be asked," Rabiah responded with a small bow of her head.

"So you will stay. Good," Mame said. "Now should we get all these men-folk out of here, or do you want them to stay too?" she asked Hadassah with a raised eyebrow.

"No. They can leave. Please."

"Mitch, can you take the men somewhere for a while?" Rabiah asked.

"Of course, Your Highness."

Rabiah removed a small bag from her belt and tossed it to him. "Take this. I was going to ask the women if they'd like to go shopping today but perhaps the men can find a use for it."

"I'm sure we can," Mitch grinned. "Come along men. Let's go spend the Queen's money."

The minutes turned to hours. Hadassah's contractions slowly grew closer. The women visited and told stories of other births. The time of the evening meal approached.

Where are you Rabiah? Tristan sent.

I'm attending a birth. I'll be back late.

Someone's having a baby? Where are you?

It's Hadassah. Her baby is coming early.

Are the healers there?

71

'Yes, and so is Mame. She's the woman who told you about the twins.'

'Let me know when the baby arrives.'

'I will.'

Mame had Hadassah get up and walk around between contractions. This time, as Rabiah helped her up, there was a small gush of fluid.

"It's about time," Mame said. "Walk if you can, but I bet that little one will be here soon."

Hadassah did not walk far before the contractions started coming hard and fast. The other women crowded around, holding her hands and rubbing her back. Rabiah stood back and watched. Mame pulled her aside and asked, "How are you with blood?"

Rabiah shrugged, "It doesn't bother me."

"Good. You can be my assistant. The first rule is to be clean. Scrub your hands well with this soap, then dump the water outside and put more on to heat."

Rabiah did as she was told. She went to the door to dump the water and almost threw it on the returning Clansmen.

"You're back already?" she asked.

"We've been gone for hours," Mitch said, "and we ran out of money."

"Have you eaten?"

"Here and there."

"The evening meal is about to begin. Take them there."

"Are you sure?"

"Mitch, you have been hanging around these Clansmen all day. Are they that different from the men around here?"

"No. They're a lot alike, actually."

"And would you choose to spend time with them again?"

"Sure."

"That's why I asked you to come with me today. I want you to be an ambassador to my people. Tonight you can practice by being an ambassador *for* my people."

"You want me to be an ambassador?"

"Yes. I've already spoken with the King. If the Clanspeople agree, I'll send you with them in the spring, if you want to go, that is."

He bowed deeply to her and said without hesitation, "It would be an honor, my Queen."

"Go. Introduce the Clansmen to your friends. See if you can keep everything peaceful."

"Yes, my Queen!" Mitch snapped to attention and saluted her. She saluted back and turned to go inside. Her personal guards were standing at attention on either side of the door.

"Have you been here all afternoon?" she asked them.

"Yes, Your Highness."

"You must be frozen. Go with them and get something to eat."

"We cannot leave you unguarded. The General would have our hides."

"Can one of you go and get some replacements?"

"We have another hour left of our shifts. We already sent someone to tell the next guards where we are."

"I'm sorry you had to stand in the cold. I'd ask to let you in but the baby is almost here."

"That's all right Your Highness. I'd rather stay out here," one of the guards said.

Rabiah went back inside.

Tristan, Mitch is coming with the Clansmen. They needed somewhere to go.'

'I'll make sure they are welcome. How's the birth going?'

'Her water broke.'

'It took that long?'

'Yes. Mame tells me this is about normal for a second birth.'

'How long does it take for a first one?'

'It can take days.'

'I hope yours doesn't take that long.'

'Me too.'

Hadassah's contractions where getting stronger and stronger. Sweat dotted her brow.

"Deep breaths. Deep breaths. Breath through the contraction," Mame coached. To Rabiah she said, "She's almost there. Any minute now she'll get the urge to push."

Mame's prediction was right. Hadassah squatted as another contraction hit.

"Gently, gently, You don't want to tear." Mame showed Rabiah how to help the skin stretch around the baby's head. "Here, you do it. Can you feel the head?"

"Yes." It was falling into her hand.

"Gently turn the baby a little so the shoulders can slide through." Rabiah did so. There was suddenly a small, wet, and slightly purple baby in her hands. Mame gently wiped the baby's mouth and nose with a clean cloth as Rabiah held her. The baby started to cry.

"Give her to her mother," Mame instructed Rabiah.

To Hadassah she said, "Try to feed her Hadassah. It will help with the bleeding."

Hadassah tried, but the baby's mouth was so small Rabiah didn't see how it would ever fit.

"It will fit. Watch." Mame demonstrated. She got the baby to open its mouth wider than Rabiah thought possible.

"You didn't cut the cord," Rabiah noticed.

"No. It's still pulsing, see? I'll cut it when it stops."

A few minutes later, Rabiah watched as Mame tied the cord with a clean string and then cut it with a pair of scissors that she had sitting in a pan of water that had been boiling earlier. The afterbirth came shortly afterwards. Rabiah suddenly had many questions.

"If there are twins, is there one afterbirth or two?"

"I've seen both. It is better if there are two."

"Do twins come out at the same time?"

"Sometimes they come out one right after the other. Sometimes they are days apart, although not often."

"The cord is so long. Does it ever get tangled?"

"Yes."

"Does it ever get wrapped around the baby's neck?"

Mame turned to her, "There are many things that can go wrong but there are many things that go right. You and I made it as did all those here. Worrying about it won't prevent anything so don't worry. Just be prepared for the worst and pray for the best."

Rabiah nodded. She *was* worried and more than a little scared if she were honest with herself. Mame gave good advice.

The Clanswomen had taken the baby and were gently cleaning her while Mame finished with her mother. The baby was small, but not dangerously so. The women wrapped the little girl in a clean blanket and handed her back to Hadassah. Rabiah marveled at the cute little face that peaked out of the blanket. She wondered what her own children would look like.

'Tristan, the baby is here.'

'Boy or girl?'

'Girl. She's very small but very beautiful.'

'Did you watch?'

'I helped deliver her.'

'And?'

'It was hard. Tristan, how am I going to deliver two?'

'If anyone can do it, you can.'

'I'll go back to the castle as soon as I can.'

'Wait for me. I'd like to see the new baby if they'll let me.'

'I'm sure they will, but you must wash your hands if you want to hold her.'

'I'll just look.'

Rabiah helped the women tidy up before the men came back from the meal. Someone knocked. Tarja answered the door, then stood back to let Tristan enter. Rabiah's stomach gave a little jump. She hadn't seen him all day and he stood out to her like a beacon among the shorter Clanspeople with his lighter hair and lighter skin. He was amused by the way she rushed to his side, grabbed his hand, and dragged him towards the new baby. Hadassah offered the bundle to Tristan but he shook his head and backed away. Rabiah took the baby and held her so Tristan could see.

"She *is* lovely," Tristan said.

"Much more so than my brother's children. At first they looked rather squashed. They changed after a few days though."

"Really? Babies come out squashed?"

"Their faces do, a little."

Rabiah gave the baby back to Hadassah. "Thank you for letting me stay. May the Spirit watch over and protect both of you, always."

"Thank you, Queen Rabiah. May the Spirit watch over and protect you and your children as well."

Rabiah nodded respectfully. They turned to leave just as the Clansmen and Mitch reached the door.

"How did it go?" Rabiah asked Mitch.

"There were a couple of hotheads but nothing I couldn't handle."

"Good. I want you to show the Clansmen around. It's easy to hate things you don't know, but if the people of Arles interact with the Clansmen, perhaps that hate won't come so easily."

"I'll do my best."

"I want you to learn their language too, at least the common one."

"Yes, Your Highness."

"I'll teach you or perhaps one of the Clanspeople will help you."

"Yes, my Queen." Mitch had an infectious grin.

"Thank you for helping today. Where did you go?"

"Oh, here and there." His grin got bigger.

"May I have the bag back at least," Rabiah said, holding out her hand. Mitch dropped the empty money bag into it, still grinning.

"He spent all my money," she groused to Tristan.

"You should know better than to give money to a soldier."

Owen was waiting outside.

"Why didn't you go in?" Rabiah asked him.

"I'm on guard duty for his Royal pain-in-the-ass."

Rabiah turned to Tristan, "What's wrong with him?"

"He'd rather be guarding a certain female."

'And?

'I've been talking to him all day and he can't talk back.' Tristan grinned roguishly.

Rabiah punched him and turned to Owen.

"Owen, go in and see the baby."

"No, I'd rather not. One baby pretty much looks like another."

"Really? Even the way you see?"

"Babies are either comfortable or they're not. That's all there is to see."

"But she's really beautiful. I think she's the prettiest baby I've ever seen. Come and see."

Owen signed and followed her back in.

"Hadassah, this is my good friend, Sir Owen. I just wanted him to see how beautiful your daughter is."

Hadassah smiled and held the baby for Owen to view. She was propped up in a sitting position. Owen looked at the baby, then the mother. He said gruffly, "She is very beautiful. Congratulations."

"Thank you."

"Yet you are sad."

"She is all that is left of my family."

To Rabiah's shock and amazement, Owen sat down on the ground beside Hadassah and wrapped his arms around her as she began to cry. She sobbed into his shoulder. Rabiah looked at Tristan wide-eyed. He just shrugged.

"He has a knack of knowing when women are about to cry."

"Shall we leave him to it then?"

"Hungry, are you?"

"Yes."

"Good thing I brought some food."

Tristan opened the door again and beckoned to two other guards she had not noticed before. They were each carrying a large basket. They placed them on the single table near the entrance of the dormitory and started unloading an assortment of food, including a large pudding.

"How did you sneak so much food from the kitchens?" Rabiah asked.

"The cook is a lot nicer to me since I became king and she seems to like you. I told her you were attending a child-birth and she pulled out the baskets and started filling them. I had to stop her from putting too much in."

Rabiah ate with the other women. After all the empty dishes were collected, she and Tristan walked back through the dark followed by their guards. The night was cold and crisp. Stars sparkled like diamond dust in the sky. Tristan offered Rabiah his arm and she gladly took it.

"I love nights like this," Tristan said.

"Do you want to go up to the tower?"

"We'd get cold pretty quickly I think."

"Even if we were to do a little exercise?"

"What kind of exercise?"

"I was thinking swords."

"Sounds intriguing."

"There won't be room for the guards."

"I'll just tell them to guard the door. They'll like that since they can stay warm."

"I'd like to change first."

"Of course."

'Shall I wear my leather tunic?

Tristan didn't respond with words.

Owen lowered his eyes behind them. From their auras he could tell exactly what his king and queen were thinking. He didn't want to start contemplating his chances with a certain female again, so he forced himself to think about the investigation. Instead though, he found himself dwelling on the warm little bundle he had held while her mother ate and the way the mother had clung to him while she cried.

Chapter 7

Esmerelda was not impressed with Rabiah's excuse for missing the lessons and the evening meal the day before.

"You can't just disappear. No one knew where you were."

"Tristan did."

"Well, don't disappear today. You have a tea scheduled this afternoon."

"A tea?"

"Yes. I've invited the ladies around the castle to spend the afternoon sharing a little food and drink and visiting. This is a way for you to learn everyone's faces and hear the latest gossip."

"I don't gossip."

"Nor do I, but it's a way to learn things that are going on that the King may not be aware of. Queen Naomi would sometimes make suggestions to the King based on what she'd heard."

Rabiah sighed inwardly. She had never felt comfortable around large groups of women, but she had enjoyed her time with the Clanswomen yesterday. Perhaps the tea wouldn't be so bad.

Esmerelda made her wear her nicest tunic and told her to wear her crown. Rabiah greeted everyone as she had been instructed, then sat and sipped her tea. Some of the women politely tried to engage Rabiah in conversation but they were talking about things she knew little about or had no interest in. The conversations quickly faded. A couple of others spoke of their husbands and issues they were having. These she recognized as petitions, which she didn't mind. Some of the ladies ignored her completely and talked and laughed amongst themselves. There were a few younger women there close to her age.

The kept looking at her and whispering. An hour passed. She'd had enough.

She stood up and said, "Ladies, if you will excuse me, I have other matters to attend to. Please enjoy your tea."

She left. Without pause she marched to her rooms and slammed the door. She stripped off the dressy tunics as fast as she could, then dawned one of the shorter tunics and the pants that Tristan had given her.

'If either of you are interested, I'm going down to the training fields where I intend to stay until I either knock a few men down or I fall down myself,' she sent to Tristan and Owen not caring what meeting she might interrupt.

'Is everything all right?' Tristan sent.

'It's fine. I just need to do something.'

'I wish I could join you but I'm in the middle of a meeting. Don't push yourself too hard.'

His voice calmed her down somewhat. She was now in full fighting gear. For Tristan's sake, she went out the back door near the kitchens instead of out the front through the Great Hall.

There were several people on the field. Rabiah found a corner by herself and started warming up.

"Good afternoon, Your Highness. Nice of you to drop by," an older, grizzly man greeted her.

"Good afternoon Roland, Master at Arms. You just became my first opponent."

He raised a fuzzy eyebrow at her, "Are you sure you wouldn't rather wait for someone younger and maybe a bit better looking to come by?"

"You'll do."

"Not having a spat with your husband are you?"

"No. Just tired of sitting around."

Roland nodded. "Let me get some practice swords."

Roland went easy on her but she didn't mind. Just going through the moves helped to lighten her mood. Roland finally pulled up his sword and bowed. "I'm glad you are healing so quickly, but I don't want to be blamed if you over-do."

She lifted her sword to him. "Thank you Roland for your concern and for helping me let off some steam."

"Any time my Queen." Roland lumbered off, leaving her alone with her guards in the corner of the field. She was not tired yet. She pointed her sword at one of them and challenged him with a look. It pleased her that he looked a little scared. He glanced at his buddy who laughingly waved him on. The guard ran to get another wooden sword. He returned a couple of minutes later, panting slightly. She gave him a few seconds to catch his breath, then bowed to indicate the start of the match. He hesitantly slashed at her. She ducked and knocked him to the ground. The other guard snickered.

"I know you are better than that. Don't worry about hurting me. You won't be able to."

"I wouldn't be so sure of that," she heard him mumble under his breath as he picked himself up from the ground. She smiled happily. The match was on.

The guard wasn't as good as Owen, but he was definitely more skilled than the new recruits she had faced before. She enjoyed herself immensely for a while, then she realized how tired she was beginning to feel. She raised her hand to stop him and then dropped down on the ground to sit for a minute.

"Your Highness, are you all right?" he asked, a sincere not of concern in his voice.

"I'm fine. I just need to rest a bit. Thank you for sparring with me."

"Should I get you a drink?"

"I don't need one, although you can get one if you are thirsty."

"No, I'm fine."

Rabiah nodded and leaned back on her hands. She closed her eyes and breathed deeply. The dizziness that had hit her suddenly started to pass. After a minute or so she opened her eyes. The guards were watching her worriedly.

"All better," she smiled.

"Shall we get someone?"

"No. Just help me up. Slowly please."

"They each grabbed a hand and puller her up. She wobbled, then steadied.

"I think that's enough for now. Let's go back to the castle."

The guards eagerly complied, walking closely lest she suddenly collapse, but she made it under her own power all the way back to the castle and up the back stairs. She turned to them at the door of her rooms.

"Thank you." She saluted them and they saluted respectfully back. "I'm going to rest. Please don't let anyone in except the King."

She walked into the bedroom, stripping off clothes as she went. Sliding into the soft bed had never felt so good. She fell asleep almost immediately.

Tristan woke her a couple of hours later with a kiss on her forehead.

"I see you wore yourself out."

"A little," she smiled sleepily at him.

"I think you scared your guards."

"Was I that ferocious?"

"No they were afraid you pushed yourself too hard." He kissed her brow again. "What happened?"

"Tea."

"Tea?"

"Esmerelda made me go to tea with all the castle ladies. Tristan, we have nothing in common. They talked among themselves and whispered. I couldn't take it anymore. I left. I'll never be a good queen, Tristan."

He sat next to her on the bed and pulled her up so he could put his arms around her. "You are already a great queen. What other queen has saved not only her husband but the whole castle from a demon? You and my mother are two very different women. I don't expect you to be like her or do what she did. I know how boring those teas can be. She made me go to some of them. I know some of the ladies are unkind, but some are very nice. I'll point them out to you. I'm sure you'll find a few good friends."

"And if I don't?"

"You'll always have me."

He shared some of his strength with her, then stood and rang the bell.

"Dinner in bed for you tonight."

She didn't argue. She didn't want to face all the people downstairs.

"What about Esmerelda? She's going to be displeased with me."

"I'll talk to Esmerelda."

"Tristan, you don't have to. You have so many other things to see to. I can speak to her."

"I want her to realize I don't expect you to be just like my mother. I want her to know I support you no matter what you decide to do. Well, within reason."

"What's that supposed to mean?"

"No more trying to take on the army when you're still weak from the last battle you fought!"

So he *was* a little upset, Rabiah thought. "Yes, my husband," she said meekly.

"You need to take care of yourself. Not just because you're you, but because, well, you know."

She lowered her head, "I know and I'm sorry. I didn't mean to push it so hard. I was feeling great, then I got tired very suddenly."

Tristan grabbed her and hugged her fiercely. She hugged him just as tightly back. Someone knocked on the door and he gently released her.

"That will be food I hope," Tristan said.

It was.

"Eat with me?" Rabiah asked.

"Gladly. Wondering what you were up to all afternoon has made me hungry."

Chapter 8

A week went by. Esmerelda had stopped pushing Rabiah to be social but had continued to teach her to read and write. Rabiah didn't mind those lessons so much. As she began to recognize the characters, words began to form for her whenever she saw them. It was as if she'd discovered a secret world that existed in plain sight.

Rabiah visited the Clanspeople again with Mitch in tow a few days after the baby was born. The baby, now named Tahirah, was doing well. The Clansmen greeted Mitch like old friends. While Mitch was talking with them, Rabiah asked Tarja what she thought of her ambassador. Tarja smiled, "He'll do."

"He needs to learn our language."

"He needs to learn many things. Send him to us every day and we'll begin training him."

While she was visiting, Owen came by. Rabiah greeted him, thinking he needed to see her about something, but he denied it and showed her the simple wooden carving that was in his hand. "I thought the baby could use a toy."

"She's only a few days old," Rabiah pointed out.

"She'll grow."

Owen walked over to Hadassah who was sitting at the table with Tahirah. Hadassah greeted him warmly. Owen showed her the toy. Hadassah had Owen sit and handed him the baby. They were still talking when Rabiah left.

The General pulled Tristan and Rabiah aside after the evening meal that night. He had found some bracelets appropriate for someone of Lydia's class. They were made of copper, gold, and silver intertwined so that each metal formed a complete circle. They looked too big. Rabiah started to try one on to check. The General stopped her.

"They will adjust to fit once they go on, so don't put one on unless you want to wear it permanently."

Rabiah handed the bracelet back to him and asked, "How is the investigation going?"

"It's clear that Lord Sauerbury was up to something. He raised a large sum by liquidating some assets and by borrowing from several different people, but what he did with it or who he gave it to is unclear. We haven't been able to determine who showed the assassin the secret passage and there's no evidence that Lord Sauerbury knew it was there, although I wouldn't be surprised. He has visited the castle often enough."

"So it is inconclusive, just as Owen said."

"Not quite. We know the assassin spent the night at an inn nearby and Lord Sauerbury was seen at the same inn, although not with the assassin. We've also acquired some of the coin the assassin used to pay the innkeeper. It has the same image imprinted on it as the coins we found in Lord Sauerbury's room. It is not a common image. We also have Lydia's statement that her father knew what the poison was. What we don't know is how Lord Sauerbury contacted the assassin, how long he had been planning the murders, and if there was anyone else involved. I find it strange that the assassin killed himself so quickly. That suggests he had some knowledge to protect."

"What about the demon?" Rabiah asked. "From where did Lord Sauerbury acquire that?"

"That was a little easier to trace since the same person that sold it to him offered it to me first. Lord Sauerbury had possession of that particular demon for at least two years."

"Why? Why would anyone want to buy a demon?"

"Why collect a piece of art that just hangs on the wall when you can have an ancient, knowledgeable being you can interact with and learn from?"

"They're dangerous."

"Only if you set them free."

"Or they just let you think they aren't free," Rabiah reminded the General.

"That won't happen again. I've had the rest of my collection tested."

"Why do people bother trapping them? Why don't they just exile them?"

"Not everyone has that power Rabiah."

She hadn't known that. How was it she had been able to exile the demon who attacked Tristan?

"Is there any evidence that ties Lydia to the crime?" Rabiah asked.

"Not so far."

"So she can be set free?"

"Yes, but I think we should put the bracelets on her first."

"Is that fair, to take away her gift?"

"She's already shown that she cannot be trusted with it."

"Perhaps, but if she doesn't know what her power is, then how can you blame her for using it. Wouldn't you want a friend if you were imprisoned?"

"You don't know Lydia."

"No, I do not, but I wonder if she knows herself. Her father has been pushing her to become queen her whole life. Now she is free of him. Perhaps she is not as bad as you think."

"What are you proposing, Rabiah?" Tristan asked.

"That we tell her of her power and let her free with the understanding that we will put the bracelets on if she uses it."

"It's too dangerous," the General said. "Think of what she could do. She could send the whole army after you."

"We don't know that. She may only be able to influence one or two people at a time."

"One is enough."

"We should at least let her know what her power is," Rabiah argued.

"Why? To have it and not be able to use it would be worse I think," the General said.

"Will a blacksmith be able to remove the bracelets?" Tristan asked.

"No. Only a wizard of great power and those are very few."

"I don't like this," Rabiah stated.

"For all we know, Lydia knows of her power and has been using it for years. Perhaps she used it to influence her father to kill my brother and his wife. It was not a well thought out plan if they were going to use a love potion to convince Tristan to marry her. On the other hand, if Lydia only needed enough time to influence Tristan, a love potion would have worked."

"We need to ask her. Owen can tell if she's lying and I can tell if she's influencing him."

"Just put the bracelets on her," the General urged.

"I will not, not until I've talked to her." Rabiah said firmly, crossing her arms.

"What possible good could come from letting those powers free?"

"My powers are just as dangerous. If I can give you energy, I can take it away. So can all the healers, but they don't. I could kill you right now with my bare hands, but I won't," Rabiah argued.

"Yes, but your powers are useful. When would anyone want to be influenced against their will?"

"Why would anyone want to die by the sword? They wouldn't, yet you yield one anyway."

"Yes, but they can see it coming."

Tristan decided it was time to cut in, "Uncle, Rabiah, you both make valid points. I've known Lydia her whole life. It's hard enough for me to believe her father was behind the deaths of my parents, let alone that Lydia somehow drove him to it. However, if she did, then she poses a real danger to the kingdom. Let's talk to her and see what she knows. If she is innocent of conscientiously influencing the events then we can give her a choice. She can put on the bracelets and be free or stay in custody until we are confident that she can and will control her power. Owen should be on his way.

"You can talk to him now too?" his Uncle asked.

"Yes, but he can't talk back," Tristan grinned.

"Maybe I should have some bracelets made for you."

"Would they work on Tristan and me?" Rabiah asked.

"Partially. They can block the transfer of energy and heat but your mental link is something different."

It took Owen only a few minutes to arrive.

"You called Your Highness?" Owen bowed insincerely.

"Yes, Sir Owen. We're going to talk to Lydia and we are in need of your services."

"What services?" Owen asked suspiciously. He had been avoiding the third floor as much as he could since he'd been freed of Lydia's influence. He'd found it hard at first to stay away, but now he was repelled at the thought of seeing her.

"We're going to ask her some questions and we need you to make sure she's telling the truth," Rabiah explained.

Owen nodded, "But I'm leaving if she tries to entrap me again."

"As you should," Rabiah agreed.

They climbed up to the third floor with Tristan's guards following behind. Servants and guests got out of the way when they saw them coming. Some followed at a discreet distance to see where they were going.

The guards posted outside Lydia's door saluted and unlocked the door for them. Rabiah scanned them. No pink. The General knocked on the door.

"Lydia may we come in?" Tristan asked.

"Go ahead. I can't stop you."

They entered. Two of the guards came with them. The room was messier than before. Rabiah supposed it was because the servants had very little access to the room now.

"So you have finally decided my fate? Am I free to leave?"

"Possibly," Tristan said. "We just want to ask you a few questions first."

"Ask me anything. I am so tired of this room."

"Lydia, what is your gift?"

"My gift? I don't have a gift."

"Yes you do. Do you know what it is?"

"What gift are you talking about?"

88

Rabiah noticed a little pink was beginning to collect around Lydia.

"Lydia, I'm talking about the special gift that each of us has. Some can boil water by looking at it. Others can heal. Others can create beautiful things. What is your gift?"

"I, I'm not sure."

"She's lying," Owen said from behind the two guards. The pink started to flow in Owen's direction.

"Sir Owen, I didn't see you there. Where have you been? I thought you were my friend. I thought," she paused, and said in a soft voice, "that we might be more than that."

"How long have you known about your power?" Tristan asked.

"What difference does it make?"

"A lot," Tristan said. "Did you use it to influence your father to do what he did?"

"Not knowingly," she hung her head. "I didn't realize until recently that I had the power of persuasion."

The pink was almost to Owen. It flowed right between the two guards. Owen was watching it come. Rabiah stepped back and pulled him out of the way. He looked at her blankly. There must be something she couldn't see.

'Owen, remember me? Remember Tristan? Remember how mad you were at Lydia?

Owen frowned a little but didn't respond.

'Remember Hadassah and her baby?

"Tahirah?"

"Yes."

Owen blinked and shook his head. The spell was broken.

'Get out of here. There's more going on than we can see.'

"She'll probably go for Tristan or the General next," Owen said in a low voice.

'I'll keep an eye on them. Go before she snares you again.'

While Rabiah had been talking to Owen, Tristan continued his questioning, "How recently?"

"After I was locked up in here. Owen suddenly started acting caring towards me and if I showed displeasure he was quick to try and please me. It was nice to have a friend. Where is he going?" Lydia strained to see around the guards as Owen disappeared through the door.

"Lydia, it isn't friendship if you are controlling someone."

The pink was flowing back toward Lydia. She must have given up on Owen. Lydia looked at Tristan, "Why not? It benefits both of us. I'm happy. He's happy."

"But you have taken away his freedom and made him a slave to you."

"Like she has made you a slave to her?" Lydia nodded toward Rabiah.

"She does not have your power Lydia," Tristan said.

The pink had changed course and was now headed towards the General. Rabiah stepped forward and touched the General's arm.

"Uncle?"

The General turned to look at her blankly, then he too blinked and shook his head.

"She's after me isn't she?"

"Yes."

He handed her the box with the bracelets. "You might just have to hold her down to slip those on."

"Whatever it takes," she nodded.

The General left. The pink had changed direction toward Tristan.

Tristan, step back.'

He obeyed. *'She's after me now?'*

'Yes, but I think there's more than I can see.'

'Let's get this done then.'

"Lydia, I'm giving you a choice. Either stop using your power against other people or we will do it for you."

"What do you mean?"

'Tristan, step back.'

'I can't keep stepping back. There's not enough room.'

'Step towards me then.'

"Why do you keep moving around?" Lydia asked.

"I take it you will not control your power."

90

"I don't know what you are talking about."

"Lydia, while I've been talking to you, you have tried to influence Owen, then Uncle, and now me. Is this why your father did what he did? Did you want to be queen so much that you convinced your father to kill my parents?"

Lydia covered her face with her hands. If not truly upset, she did a good job of acting like she was. "I don't know. I didn't mean to if I did. I didn't want your parents dead. I didn't want my father to sell his soul. All I ever wanted was you Tristan and you were never interested."

Tristan stepped forward into the pink before Rabiah could stop him. It didn't climb up his leg the way she expected. Instead, it fell back as if it were repelled by him. Tristan sat next to Lydia on the bed.

"Lydia, I'm only one man. There are many in this world. I can't explain why I have never been interested in you that way, I just wasn't. That doesn't mean I didn't think of you as a friend."

"I didn't want you as a friend."

Tristan nodded to Rabiah. She brought the box and opened it for him. Tristan picked up one of the bracelets and showed it to Lydia.

"This is for you. This will prevent you from using your power to assert undue influence on others whether purposely or not. It you put them on willingly, you may leave this room, although we must verify that they are working before you can go home. You will not be able to remove them."

The pink was heading for Rabiah now. Her necklace heated and the pink wave parted.

"How is it you are unaffected?" Lydia asked Tristan.

"Lucky I guess," Tristan shrugged.

"Do I have a choice?" Lydia asked.

"Yes. If you don't put them on I cannot let you free. You must remain a prisoner and I cannot allow you many visitors since you might try to influence them."

"Will you come to see me?"

"Perhaps, but I'm a busy man. It wouldn't be often."

91

"Does it matter?" Rabiah asked. She could feel a force that Lydia was sending her way, but she was able to resist it.

"No, I suppose not." Lydia put her arms out in front of her. "Put them on."

Rabiah took the other bracelet and she and Tristan slid them on at the same time. Both bracelets immediately shrunk so that Lydia could not slide them off, but they were not tight.

Lydia inspected her wrists. "I suppose it could be worse. You could have just put slave bands on me."

"I know you better than that, Lydia," Tristan said.

The pink was gone except for that twirling around Lydia herself. Whatever force Lydia had been trying to use against her was gone too.

'It's working.'

"You are free to roam the castle with an escort of course. We are still conducting the investigation but so far you have not been implicated," Tristan said.

"Even though I'm the reason it may have happened?"

"Did you do it on purpose?"

"No! Never."

"Then yes, even if it was ultimately your fault. My own gift revealed itself unexpectedly. He looked at Rabiah with a smile. I am just lucky it wasn't quite as troublesome as yours."

"What is your gift, Your Highness?"

"It's more like our gift." He nodded to Rabiah. "We seem to share one."

"But what is it?"

"We are soulmates."

Lydia shook her head, "That's not a gift."

"It is to us."

Lydia looked at Rabiah speculatively, "Soulmates? I wonder if that's why the love potion didn't work."

"Probably," Tristan said, "although it did work, just not the way you intended."

"And why I could never get your attention. You knew, or your subconscious knew that she was out there somewhere."

"Perhaps."

"They lied then."

"Who?"

"The priests. They said that I was destined to be queen."

"Perhaps you are, just not here and not with me."

Lydia sighed. "What do I do now?"

"Because of his actions your father has been stripped of his title and property. You will be allowed to retrieve any personal belongings from the manor. However, your father incurred a great debt recently so there's not much left in terms of a fortune for you, but there is enough to live on if you live frugally."

"So I'm to be turned out into the cold?"

Rabiah spoke up, "No. You may serve me if you wish."

Lydia and Tristan looked at Rabiah in surprise. "Serve you how?" Lydia asked

"I need a helper, a personal assistant. Esmerelda is very good, but I think it's too much for her to run the castle and try to train me to do it."

"You want me to help you?"

"You want to be queen, you can see what it is like."

'Are you sure?' Tristan asked silently.

'How better to keep an eye on her?' Rabiah responded, still looking directly at Lydia. Lydia studied her.

"I don't understand. I tried to steal your husband away from you. Why would you want me around?"

"Just don't try to steal him again and you'll have a roof over your head and food in your belly."

Lydia looked at Rabiah an uncomfortable amount of time, then finally nodded.

"Good," Rabiah said. "It is late. You can go to your old home in the morning to collect your things."

Lydia bowed her head. "Thank you, Your Highnesses, for giving me this opportunity."

"Don't waste it," Tristan said.

They left the room. Owen and the General were waiting outside the door. Tristan instructed the guards to stay but not lock the door. Lydia was free to leave her room and walk about the castle and the grounds but she was to have an escort at all times. Tristan waited until they'd turned the corner before he said, "Rabiah, I don't like this idea. I don't want you near her."

"Tristan, think what mischief she could get into if she was allowed to live alone somewhere. Do you think she would be happy living frugally by herself? I will be on my guard and I will give her jobs that don't give her any opportunity to interact with people elsewhere in the kingdom."

"So no correspondence?"

Rabiah sighed, "No. I think that is something I must do."

"What has happened?" the General asked, "Did the bracelets not work properly?"

"They worked as expected," Tristan said. "When I told Lydia that her father did not leave her much to live on, Rabiah hired her as an assistant."

"Trying to keep an eye on her?" the General speculated.

"Yes."

"Just watch your back."

"And your front and everything else," Tristan added.

"Owen, you had Sauerbury's home searched, correct?" Rabiah asked.

"Yes."

"Is his house far?"

"Only a couple of hours."

"I think you should go with her tomorrow in case there is something that was missed."

He nodded, "As you wish my Queen." Rabiah could tell he did not want to go.

"I'll go too. Does she have a carriage?"

"No. The creditors came and took it away," Owen said.

"Then we'll use mine."

"Rabiah, I don't understand. Why are you being so nice to her?" Tristan asked.

"We are all children of the Spirit. I get the feeling that she does not have many friends and she is alone now. She needs someone and I am here."

Chapter 9

The next day dawned clear, bright and almost warm. It hadn't snowed in several days so the roads were passable. Rabiah went upstairs to make sure Lydia was awake as soon as she had dressed. She ordered her carriage made ready and then ate breakfast. She was waiting with Owen when Lydia finally emerged with a guard in tow.

"I get to ride in the royal carriage?"

"Of course. I'm coming too."

"Why?"

"I thought you might need some help."

"Queens don't help people that way."

"Why not?"

"They have more important things to do."

"This is important. You are my assistant. I'd like to learn more about you. What better way than to see where you grew up."

"It's not as big or as fancy as the castle."

"I would not expect it to be."

A servant helped Lydia climb in. Rabiah climbed in unaided and sat on the seat opposite from Lydia. Owen climbed in behind Rabiah and sat beside her. Two guards followed the carriage on horseback while two others rode on top. Lydia didn't seem interested in talking. She gazed deliberately out the window. Rabiah watched the city pass by with interest. She hadn't gone this way before. The houses were larger and more spread apart than those close to the main gate.

"Who lives here Owen?"

"Politicians, merchants, businessmen. People with lots of money but no land. Well, some of them have land and also have a home here in the city, close to the castle."

"The houses are very grand."

"You should see them in the warmer months when they are covered with vines and surrounded by flowers," Lydia said, without turning from the window.

"Do you have a house somewhere Owen?" Rabiah asked.

"I do. I have some land too, but in the winter I prefer to stay in the city."

"How far away is your house?"

"About a day's ride. I haven't been back in several months. I have an excellent steward who cares for it in my absence."

"You hope he does anyway," Lydia said, still looking out the window.

"What's that supposed to mean?"

Lydia looked at Owen, "You trust people too much Owen."

"He's been with my family for years and we've had no complaints."

"You are lucky then. It's hard to find trustworthy servants."

Lydia looked back out the window. The conversation died. They were now outside the city. The space was open with a few trees dotting the land. Rabiah got lost in her own thoughts as she stared out the window. A rubbing sound distracted her. Looking beside her, she discovered Owen diligently rubbing something with a rock.

"Owen, what are you doing?"

"He held open his palm and showed it to her. "Do you recognize it?"

She took it from him and inspected the small carving. "It looks like a baby."

He nodded. "I made it for Hadassah. She wants to have a Thanksgiving ceremony for Tahirah. She explained to me what that was. I told her you were sure to say yes. I offered to make the figure since her husband could not."

"That was very kind of you, Owen. And you are right. I will agree. I'm sure Tristan will too. We have much to be thankful for."

"What's a Thanksgiving ceremony?" Lydia asked.

"It's a celebration to tell the Great Spirit thanks for the special things he sends us. There's a big fire and we send him offerings representing the things we are thankful for. Hadassah just had a baby, so she will throw a carving of a baby into the fire. She could also draw or sing or dance, but traditionally it is a carving."

"Who is Hadassah?"

"She is one of the Clanswomen captured by your army as a slave. She has been freed. When the weather is warmer all the Clanspeople will go home," Rabiah said.

"You cannot allow them to have a celebration."

"Why not?"

"The country is in mourning. We have lost both a king and a queen. It would be wrong to celebrate when someone is in mourning."

"How long will the country mourn?"

"A year, although after a month quiet, private celebrations are allowable."

"It is traditional to hold the Thanksgiving ceremony within a month after the child is born. Hadassah can wait a week, but the Thanksgiving ceremony is not a quiet one."

"It must be. They are foreigners, prior captives. You cannot put their wants over the traditions of our country."

"They are unwilling visitors to a hostile land. We are trying to forge a peace. We must be hospitable."

"They are your people Your Highness. People will not look favorably on you if you allow a wild party by your people in our time of mourning."

"She's right, my Queen," Owen said. "I'm sure Hadassah will understand. They can have a quiet party now and a loud one when they finally return home."

Rabiah nodded and turned to look out the window again, hiding a tear that escaped, unbidden from her eye. She used to love the Thanksgiving ceremonies. Would she ever get to attend one with her brothers and her father again? She had suddenly envisioned her and Tristan performing the Thanksgiving dance for a good marriage. She hadn't really thought of it before because there had not been any Clan to celebrate it with. That was not a good reason though, she realized. The celebration was not for the rest of the Clan but to express gratitude for the gifts of the Spirit. Perhaps they could do the dance in their rooms.

'Rabiah, are you all right?' Tristan sent.

'Yes, why?'

'You felt sad suddenly.'

'You can feel what I feel?'

'Yes. It's usually very faint. It suddenly got stronger.'

She explained what she had been thinking about.

'I'd be glad to offer thanks for you. Lydia is right about the party, but I will dance with you whenever you wish.'

'Thank you Tristan.' She sent a wave of love down their link and received a large one back.

"Ah-hem." Owen cleared his throat behind her. She turned to look and found him glaring at her. She grinned and sent him some love too, although much tamer than what she'd sent Tristan. He frowned harder and she laughed.

"What is so funny?" Lydia asked, turning away from her window.

'Sir Owen. He's too sensitive sometimes."

"Me, sensitive?"

"And moody," Rabiah nodded.

"I am not moody," he said grumpily.

Rabiah raised her eyebrows at him and turned to look back out the window.

'Tristan, send Owen some love. I think he's feeling left out.'

Tristan sent them both love.

'Rabiah!' Owen growled.

"It wasn't me," she said, grinning impishly at him.

Lydia was watching them curiously.

"You travel with someone long enough, you figure out their little quirks," Rabiah explained.

"But you didn't do anything."

"Ha," Owen said, "Do you have any idea what it's like to travel with two people who keep kissing all the time. You walk around a horse and they're lip-locked. You try and find a quiet tree and there they are. I'm surprised I'm not blind."

"It must have been an interesting trip," Lydia said.

"I'm sorry we disturbed you so, Owen," Rabiah said sincerely.

Owen sighed, "It's not your fault. I'm glad you found each other."

"Perhaps you will find someone soon too Owen, then our children can grow up together like you and Tristan did."

"Perhaps."

Rabiah turned to Lydia. "I've heard of a few things they did as children. Did you get to visit them much?"

"No. They were gone most summers and had lessons during the winters."

"What did you do as a child?"

"Took lessons, wandered about my family's land. There wasn't anyone my age to play with."

"What kind of lessons?"

"Music, art, dancing, reading, and writing mostly. I also took classes in proper social etiquette and deportment."

"Do you sing? I haven't heard anyone sing since I've been here."

"Sing? No. I play the harp. No one sings. It's distasteful."

"Not for my people. Everyone sings. Well, almost everyone. My brothers and I have banned my second brother from doing so."

"Really? You sing?" Owen asked.

"It's not hard."

"Sing something."

Lydia frowned at them.

"You should ask Hadassah. I'm sure she's better than me."

"Come on, Your Highness. You owe me for all those times I had to avert my eyes."

"It's not proper," Lydia said.

"Who is going to know?" Owen asked.

"I will not sing if it will offend you," Rabiah said to Lydia.

Lydia sat with her mouth in a firm line for several seconds, then said, "Go ahead, if you must."

Rabiah didn't know any songs in the common language so she sang them one in hers. It was a love song that told of a maiden who searched for her love amidst all the travelers she met, not realizing he was her neighbor the entire time. She felt uncomfortable singing in front of Lydia so she looked out the window as she sang and imagined she was singing it to Tristan. There was silence after she had finished, except from Tristan.

'What was that?'

'You heard that?'

'Loud and clear. I had to excuse myself from the meeting so I could listen without interruption.'

'Sorry, I didn't mean to disturb you.'

'I didn't mind the disruption. It was beautiful.'

'Thank you.'

'Will you sing for me again tonight?'

'If you wish.'

He sent her another pulse of love.

Lydia and Owen still hadn't said anything. Rabiah turned to Owen. "What did you think?"

"Did you sing that to Tristan?"

Rabiah knew what he was asking, "I was thinking about him, yes."

"It's no wonder he loves you," Lydia said quietly, "I could just feel your love for him."

"It gets to be a bit overpowering after a while," Owen groused.

"You asked me to sing."

"I will not make that mistake again."

Rabiah turned back to look out the window. His comment had hurt. So he didn't like her singing. So what. She was becoming too sensitive.

"I think your singing was lovely," Lydia said. "I don't know what you were singing but it gave me chills."

"Thank you." Rabiah turned to look at her. "I'd like to hear you play your harp. I've never heard one before."

"It's at the manor. We can bring it back to the castle with us."

They were quiet the rest of the trip. Rabiah was only too glad to get away from Owen when they finally stopped. She followed Lydia inside the manor. It was smaller than the castle but much more lavishly decorated inside. They walked into a spacious, open room with a grand staircase leading up to a balcony above. They were met by a bevy of servants.

"Your home is beautiful Lydia," Rabiah said.

"My former home," Lydia corrected. Lydia introduced the servants to Queen Rabiah and Sir Owen, then ordered several of them to follow her up the stairs. Rabiah and Owen followed behind them. Lydia had a large suite of rooms to herself. The space was much bigger than Tristan's. Lydia ordered the servants to bring several large trunks and pack it all.

"I'm not sure all those trunks will fit in the carriage," Owen said, "But we can come back later and get the rest."

"This way, Your Highness. I will show you my harp."

She led Rabiah downstairs to a room behind the grand staircase. Bright light poured in from a large window illuminating specks of dust as they floated above a threadbare floor. Empty shelves stretched from floor to ceiling on one wall. Lydia stopped short.

"It's gone!" Lydia ran to the center of the room and turned. "It's all gone - all my father's books, all my mother's art, my harp. It's all gone."

A manservant who had followed them down the stairs stepped forward. "Yes, milady. The creditors came and took everything of value. I'm afraid they took some of your personal things as well."

Lydia pressed her lips together and didn't say anything for a moment. Then, she walked purposefully out of the room and into the next one. She stopped in front of a narrow, closed door. "They won't have taken anything from here." She pulled a key that was hanging on a chain around her neck out from under her tunic and bent to unlock the door.

"Wait, milady. They did try to take something from your father's laboratory. I fear it is unsafe to enter now."

"Nonsense. It will be safe for me."

The servant looked frightened. Rabiah thought it better to be safe.

'Owen, we might have a problem. Sauerbury's laboratory downstairs. The servants are warning Lydia not to enter.'

The key turned and Lydia pulled open the door. Rabiah tensed, then relaxed when nothing happened. It was a small, cramped, dark closet. Lydia stepped inside and lifted a heavy glass bowl off the shelf. Something clicked. Lydia bent again with the key in hand. She put it somewhere Rabiah couldn't see, then stood and pushed on the back wall of the closet. Rabiah was unprepared for the smell that assaulted her nostrils. Something was dead, very dead. Lydia stepped out of the closet, waving her hand in front of her nose.

"How long has the body been in there?"

"A couple of weeks milady."

"Did the creditors get anything?"

"No. Your Father's safe-guards worked as planned. The first one to enter was inhabited and he chased the rest away."

"How did he die?"

"He could not leave the office and he would not eat or drink, although we put food outside the door. Perhaps he starved."

"By the Bull, that's an awful stench," Owen said, coming up behind Rabiah.

"Lydia, what did your manservant mean by 'inhabited'?" Rabiah asked.

"Father trapped a demon inside his laboratory. The deal was that the demon could inhabit anyone who entered without my father's permission. The demon knows me and will let me pass."

"I'm glad we didn't find this room when we came to search for evidence."

"How did the creditors know the laboratory was here?" Lydia asked the manservant.

"They walked behind the manor and saw the window. They realized there must be a secret room somewhere."

"Is the demon still in the body or did he come out?" Rabiah asked.

"Oh, he will be out. He only likes living bodies," Lydia said nonchalantly.

"Can you invite us in so we can get the body out of there," Owen asked.

"No, only Father can do that," Lydia replied.

"Can you trap him in one of those black bottles then?" Rabiah nodded to several small ones sitting on a table across the room in the laboratory.

"He won't like that."

"Yes, but can you do it?"

"As long as he doesn't get suspicious. He'll know as soon as I reach for his bottle."

"So use a different bottle."

"My father has many bottles. I don't know which ones are empty."

"What happens if he gets mad?" Owen asked.

Lydia shivered, "He won't inhabit me, but he likes to cause pain. I've seen him do it to a servant who stepped too far across the threshold."

"Then we will distract him while you get the bottle. What is the demon's name?"

"Gaap."

"Your Highness, you stay back. I'll do the distracting," Owen said.

"Where can Sir Owen stand so he will be safe?" Rabiah asked.

"He can stand in the closet. As long as he doesn't cross the threshold into the laboratory, he should be fine."

Lydia pulled a handkerchief from a hidden pocket and put it over her nose. She walked back into the closet entrance. Owen followed. Rabiah could just see the light from the laboratory window around Owen's big frame. She heard him say, "You're right Lydia. Your father does have a lot of bottles."

Then she heard another voice, a dry, raspy voice that made chills go down her spine.

"So you've come back at last little Lydia, and you've brought a friend, but where is your father to let him in?"

"He is not of your concern."

"But he is. I know he's still alive because otherwise I would be free. That was our deal. I guard this room and upon his death I could have anyone I wanted except you and your children."

"What did you do to him?" Lydia asked, sounding horrified. Rabiah guessed she had found the body.

"Oh, I had a little fun. It makes it hurt that much more when you cut off your own body parts and then cauterize the wounds so you don't bleed out."

"You're horrible!"

"I know. So why are you here? Did you come to feed me?"

"Feed you?"

"Yes. Give me a little of your pain."

"Didn't that man suffer enough to satisfy you?"

"Oh, yes, but that was days ago."

"No, I'm not here to feed you. I've come to get something for my father."

"Liar. His grand scheme didn't work or else that man would not have come."

"That man was greedy and impatient."

"So your father's plans did work? Is this your new husband then? Should I offer my congratulations?"

"Get away from him."

Owen took a step back.

"Not very brave is he?"

"He is brave and he's smart too."

"Brave and smart. Worthy qualities in a prince, or is it a king? I've never had a king before."

"And you won't have this one. Let's go dear." Lydia exited the room holding one hand close to her chest. She was pushing Owen in front of her.

"Little Lydia," the demon said in a sing-song voice. "There's something I forgot to mention. Since I didn't think your father would be back I had my last guest damage the markers that were holding me here. You broke it completely when you opened the door. So now," the voice got louder and clearer, "I am free."

A large creature bounding on all fours who looked like he'd had all his skin burned off came charging out of the room behind them. Its shoulders barely fit through the door. He charged right at Owen. Rabiah flicked her belt off and tried to stop the demon, but the belt when right through him. He didn't even seem to notice. He hit Owen's chest and disappeared.

Owen drew his sword and the demon's voice echoed around the room, "Ooo, a big one. This will cause a lot of pain. What shall I stab first? His foot? His hand? Maybe I'll just chop along his ribs."

"Stop. Gaap, I command you to come out of him. You are bound. I bind you. Into this bottle you must go."

"Too late little Lydia. You'll have to wait until I get tired of the body. He's very strong so this might take some time."

Owen lifted his sword. Rabiah kicked it out of his hand before he could bring it down. "Tie him up so he can't hurt himself," she yelled at the servants and any guards who might be able to hear her. Owen pulled out another knife. She knocked it away. He went for one in his boot and she knocked him flat.

"Ow. That felt good. Who is this woman? I think I'll have her next."

One of the guards flung himself on top of Owen's legs to hold him down. Rabiah laid across his chest and held down his right arm while a manservant held the left. Someone brought ropes. They tied Owen to the stair bannister with his legs and arms spread apart.

"Now what are you going to do little warrior woman? He's stuck with me until I leave."

Rabiah stood in front of Owen and looked within. This demon wasn't clouding his soul, he was torturing it. She could see a miniature form hitting and poking at Owen's soul like a boy with a stick might poke a snake. The demon liked pain. Would pleasure work?

"Lydia, kiss him."

"What?"

"This demon likes pain. Maybe we can chase him out with pleasure."

"But I," she came closer to Rabiah and whispered, "I've never kissed anyone before."

"Just press your lips against his. If he responds then do what he does."

Lydia walked up to Owen and stood before him. Owen did not look at her. He had his eyes closed. She stood for several seconds then turned away. "I can't do this."

Rabiah spied a younger female servant watching from behind the stairs. She beckoned to her and asked in a low voice, "Do you have a husband or someone special?"

The girl shook her head.

"Have you ever kissed anyone before?"

She nodded in the affirmative.

"Would you mind kissing him for me?"

"Me?"

"The demon likes pain. I want to fight him with pleasure."

"Really? You want me to kiss Sir Owen?"

"You know him?"

"Who doesn't know of him?"

"Please?"

The girl didn't need any further persuasion. She walked up to Owen and ran her finger down Owen's cheek. She was much shorter than he was. A male servant foresaw the problem and quickly brought her a stepstool. The girl nodded a thanks to her fellow servant and stepped up. She could reach Owen now, but she didn't immediately kiss him. She ran her fingers along his hairline and down behind his ears as if she were memorizing his face.

"What is she doing?" Lydia whispered.

"She's giving him pleasure."

The servant girl had worked her way to the back of Owen's head. She gently brought his head forward and place her lips on Owen's. Rabiah was watching the demon. Owen's light pulsed suddenly. The demon backed away. Rabiah stepped closer in case she had to pull the girl away.

"Lydia, give me the bottle." She whispered, holding her opened hand behind her back. Lydia did as she was told.

Owen was kissing the girl back. She seemed to be enjoying it. Her hands were now resting on Owen's broad chest, her fingers making broad circular motions.

"Ugh. What is this? Stop that you, you loose woman!" Rabiah heard the demon say.

The girl pulled away, not to leave, but so she could run her hands over Owen's shoulders and strong upper arms. The demon retaliated by trying to make Owen bang his head against the rail. The servant girl gently put her hand back behind his head and pulled him in for another kiss. Owen's arms strained at the ropes as he tried to put his arms around the girl.

The demon was coming out. Rabiah stepped back right before he appeared before her. She held the bottle out in front of her.

"Gaap, I exile you to this bottle where you will stay forever and a day."

Nothing happened.

"That's not going to work warrior girl. Shall I try you next? Will anyone be brave enough to try and tie you down?"

'*Great Spirit, help me!*' Rabiah prayed desperately as the demon sprang toward her. She stepped back.

The name, the name was key, something told her. It was from a country far to the south. Her people had traveled there. She knew the language although not well. The demon leapt at her and her ring jumped. He was frozen in mid-flight. She tried again to banish him but said the words haltingly in the language of the Southern people. Putting all the spiritual force she could muster into the words, she said, "I banish thee Gaap forever from these lands to the dark spaces between the stars where nothing lives and nothing dies and no one feels pain."

"No. You can't..." The demon shrank in midair and disappeared with a pop.

The girl and Owen were still kissing. She finally pulled away, gave him a smile, and one last peck on the cheek. She stepped down from the stool and walked away, smiling. The servant who had brought the stool picked it up and followed her as if in a trance.

Rabiah suddenly felt very tired. She sat down before she fell.

"Rabiah! Are you all right?" Owen asked.

"Yes. I'll be fine in a few minutes."

"Think you can cut me down then?"

Rabiah leaned back on her hands and studied him, "Are you sure? I bet there are some other girls who would like to try kissing the famous Sir Owen while he's helplessly tied up."

One of the guards snorted. Owen growled at her, but she could see he was trying to hide a blush.

"Cut him down. The demon is gone," Rabiah ordered.

She turned to look at Lydia, "Are there any other demons that are loose on the property waiting to trap someone?"

Lydia looked paler than normal. "None that I know of."

"Do you know of any?" Rabiah asked the servant who had warned Lydia not to enter the laboratory.

"No, Your Highness. Might I get you a chair?"

"Not yet. I'd probably fall out of it."

Owen was free. He came to stand before her but dropped down beside her when he saw how pale she was. She leaned on his arm.

"You're not all right."

"I guess banishing demons takes a lot of energy."

"Take some of mine. I've got plenty. More than enough right now, in fact."

"Are you sure?"

"Please."

She placed her hand on his arm and took a little. Just enough to calm the sick, dizzy feeling.

"Thank you."

"No, thank you. Take more if you need it."

"I'm fine now. I could probably handle a chair."

Owen scooped her up and the manservant led them to the room where the harp had been. There was an old, worn couch in the corner.

"Is everyone all right?" Owen whispered as he sat her down on the couch.

"I think so," she said quietly.

"Can you bring her something to eat and drink?" Owen asked the manservant.

"Yes sir. It will be my pleasure. Would you like anything milady?" he asked Lydia who had followed them and now stood beside Owen.

"Just something to drink."

The servant bowed and left.

"I'm going to go ask the other servants if they know of any other demons," Owen said.

Rabiah raised her eyebrows at him. He turned and hurried out of the room. The tops of his ears were bright red.

"How did you know what to do?" Lydia asked.

Rabiah lay back on the couch, "I asked the Spirit to help me."

"What spirit?"

"The Great Spirit who made all things."

"What language was that?"

"It's the language of the Southern tribes. The demon's name sounded like some of their words."

"How many languages do you know?"

"I don't know. Many. My brothers and I are all very good at learning new languages."

"Yet you can't read or write."

"No, but I'm learning."

Rabiah closed her eyes. She must have dozed off because suddenly the servant was back with a simple tray of food and some steamy mugs. Rabiah suddenly realized how cold she was. There was no fire in the fireplace and the room was very chilly.

"Milady," the servant said to Lydia after he had deposited the tray, "Can you tell us of Lord Sauerbury? What has become of him? We heard that the King and Queen had died and that Lord Sauerbury had been arrested. Will he be returning soon?"

"He may never return," Lydia said. "My father has been stripped of his title and his lands. I am no longer your mistress. I work for the Queen."

"But what will become of us? We cannot leave."

Rabiah was sipping her warm drink and only partially listening, but the panic in the man's voice as he asked the last question caught her attention. "Why do you say you cannot leave?" she asked the servant.

"They are bound to the house," Lydia explained. "We had trouble keeping servants so my father found a way to keep them here until he released them. They can leave for up to two weeks but then they must return or they will die."

"Is that common in Arles?"

"No," Lydia said, "but my father had more secrets than most."

"Can you release them?"

"No. It's a blood link. Only my father's blood can release them."

"How?"

"You just have to drop some on the soil and say the person's name and that they are released."

"Sounds simple enough. Tell Sir Owen. He can see to it," Rabiah said to the servant.

Rabiah drank more of the drink. She was feeling weaker again. She put the mug down and lay back. She didn't want to disturb Owen. Tiredly she called, *'Tristan.'*

'Rabiah, what's wrong? You sound worn out.'

'Demon. He's gone. I'm tired.'

She felt his strength seeping in.

'Not too much.'

'I'll live. You come home.'

'Yes, thank you.' Her groggy mind cleared a little and she remember to say thanks to the Great Spirit for his help and to ask for more strength.

Owen came into the room a minute later. "I've called for the carriage. Lydia, is there anything else you wish to take with you? I think the servants are done with your room."

"There's not much left. May I walk through the house one last time?"

"Yes, as long as you don't release any more demons."

"I'll try not to."

Owen sent one of the guards with Lydia. Rabiah looked even paler that she had before. He watched as she lay down and tucked her arms under her head. Her eyes closed.

"My Queen."

She didn't respond.

"Rabiah?" He touched her face. She was cold.

Rabiah dreamt of her mother. They were sitting on a boulder near a stream. Her mother pulled a necklace out of her pocket. Rabiah recognized it as the one her father had given her. Her mother put it around her neck.

"Wear it close to your heart and think of our people when you use it," her mother said.

"But how do I use it?" Rabiah asked. It was too late. Her mother had disappeared. Someone was calling her name and touching her cheek. Tristan. She smiled and opened her eyes.

"Hello." He was sitting on a chair next to her.

"Hello my fearless wife."

"What are you doing here?"

"I've been here for two days."

"What?" She looked around and realized she was in their bed back at the castle.

"You, my little warrior Queen vanquished a semi-corporeal demon into space. That apparently takes so much power that no one dares to try it without at least two other demon vanquishers to help. Yet, you did it all by yourself. I almost lost you again."

He was smiling, but his eyes were shinier than normal.

"I'm sorry Tristan. I didn't know. It came at me and I couldn't get it to go into the bottle."

"No more vanquishing demons until you know how to do it properly, all right?"

"All right," she nodded.

He kissed her forehead, then leaned over and gently hugged her. Rabiah felt something wet fall on her cheek.

"Are you hungry," Tristan asked as he pulled away.

She realized she was very hungry, "Yes!"

He chuckled and stood to ring the bell to call for food.

The sun was shining brightly in the sky. It was well past noon. "Why aren't you in a meeting?" she asked.

"Don't you want me here?" he asked, sitting back down beside her.

"Yes, but you always seem to have a lot to do."

"I had a feeling you would wake today and Healer Marion told me to stay in bed."

"Why? Are you ill?"

"No. After you asked for some energy, I realized you needed more. A lot more. I ran down to the infirmary and grabbed all the healers I could find. We drove to the former Sauerbury manor as fast as the horses could get us there. The servants had built up the fire and Owen had you under a pile of blankets but you were almost ice cold and pale as a ghost. The healers crowded around you and got you warmed up again but you wouldn't wake. We bundled you up and brought you back home in the carriage. I tried to wake you by kissing you but even that didn't work. It left me so weak that Healer Marion yelled at me. Owen had to help me up the stairs."

"You've been here the whole time?"

"No. I was better by the next day. I think I ate enough for three people."

"Did Owen tell you how I got the demon to leave him?"

"He said something about being tied up and a girl kissing him." Tristan sounded amused.

"I think he liked it. Watching them made me wonder what it would be like to tie you up and kiss you."

"Rabiah! Now I know you're feeling better." He kissed her head again, a little more firmly than before, then he pulled her into a sitting position and propped her up with some pillows. Someone knocked. Tristan went into the sitting room to answer the door.

Rabiah heard Owen ask, "Is she awake? Can I see her?" A maid appeared carrying a tray with a large bowl of soup and some bread. Owen was behind her, a large smile brightening his face.

"So you finally woke up. How are you feeling?"

"Hungry."

"That's nothing new." He came to stand beside her. His smile faded into a look of remorse. "I wanted to apologize."

"For what?"

"For what I said about your singing. It was very nice. I was feeling a little, well, mean at the time I guess."

"That's all right Owen. I know Tristan and I annoy you sometimes."

"Sometimes? Do you know how loudly Tristan can yell without saying a word? I didn't know he knew so many swear words, in different languages no less. I'd still be cleaning my ears if he'd used them."

"Did you get to ah, speak to the girl who helped drive the demon out?"

"I did. I just thanked her and left."

"Why?"

"I think her display made one of the other servants realize what he'd been missing. I could tell they were attracted to each other so I left them to figure it out."

"I'm sorry Owen."

"I'm not. She was a great kisser and I got away without any encumbrances."

Tristan put the tray across Rabiah's lap. "Eat Rabiah. You can talk about Owen's love life, or lack there-of, later."

Rabiah obediently took a few bites.

"I have something for you," Owen said. He dropped something onto her tray. It looked a bit like a carving of a dog but she wasn't sure.

"What is it?"

"It's the demon. I am thankful you helped me be free of him. I thought we could burn it during the Thanksgiving Celebration. I told the Clanspeople what happened. They've been praying for you. They also started teaching Mitch your language."

"Thank you Owen. I must have Tristan carve one to represent the other demon."

Owen seemed to want to say more but after a few seconds' pause he simply said, "Enjoy your meal, my Queen." Then bowed and left.

Rabiah had only eaten a few spoonfuls of soup when Esmerelda appeared at the doorway to the bedroom.

"May I come in, Your Highness?"

"Yes. How are you Esmerelda?"

"I am well." She walked to the side of the bed. "I'm glad to see you are doing better Your Highness."

"Thank you, Esmerelda."

"Can I do anything for you?"

Rabiah suddenly realized she did need some assistance. Esmerelda took the tray and she and Tristan helped Rabiah out of bed. She could walk but she felt very weak. After relieving herself, she was very glad to climb back into the stable warm bed.

The tray was returned. Rabiah picked up the spoon and asked, "What has Lydia been doing?"

"I've put her in charge of purchasing food, supplies, and the upkeep and assignment of guestrooms," Esmerelda said. "So far there have been no complaints."

Rabiah detected a note of displeasure in Esmerelda's voice. "But?" she asked.

"She questions everything," Esmerelda expounded. "'Why do you serve fish only on certain days?', 'Why do you have so many servants?', 'Why do I have to do it this way?'"

"Should we give her a different job?"

Esmerelda sighed. "No, this is good. I've told all the head staff to report to you or me is she does anything suspicious. There are many eyes watching her."

Rabiah nodded and ate another spoonful of soup.

"I've brought you something, Your Highness."

Rabiah looked as Esmerelda in surprise. "What is it?"

"Since you won't be able to run off for a while, I thought you could work on your reading and writing." She put a basket containing a book and a slate on the table next to the bed.

"Thank you Esmerelda."

114

"Would you like me to stay with her for a while, Your Highness?" Esmerelda asked Tristan who had been looking out the window while they spoke.

"Not right now. I'll send someone to find you if we need you," Tristan responded.

Esmerelda bowed and left, holding the door to the hallway open for Tristan's uncle to enter.

"I hear someone has finally awakened," he said, stopping at the bedroom door.

"Come in, Uncle," Rabiah said.

The General walked up to her side, leaned over, and kissed her forehead.

"What was that for?" she asked in surprise.

"Just glad you're back." He sat down in the chair next to the bed. "I've called in some expert demon hunters to take care of Sauerbury and to make sure his house is safe to inhabit. They were very impressed when I told them about you. Three out of three and you haven't had any formal training.

"I did have help."

"Not much. Anyway, since you seem to have a knack for getting into these situations, I thought you might want to learn more." From behind his back, he pulled an old, scruffy book bound in black leather with an enlarged, embossed eye in the center.

"This is a book of demons. It tells of their history, their names, how to trap them, and how to control them. I have others if you want to read them after you are finished with this."

Rabiah took the book with interest, "Thank you."

"Some of the pictures are disturbing so you may not want to read it right before you sleep."

"I won't."

The General took the book from her and put it on the table. "I'll leave you to your meal. Get better soon. I'm tired of seeing so many empty chairs at mealtimes."

Rabiah had just finished her food when Lydia knocked on the door. Tristan let her in. She came and stood at the foot of the bed for a few seconds, then curtsied. "Your Highness."

"Hello Lydia."

"Might I speak to you for a few minutes in private?"

"Of course."

Tristan frowned behind Lydia's back, but he said, "I'll be right out here in the sitting room if you need me," and left the room, leaving the door opened a crack.

"May I sit?" Lydia asked, indicating the chair by the bed.

Rabiah nodded. Lydia gracefully floated to the chair and sat but didn't immediately say anything. Rabiah waited patiently. Finally, Lydia spoke. "You were very brave," she paused, "You almost gave your life to save Owen and I couldn't even kiss him."

"Lydia, that's all right. I only asked you to kiss him because I thought you were interested."

"I am, I think. Were you nervous when the King first kissed you?"

"I was expecting a sword through my heart so nervous wasn't what I was feeling."

Lydia studied her for a minute. "How did Tristan know? How did he know to bring all the healers? Is it because of your shared gift?"

"Yes," Rabiah answered simply.

Lydia sat silent for a minute, then said, "I do not hate you."

Rabiah smiled, "I don't hate you either, Lydia."

It was another three days before Marion would allow Rabiah to go downstairs.

"And you are to take it easy. My kind of easy, not yours! No running, no jumping, no swordplay. You can walk and sit."

"Can I go to the archery range?"

"Only if I am with you," which meant never to Rabiah's ears.

Thanks to all the bedrest, Rabiah's reading skills progressed rapidly. With Tristan and Esmerelda's help she made it through 2 chapters of the demon book within a few days.

"I hope you don't teach your children how to read with this book," Esmerelda complained during a very gruesome description of what a hunger demon could make a person do. Rabiah had to catch herself from touching her belly protectively. Somehow the two little lights were still shining strongly. Neither Tristan nor Rabiah were ready to announce her pregnancy. It was barely past a month since Rabiah had discovered she was expecting twins and already so many things had happened to endanger them. Healer Marian arranged a secret meeting between Rabiah and Mame. Mame's words were encouraging.

"They're fine as far as I can tell. Don't be surprised. Babies can be a hardy bunch."

A week later, the day after the official forty days of mourning for Tristan's parents had passed, the Clanspeople had a quiet celebration of Thanksgiving in their dormitory. The fire in the fireplace was built as high as was safe and everyone took turns offering their thanks. The Clanspeople were impressed with Tristan's rendition of the traditional wedding dance, although they didn't say so. Owen could see the approval in their auras. The dance probably did more for their relationship than anything so far he surmised. Owen held the baby while Hadassah threw the figure he had carved into the fire. She also sang a song of her own making as thanks for freedom and new friends. She did have a beautiful voice Owen thought.

Tristan, Owen, Mitch, and Marion were the only non-Clanspeople there. They walked back to the castle well after the evening meal was over. There had been several warm days in a row and the brown earth could now be seen in some places. The sky was clear and the stars were bright. Tristan and Rabiah parted from the other three and went for a walk to the lake. Their guards waited patiently while they stood staring out over the water, her head on his shoulder and his arm around her waist.

Chapter 10

Owen took it upon himself to discover what had happened to Hadassah's older daughter. The little girl had been so sick the soldiers thought she would surely die if she stayed with the slaves. They took her from her mother and left her at an orphanage where she might receive better care. The orphanage was run by a group of women dedicated to the service of the goddess of love and wisdom. With Tristan's permission, Owen took a horse and a fellow soldier to make the three day journey to discover what had become of the girl. They came back eight days later in the midst of a nasty storm.

Rabiah happened to be walking through the Great Hall when Owen and the other soldier stomped into then entry looking like two huge buffalo covered in snow. She smiled and ran to greet him, unmindful of the glances she received from some of the other women in the hall.

"Owen, welcome back!"

"Hello, my Queen." He said pleasantly and bowed so that several blobs of snow landed on the floor in front of him.

He began to shed his outer garments in the entry way, knocking snow all over the floor.

"You are making a mess."

"So I am."

"What did you discover?"

"Aren't you going to ask me how I am?"

"I can see how you are. So what did you discover?"

"Well, it's very cold outside. The wind is blowing hard enough that the snow is down inside my tunic, and you are very impatient."

"If you will tell me, I'll go order some warm mead for both of you and have it served in the guest washroom. I might even send someone to the barracks to fetch you some fresh clothes."

"No need for that. I'll just borrow some of Tristan's. They're probably mine anyway."

"Well?"

Owen gave his cloak a final shake and looked at her as if he were irritated with her, then his face broke into a smile. "She's alive. At least she was. A merchant's wife gave the orphanage a handy sum to acquire her, for what purpose we didn't discover. At least though, I can give Hadassah some good news. Her daughter didn't die."

"That's wonderful. I'm surprised you didn't stop there first."

"We barely made it to the castle. The snow is so thick we had to feel our way along the wall to find the entrance."

"Well, I'm glad you are back." She slipped around the piles of snow and quickly gave him a hug. He smelled of cold, snow, and wood smoke.

"You too, Richard." She threw the other soldier a bright smile. He bowed to her.

"I'll go see to your mead."

Owen was a little afraid Rabiah herself would deliver the drinks so he delayed stripping down to get into the big sunken pool until they came. It wasn't Rabiah who delivered them though, it was Tristan.

"I'm very honored to have my king serve me a drink," Owen said as Tristan handed it to him.

"Don't get used to it."

"Why did you come? I was hoping it would be that new buxom lass I've seen around the kitchens."

"Sorry to disappoint. I just wanted to ask if you'd like to join Rabiah and me on a trip south."

"South, as in away from the snow? Yes." Owen finished undressing and slid into the water.

"Lydia is coming."

"Lydia? Why Lydia?"

Rabiah asked her. Lydia and Esmerelda don't appear to work well together. Rabiah thought it would be best to take Lydia rather than Esmerelda so we can keep an eye on her. Since she left you, ah, hanging, I thought you might not want to go."

Owen waved the thought away. "I'm glad she did. To tell you the truth, I don't know which would have been worse, her or the demon."

"What about Hadassah's daughter? Are you going to continue the search?"

"I am doing so as we speak. I left instructions everywhere we went to contact the Warrior Queen if anyone saw or knew of the merchant or his wife. Esmerelda can monitor the Queen's correspondence and you can put someone in charge of following up if anything should come to light."

"Warrior Queen?"

"Yes. They seemed pretty eager to comply after I corrected all the rumors they were hearing."

"What rumors?"

"They had me tied up naked in front of everyone and three girls refusing to kiss me because of the demon. They thought the Queen had finally kissed me herself. I didn't think you'd want me to leave it like that." Owen took a long sip from his mug. "When will we leave?"

"As soon as we can. King Abbus received word of my father's death and immediately sent a messenger to declare the treaty void since it was between him and my father, which is preposterous. It was between him and Arles."

"You'll just have to make sure it's worded more explicitly."

"It *was* explicit but he's ignoring it. Unfortunately, the only other option is to tell the sailors to go around the long way and let the trade we've developed with the south dry up."

"You could send in the military."

"I'd rather try diplomacy first. He has a powerful navy."

"Glad you're the king and not me."

Owen took another sip and sunk lower in the water. "Are you sure you want to take Rabiah? Their society is not as liberal towards females as ours."

"I don't want to leave her here alone. Besides, Father suggested I take her on this trip and if she's on a ship she'll be less likely to overdo or run into another demon."

"Mmm," Owen said as he took another long sip.

"What?"

"I was just remembering how peaceful and quiet it was on my trip. No king ordering me about. No queen to rescue from dangerous situations."

"You don't have to go," Tristan said crossly.

"Of course I'll go. Who knows what mischief you two will get into by yourselves. Besides, I wouldn't mind getting in a little fishing."

They set sail on the next warm day with three ships. Rabiah waved to everyone dutifully as they left, but as soon as they were far enough from the docks, she ran back to their spacious cabin and changed into something she could move in more freely. Tristan caught her as she ran out the door.

"Where are you going?"

"Exploring. I've never been on a ship before."

"Wait for me. I'll come with you and show you around."

They spent the next several hours exploring the ship from bow to stern. They ended at the center mast of the three on the ship. Tristan called it the mainmast. Rabiah saw a platform high up the mainmast.

"Can I climb it?"

"Yes, but be careful." He had to finish with a yell as she was already half-way up. She shimmied up the net-like shroud as if gravity didn't exist.

"I think she has recovered," Owen said behind him.

"I hope she stays that way," Tristan said, looking down and moving his head to loosen his neck. Rabiah had safely made it to the top.

121

"Looks like she might be up there for a while."

Tristan was quiet for a few seconds, then nodded. "Yes. She says the view is lovely."

"Good. The captain wants to speak to you about our route."

"Don't we have it all planned out?"

"He wants to add another stopover."

Tristan sent Rabiah another message telling her where he'd be, then followed after Owen. Rabiah stayed to watch the land slip away. When he got back she was still up in the crow's nest.

'Are you going to stay there the whole trip?'

'Maybe. It's very peaceful. I went and got a book, a blanket, and some apples. Do you want one?'

'I am getting a little hungry.'

'Here. Catch.'

He barely managed to get out of the way in time. The apple bounced on the deck. He looked up at her and sent, *'So this is how it's going to be? You're going to sit up in your perch and throw food at me? I thought we might explore our quarters a bit, maybe have some lunch, but if you want to hang out up there by yourself, I'll just go sit in our quarters alone.'* He bent to retrieve the apple, then turned to find Rabiah standing behind him.

"How did you get down so fast? No. I don't want to know."

"Race you to the cabin."

She took off before he could agree. He followed after her and caught up to her just as she reached the door. She gave him a look that made the hairs on the back of his neck stand in anticipation. He quickly looked to the right and left to make sure no one was coming to disturb them, then he shut and locked the door.

The first two days were wonderful. Tristan had not had so much free time to spend with Rabiah since the day after his parent's funeral. With all the advisors and other nobles aboard the other two ships, neither felt a need to conform to the normal dress code. Rabiah was fully healed and eager to retrain her muscles for what they seemed to do best. The ship, with all the ropes to climb and the open space on the deck seemed to her a perfect place to train. The captain was not so excited to have the Queen scampering all over the ship but he held his tongue as Rabiah, Tristan, and Owen fought mock duals on his polished decks.

Since she was filling the role of Rabiah's assistant, Lydia was aboard the ship with them. She sat on the deck and primly watched the duals, silently in awe of Rabiah's fighting skills. Rabiah's knife throwing skills were just as impressive. She bested all but one of the sailors she challenged and that was only because a wave jarred the boat just before she threw. Lydia watched Tristan carefully. Rather than being dismayed by Rabiah's unladylike behavior, he seemed to enjoy and even encourage her. The only sign Lydia saw that he might be at all displeased was when Rabiah mentioned wrestling. She wanted to challenge one of the sailors who was well-known for his skill. Tristan gave Rabiah a little frown then whispered something in her ear. Rabiah grinned and nodded in return, then gave him a quick peck on the cheek. From the thumping and laughter that came from their room later, Lydia surmised that Tristan had offered to wrestle with her.

In the afternoons Rabiah brought out books and a slate to practice her reading and writing. Tristan brought out a book and sat with her. Their affection for one another was obvious. Lydia found it hard to watch. She could see why Owen often complained about being around the two of them. Lydia still felt a little jealous of Rabiah's position at Tristan's side, but she found herself admiring Rabiah's bravery and her easy comradery with men, which lacked the flirtatious element most women seemed to use. And whereas Tristan treated Lydia with politeness and Owen continued to keep his distance, Rabiah treated her with a kindness that Lydia did not understand. It was almost as if she wanted to be friends.

Some time on the third night the weather became rougher and the waves higher. Rabiah awoke feeling slightly nauseous. She rose and took a bite of the flatbread Marion had insisted she keep on hand in case the pregnancy sickness some women got set in. It did help. Then Tristan woke. He tried to rise, but instead rolled over and threw up on the floor. As soon as the smell assaulted her nose, Rabiah had to run for the door to keep from doing the same thing herself. She managed to make it to the rail before she lost the crackers she had just eaten. One of the sailors saw her sitting on the cold deck with her back to the rail, looking very pale. He was not surprised. The rougher waters caused many a proud passenger discomfort.

"Are you all right Your Highness?"

Rabiah nodded. She felt fine. What she needed was a drink.

"Would you like me to get you a drink?" It was as if he had read her mind.

"Yes please."

He left and came back a minute later with a cup of water. She drank it carefully. Her stomach handled it well.

"Would you like me to help you back to your cabin so you can lay down?"

"No. I can't go in there. Tristan, the King, he'll make me sick again."

Puzzled, the sailor went to the cabin by himself. He knocked and heard what he thought was a moan. Concerned, he opened the door and immediately realized what the Queen had been referring to. The sailor gave Tristan a drink and a bucket and went to find the cabin boy to clean up the mess.

Owen was quite amused the next morning when he found out Tristan had motion sickness. They had been on many ships when they were younger and neither had experienced any trouble. Now he was the only one standing. He couldn't help but gloat. "So you lost your sea legs, eh? Become a true land-lover."

"Go away," Tristan said, pale faced.

"Never thought I'd see the day. The water's not even that rough. Remember that storm that hit the last time we were on a boat? Now that was rough!"

"Go Away!" Tristan said as the memory of those waves caused him to heave up the water he had just drank.

Owen took pity on him. "Here." He handed Tristan a towel to clean his face and a cup of water to rinse out his mouth. He then took the bucket and dumped it over the side of the boat.

"Let's let the room air out a little. Shall I take these to Rabiah so she can dress?" he asked, indicating the tunics he recognized as the ones she'd worn the day before.

"Yes," Tristan said weakly.

"I'll be back for you. A little fresh air might help."

He took the clothes to Rabiah and let her into his cabin, then returned for Tristan. Tristan had gotten dressed himself without any more incidents. The fresh air did help, and after eating a few of Rabiah's crackers, which was all he could find to eat in their room, he felt much better. Owen managed to contain his glee to only a few snide comments throughout the day. He did not tease so much when it happened for a second morning and then again on the third morning in a row. Owen had Healer Marion come over from the other ship to a look at Tristan and at Lydia, who hadn't been able to keep much down either.

"You say this only happens in the mornings?" Marion asked Tristan. "What about you, Rabiah? How have you been feeling?"

"My stomach is a little upset in the mornings, but after I eat a few crackers I'm fine."

"So you are both sick only in the morning?"

"Yes," they said in unison.

"So you both have morning sickness?" Marion began to laugh.

"Yes. What's so funny?" Tristan asked.

"Of course it would happen with you two."

"What?" Tristan asked.

"You, Tristan, are one of those special men who take on the sickness that some women get from being pregnant either to help them, or because you are sympathetic. No one is sure. Since your symptoms are worse than hers, perhaps you are actually helping her. With you two, anything is possible."

She gave them more crackers and left chuckling. Owen came in right after she left.

"Why was Healer Marion laughing?" he asked.

Rabiah looked at Tristan. Owen could tell they were communicating silently. Tristan shrugged and looked away.

Rabiah turned to Owen, "He has morning sickness."

125

"What? But he's a man!"

"He is helping me," Rabiah said, laying her head on Tristan's shoulder.

"Ugh. You two! Are you going to birth the children for her too?"

"Gads, I hope not," Tristan said. "Marion said this might go away after we get off the water."

"I hope so. It will be hard to explain to our host that you can't come to an early meeting because you have morning sickness." It took a few seconds and a couple of snickers, then Owen burst out laughing. Tristan and Rabiah couldn't help but join them. Marion heard their laughter in Lydia's room where she was helping the poor girl to clean up and smiled.

"What do you think they are laughing at so hard?" Lydia asked wistfully.

"The King I suspect," Marion answered.

"Because he's sick?"

Marion just smiled and wouldn't say anything more.

Chapter 11

It took eight days in total to travel to visit King Abbus with the wind behind them. Lydia emerged pale and fragile looking, but beautifully attired. The weather was much warmer. Rabiah found she did not need a cloak or even the heavier woolen tunics they had been wearing in Arles. She dawned a couple of the lighter summer tunics Esmerelda had packed for her. Before they'd left, Esmerelda had also spoken with the experts on the Kingdom of Ibirann to make sure Rabiah and Lydia dressed and behaved appropriately. Outside the confines of their homes and when guests were present, women were to keep everything covered except their eyes. They could not speak when spoken to unless their husbands, brothers, grown sons, or masters gave them permission. In addition, they could never make eye contact with any males.

"Why?" Rabiah had asked.

"Apparently the men in Ibirann are easily seduced and can't keep their hands to themselves," Esmerelda had said disdainfully. "If one does touch you, it's your own fault for looking at him or being near him."

"How do the women live that way?"

"I guess they are used to it."

Esmerelda had showed them how to wear the scarves she had made for them. Rabiah donned hers now. It looked ridiculous with her crown so she left it off although Tristan wore his. Instead, she wore the other stone from her Mother's earrings on her forehead the way she had first worn the large one to meet Tristan's father. Since her dream, she had begun to wear the large stone on a chain so that it hung close to her heart as her mother had instructed her. Underneath it all, as usual, she armed herself with all her little knives. Tristan was always silently amused as he watched her put them on, but he didn't say anything. They might come in handy.

Rabiah thought she looked silly but Lydia looked regal and mysterious in her veils. It didn't help that Owen chuckled a little when he saw Rabiah. "You look so sweet and innocent, almost like a female, my Queen." She scowled at him, squinting her eyes. That just made him laugh.

According to Esmerelda, Rabiah was to follow behind her husband, not stand at his side. As they departed the boat, Owen exited first, followed by Tristan, then Rabiah, then Lydia, with more guards behind. King Abbus greeted Tristan warmly, as if he had not forced them to come visit by breaking the treaty. Rabiah kept her eyes as downwards as she could without bumping into anything. She stopped when Tristan stopped. "King Tristan, I heard rumors that you had taken a bride. Which is she or did you take two?"

Tristan reached behind him and pulled Rabiah forward. "This is my wife, Queen Rabiah of Arles. The other woman is her handmaiden."

"Welcome Queen Rabiah." To Rabiah's surprise he took her hand and kissed the back of it. He managed to hit a splinter from the ship that she had yet to work out. It made her flinch a little just as her lips touched her.

"Is this not the proper greeting?" He asked Tristan.

"It is one of them," said Tristan calmly.

King Abbus also took Lydia's hand but he only made a little bow in her direction.

"Come. Your carriages are here. My men can see to your luggage."

"We don't want to impose," Tristan said. "We don't mind sleeping on the ship."

"What kind of host would I be if I did not provide you with a place to rest your heads. Come!"

"Thank you. That is very kind of you. The sailors can show your servants what to bring."

On the advice of the expert, everyone had packed a chest in the event that they would not be staying on the ship. King Abbus liked to keep an eye on his guests. "It is a bit like sleeping in the lion's den. Just don't show any fear," were his encouraging words.

The route to the palace was very pretty, Rabiah thought, especially compared to the cold winter scene in Arles. She learned the odd tress with the straight trunks, big leaves, and huge nuts were the palm trees Tristan's father had told her about. Even though it was winter and the weather was slightly cool, there were many flowering trees and bushes. She was so busy watching the scenery it was easy to remain silent on the coach ride as King Abbus and Tristan exchanged pleasantries. As they got closer to the palace, the number of buildings increased. Many of them were made of white stone. She saw men dressed in light colored tunics and loose pants and women in many different colors of dresses and scarves. Some of them had jewels and beads sewn along the edges of the veils. Rabiah smiled to herself. No matter how much they had to cover, they still managed to make themselves beautiful. Occasionally she saw a man walking in front of a woman who was leading several children behind her like so many ducklings. The female children were dressed like their mothers but their faces were not covered. She waved at one little girl who stood watching the carriages go by with her mouth hanging open. The little girl waved enthusiastically back.

They arrived at the palace and exited the carriages. What looked like the entire household was there to greet them. King Abbus introduced them to his three wives, three out of his nine sons who were present, several of his many daughters, his sons' wives, and some of their children. The palace itself was very grand. It was two stories high and built of smooth white stone. It covered an immense plot of land and was surrounded by gardens of lush tress bearing colorful flowers or fruits. Rabiah recognized some of the fruits from the Southern lands her Clan had traveled to during the winter months. There was a tree full of oranges near the edge of the garden. Oranges had always been one of her favorite fruits. She had a sudden strong craving for a big, juicy bite. She was staring so hard at the tree, she didn't notice the amused look Tristan sent her way.

"Are those oranges?" Tristan asked their host after all the introductions had been made.

"Yes. Do you like them?"

"My wife likes them very much."

Rabiah looked at Tristan in surprise.

"I'll have some sent to your rooms."

"Thank you."

They entered the palace as a large group. King Abbus' family melted away so that is was just him and two of his wives. It was cool and airy inside the palace. The walls and floor were of white stone or lightly colored tiles, accented with colorful art, vases of flowers, and rich, wooden furniture. King Abbus gave them an extensive tour of the palace's first floor and the gardens. He even picked an orange and tossed it to Rabiah. She caught it easily. King Abbus gave her an approving nod and continued his tour. She did not want to be rude, so she waited to eat it.

An hour later they were finally shown to their rooms. Tristan had sent word ahead by one of the faster messenger ships that he would be coming along with several of his advisors and staff. Thus, there were several rooms ready for them.

Tristan was given the biggest room. Like the rest of the house it was white but it was decorated with pillows and art in rich reds and golds. The bed was big, but low and there was a sunken pool big enough for at least six people to sit in.

"The women's room is over here." King Abbus led them through another door into a large room with several smaller beds. The connecting door to Tristan's room was the only door in the room.

"We will have a feast in your honor in about an hour. I will send someone to guide you when it is time."

Tristan gave him a respectful bow, "Thank you for your time and attention. Your palace is very impressive."

"So it is. I look forward to our meal together." King Abbus bowed politely to Tristan and Rabiah and left. As soon as the door was shut, Rabiah took off her scarves and threw them on Tristan's bed. Lydia wandered into the women's room.

"Not liking the scarves?" Tristan asked.

"No, I want that orange. That's all I've been able to think about." She plopped down on a cushion and began peeling it.

"I noticed. Apparently it's not just morning sickness I'm sharing with you," Tristan said in a low voice as he sat next to her. "Can I have some?" She tore off a piece and placed it in his mouth.

"Did you notice I didn't get a room?" Owen said.

"You are my body guard. You don't sleep." Tristan said.

"Or, you are supposed to sleep with him. The bed is big enough," Rabiah said.

"No, thank you. Not if he's going to do what he's been doing lately."

"We should probably get a bowl, just in case," Rabiah said.

"If you need a bowl, there's plenty in here," Lydia said, floating back into the main bedroom. She looked around, "Where's Owen going to sleep?"

"He's going to sleep with the King," Rabiah said.

"I am not!"

"Then you'll have to sleep in the women's room," Rabiah teased.

"Not with me. That wouldn't be proper," Lydia said.

"We'll just pull one of the beds in here," Tristan said, "It will be just like we're camping again, except on much softer ground."

"That's what I was afraid of," Owen grumbled.

After an hour they were led into a large room divided into two parts. The men were led to one half and the women to the other. A gauzy curtain separated them. Instead of chairs there were thick mats and cushions arranged at low tables. Tristan was directed to sit next to King Abbus. As body guard, Owen did not sit, but took up a place behind Tristan. King Abbus had his own bodyguards. Rabiah was seated next to the oldest wife while Lydia was seated far down toward the end of the table. The women removed the scarves over their faces so they could eat. Rabiah did as well. The wives were friendly toward her but did not speak the common language well, so she listened to them talk among themselves. She vaguely recognized some of the words as one of the languages of the Southern tribes. As the first wife placed dishes before her, Rabiah indicated that she

131

wanted to know the names. She repeated them. She did know the language, it was just a very different dialect from the one she was familiar with. By the end of the evening she could understand what they were saying, although she doubted they would understand her if she tried to speak it.

When the meal was finished, the women refastened their scarves and the partition was removed. The first wife indicated Rabiah could go sit with her husband if she wished. Rabiah bowed in thanks and went to Tristan who moved over to make room for her.

"Now we will have some entertainment," King Abbus said. He clapped his hands. Some musicians began to play. Several young women came out and began to dance in unison while waving colorful scarves. It was somewhat mesmerizing. Rabiah noticed Tristan staring so she poked him. He looked at her and sent, "*What? I was being polite.*" She made a face at him but he couldn't see it.

The music got faster and some young men came out. The women rushed out of the way. The men wore tighter clothes and performed energetic flips and feats of strength and skill. Tristan poked Rabiah back. '*What? I was watching how they did it,*' she sent.

"Does your wife like our dances?" King Abbus asked Tristan.

"Yes, I'm sure she does."

"Do you have something similar to this?"

"No. Ours are quite different. Usually the men and women dance together."

"So I've heard. I've never seen it though."

"Would you like to? My wife and I can dance one for you."

"I would be pleased if you would."

'*Tristan, we haven't practiced!*' Rabiah sent.

'*All you have to do is follow my lead like you did before. It won't matter if we mess up. They won't know.*'

He pulled Rabiah up then went to talk to the musicians. Luckily, one of them could speak the common language. Tristan instructed them to start slow and play faster and faster.

"What are we dancing?" Rabiah whispered as he led her in front of everyone.

"Remember that last dance we did for my Mother?"

132

Rabiah looked at him as if he'd grown horns, "That almost made me sick then. If I get sick now you'll get sick too."

"Don't worry. We'll be fine. I won't spin you as fast or as much. I'm going to do little bits of several dances."

Tristan nodded to the musicians. Behind the veils, Rabiah found she didn't feel as nervous as she had expected to. She followed Tristan's silent instructions as best she could. At first the steps were very easy. As the music sped up, they became more and more challenging. At some point it was almost as if his mind took over for both of them. He started spinning her. He told her to lessen the dizziness by focusing on one spot as she spun. Then came the end. She threw herself back and he caught her. He could tell she was smiling under her veil.

'*How do you feel?*' he sent.

'*Better than last time. How are you?*'

'*Just a little nauseous. Nothing I can't handle.*'

'*Good.*' She moved to get up.

'*Maybe more than a little.*'

She touched his arm and tried to send calm and soothing energy. He took a deep breath. '*That's better.*' He let her up.

Meanwhile, their audience was clapping politely. Tristan gave a nod of his head to acknowledge them and then escorted Rabiah back to her cushion.

King Abbus seemed impressed. "Are all your dances like that?"

"No. Most are more like those at the beginning. That last one is one of the more challenging ones, but very fun to do when you have a good partner."

"So I saw," King Abbus said. "Is it only married couples who perform the dances?"

"No. Anyone can dance them although the single men and women are generally well-supervised."

"So I could dance with your wife?"

"In Arles, of course. As an honored guest she would be glad to dance with you. You would have to learn the dance first though. It is the men who lead the women."

"Of course."

Chapter 12

The next morning, Rabiah felt fine but Tristan had to eat a few crackers before he would consider rolling out of bed. She felt so sorry that he was ill and so much love that he was taking it all in stride that she couldn't help but pull him under the covers and give him a big kiss.

"Just like camping," she heard Owen sigh from across the room.

I think that worked better than the crackers,' Tristan sent.

She kissed him again, more deeply, and had to remind herself that they weren't alone.

What will happen today?' Rabiah asked, pulling down the covers a little and laying her head on his shoulder.

'King Abbus said something about a hunt.'

'Can I go?' Rabiah asked immediately as he knew she would.

'Yes. I mentioned that you would be interested and King Abbus said his second wife and one of their daughters often go hunting with the family men. He said he would have them send some clothing that is more appropriate.'

There was a knock on the door. She bounded out of bed to answer it but Owen beat her to it. He said something, then shut the door and turned. There was a bundle of clothes in his arms.

"For you and your handmaiden, my Queen," Owen said with a bow.

Rabiah grabbed them eagerly, then gave him a quick kiss on the cheek as a thank you before hurrying to the women's room to take the clothes to Lydia.

"She's chipper this morning," Owen commented.

"I told her we were going hunting," Tristan said, laying back with his hands behind his head.

"That was some impressive dancing last night," Owen said, "I didn't realize you could dance so well. I'm surprised you didn't get sick."

"I almost did."

"Why on earth would you do the spider dance?"

"King Abbus was trying to impress us with his family so I thought I'd show off mine."

"And here I thought you were finally showing signs of maturity."

They dressed and were ready and waiting by the time Rabiah and Lydia emerged.

"These are almost like my Clan clothes, just a little lighter and finer," Rabiah mused, spinning in the shorter tunic.

"Do I have to go?" Lydia whined, "I feel so underdressed and hunting is a male sport."

"It would look odd, I think, if the Queen was the only female. You are supposed to be her handmaiden. You won't know most of the people there. Wearing pants for a day won't hurt you," Tristan concluded.

Lydia bowed, "Yes, Your Highness."

There was food laid out in a long buffet for anyone who was hungry to eat before joining the large group of men that were collecting outside. King Abbus greeted Tristan warmly and directed Rabiah and Lydia to go with his second wife and daughter. Rabiah easily swung herself into the saddle of the horse provided for her. A female servant stationed nearby helped Lydia to mount. One of the servants handed Rabiah a bow. She tested it and gave it back, pointing to the one Owen had. Looking doubtful, the servant handed her a stouter bow. She nodded her thanks and slung it over her back, wishing she'd thought to bring her own bow from the ship.

Rabiah wasn't sure the second wife knew the common language as she hadn't spoken the night before, but she thought she'd try it before trying to make herself understood in their language. "What are we hunting today?" she asked, riding up alongside the second wife.

"Deer," the woman answered after a pause.

"With all these people, how will we see any deer?"

The second wife chose her words carefully. "They chase them out for us."

Rabiah didn't like the sound of that. Still, she was glad to be outside, riding on such a fine day. Lydia was dragging behind. Rabiah dropped back to see why.

"Why are you riding so far back?"

"My stomach hurts," Lydia said.

"Are you unwell?"

"Yes."

"Why didn't you say so?"

"Because the King commanded that I go."

"He would not have if he knew you were ill."

Lydia shook her head, "I could not let you go alone."

"I'm not alone. The second wife and her daughter are here. You can go back."

"No. I will stay with you."

"Do you want me to go back with you?"

"No. We should stay with the King and Sir Owen."

Rabiah nodded and stayed alongside her. They got further and further behind the main group. Some of the servants stayed with them.

"I need to relieve myself," Lydia said. They were riding through a somewhat open area but there were plenty of bushes and trees around.

"You can use those bushes over there. I'll keep everyone away." Rabiah slid down and helped Lydia dismount. Some of the servants stepped forward but Rabiah waved them away. Lydia walked into the bushes. Rabiah turned to face the servants and waited. The servants understood and did not approach again.

A couple of minutes later, Lydia emerged. Rabiah helped her onto her horse. They rode faster to catch up with the rest of the group. They had almost reached the other women when Lydia said she needed to go again. Rabiah stopped at another cluster of bushes and helped her down again. Lydia seemed to hesitate, then went ahead into the bushes. They had climbed back on their horses and almost caught up with the group again, when Lydia said she needed to stop a third time.

"Are you sure you don't want to go back? I don't mind," Rabiah said.

"Perhaps we should," Lydia paused, "I was hoping to find some clean moss."

"Is that why your stomach hurts?" Rabiah asked, realizing it was probably a women's issue rather than something else.

"Yes."

"You can use the moss that hangs from the trees here. We can get some when you are done, then we can go back."

Lydia had just emerged when one of the servants approached and urged them to hurry. Rabiah helped Lydia up, then mounted her own horse. Together they hurried to where the servant pointed. Rabiah slowed when she saw the second wife and her daughter waiting at the edge of an open area. The second wife pointed across the grass, "They will chase them out now."

Rabiah got her bow ready and waited. Soon, a cautious doe poked her head out. Another followed. Presently, several were running across the clearing. Rabiah put her bow down. There were fawns with the does. The other women had not shot either, but they were still aiming. The second wife hissed, "Why you not shoot?"

"They have young."

She nodded and lowered her bow. Her daughter did the same. "You right. We not kill mothers."

Some servants came out of the trees where the deer had emerged.

"Where are the men?"

"They far ahead. Why so much stop?"

"Lydia has women's pains."

It took a few seconds for the second wife to decipher her words. Then she nodded, "We go back then."

"She needs moss."

"We help collect."

"Thank you."

137

The women collected some moss as well as some other plant materials they found.

"This good for pain." The second wife showed Lydia the bark of a white willow. "And this just good." She popped a berry into her mouth. They had collected all they needed when Lydia had to stop again. Rabiah went with her while the other women waited. She turned her back as Lydia walked behind a tree. Suddenly, Lydia screamed. Rabiah turned as a boar charged towards Lydia. She pulled off her belt and whipped it around the boar's head as he ran past.

"Be still Lydia," she yelled.

Rabiah jerked hard on the belt. The boar turned her way. She didn't have time to get her bow ready. She turned and ran, hoping he would follow her. Based on the noise behind her, he did. She ran as hard as she could for a tall tree nearby, grabbed the nearest tree branch and swung herself up. The second wife had heard Lydia's scream and waited for Rabiah to get out of the way. She and her daughter were ready with their bows. They both hit the animal, but neither hit was instantly deadly. The boar thrashed about beneath her. Rabiah leaped down and found a way past its sharp tusks to slit its throat, giving thanks as she did so that no one had been hurt.

"Now that's hunting," the daughter said to her mother in their language. Rabiah silently agreed. They left the servants to carry the boar back and helped a disheveled Lydia back on her horse.

The men came back a couple of hours later. By that time the boar had been prepared and was already roasting. Rabiah and the second wife, whose name she had learned was Niyaf, met their husbands as they were dismounting.

"How was the hunt?" Rabiah asked Tristan.

"We got a couple of deer but that was it. What happened to you?"

"After we killed the boar, we decided to come back because Lydia wasn't feeling well," she said nonchalantly.

"You got a boar?"

"Yes. Lydia surprised it, Niyaf and her daughter shot it, and I cut its throat."

138

"Why do I get the feeling you are leaving out some details?"

Rabiah shrugged. "I did spend a little time in a tree, but not much."

King Abbus finished talking to his wife and came and clapped Tristan on the shoulder. "I hear your wife is a hero and that we are having pig tonight. Let us go refresh ourselves and you can tell me more of this remarkable wife of yours."

Tristan turned to Rabiah to give her a stern look as King Abbus dragged him away. She winked at him since he couldn't see her smile.

An hour later, Tristan finally rejoined her in his room wearing only a robe. Owen came in behind him fully dressed and still dusty from the hunting trip.

"What have you been up to?" Rabiah asked.

"Communal bathing with King Abbus and his sons. Then I had a massage from his second wife. Tristan fell back on the bed. "She requested the honor. I think she enjoyed hunting with you." He let out a breath, "Diplomacy is so exhausting."

Owen snorted. "If you don't mind, I'd like to get some food and clean up myself."

"Be my guest." Tristan waved his hand randomly in the air.

Owen sent one of their other guards inside. He still didn't trust Lydia.

"Anything happening this afternoon?" Rabiah asked, sitting next to Tristan.

"We're going to discuss a new treaty."

"May I go?"

"You may, but it probably won't be very interesting."

"I'm interested and I can understand their language."

Tristan took his hand off his eyes and looked at her, "You can?"

"Yes. It's similar to another one I know."

He pulled her down to lay beside him, "You are amazing."

She cuddled against him and eventually fell asleep.

An hour-and-a-half later, a servant came to get Tristan for the meeting. Rabiah dawned her veil and followed. They were led to a room with a low table and cushions like the dining room but smaller. King Abbus and several of Tristan's advisors were already there.

"Ah, King Tristan. Is your wife looking for the women?"

"No. She wanted to attend."

"Women and politics are not a good mix in my experience."

"She only wishes to learn more about Arles and the people we associate with. It is difficult to be a queen in a country you know nothing about."

"If it is truly your wish, then she may stay," King Abbus acquiesced.

Rabiah found a cushion along the wall behind Tristan and seated herself. Owen stood against the wall by Rabiah. The rest of the advisors slowly trickled in. Servants put bowls of nuts and fresh fruits on the table and a drink in front of each person. One of the servants even handed a drink to Rabiah. There must have been a signal she didn't see because the servants all left at once, closing the door behind them.

King Abbus took a sip from his cup and said, "King Tristan, I have looked over your proposed treaty and I do not accept."

"It is exactly the same as the one you agreed to with my father. Might I ask why you decline," Tristan said politely.

"You may. Here is the problem. Back when I made that treaty with your father I did not have so many children and you were but a few years old. I suggested at the time that an arrangement could be made between one of my daughters and yourself. Your father declined. He told me that he didn't plan to tie you to anyone until you came of age. You reached the age of eighteen and I sent a message to your father. He said you were exploring the world and not yet ready for a wife. I waited. Word came that several other parties had expressed an interest but your father waved them all away. I sent another message to your father and he said you were still not ready. You were twenty-one by then. Plenty old enough to take a wife. I decided to start increasing the tariffs to force your father into action. He ignored me. I increased them more. That was this summer. He sent me a message inquiring why I was ignoring the treaty. I told him I wanted to make a new deal with you. He promised he would send you when you came home, but as I feared, it was too late. You had already found yourself a wife. That leaves us at a bit of an impasse. I have many daughters and granddaughters and I wish to link our kingdoms through marriage, but your father has only one living son. So, either you need to put your Clan wife aside or provide me with another acceptable male for one of my daughters. Then and only then will I accept the terms of your treaty."

"What would you deem acceptable in terms of rank?" Tristan asked.

"They must be propertied and they must have some connection with you. I want my son-in-law to have access to you if I need you."

"Might I ask why this is so important to you?"

King Abbus said something to his advisors which Rabiah interpreted as "Leave us." Tristan nodded to his advisors and his guards, including Owen, to follow. Rabiah stayed where she was. King Abbus waited until they were alone before speaking. He turned to Rabiah and spoke directly to her, "You will keep this to yourself?"

Rabiah nodded.

King Abbus turned back to Tristan. "I am blessed with a large family and many sons. Only one can become king after I am gone, but several believe it should be them. I could pick any of them to be my successor. Sadly, some of my sons, or their close relatives, seek to decrease the competition. I suspect that is the reason my eldest son died four years ago. Several of my other sons have narrowly escaped death or grave injury. I have chosen my successor but he is still young. Your kingdom is far enough away that I could send a couple of my younger sons and grandsons to visit their sister for an extended time without causing too much speculation. I knew your father for many years and I have received good reports of you. I know you would do your best to watch over him."

"But you do not need marriage to send them to Arles. You can send them as goodwill visitors to train in the army or to learn to be ambassadors."

"Yes, but as I said, I have many children. It is hard to find good mates for all of them. I ask that you humor me in this request. I will agree to the treaty as soon as a marriage takes place."

"I must think on this," Tristan said.

141

King Abbus nodded. "Then we are done for now. We can meet again tomorrow."

King Abbus left. Rabiah sat down next to Tristan and waited. After a few minutes he spoke. "I can think of at least eight eligible men who fit the requirements."

"Who?"

"My uncle for one."

Rabiah raised her eyebrow doubtfully and waited.

"Then there's the son of one of my advisors although he is a bit loose, if you know what I mean. There's also old Lord Landsbury."

"He's older than King Abbus."

"He didn't mention an age requirement."

"No, but would you want your daughter to marry someone that old?"

"I suppose I could marry one. You would still be the first wife."

Rabiah punched him.

"Then there's Owen."

"Owen would do it," Rabiah said quietly, after a thoughtful pause.

"But I don't want to ask it of him."

"No. And I think he likes Hadassah," Rabiah said.

"But she is still mourning her husband."

"He is patient and he is so sweet with the baby."

"And he is already here. We could get this over and done with. His new bride could come home with us," Tristan pointed out.

"What's a few more months compared to a lifetime in an unhappy marriage?"

"They might be happy."

"Perhaps," Rabiah conceded.

"I will ask him to look over the girls and see if he finds anyone interesting."

"And if he doesn't?"

"We'll go back home and get my uncle."

"Is this truly so important?"

"It's not just about the treaty. They are a seafaring nation as we are. King Abbus gives each son a ship when he comes of age. They are out in the waters with our ships. Right now they are friends. If pirates attack, they help us. If a storm hits, they offer our ships safe port. It would be very bad for trade, for travel, and even for fishing if they became our enemies."

Rabiah nodded. Tristan silently requested Owen's presence. Owen came in a few seconds later.

"You called Your Highnesses?"

"Please sit down Owen," Tristan said.

"You want me to be the sacrificial lamb, don't you?"

"No, but you are the best candidate. I'm not going to order you to marry anyone. If you did though, it would certainly simplify matters."

"Owen, if you have feelings for someone else, we can end this discussion right now." Rabiah said.

"I don't, but…"

"What about Hadassah?"

"We are just good friends."

"Nothing more?"

"Her husband has only been gone a few months. She saw him killed, by the way, by an Arles man. I would not ask her to marry me even if I wanted to. That just seems wrong."

"That's horrible," Rabiah said, imagining how she would feel if she saw Tristan cut down.

"King Abbus said we would talk again tomorrow. All I'm asking is that you keep your eyes open. If you see someone you like, point her out and we'll find out who she is."

"Maybe you should just have King Abbus line up all the eligible females and introduce them to you," Owen said sarcastically.

"That's not a bad idea."

"I was joking."

After the evening meal, Tristan asked King Abbus if he had any girl in particular in mind.

"I have several," King Abbus replied, "Let me show you." He called up eight girls. They included his three youngest daughters

143

ranging from twenty to sixteen, and his five oldest granddaughters ranging from seventeen to twelve.

"That's a lot to choose from," Tristan said.

"Yes. I prefer to marry off the eldest first, of course."

"Of course. What can I tell a perspective husband about them?"

"What's to tell? They are women. The one chosen will warm his bed and bear his children. All my daughters know how to run a household. They have all been trained to be obedient and loyal to their husbands."

"If there's one thing I've learned from having a wife, is that women have definite likes and dislikes. Might I ask them a couple of questions? They won't have to answer verbally."

"Be my guest."

"Do they all know Common?"

"They should."

Tristan addressed the girls, "Please step forward if you'd like to leave here and travel to Arles to be someone's wife."

All but the youngest and one in the middle stepped forward.

"Step forward if you'd like to marry a soldier such as Sir Owen here." He motioned for Owen to step forward. Owen frowned to be commanded to stand on display. Only two of the girls stepped forward without hesitation.

"That narrowed it down," Tristan said.

"You think to offer Sir Owen as a son-in-law?"

"He's one possibility. But I will not make that offer unless he wishes me to."

"So, Sir Owen, do you like what you see?" King Abbus asked.

"They are all very nice," Owen said politely. He scanned the girls and paused when he came to the youngest. "Do you have another daughter close to these ages?"

"I have a granddaughter who is eleven, but she is much too young and small for someone of your stature."

"No, someone older."

"Well, yes," King Abbus said somewhat reluctantly, "But she, well, she is hard to find."

144

"Ask if the one who was outside your room today when I left to bathe will step forward," Owen said quietly to Tristan. Tristan did so. None of the other girls moved, except to turn their heads to see if anyone else did. Owen, however smiled, and walked toward the youngest. She looked frightened and took a step back. Owen passed her without a look and stopped just past her where no one stood. He put out his hand, "If you are interested then so am I, but don't you think it unfair that I've only seen a little of you whereas you have seen most of me?"

A hand appeared in Owen's which led to an arm, then a torso, then the full body and head of a petite female clothed as was proper in a veil. Owen's face brightened with a dashing smile. She looked up at him with a smile in her eyes.

"He can see her!" King Abbus exclaimed. "Do you know how hard it is to raise a child you cannot see? She started disappearing when she was three. We had to lock all the doors so she couldn't escape and get lost. Who is this man, King Tristan? Why can he see her?"

"He is my best friend. We grew up together. Seeing what other people cannot is his gift."

"And he is in need of a wife and has land?"

"Yes, and he's fifth in line for the throne as well."

"And he's your bodyguard?" King Abbus asked with some surprise.

"Who better? I trust him with my life. He saved me last summer and he and my wife saved the whole city little more than a month ago."

"Did you inform him of my wishes?"

"No, but I'm sure he will be happy to comply, although he likes to be asked."

"Of course." King Abbus popped up from his pillow and strolled over to where Owen and the girl were talking. He took the girl's hand out of Owen's hand then gave it back to him. "She is yours. Take her and make her your wife. I will sign the treaty immediately."

Owen opened his mouth to say something and even looked a little frightened Tristan thought, but his new wife tugged on his hand to make him look at her. Tristan thought he saw her removing her veil and pulling Owen closer but they disappeared from sight before he could be sure.

'What just happened?' Rabiah sent from across the room. *'All the women suddenly started talking very excitedly and the servants are running around in panic.'*

'Owen just got married.'

'What? Where is he?' Rabiah stood up to get a better view. *'Who did he marry? I can't see them.'*

'She can turn herself invisible and Owen too it seems.'

Rabiah switched to her soul sight. *'Oh, there they are. They must be hugging or kissing. They are very close to one another.'* Rabiah paused, *'Owen seems to be enjoying himself.'* She paused again. *'It looks like she's leading him somewhere. I think Owen is trying to slow her down.'*

To Owen, Rabiah sent, *'Go. I told Tristan you were leaving.'*

Rabiah watched as their two lights got closer again and they disappeared through a door.

'They're gone.'

'I at least had the decency to wait a couple of weeks so you could get to know me.'

'You were unconscious for part of the time, remember. Besides I don't think Owen had much choice. She was the one dragging him away.'

'The boat ride back should be interesting.'

Rabiah agreed.

The first wife rose and went through the door where all the servants entered and exited. Shortly afterwards, the servants began bringing in more drinks and food to celebrate the marriage, Rabiah guessed. The third wife had begun to cry and was now surrounded by women and girls who were trying to console her.

"Why is she sad?" Rabiah asked Niyaf, who was sitting near her.

"Senna her daughter."

"Owen is a good man. Would it help if I were to tell her that?"

"No. She always cry."

146

King Abbus stood. "My family and friends," he waved his cup towards the people from Arles, "today we celebrate the marriage of my daughter Princess Senna to Sir Owen of Arles. Their marriage fulfills the conditions I set for the proposed treaty, which I will now sign."

With great gusto, he used a feather to sign the paper his advisor held before him on a sturdy board. He handed the feather to Tristan who also signed.

"There, it is done!"

Everyone cheered.

"I would toast the bride and groom in person but they seem to have disappeared." His family laughed. "So here's to long life, health, and happiness, wherever you are."

Everyone drank, even the women. Rabiah took a small sip of the drink that was handed to her. It was very bitter. Tristan made a toast as did several of the advisors. Rabiah saw Owen come back into the room. She turned on her soul sight. He appeared to be alone. *'Owen has come back by himself,'* she sent to Tristan.

'Uh oh. Trouble already. Do you see her anywhere?'

Rabiah expanded her search. *'I see her. She's behind a plant in the corner.'*

Owen saw her too and approached the plant. His new bride slipped out from behind it and moved toward the women's side of the room. Rabiah watched as the girl's glow went past and entered the women's quarters. Owen stopped short at the line where the curtain normally stood. The men guarding the women's side stepped in front of him. He lifted his hands palms up as if asking Rabiah what to do.

'I'll go talk to her,' she sent to Owen. Rabiah stood. Niyaf looked at her inquiringly. "The new bride has run away," Rabiah explained, nodding towards Owen. "She went through that door."

"Good luck finding her," Niyaf said, turning back to the table. She clearly thought it a lost cause.

The door through which the girl had gone led to a long hallway with many other doors. *'This might take a while,'* Rabiah sent to Owen. She began systematically trying every door. Some opened at her touch and others were locked. She extended her sense to search for

147

souls, but as usual she couldn't see through the doors or walls. She was just about to shut the eleventh door when she thought she saw a small glow coming from behind a large piece of furniture. She entered the room and shut the door to block the light from the torches in the hallway. There *was* a glow.

"I can't see you like Owen can but I know you're there. Why did you run from him?" Rabiah waited but there was no response.

"It looked like you were really enjoying each other so I'm guessing he did or said something you didn't like." Rabiah waited again. The light didn't move.

"Owen is a good man and he is my friend. He's very brave. He saved my husband's life. He refused to leave his side although people were pointing spears at him. He's smart too. He figured out how to break into a castle that had been taken over by a demon who could see and hear through its victims' eyes and ears." The light got brighter as the girl stepped out from behind the furniture.

"He's also very kind. A woman who had recently lost her husband had a baby. He comforted her when no one else thought to do so."

The light approached her. In the very dim light coming from the crack under the door, Rabiah saw a tunic-clad body appear before her, sans veil.

"Why did he reject me then?"

"Reject you? It didn't look like he was rejecting you to me."

"I wanted to…I've seen other people and they looked like they were enjoying themselves. I wanted him to, to make me fully his wife and he said no."

"Did he say 'no' or did he say 'wait'?"

"He said, 'No wait.'"

"I told you he was smart."

"How so?"

"You and Owen have only just met. He wants to get to know you first. My husband and I waited several weeks before we came together."

"Weeks!"

"There were extenuating circumstances, but when we finally did come together, it was, it was, I can't think of a word good enough to describe it."

The girl sat on the bed. "It would be hard to wait that long. I really like kissing him."

"Have you kissed anyone before?"

"Yes, but I didn't let them see me."

"That must have been interesting for them," Rabiah chuckled.

The girl laughed. "I think they thought they were kissing a ghost."

"There's a lot more to Owen than just his lips you know," Rabiah said, hoping to get the girl to think beyond her physical attraction. It didn't work.

"I do. I followed him into the bath earlier."

"You did?"

"He knew I was there. He wouldn't finish undressing until I left."

"Do you do that often? Follow men into the bath?" Rabiah asked, her eyebrow raised.

"No, but there's something about him. I couldn't help myself."

"It's like that for me with King Tristan."

"What should I do?"

"Go back to him and drag him away again. Tell him you will wait. Let him set the pace."

"Will he be mad?"

"No. I can tell he really enjoys kissing you. He's waiting for you. Just don't rush him. Take your time. Enjoy getting to know him."

"Getting to know him?"

"Both mind and body."

The girl smiled and bowed.

"Thank you Queen Rabiah."

"You're welcome. Go quickly before my husband has a chance to tease him too much."

The girl hurried out of the room. Rabiah followed behind more slowly. She saw the girl disappear right before she reentered the main hall. Rabiah looked toward Tristan as she reentered the hall herself. Owen was sitting next to Tristan sipping from a mug. He didn't appear upset. Tristan was saying something to King Abbus. Then Owen's face brightened. Rabiah watched as the girl's light got close enough to whisper in his ear, then they both disappeared again. King Abbus nudged Tristan. Tristan put his hand out to see if Owen was still there but Rabiah knew he had already left the room.

Lydia had not come to the meal that evening and she was already sleeping when Rabiah and Tristan returned to the room. The guards posted themselves outside of Lydia's door and in front of the main door. Owen didn't come back at all that night. They didn't see him until late the next morning. He walked into the room, his face a mask, but at one look from Tristan, his face cracked with a broad grin.

"Where is your wife" Tristan asked, "or is she right behind you?"

"Senna is busy packing. Her mother was leaking tears all over the place so I got out of the way."

"Did King Abbus speak to you?"

"Yes."

"Did you agree?"

"Yes. What else could I do?"

Owen was still smiling.

"So where did you go last night? Does Senna have her own room?"

"Where did I not go is what you should ask. Senna seems to know all the secret places in the palace and I think she showed me every one."

Rabiah noticed Tristan was grinning now too, as was she.

"Just showed?" Tristan asked.

"Well, no," Owen's grin grew larger.

"So you are not upset at this marriage?" Rabiah asked.

Owen crossed the room, picked Rabiah up into a huge hug and spun her around. "Thanks for sending her back to me," he said softly before putting her down.

"You're welcome," she squeezed out.

Lydia walked out of her room just as Owen put Rabiah down. "Good morning Your Highnesses, Sir Owen. She looked at all of them closely. "Why are you all grinning?"

"Owen had a good night," Tristan said, grinning even bigger.

Lydia looked between them, "What is that supposed to mean?"

"He and his new wife hit it off well I'd say."

"Wife? How did that happen? No. Don't tell me. King Abbus caught him with one of his daughters and made them marry."

"More like he saw the girl that no one else can see. King Abbus was so impressed that he immediately gave her to him to be his wife before she could disappear again and then no one is sure what happened because they both disappeared," Tristan laughed.

"That makes no sense."

"You'll see. Or you won't."

Lydia frowned at him.

The door opened and closed. Owen turned, looked down with a soft smile, then faded before their eyes.

"Where did he go?" Lydia said in shock.

The door opened and closed again.

"Out," Rabiah said.

Chapter 13

The captain of Tristan's ship urged Tristan to take advantage of the trip and do some trading with the countries even further south once the treaty was signed. Since they had concluded their business so quickly and no one really wanted to go back to cold Arles, Tristan agreed. He told Owen it was a wedding gift: a wedding trip for him and his new wife.

"Then why are you going?" Owen asked.

"It's my boat."

Owen snorted and walked away, but he was happy to go.

The next day, they took two of their ships farther south while the third ship, full of advisors and lawyers who would help Tristan's uncle take care of the kingdom in Tristan's absence, headed back to Arles. For safety, Yusri, one of King Abbus' sons, joined them with his ship. Marion mixed a fresh potion for Lydia and Tristan that helped them with their sea sickness. Because she was expecting, Rabiah couldn't take it. Since it was partially a pleasure trip, they stopped often to visit beaches sparkling with white sand and little villages with lots of coral and pearls to trade. As soon as the people in the villages stopped wearing veils, Rabiah took hers off. She even went swimming when there was no one but them around. Senna followed Rabiah's lead, although she was a poor swimmer. Owen started giving her lessons. He offered to teach Lydia. She declined. Instead she spent her time wading in the water looking for shells.

After a week, they made it to their destination. It was a large port with a market where everything from cows to coconuts to diamonds could be had for the right price. It was not a safe place.

Rabiah dressed in what Tristan had started calling her warrior wear. She strapped on all her throwing knives and a short sword. Yusri's eyebrows rose when he saw her but he didn't say anything. Owen armed himself with a sword and several smaller knives as well. Senna stayed by his side. Tristan carried a sword. Everyone who saw them assumed Lydia was a lady on an outing with her female servant and several guards.

Their display of arms worked. No one accosted them. Lydia found booths selling beautiful light-weight fabric. She insisted Rabiah purchase some. Rabiah didn't take much persuasion. She loved the feel and the look of the smooth fabric, as did Senna. They bought so much they had to have their purchases delivered directly to the ship. The also shopped for gifts for the General and other close associates at the castle. With Senna's help, Owen even bought something for his new mother-in-law.

They spent the next day walking around the rest of the city, Senna's brother acting as their guide. The Captain, meanwhile had been busy buying goods they could sell when they got back to Arles. They left port the next day with a loaded ship to travel back to the Kingdom of Ibirann. It was, Rabiah thought as she snuggled next to Tristan that night, a very nice wedding trip, especially since Owen could enjoy it too.

It was slow going back. The wind was against them. On the fifth day, the wind died completely. They waited impatiently for a breeze within sight of a distant coast. Senna's brother was nervous. He warned them to be on guard against pirates.

"If we can't move, then they can't either," Owen pointed out.

"Don't be so sure of that. It is said the pirate captain can control the wind."

"Surely he is not powerful enough to move enough ships to take on three of ours," Owen said.

"According to the reports, he is extremely powerful, able to control the wind at a great distance. One of my friends just barely escaped with his ship, and that was only because all the other merchant ships he was traveling with were more heavily loaded and were captured first."

"Then we just have to be ready for them," Tristan said. He called a meeting of all the captains and they made a plan, just in case. Several of the guards and many of the sailors were excellent archers. Archers and arrows were divided evenly across the ships. They set an extra guard, and at dusk, before she went to bed, Rabiah climbed the tall mast and searched as far as she could for souls. She found a few on the shore and a far distance away, but they didn't seem to be moving any more than they were. She climbed up again in the middle of the night but couldn't sense anything.

Another day passed. The wind remained still. "How long do you think this will last?" Rabiah asked Tristan.

"There's no telling, but it usually doesn't last too long."

"There's a storm coming," the ship's captain said, "but it is a day away yet."

"How can you tell?" Rabiah asked.

"It is the cook's gift. He's always right about storms."

"Can he tell how bad it will be?"

"He can if it's going to be really bad. This one won't be and it should get the wind moving."

"Good. As nice as it is, I don't like being stuck here," Tristan said.

Rabiah climbed up the mast again at dusk. All was clear.

"How can you see anything up there?" Lydia asked when she came down. "It's almost completely dark."

"I'm looking for lights," Rabiah explained.

"Why must it be you? Why can't the look-out find them?"

"He will and he can, but I can see different lights than he can."

"What do you mean, different lights?"

"It's part of our gift."

"Why doesn't King Tristan climb the pole then?"

"We share some parts of our gift, but some parts are different."

Lydia sighed inwardly and went into her cabin. Trying to get information out of Queen Rabiah was difficult at best. They seemed to have a very useful gift, whatever it was.

Rabiah went into her cabin. Tristan was still on deck somewhere, but Rabiah was feeling very tired, so she quickly fell asleep.

Around midnight she awoke. Tristan was beside her and all was quiet, yet something seemed off. She grabbed her bow and slipped out to climb to the crow's nest again. She didn't need to go that far. She could sense the approaching souls as soon as she reached the open air. There were seven different clusters of souls approaching their three ships. The souls were lower in the water than the Arles ships. They must be on much smaller boats, Rabiah surmised. The water rocked gently from their movement. With just her normal sight, the boats were pitch black. She should have been able to see something in the starlight, but it was as if the ships absorbed the light. She rang the warning bell. Tristan, the captain, and the sailors on guard responded quickly.

"Where?" Tristan asked.

She pointed.

"I don't see anything."

"I know. Their ships are absorbing the light."

"But you can see people?"

"Yes, seven clusters."

The captain was doubtful until Owen joined them. Owen knew where the pirates were without being shown. "Looks like we're going to be busy." Rabiah nodded and ran to the back of the ship. Owen left to cross to the nearby ship so he could help them find the boats. He took Senna with him. The pirates were still too far away to hit, but Rabiah wanted to be ready. Tristan came up beside her with his bow.

"Just in case they suddenly light some lamps," he said.

Rabiah squeezed his arm as an idea came to her. She tried to send a picture of what she was seeing to Tristan. He gave a low whistle. "We do have our work cut out for us. Just point me and I'll probably hit something."

"I can't shoot until they do," Rabiah said. It was Clan law. She could not attack unless she was attacked first.

155

"They may not fire if they think we're asleep. They'll try and surround and board us without warning."

"I guess I'll let them know we're awake then." She shot an arrow high and long. It landed in the first boat, she thought. She was aiming for just in front of the soul she saw there. She waited. A hail of arrows rained down just short of the boat.

"Can you fire now?"

"Yes."

They were still at the limits of her range but she could hit the ones in the front. She aimed low, hoping to maim, not kill.

"Point me," Tristan said. "She pushed his arrow towards a large cluster of souls. He released three arrows in quick succession. Two sailors standing with them aimed in the same direction.

Rabiah aimed for the people who weren't moving. She assumed they were the leaders. She had fired about twenty arrows when a stiff wind began to blow toward her. She lowered her bow.

"The wind is too strong. The arrows can't fly in this."

"But we can sail or we could if we weren't in formation."

The wind died. Rabiah shot five more arrows. At least three of them hit their marks. Another stiff breeze hit and kept blowing.

"Who is controlling the breeze? If we take him out we'll have a good chance," one of the sailors said.

Rabiah searched the souls in front of her. She couldn't tell. She sent a message to Owen, *'Owen, who is controlling the wind?'* After a minute she thought she heard him yell "Last ship." She looked. One ship was hanging far behind the others. There was someone on the deck but he was much too far for her arrows even if the wind was not blowing.

"We can't stop him," Rabiah said.

"Then we should use what they are giving us. Captain, let's move," Tristan said to the captain of the ship who was standing next to them.

The captain barked some orders. They began to move away from the other two ships and the pirates. The wind died down. Rabiah waited until the pirates were in range again and fired. She hit another eight targets before the wind started again.

"How are they communicating so fast?" Tristan asked.

"How do we communicate so fast?" Rabiah responded.

"Guess the bad guys have gifts too."

They were moving again. The other two ships were taking advantage of the wind too.

"How long do you think we'll keep this up?" Rabiah asked.

"All night, I hope," Tristan said. Then we'll all be able to see them and perhaps I'll be able to aim."

The wind died. Rabiah hit another five targets. Tristan was frustrated that he couldn't see. As the wind picked up again, he put his arms around Rabiah to share some of his strength since she was the one doing all the shooting.

"Here my love." She felt his strength seep into her arms. She leaned her head back on his shoulder to let him know she appreciated it.

"Is everything all right?" Lydia asked behind them.

"Yes. We're just waiting for the wind to die again," Rabiah said.

"Where's Owen?" Lydia asked.

"He's on the other ship, helping them aim," Rabiah replied.

"And Senna?"

"She's with Owen?"

"What can I do?"

"Find me more arrows," Rabiah said. She pushed herself out of Tristan's arms and stepped forward. "One of the boats is speeding our way. Looks like they have another plan. If it gets close enough, the wind won't be so much of a problem."

The boat came closer. A flame flared on its deck. Tristan could see the boat now too. "They're going to try and catch our boat on fire," he said.

"They can't if they're all dead," Rabiah said. She left the ones near the flames for Tristan and focused on the ones on the edges. The ship kept coming, powered by the wind pushing it, but it veered away as the captain fell. The lighted rag and the flagon of oil they had been about to throw on the Arles ship fell on the pirate ship's deck as the pirate holding it succumbed to Tristan's arrow.

"There's another attacking Senna's brothers ship." Rabiah cried, looking up in alarm. *'Owen, they're attacking the other ship.'*

"I see it," Owen yelled. There was nothing he could do. The archers on the third ship sent a volley of arrows at the attacking ship. They hit a couple of pirates but the pirates still managed to deliver one of their flaming packages.

"Their ship is on fire!" Rabiah exclaimed.

"Not for long. Jaxon is on that ship. He can control fire, but only at short distances," one of the sailors said.

"Here comes a third one," Rabiah said, "It's heading for Owen's boat."

Since Owen could see the pirates, he and the archers with him made short work of the pirates on the third boat. The pirate boat sailed past, barely missing its target.

"What do you think they'll try next?" Rabiah asked.

"Where did the second boat go?" Tristan asked.

Rabiah searched, "It's ahead of us, waiting I think."

"They'll try again or they'll try to board," Tristan said.

"They're in range. Can you see them?" Rabiah asked.

"I can see a glow."

"I'll take them. You keep an eye out here," Rabiah said

She ran to the front of the ship. The stash of arrows she had placed there was gone. She looked around. Lydia came puffing up with a loaded quiver.

"I'm sorry. I didn't think you'd need them here."

"It's fine. Just make sure to leave a few in each spot just in case."

On this side of the boat, the wind was with her. Rabiah took a handful of arrows and fired them in rapid fashion. She hit three pirates. The others disappeared in the lower part of the boat, she assumed.

"Did you hit anything?"

"I got three."

"You killed three people?"

"No, just injured them."

"How can you tell?"

Rabiah looked at her and Lydia noted with a shock that Rabiah's eyes seemed to be glowing. "They still have their souls," Rabiah explained.

Rabiah waited to see if anyone would come back onto the deck of the smaller ship. Nothing happened. She finally asked Lydia to get her one of the rags she had dipped in pitch and oil and a torch. Lydia returned quickly with both. Rabiah wrapped the cloth around an arrow, had Lydia light it, and fired. She hit the center of the pirate's craft.

"That's so the other archers can see it," Rabiah explained. "Keep an eye on it and let me know if it goes out."

The wind died down again but this time the remaining ships stayed out of range.

"Why don't they give up?" Lydia asked, coming to stand beside Rabiah and Tristan. The fire on the pirate's boat had spread. There was no danger of it going out soon. "They've already lost three boats."

"I don't know," Tristan said.

Rabiah looked all around them. "I do," she said quietly, "There's more."

"How many?" Tristan asked.

"At least ten more."

"What do they want so badly?" Lydia asked.

"Our ships, I would guess," Tristan said.

"We can't hold them off forever," Rabiah said.

"We don't need to. We just need to keep them at bay until the storm arrives. Then there will be wind and we won't be sitting ducks anymore."

"They're coming."

This time the pirates approached from all sides. The wind twirled around them and seemed to come from all directions. Rabiah was impressed. "The person controlling this is really powerful."

"Too powerful I think," Tristan said. "Can you see him?"

Rabiah squinted. "Yes, barely."

"Does he look normal?"

"I can't tell."

"Where are the ships coming from?" Tristan asked.

"Everywhere."

"Light them up so the rest of us can see," Tristan ordered her. He sent the same order to Owen.

"Lydia, bring the rest of the cloths and the torch," Rabiah ordered.

The lit arrows were heavier and didn't fly as well. Rabiah hit the two ships closest and then she and Lydia ran forward to hit the ones approaching the front of the ship. Tristan and the other archers targeted the pirates as they put the fires out.

Rabiah hit all the boats she could reach from her ship, then ran and leaped to the ship Owen was on. The ships from Arles were closer now that they had stopped moving. The sailors handed her arrows ready to light, and them lit them for her. She hit another boat approaching the bow of the ship she was on, and then one approaching the third ship. She targeted the captains of the pirate ships while the sailors targeted what they could see. One of the ships crashed into the bow of the third ship but the pirate's ship was more damaged than theirs.

"They're boarding!" she heard someone call from the third ship. She ran and leaped the small gap between the boats. She could see faces appearing over the edge of the ship. She fired. She had five arrows with her and she made five hits. There was a pirate fighting a sailor. The sailor looked to be winning. Looking down over the side she spied two boats. More pirates were crawling up the sides.

"I need arrows!" she yelled. Someone put some in her hand. She hit three of the invading pirates.

"Give me fire!" A sailor wrapped a cloth around her ready arrow and a soldier lit it. She fired on the closest ship.

"Again!" They were ready for her. She fired on the second boat. Someone fired an arrow at her. It struck the wood in front of her. She pulled it out and fired it back, hitting the pirate with his own arrow. The sailors could see the boats now. Someone yelled elsewhere. She ran towards the sound. More pirates were approaching the ship Tristan was on. Rabiah leapt over gaps that most men wouldn't dare attempt in order to reach him.

160

'I'm coming.'

Tristan had an arrow ready to light waiting for her. She hit the two boats at the side and the one coming up behind. Tristan and the sailors picked off the pirates climbing up. She heard a call for help and looked back to see someone she recognized as Owen and perhaps Senna surrounded by three other souls. She turned and running, shot two of them dead. Owen finished off the other one. Rabiah looked around. Pirates were boarding on all sides but the sailors were holding their own. She needed more arrows. There were some stashed in the crow's nest. Quickly she climbed. Her arms were beginning to feel heavy. The arrows were there but from this vantage point it was difficult to tell who was who in the dark.

Rabiah could see everything around them. She could see eleven spots with at least one soul around their three bigger ships. There was a cluster of souls which appeared to be on a ship much bigger than any of theirs. Now she could clearly see the one who must be controlling the wind. His soul was encased in pink like Lydia's. The pink was flowing from him to the sky. He was too far away for one of her arrows.

She climbed back down, carrying the arrows with her. She used a few as she ran to find Tristan. The sailors were doing a good job defending their ship. She found Tristan close to where she had left him. He was trying to wrestle a knife out of someone's hand. She hit the pirate from the side and flipped him over the rail.

"Tristan, I saw the person controlling the wind. He's pink, just like Lydia. He's on a huge boat. Much bigger than ours. If it's full of pirates, we're in trouble."

"We need to take him out. If they don't have wind, they can't move."

"I can try to hit them when he gets a little closer."

"He'll probably just knock your arrow away."

"If they board us maybe Senna can disguise Owen so he can get close enough to take him."

"It would be very dangerous."

"If they board us they may kill us all anyway."

"I'll tell Owen. Go see if you can get a shot."

161

Rabiah ran back to the crow's nest. If the ship got close enough she would have a shot from there. Before she was half-way to her destination, she heard Lydia scream. Rabiah turned and ran back. A pirate had climbed over the side and grabbed her. He was holding her between himself and Tristan with a knife at Lydia's neck. The pirate's back was to Rabiah. She ran lightly up behind him and forced her arms up between his arms and Lydia's body, trapping them so that Tristan could pull Lydia out of the way. Rabiah flipped the pirate over the side. She kicked a second pirate peering over the edge in the face. He fell too.

Tristan was helping Lydia up. "Are you all right?" Rabiah asked her.

"Yes," she said, rubbing her neck, "Go do what you need to do." Rabiah headed back towards the crow's nest.

"Rabiah," Tristan called. She turned. "Be careful. I can feel how tired you are. Don't overdo again."

"I'll try not to." Rabiah ran off into the dark again.

"She can't tell when she's tired?" Lydia asked.

"She can, but she ignores it. She doesn't give up easily."

"I've noticed."

"And somehow she keeps ending up in situations like this and there's nothing I can do to help her," Tristan sighed.

"She'll be all right. There are no demons this time."

"It's not just her," Tristan said, after a pause.

"What do you mean?"

Tristan looked at her, considering. Then he said, "She's expecting. Please keep it to yourself for now."

Lydia shook her head, "Of course she is. How could she not be with the way you two carry on? Senna and Owen are even worse. Disappearing all over the ship and why? Everyone knows what they are doing. I think I almost sat them the other day."

Tristan looked around. The onslaught of pirates seemed to be lessening. "I suppose we are a little freer than we should be, but it's supposed to be our wedding trip."

"Then why am I here? Rabiah doesn't need me. She dresses herself and doesn't listen to my suggestions."

"It would look odd for her not to have at least one servant or handmaiden. Besides, isn't it nice to be away from the snow?"

"It was until the pirates found us," Lydia conceded.

Tristan looked down over the side of the boat. He didn't see anything *'Rabiah, are you up there yet?'*

'Almost. The big ship is much closer. I can see the wind-mage.' There was a pause. *'I'm ready. Here it goes.'*

Rabiah let loose her arrow. It flew straight towards the mage. There was so much pink surrounding his soul that she could almost make out his face in the glow. The arrow dropped right in front of him as if it had hit a wall. He paused and looked about, searching for the source of the arrow. Rabiah ducked down. She didn't think he had seen her, but the boat began to rock violently as the wind-mage sent the wind against it.

'I think I made him mad.'

Tristan was hanging onto the side of the boat to keep from rolling across the deck. Lydia had fallen against a large crate and was hanging on to the ropes which held it.

'I'll say.'

Tristan felt the bile rising and leaned over the side to puke.

'Hang on Rabiah.' He could feel her getting sick. He took it on himself and puked again. Rabiah was more than 100 feet up. He knew from experience that little waves below felt like big waves up there and they were having huge waves below.

After what seemed like an eternity, the tossing finally stopped. Rabiah slid down from the crow's next and lay on the deck. To say she did not feel well was an understatement.

'Rabiah, are you all right?'

'That was worse than being stuck in a tree during a wind storm.'

'The good news is, the pirates ships have to have been knocked away.'

'What about our other two ships?'

'I don't know.'

Someone was shaking him. Tristan opened his eyes to see Lydia staring down at him, a frantic look in her eye.

"We're being boarded."

"How many?"

163

"Too many. The sailors are fighting but it looks like there are two for every sailor."

"Then there's nothing I can do." He closed his eyes again. The world was beginning to calm down but not enough that he felt like moving yet. Lydia yelped suddenly. Tristan's adrenaline pulsed briefly but it wasn't enough to rouse him. He resigned himself to his fate. Death had finally caught him.

'I love you Rabiah.'

'I love you too.'

Something dug into his ribs. "Ow," he said.

"This one's breathing. A land lover for sure. He smells of puke."

"Put him with the others."

Someone hauled him up. The world spun and he retched again. The pirates handling him stepped out of the way just in time.

"Sorry," Tristan said, embarrassed. He wiped his mouth with the back of his hand. The pirate pulled out a long knife and used it to prod Tristan towards the mainmast. Rabiah was sitting with her head in her hands. The pirate pushed Tristan down next to her.

"Here. Puke on each other all you like."

Lydia was sitting next to Rabiah. She looked furious. Several sailors had been tied up and tossed next to mainmast as well. One of the pirates kicked Rabiah's foot out of his way.

"You can't treat them like that!" Lydia said.

"Like what? I didn't do anything to them. Not like you did to our boats."

"You attacked us."

"We're pirates. That's what we do."

"Who was the one controlling the wind," Tristan asked, "That was a pretty impressive feat."

"It was, wasn't it?" a voice said behind the pirates. The pirates stepped aside to let a tall, thin young man in a dark cloak step through. The man's long hair and cloak moved about even though the prisoners could feel no wind.

"Which one of you loosed that arrow towards me?"

164

Before Rabiah could respond, Lydia spoke, "What difference does it make? It didn't hit the mark."

"No, but it came close. You put up a good defense. We've never lost so many ships at once. In fact, we usually don't lose any at all. How is it you could see us?"

No one answered. One of the pirates stepped forward. "We found several bows. This one was on the one with the odd hair." He showed the wind-mage the ornate bow Rabiah's brother had given her as a wedding gift.

"One of you is responsible. It is a good gift to have. Tell me or shall I see how well the sharks like human flesh?"

"Stop!" Lydia said. "Leave my people alone."

"So it's you? You can see in the dark?"

"No, but this is my ship. These are my people. What do you want with us?"

"It's my ship now. These are now my people, as are you. He pulled Lydia to him. Lydia tried to pull away but the pirate kept a tight hold of her wrist. Tristan noted how regal Lydia was compared to Rabiah with her full length, flowing tunic and wavy, golden hair spilling down her back. He was glad of the difference. Perhaps it would keep Rabiah safe.

"What's this? That's a fancy bracelet. Take it off," the wind-mage commanded Lydia.

"It doesn't come off. It was a gift from the Queen of Arles. It is held on by magic. It is for protection."

"It doesn't seem to be working."

"Not *my* protection."

The pirate dropped her hand and pushed her back so that she stumbled.

"I am tired. Lock them up. We'll deal with them in the morning."

The pirates searched everyone and removed their weapons. They even took Rabiah's belt. Rabiah did nothing to prevent it. There were too many pirates and too many prisoners who could get hurt and she still felt very sick. They were all escorted below deck to the hold, told to sit on the floor in front of the crates and boxes, and

165

locked in. Two of the pirates remained with them. They took up posts near the door where a single lantern hung. One of the pirates touched the unlit wick. It started to burn.

"My gift is to burn with my touch. If you try anything I will make you go up in flames just like this wick," the pirate warned.

Rabiah and Tristan had sacks of something behind them. She knew they should work on an escape plan, but Rabiah was so tired and felt so bad, she just wanted to lay back and sleep. Her sensitive nose and more sensitive stomach wouldn't let her.

'Take off your tunic,' she sent.

'Do I smell that bad?'

'To a person with a sensitive stomach, yes.'

He smiled at her fondly and complied. She snuggled against him. He kissed the top of her head.

"What are you doing?" Lydia whispered harshly. "We've been captured by pirates who will probably kill us or sell us as slaves and you're kissing again?"

"No, just cleaning up a bit so she can stand to be near me," Tristan explained. He tossed the offensive tunic far to the side then lay back with his arm around Rabiah.

"Do you not have any decency?" Lydia hissed.

"Lydia, let me see your arm, the one with the bracelet I gave you," Rabiah said tiredly.

Lydia stuck it impatiently in front of Rabiah's face. "There. It is still on. I can't even defend myself."

Rabiah took her arm gently. "I know. I realized that when the pirates were talking to you. It is your gift. We have no right to take it away. The Spirit gives what he gives for a reason." Rabiah put her hand over the bracelet. It grew bigger at her touch and she slid if off of Lydia's wrist.

"I thought only a great wizard could remove that," Lydia said, rubbing her wrist.

"That's what Tristan's uncle said, but he doesn't always share all the details. It makes sense that the one who put it on should be able to take it off."

Tristan removed the bracelet from Lydia's other wrist. Rabiah stuffed them both under her tunic in the wrap she wore around her chest.

"Lydia, you have a powerful gift. I don't feel right asking you to use it to get us out of this after we tried to stop you from using it at all. Just use it to defend yourself."

Lydia looked down at her unbound wrists, "This was not my gift."

"What do you mean?" Rabiah asked.

"My gift, the one I was born with, is to make flowers bloom."

"That's a lovely gift," Rabiah said.

"No. It's useless unless I want to marry a farmer. My father wanted me to have a gift fit for a queen. He took me to the temple and paid a lot of money so they could give me a better gift."

"When did he do this?" Tristan asked.

"After you came back from the Clanlands with your wife."

"How much did he spend?"

"I don't know, but it must have been a lot. The priests only rarely augment abilities. Few people can afford it."

"If your natural ability is to make flowers bloom, I wonder what would happen if you had some seeds," Rabiah said, nearly asleep.

"There might be more of that seedy fruit down here somewhere," Tristan said, pulling Rabiah closer to him as her head was putting his arm to sleep.

"I wonder how Owen and the rest are faring." Rabiah mumbled. Tiredly she followed his link. "He's still alive."

I'll tell him where we are. Go to sleep my little warrior Queen.'

It was sweet, Lydia thought, how much Tristan obviously cared for his Queen. A little disturbing for someone not used to witnessing that much physical affection, but sweet. She flexed her hands. She could feel the power swirling around inside her again. Should she target the guards first? Tristan and the Queen seemed unconcerned with things as they stood as they had both fallen asleep. They weren't in any danger at the moment. Queen Rabiah's comment about the seeds intrigued her. Could she now make plants do more than bloom? Could she command them to grow? The corners of the hold

167

were dark but she could smell some overly ripe fruit somewhere. She stood and started to follow the smell.

"Hey there, what are you doing?" One of the guards asked, starting her way.

"I'm looking for something to eat. I smell something fruity."

"Just sit down."

"But…"

He came closer and grabbed her elbow. She let her power flow into him.

"Please?"

The pirate let out a breath, "Well, I suppose it can't hurt." He returned to door, the grabbed the lantern, and started to help her look. They found the basket of fresh fruit. Some of the fruit was beyond ripe, but there were several good pieces left. Lydia took a few.

"Why don't you take the whole thing?" The guard asked.

Lydia hesitated, it was a big basket, then she realized the other prisoners, in particular the Queen, who had the largest appetite of any woman she knew, might be hungry later. "Thank you. I will."

The pirate carried the basket for her and placed it beside her as she sat near her King and Queen. He lifted the lantern to view Rabiah asleep on Tristan's naked chest with Tristan's arm around her.

"Well, ain't that sweet."

"It gets a bit tiring after a while," Lydia said.

"Want me to separate them?"

"No. Let them rest. Who knows if they'll ever get the chance to be together again after tonight."

The pirate gave her a little bow and returned to his post. The other pirate frowned at him questioningly. The first pirate shrugged. Lydia took a bite of the fruit. Juice dribbled down her chin. It was delicious, but it was also very seedy. She spit a few seeds into her hand and concentrated. Roots and stems popped out so quickly it scared her. She dropped her hand into her lap and looked toward the guards. The one she had entranced nodded to her. He hadn't notice the seeds sprout.

Seeds needed dirt to grow, and water. Would they need dirt if she grew them with magic? She focused again on the sprouts in her hand. They got bigger but the roots were obviously seeking something. The sprouts slowed and stopped. She needed dirt. She got up again, leaving the sprouts on the floor behind Tristan's foot.

The same pirate approached her again. "What are you searching for now?"

"Dirt so I can plant the seeds from the fruit."

"Dirt? They won't grow here in the dark."

Lydia shrugged, "I like to plant things. Don't they sometimes keep bags of dirt as ballast?"

The pirate turned to one of the captive sailors, "You there, do you have any dirt down here?"

The sailor nodded to a pile of bags.

"Thank you," Lydia said to the pirate. "Do you mind if I put the bag near the door so the seeds get light from the lantern?"

"That won't be enough."

"I know," Lydia said, "but I'm a prisoner. It will have to do."

The guard shrugged and carried the bag of dirt near the door. The other pirate watched suspiciously. "Here, now. Why are you doing that? Tell her to sit down."

"She just wants to plant some seeds."

"You can't grow plants in the dark!"

"I know, I just like to plant things," Lydia explained calmly.

She opened the top of the bag and dropped in a couple of seeds. "Now I just need a little water."

The helpful pirate handed her his canteen. Lydia thanked him and poured a little on the seeds.

"There, now maybe they'll grow." She sat on the floor in front of the bag as if she were going to wait. The guards looked at one another.

"It might take a while," the first pirate said. "Several weeks, in fact."

"Mmm," Lydia said, concentrating. She put her hands on either side of the bag. She could feel the power encircling the seeds and urging them to wake. Suddenly, the sprouts exploded out of the dirt.

169

They started to climb. Lydia encouraged them to head for the hatch and bind up the pirates on the way. One of the pirates tried to draw his sword but the plant was too fast. The one who could burn with his touch grabbed a branch. It withered and started smoking. Two other branches wound around his arms and pinned his hands far apart so he couldn't touch anything. Lydia encouraged the vine to cluster beneath the hatch, but not to bust through yet. "Wait for the sun," she whispered to the plant. It was late. She was tired. She left her bag of dirt and went to lay next to her king and queen.

A few hours later she was awaken by the sailors. "Your plants, mistress, they're growing."

Lydia sat up and stretched. Her shoulder hurt from lying on the floor. The hatch was open and her plants were crawling through it.

"Did the plants push it open?"

"No. Someone opened it from outside."

Lydia climbed the steps and peered out. The vines were already all over the ship. Pirates were hanging everywhere like so many ugly fruits. She saw one man jump over the side before the vine could reach him. There was no one left standing on deck. She called down the steps, "The deck is clear. The plant has captured everyone."

The sailors spilled out of the hatch and took control. The plant seemed to know not to attack them. Some of the pirates tried to wiggle free, but the plant tightened its hold.

Rabiah woke as the sailors were charging the deck. She shook Tristan awake. Lydia came back down and waited for them at the foot of the stairs. They climbed out of the hold and looked around in awe.

"Did you do this?" Rabiah asked in amazement.

"Yes," Lydia said, pride in her voice.

"It's wonderful."

They could see their other two ships bobbing nearby. The big pirate ship and several smaller boats were clustered a short distance away.

"Do you think you can grow more vines, Lydia?" Tristan asked.

"Yes, why?"

"If we can figure out a way to get the plants on the other ships, it will be easy to take them back. The challenge will be keeping them," Tristan said.

"How close do you have to be Lydia?" Rabiah asked.

"I don't know. I was sleeping. I just told the plants to wait until morning and they grew themselves."

They heard yelling and a bell on the other ship.

"I think they've noticed the plant," Rabiah said. "Lydia, go start another one and tell it to grow when it feels a big bump. I know how we can get it to the closest ship at least."

"The old arrow with a rope trick?" Tristan asked.

"Yes, how did you know?"

"I saw you eyeing that rope." Tristan walked up to the captain and explained their idea. By the time a sailor had carried the new plant out of the hold, a second sailor was ready with an arrow and a coil of rope. One sailor climbed up into the crow's nest with the arrow while another quickly fashioned a harness for the bag of dirt with the little plant and climbed after him. The first sailor shot the arrow into a beam where it would be hard to reach, then he tied the plant onto the attached rope and let go. The plant slid quickly down the rope and hit the beam with a thump. Immediately, branches began to pour over the top of the bag, spreading throughout the boat. The pirates tried hacking at the branches with their swords but quickly gave up and ran. Some dived into the water and swam towards the cluster of pirate ships.

Lydia came back up the steps with another sailor carrying a bag of dirt and a new plant.

"Do you have enough rope to reach the other ship?" she asked.

"It's too far," Rabiah answered.

"We can get it there," the captain said. "Now that we can see the pirate ships, my men have a few talents of their own." He nodded to a sailor who approached Lydia to take her new vine.

"What are you going to do?" Lydia asked as the sailor took the plant.

"He's going to swim it over."

"The plant won't like the salty water."

"We will wrap it in oilskin," the captain said.

"Wait. Let me tell it what to expect. I'll tell it to grow when it is exposed to the light." Lydia put her hands on either side of the plant and closed her eyes. With her second sight, Rabiah could see the pink flowing from Lydia's hands into and around the plant. The plant and the soil were glowing with pink when she was through.

The sailors wrapped the plant with oilcloth and tied it securely with a rope. They left loops so it would be easy to carry. The sailor the captain had pointed out, took off his tunic, shouldered the plant, and climbed quickly down the side of the boat where none of the other boats could see. When he reached the water, he slid under and disappeared. Rabiah waited for him to resurface farther away but he never reappeared.

"Where did he go?" she asked the Captain.

"He can breathe underwater," the Captain explained. "It comes in handy when you're a sailor."

The Captain sent another sailor over the side. This one swam to the nearest boat and climbed aboard. The vine raced toward him.

"Miss Lydia, can you call off your plant?"

She tried, but she could not keep the vine from snagging the other sailor.

"I think I have to be closer."

"We'll get you over there," the captain said. He had Lydia and two other sailors lowered in one of the small boats stored on deck. They rowed to the next ship. One of them used one of the ropes the pirates had left to climb up the side of the ship. Moving quickly to stay ahead of the vine, he unfurled a ladder down the side. The vine grabbed him. The sailor still in the boat urged Lydia to climb. She refused to take hold of the ladder.

"She's probably afraid to climb," Tristan commented.

Lydia put her palm on the side of the ship. On the deck above her, the vine released the two sailors. One of them ran to the hold and threw open the door. Two pirates came out, swords drawn. The sailor backed away. The two pirates saw their fellow pirates hanging from the vine and began hacking at the plant to try and release them. The vine retaliated and wrapped around their ankles. They fell as the vines retracted, dragging them across the deck and up in the air so that they were soon hanging upside-down like the rest of the pirates.

"That was a bit scary," Tristan remarked.

There was a sudden burst of green on the third ship. They could see people running everywhere. Within a few minutes all was silent except for a lone figure climbing over the edge of the ship and racing for the hatch.

"Why didn't the vine stop him?" Tristan wondered.

"Maybe Lydia remembered to tell it not to."

"I'm glad she's on our side," Tristan said.

They could see people coming out of the hold on the third ship. The plant didn't grab them.

"Now all we need is the wind," the captain said.

"It's coming Sir. Look, there's the storm."

Several miles away they could see tall, white, puffy clouds building, but there was still no wind. The pirates could easily attack again and there was nothing they could do about it.

There was motion on the big pirate ship. Rabiah saw a man with a billowing cape look down over them. With her soul sight she could see the pink flowing around him. She could almost see the scowl on his face. "The wind-mage is awake and he doesn't look happy," she said.

"Which one is he?" Tristan asked. "Let me guess, the one with the cape."

"Yes."

The wind picked up and the water started getting choppy.

"He's going to do the same thing he did last night," Tristan said.

"Lydia's still in the little boat. They'll get tipped over. She can't swim," Rabiah said worriedly.

"The sailors will take care of her," the captain said.

They heard a splash. Rabiah ran to the side of the ship and looked over the edge. Lydia and two sailors were still in the little boat. Then, before her eyes, they disappeared. Rabiah and Tristan looked at each other and said in unison, "Senna."

"Lydia might need more dirt," Rabiah said, "And seeds."

One of the sailors ran down the steps and returned with a bag of dirt and some fruit. They quickly wrapped it in oilcloth and tied it to a buoy.

"I bet Owen is with Senna. I'll let him know it's coming," Tristan said. He and a sailor picked up the bag of dirt. Tristan waited. He saw a hand wave in midair. They threw the bag near the hand, but not too close. After a minute, the bag of dirt disappeared.

The tossing was getting worse. Tristan and Rabiah moved away from the edge and toward the middle of the boat. They found a place out of the way and held on. The rocking seemed to last for an eternity. Rabiah prayed that it would end.

Chapter 14

The expanse of water between their three ships and the fleet of pirate ships was a little choppy but the dinghy escaped the worst of the waves tossing the big ships. Lydia sat regally with her back straight and her face determined. She held the bag of dirt between her knees. Owen could see the power coursing from her and through the soil. Senna sat beside Lydia, eyes closed, gripping the sides of the boat. Owen knew she was not scared, just concentrating to keep them hidden. He could see the invisible shield Senna had woven around them. It made him want to kiss her again. How many times had she pulled him inside that same shield over the last couple of weeks to do just that he mused. She had spent so much time hiding as a child that she could form and hold the invisibility shield over herself or a second person standing close almost effortlessly. To hold it over a boat with five people was more of a strain, but she was doing it. He wondered if she could hide an entire ship.

"Sir Owen….SIR OWEN! Stop staring at Lady Senna and pay attention!" Owen switched his view to Lydia but not before he saw a little smile creep onto Senna's lips.

"Yes Lydia."

"How are we going to get the seedling onto the ship? I need to know when to tell it to grow."

"See all the lines below the bowsprit in the front of the ship? I'm going to try and get a rope over one of the lines and raise the plant up. I could give it a good tug once it's there."

Lydia remembered the bowsprit was the long, pointy piece at the front of the ship. There were three smaller pirate ships floating within easy sight of the bow, but none were right under the bowsprit. The sailors rowed underneath. Owen prepared to toss the grappling hook that he had brought with him.

"Sir," One of the sailors said, "If I may. We practice all the time." He nodded towards the hook.

"Please then," Owen said, handing him the hook. They exchanged places, managing not to tip the small boat over.

"Senna, can you extend the shield up a couple of feet so he has room to swing?" Owen asked.

"I'll try."

The sailor stood in the bow of the small boat and swung the hook in an increasingly larger vertical circle. He let go on the fourth swing. "Watch your heads in case I missed," he warned.

They all ducked warily. He did not miss. The hook went over the lowest cable. The sailor started to pull it tight but Owen stopped him. "Let it down. We can hook the plant on and pull it up."

"The rope will be too short."

"How short?"

The sailor let the rope slide through his hands until it was near the end. "About fifteen feet Sir."

Owen took off his tunic. "Everyone give me a piece of clothing. We'll make it long enough. Senna, you just keep us invisible."

The sailors removed their tunics. Lydia removed her over-tunic, careful not to rock the boat too much. Owen tied them all together and then to the other end of the rope. He had a foot to spare. The sailor held the rope while Owen attached the plant securely to the hook. Together, they pulled up the bag as fast as they could. It wasn't fast enough. Someone noticed the bag rising in midair. Arrows started flying from the smaller pirate ships. Owen stepped into the water with the rope in his hands. He dropped with a splash.

"Go. Get the girls away from here. I'll pull it the rest of the way up and tie it off somewhere. I'll swim to you when I'm done."

Two arrows planted themselves on the boat as the sailors paddled away. Owen dived, taking the rope with him. He swam towards the bow of the big ship. The pirates were now targeting him but their arrows could not penetrate deeply into the water. He swam

176

below as long as he could. There was a tug on the rope. Flipping onto his back and looking up through the water above him, he thought the plant must have reached the cable. He gave a firm tug. Green sprouted from the bag and began crawling up the cable. Perhaps it was enough to hold the plant in place. He experimentally let the rope slip a little. It remained slack. He had to breathe. Arrows were peppering the water above him. He let go of the rope, swam a few feet into the shadow of the big boat, then carefully surfaced.

He wasn't sure which way the sailors had rowed. He spun all around before diving again. He saw the two ships from Arles and swam in that direction. Somewhere there was a yell and a splash. The dark shadow of a boat passed above him. He swam for it, hoping to surface where they couldn't see him. He felt a sharp pain along his right side and turned in surprise. A man was beside him, holding a knife with blood flowing from the tip – his own, Owen realized. Someone grabbed his elbow from the other side. Owen jerked his arm away from the pirate holding it, elbowed him in the nose, and punched the man with the knife in the face. He needed air. The surface was just above him. Swimming hard, he escaped the grasp of the pirates and made it to the surface where he quickly scanned the water as he took a deep breath. He still couldn't see the dinghy. Someone grabbed his leg. He kicked and connected with something. Free, he started swimming as quickly as he could toward the Arles ships. His attackers were faster. They grabbed his legs and pulled him under. Both pirates had knives out now. There was more blood in the water. Not his this time. It was from a pirate's nose. Owen did his best to defend himself. Fighting in water was not like fighting on land. Two other pirates dove in. He was out of air. He blacked out.

'*Owen's in trouble,*' Tristan sent to Rabiah. They were laying side-by-side on the deck still waiting for the waves to subside. They'd both been sick but it didn't matter because they'd had nothing to eat.

'*How can you tell?*'

'*I can feel his pain.*'

177

'How bad is it?'

'Worse for him, I'm sure. It feels like he's been stabbed in the side.'

Rabiah squeezed Tristan's arm, 'There's nothing we can do right now except pray.'

'Let's pray then.'

Senna could keep everyone invisible with her eyes open, it was just a little harder to concentrate. She watched in fear and admiration as Owen swam away amidst all the arrows. She saw him leave the rope and resurface to look around. There was a dip in the water as he looked their way and she knew he hadn't seen them. She saw two pirates dive into the water from the smaller boat near him and almost lost her control of the invisible shield. He had been too long under the water. Two more pirates dove in. They came up dragging something. Owen. His eyes were closed and he hung limp. The pirates pulled him aboard. There was red running down his side.

"He's hurt." Lydia exclaimed.

"Good thing he's getting out of the water then. There are a lot of sharks around here," one of the sailors commented.

"Do you think he's still alive?" Senna asked, a tremor in her voice.

"Probably. His injury did not look that severe," the other sailor said.

"Take me to him," Senna ordered, "I will hide him."

"But we would be left exposed," Lydia said. "There are three of us and one of him and they are looking too closely at him right now for him to just disappear. It would be wiser to wait."

"We will row next to their boat and wait. If you can keep us hidden for a while longer, we can attempt a rescue when the opportunity presents itself," one of the sailors said.

"I can keep you hidden all day if I have to," Senna said.

"If I had more dirt, I could start another plant," Lydia said, "I still have several seeds."

"We have no way to get any dirt right now," a sailor said. "The water is too choppy to return to our boats."

"That shouldn't be a problem soon. I told my seedlings to secure the wind-mage well and put leaves over his eyes. He won't be able to control the wind if he can't see what he's doing."

The sailors placed the dinghy just behind the pirate's boat, right up next to the hull. They were too low in the water to see the deck of the mother ship which floated several hunded feet behind them, but they could see the vines racing along the edge and up to the tops of the masts. Suddenly, a swirl of leaves arose along the side of the ship, twirling around as if there were a small tornado on deck.

"The wind-mage is fighting, but I told my seedlings not to give up," Lydia said smugly.

The leaves kept swirling. They noticed the violent waves rocking their own ships began to calm.

"He's too busy fighting my plant," Lydia smiled.

"We must take advantage of this quickly before the mage has a chance to escape," the sailor said. "The wind is starting to pick up from the storm. We can sail. We must get back to our ships."

"What about Owen?" Senna asked. "We can't leave him."

"He is one man," Lydia said softly. "He would not want us to be captured just because of him."

"He is my man," Senna said. "I will not go without him. I will climb onto the pirates' boat. If you won't help me, you can row back to the ships without me."

"We could try and take the pirate's boat, then we could catch up to ours later," one of the sailors said.

"How are we going to do that?" Lydia hissed.

The sailor grinned, "You aren't the only two with gifts."

The sailors rowed up right next to the pirate's boat where they couldn't be seen by any other boats. The sailor who had spoken offered his oar to Lydia. She took it reluctantly. He stood and touched the sides of the boat with his fingertips and palms. Then, he raised one bare foot, then the other to the side of the ship so that he was crawling along the side like a spider. Senna kept him hidden as long as she could. He was almost to the top before she could no longer cover him.

"What is he going to do?" Lydia whispered to the other sailor.

"He'll probably just look and see how many pirates are on board and find out where they have Sir Owen."

They watched as the sailor scuttled along the side of the ship. Occasionally he peered over the side. He made it all the way to the front, then turned and hurriedly crawled back down toward them. Senna engulfed him with the shield when he was close enough. The sailor unstuck himself from the side of the ship and stepped into the dingy.

"I counted twelve."

"What about Owen?" Senna asked.

"They are questioning him." The sailor raised his eyebrows at the second sailor as he said it.

Senna didn't notice, "So he's alive?"

"For now, but we need to move fast. Lady Senna, if you can hold on to my back, I can take us both onto the boat. I will take care of the pirates if you can keep me hidden."

"Gladly."

"What about us?" Lydia asked, indicating herself and the other sailor.

"Your plant has provided a great distraction. Everyone's attention is on the big ship. You can wait here. I think it will be safe enough."

"I hope you're right," Lydia said unhappily.

The sailor affixed himself to the boat again. Senna wrapped her arms around the sailor's shoulders and her legs around his waist. He crawled carefully upward. They disappeared as they reached the range Senna could still keep hidden. Lydia could no longer see Senna. She suddenly felt very exposed.

The sailor stopped at the edge. Senna let go and climbed over, staying close enough to keep him hidden. He nodded towards a pirate who was alone near the bow, watching the big ship. Senna put her hand on his shoulder and let him lead her.

"Look away. This might be messy," he whispered as he pulled a large knife from his belt.

"Don't kill him. Toss him overboard," she whispered back.

"There would be a splash and they'd find our dinghy."

She nodded. The sailor snuck up behind the man and put his hand over his mouth right before he cut the pirate's throat. Blood welled. Senna looked away. They left the body propped up, facing away so that it looked like he was just resting.

They picked off two more in the same way. That left nine. They were all clustered around Owen. One of them was asking questions while two others were holding Owen and punching him in the ribs. They seemed to enjoy hitting the cut on his side. Anger welled in Senna. Owen was the nicest, most considerate man she'd ever met. He treated her like a person, not just a female, and he was hers. There was a sword lying discarded on the deck. She picked it up. She knew how to use it after watching all her brothers learn and practicing in secret.

"You go that way. I'll go this," Senna whispered to the sailor.

"Are you sure?"

She nodded, her eyes angry and her face determined. He agreed. She attacked, still invisible. A man fell. The pirates turned in confusion. They saw one man, but he was far away from the one that fell. Another succumbed. It was as if the sailor was stabbing them remotely. Two pirates attacked the sailor. The sailor stabbed at them and backed away, drawing a third away from Owen. The two holding Owen fell, then the questioner. The one who was doing the punching looked around frantically, then found Owen's fist in the center of his face. Owen watched as the glow he knew to be Senna moved towards the two remaining pirates who had cornered the sailor against the rail. He was defending himself with his long knife against the much longer short sword of his opponent. One of the pirates fell, distracting the other. It was just the opening the sailor needed. He stabbed, then flipped the last pirate overboard.

Senna ran back to Owen. He was kneeling, and bending forward as he spat out blood from a split lip. She dropped to her knees beside him, covering him with her invisible shield and put her arm around his strong shoulders. "Are you all right?"

"I've been better."

"Is there anyone below deck?" the sailor asked the air where he knew them to be.

181

"I think so," Owen said, "I lost track of everyone."

"Understandable, Sir. If you or the lady will stand guard, I will pull our other two members aboard before I inspect below."

"Gladly." Owen coughed. Senna stood and picked up another sword. She handed it to Owen while brandishing her own. Owen stood painfully, put his free arm around her and squeezed. "You were magnificent. Dare I bother to ask how you learned to handle a sword?"

"You know me. I always went where my mother told me not to. In this case, to watch the sword-fighting lessons my brothers took." She paused and looked around, "It was easier than I thought it would be to kill someone."

Although she didn't say anything, Owen could see from her aura how upset she was. He hugged her again. "They aren't completely gone, their souls go somewhere. Queen Rabiah would pray for them."

"I didn't want to kill them," Senna whispered, "but I couldn't stand seeing them hurt you."

The door to the hold slowly opened. Owen pushed Senna behind him and held his sword in readiness. A boy of about six crept out. He walked up to the pirate who had been doing the questioning and nudged him with his foot. He looked around at all the bodies lying on the deck, then kicked the pirate at his feet.

Going back to the hold entrance, the boy pulled open the doors to the hold and called down in a language Owen didn't know. A very worn-looking woman emerged. Her clothes were torn and her hair messed. She looked around silently at the men, then fell to her knees, wrapped her arms around the boy, and began to sob.

Senna couldn't tell if she was sad or happy, but Owen could. "She's relieved. She must have been a prisoner. Show yourself," he whispered.

Senna obeyed. The boy noticed them first and cried out. Senna dropped her sword and put her hands in front of her in a gesture of peace. The woman spoke rapidly. Senna shook her head to show she didn't understand. Then, she pointed to one of the bodies and mimed swinging it overboard. The woman smiled and nodded.

Owen stopped them. "Not yet. We don't want to draw anyone's attention." He took a slow breath. It hurt. His bare chest was covered in red blotches where the pirates had punched him and his wound was still bleeding sluggishly. The woman got a good look at him and exclaimed something. She turned and gave rapid instructions to the boy. The boy turned and disappeared back into the hold. The pirate with the meaty fists who had so enthusiastically used Owen as a punching bag moaned.

"Find me some rope so I can tie him up Senna. I'd throw him overboard but I don't want him to come back and cause more problems."

Senna quickly found some rope. She thought Owen might be too sore to tie the man up himself, so she flipped the man over with her foot and did it herself. The woman helped as soon as she realized what Senna was doing. They tied his hands and feet together as if her were a hog. The woman spat on him when they were done.

Meanwhile, the sailor appeared with Lydia. Lydia had refused to climb on his back. Instead, she had insisted that he drop a ladder for her to climb. The second sailor appeared soon after. The boy came up from the hold carrying a bag and a bottle. The woman handed the bottle to Owen and mimed sipping it. He sniffed it, then took a drink.

"Strong stuff," he said to Senna with a grimace.

No one could understand what the woman said, but they understood her motions. She indicated that Owen should drink up, then had him lay down. She wiped his wound and bruises with a rag and some liquid from a bottle in the bag. When she was done, she pulled out a purple leaf, placed the leaf and her hands over his stab wound and closed her eyes. Owen's head was in Senna's lap. He opened his eyes as he felt hot and then cold around his wound.

"She's a healer," he said groggily and fell asleep as the woman used his energy to help him heal.

Chapter 15

The waves lessened. Tristan and Rabiah cautiously climbed to their feet. Rabiah's head hurt and she felt nauseous, but not so much she wanted to throw up again. "I hope that never happens again."

"Me too."

Wind from the oncoming storm had finally reached them. The sailors scrambled around them, preparing the ship to sail. Lydia's vine had crawled all over the ship but it seemed happy to move if the sailors asked politely.

"What about Owen?" Rabiah asked.

"It doesn't hurt as much and, I think," Tristan paused, "I think he's a little drunk." He grinned. "He must have found a healer."

"That's good then. He must have made it back to one of our ships."

"Maybe."

The ship began to move as the sails unfurled.

"I hope we aren't leaving them behind," Rabiah said.

"As do I."

"We should make sure they are aboard."

"There's not enough time. We must take advantage of the storm and get everyone else away while the pirates are distracted. Owen has Senna and Lydia and two experienced sailors with him. He will be all right," Tristan said, as much for his sake as Rabiah's.

The two sailors scrambled to get the boat ready to sail. Neither Lydia nor Senna know much about sailing a ship, but the woman and the boy were eager to help. Senna did as she was told. By the time they were underway, the Arles ships had already sailed a good distance away. Most of the smaller pirate ships stayed with the mother ship but a couple followed after them. The wind from the oncoming storm made them fly across the water but they were not as fast as the larger ships ahead of them. The storm was catching up. The waves got rougher. The other two pirate ships slowed and lowered their sails.

"Shouldn't we stop too?" Lydia asked the sailors.

"Yes, but it would be better if we could ride out the storm in our bigger ships. They will stop, if they haven't already. If we keep going we may catch up with them."

"And if we don't catch them?"

"Then we may go swimming."

The boat leaped over a strong wave and crashed down. Lydia only managed not to fall by grabbing onto a rope. Senna threw herself over Owen who was still sleeping on the deck. The woman and the boy had gone down into the hold. Two of the bodies rolled off the side of the boat.

Lydia straightened and glared at the soldiers. "I don't know how to swim."

"Give us a few more minutes. If we don't see them we'll stop and prepare for the storm."

It was only a minute later that one of the sailors spotted the three ships in the distance with their sails furled. They adjusted the course of the pirate ship. The waves were becoming too big for the speed of the boat.

"We have to slow down," Lydia yelled, hanging on desperately as a wave crashed over her. Owen wouldn't wake. Senna held on to him and a thick rope as the water washed over them. He almost floated away. She found a smaller rope, pulled his head and shoulders into her lap, and tied them both down. The hog-tied pirate caught the rope holding him under a hook on the deck. All the other pirates washed overboard.

The sailors adjusted the sails to decrease the speed of the boat, but they continued forward toward the three ships.

"Senna, we need to move Owen below deck," Lydia encouraged.

"I know, but he's too heavy and the sailors are busy. We are almost to the other ships."

"Almost. The sailors will get us if we make it. I will help you carry him down."

"Thank you."

Senna untied herself and Owen. She tried once more to wake him but he didn't respond. Each girl took a shoulder and dragged him toward the hatch, moving slowing to keep their balance as the boat tilted. The healer woman opened it as they approached. The boy was with her. She seemed upset. She wouldn't let them take Owen down, but instead took Lydia's hand and dragged her down the steps. Lydia came up a few seconds later.

"There's a leak. We're sinking," she told the sailors.

One of them ran down to inspect. He came back shortly. "We'll be all right if we keep up this speed. Look, we're within half a knot of the ships."

A cold rain caught up to them. Senna put her arms around Owen to keep him warm. The woman found a tarp that she wrapped around the boy, Senna, and Owen.

They could not keep up the speed. The water pouring into the boat slowed them down. They were within 200 yards of the first boat but they could go no further. No one had noticed them either.

"What happened to the dinghy?" Lydia asked.

"We let it go. We'd be swamped as soon as we attempted it anyway."

"What's your gift?" she asked the second sailor.

"I can call rats," he shrugged.

"Do you have any dirt?" she asked the woman. The woman shook her head to show she didn't understand.

"Dirt, dirt!" Lydia showed her a seed and mimed planting it, then she held the seed in her hand and made it sprout.

The woman smiled and searched in the bag she had brought with her. Instead of dirt, she pulled out some seeds.

"What are these?"

The woman nodded at her as if to say, go ahead, make them grow. Lydia held one in her hand. A thin vine snaked out.

"That's snareweed. It grows in shallow ocean water. Devilish to remove if it gets tangled on the rudder. It grows as a long, strong, thin vine," the rat-calling sailor said.

"Do you think it will grow long enough to reach the ship?"

"With your talent, maybe. Maybe you can grow several so they wind around each other. If you can reach the boat, we can use it to pull us closer."

"Does it need dirt?"

"It needs salt water."

Lydia put two more seeds in her hand and started them. The new vines wound around tightly around the first one. It was disturbingly easy to reach the water with her fist. The vines raced towards the ship while the roots wrapped around her arm. After a couple of minutes, Lydia felt a tug.

"Hold on to me."

The sailors grabbed her shoulders as the boat began to move. She tried transferring the roots to the ship but they didn't want to let go of her. She could feel them piercing her skin.

"I think they like blood too."

Lydia held her arm out purposefully as the vines pulled. The boat was barely above the water now. As soon as they could touch the ship, the sailor who could climb leapt onto the side of the boat and scurried up.

"Tell the weed to let go Miss Lydia. We are here," the other sailor said.

"It won't listen."

The healer woman said something to her but Lydia couldn't understand. She was beginning to feel faint.

The woman pointed to the sailor's knife and mimed cutting. The sailor understood and quickly hacked through the three main branches. Blood dripped from the stems. Lydia fell back onto the deck.

The woman took the knife and cut through the roots that had punctured Lydia's arm. She pulled out the tips and threw them in the water.

"I don't think I'll be growing that plant again," Lydia mumbled. The sailor held her as a wave washed over the side.

A ladder and several floating rings dropped from above.

"Go on up miss, you and the boy", the sailor said, pointing to the healer and the boy and then upward. The woman understood and pulled the boy out from under the tarp. Their sinking boat was being pushed and pulled into the larger one by the waves. The sailor held the ladder and their boat, trying to keep them close. The woman made the boy climb ahead of her.

Senna was holding Owen's head above the waves. "How are we going to get him aboard? He's still sleeping."

"They'll send down a basket. See, here it comes. Miss Lydia, would you like to go first?"

"No. Put Sir Owen in the basket. I can climb."

"Are you sure? That plant might have taken a lot of blood."

"I can climb."

"Go ahead then. Lady Senna and I will get Sir Owen into the basket. We'll come right behind you."

The other sailor had come back down. He held the ladder for Lydia to start climbing. About ten rungs up she wished she had listened. The rocking of the boat made it difficult to hang on to the ladder and she felt very weak. Her hand slipped. Someone pushed her rear from behind.

"Keep moving Lydia." Senna said. Owen passed, still sleeping in the basket. Lydia took a deep breath and pressed on. She could see the top of the ship impossibly far ahead of her.

"Go on Lydia." Senna said.

"I can't. I don't have the strength."

"I'll wait with you then, but we'll have to wait a while for the basket. We have to rescue the pirate too."

"We should just let him drown."

"Perhaps, but that doesn't seem right. Try another rung. They don't go on forever."

Lydia reach up and pulled herself up another rung. The empty basket went past and the pirate came up, still hog-tied and cursing.

"Miss Lydia, is everything all right?" the sailor called from below.

"She's too weak," Senna yelled down.

The sailor yelled to the men above them. The ladder began to move. "Hold on," the sailor warned. Lydia wrapped her arms around the rope legs of the ladder. Her body twisted in the wind and the heaviness of her wet clothes dragged at her. She had never been so scared.

The top was near. Hands reached out and grabbed Lydia, then Senna. Senna found herself in front of her brother.

"Brother?" He was grinning at her.

"This is probably the first time you've ever been visible long enough for me to get a good look at you."

"You're not going to scold me for being without my veil?"

He shrugged. "We are not at home and your husband is in charge of you now."

"Where is he?"

"The healers took him below deck. What happened?"

"He delivered the plant to the pirate's mother ship and then the pirates captured him."

"And you captured one of them."

"Owen did. I killed most of the rest."

She hadn't meant for a sob to escape. She ran from her brother and turned invisible as she went below deck. Her brother frowned after her. He stopped one of the sailors who had been with his sister. "Tell me what happened. Senna said she killed someone. Where was her husband?"

Senna let her invisibility shield fall as she went down the stairs. Why she'd felt the need to hide from her brother she didn't know. It was crowded below decks due to the storm. She asked loudly to the wall where she could find her husband and was quickly pointed in the right direction. He was lying in a cot under a thin blanket, still sleeping. She found a stool and sat beside him.

"Sir Owen, I see you have a visitor. I assume she is your wife?" A male voice asked behind her.

Senna nodded. There was a healer behind her dressed in white as was the custom in her country. He was not permitted to speak to her directly without her husband's permission, so he spoke to Owen.

"You will be fine Sir Owen. You will probably wake up sometime tomorrow. Whoever healed you did a nice job."

Senna nodded again and turned back to Owen.

"Sir Owen, if your wife hasn't had anything to eat recently, there is food in the kitchens. I'm sure you would not want her to go hungry on your account. I am going there now if she would like to follow me."

She *was* hungry. Senna squeezed Owen's hand, then got up to follow the healer to a small table set up near the ship's kitchen. Lydia was there getting her arm bandaged by the woman healer. She looked much paler than she normally did. The boy was there too, hungrily stuffing food into his little mouth.

"There are plates on the shelf and food in the bins. We had to extinguish the fire in the stove due to the storm so there is no hot food," the healer announced to the wall.

Senna nodded. The male healer left. She got a plate of food for Lydia and offered another one to the woman. The woman refused. Senna sat down to eat it herself. She watched as the woman finished with Lydia's arm. It was obvious that she was an experienced healer. Senna wished she could understand her words. Perhaps they could start with something simple.

She tapped the woman on the arm and patted her chest. "Senna." Then, she pointed to Lydia, "Lydia."

The healer patted her own chest "Kaawa" and pointed to the boy "Ice". Senna repeated the names. She couldn't decide what to try next.

"I wish we could understand her," she finally said to Lydia.

"We'll ask the queen when the storm is over. She knows many languages."

Yusri appeared in the doorway.

"Pardon me sister, but may I have a word with you?" he asked, bowing politely.

"I'll walk with you brother," Senna said and set her plate of half-eaten food on the shelf so it wouldn't slide on the floor. They walked out of earshot before her brother began.

"Senna, the sailors told me what happened. You should never have been in a situation where you had to kill someone. Your husband was irresponsible. He should not have taken you with him."

"How else were we to sneak a plant onto the pirate ship? Do you know of anyone else who can turn invisible?"

"No, but we have many sailors with many gifts. I'm sure we could have come up with something."

"But you didn't and Owen did. He didn't force me to go. He asked. Just like he didn't force me to kill anyone. I insisted on rescuing him. In fact, I refused to leave without him. Owen is a good man."

"But he should not have asked. He should not have used you or your talent in that way."

"What is my talent for, if it is not to be used?"

"You are a woman. You are to be cherished and loved and kept safe, not thrown to the lions and wolves of the world."

"He *was* keeping me safe. We were in a ship overrun by pirates. He stayed with me all night and insisted on keeping watch. When the plant took over the ship he was afraid it would capture us too. We ran to the side to jump. That's when we saw Lydia and realized who was controlling the plant. Owen asked if I wanted to help save us all from the pirates and I said yes, because I did. He was injured trying to keep Lydia and I safe."

"I still think he was irresponsible."

"What would you have done in his place?"

"Left you in the hold with the other prisoners."

"We were never in the hold. I hid him when the pirates boarded. He didn't ask me to, I just did."

"I shall speak to Father of this."

"Do what you must brother." She bowed to him and returned to her food. She couldn't eat it. What if her father took her away from Owen? He had that right if he thought her husband unsuitable. A tear slid down her cheek. Why had she told her brother anything?

191

Why did Owen have to get captured? Why did the pirates have to attack? She put her head down and let the tears fall. A warm hand touched her arm. She looked up into the kind brown eyes of the healer woman they had rescued. The healer said something to the boy. The little boy nodded and said, "She says thank you for rescuing us." He noticed the tears on her face. "Why are you crying?"

"I don't know." She swiped at the tears on her face. "Tell me about the pirates on your ship."

"They were bad men. They used to hit and kick me. They would make Kaawa scream sometimes."

"Is she your mother?"

"No. My mother is dead."

"How long were you on that boat?"

"Not long, but we were on another before that. I was on that one as long as I can remember."

"Was Kaawa there?"

"Yes. Part of the time. There was another woman before. She died."

"You've had a rough life."

The boy shrugged.

"How do I say thank you?" Senna asked.

Senna repeated what the boy said and finished "for healing Owen." She pointed to her torso in the same spot where Owen had been injured.

Kaawa smiled and nodded.

Senna felt better. Perhaps she had simply been an instrument in the god's hands. Still, she asked for forgiveness. Whether it would be granted to her, a woman, she doubted.

Senna had planned to return to Owen's side after she ate but her brother insisted she stay with the other women in a room just for them. There was a cot for each of them and for the boy and some dry tunics her brother must have purchased at the port. A sailor stood guard outside the door to 'keep them safe,' her brother had said. From whom it was unclear.

The storm ended sometime in the middle of the night. Lydia had a high fever by morning and was rolling about as if she couldn't get comfortable. Kaawa awoke Senna and poured forth an incomprehensible string of words. The boy was beside her.

"She says get the other healer. Lydia needs a potion."

Senna opened the door. The sailor standing guard came to attention but because she was unveiled he would not look directly at her. Per the custom of her people, she could not speak to him. She tried to pass but he put out his arm to stop her without touching her and shook his head. He spoke to the wall. "All the women must stay here. The ship is full of men. I will inform Prince Yusri that the women are moving about."

No need. I will get the healer myself, Senna thought and disappeared. The sailor tried to step in her way but she avoided him easily. She ran first to Owen. The healer was not there. Owen was still sleeping. She searched everywhere below deck. She finally went above deck, sliding out as someone else opened the door. She found the healer speaking to her brother.

"Sir Owen should wake any time now," the healer said.

"Keep him drugged. I do not want him to speak with my sister until I can speak with my father. He is a bad influence on her."

"Yes, sir."

The healer turned to go back below deck. Senna ran ahead of him, squeezed through the door behind someone, and slipped down the stairs. She dropped her invisibility shield and walked out of the shadows to greet him so that it looked like she had been downstairs the whole time. She beckoned to him to follow. He fell into step behind her. She led him close to the cabin where Lydia lay and pointed, well out of reach of the guard.

"Why did you let her pass? Women should not be wandering about the ship," the healer said to the guard.

The guard opened his mouth to protest, then waved his hand toward Senna as she disappeared again. The healer gave a nod of understanding, then stepped toward the door. The soldier blocked him.

"Lady Senna directed me here. There must be someone who needs help," the healer said.

The soldier nodded and stepped aside to allow the healer to knock on the door. Kaawa answered and waved the other healer in. The guard kept the door open after the healer passed. Senna peered in. The healer felt Lydia's forehead, then dug into the bag he had been wearing. Kaawa said something and held up Lydia's unbandaged arm. The puncture wounds were swollen and dark. The healer shook his head and went back to his bag.

Senna sighed inwardly and pushed past the sailor-guard. She walked to stand on the other side of the healer and began speaking without showing herself.

"Yesterday when Lydia saved us with the snare weed, the weed punctured her skin and used her blood. Could she have an infection?"

The healer looked at Kaawa as if she were speaking. He didn't seem to notice her mouth wasn't moving.

"It's possible."

"The healer's name is Kaawa. The boy can speak to her. She gave Lydia the seeds. Ask her."

The healer turned to the boy, "Ask Kaawa what she believes is wrong with this woman."

"She already told you. The snare weed poisoned her."

"Ask her what antidote she would use."

The boy said something to Kaawa. Kaawa pointed to the healer's bag. He seemed hesitant to let Kaawa look through it. Senna took it from him and gave it to her. Kaawa looked through the bag carefully so as not to displace anything. She pulled out three small vials and showed them to the male healer, then she pulled out a small mortar and pestle from her own bag and proceeded to mix a little from each vial. She put a small amount of the mix in a cup. The rest she mixed with some oil from her own bag. Kaawa pointed to the cup and spoke to the healer.

"She says put some fever powder in that and make a warm drink," the boy said.

The healer nodded and took his bag back to search for the powder. Senna slipped out the door. The sailor didn't notice.

Senna hurried back to Owen's side, skirting around the few sailors she passed in the hallway.

"Wake up. Wake up, my husband," she said softly, shaking his shoulder.

He turned his head but didn't open his eyes.

"Owen! Wake up!"

He took a sudden breath and opened his eyes. He blinked a couple of times. "Senna?"

She wrapped him in her invisibility so he could see her and kissed his forehead.

"How do you feel?"

He took a deep breath. "A little sore but much better." He pushed down the blanket. He was still tunic-less. All that was left of the stab wound was a dark line but he had bruises all along his rib cage. Senna felt tears threatening again. Owen sat up and swung his feet over the side of the bunk. Senna sat on the bunk next to him and leaned on his shoulder. He put his arm around her.

"What's wrong?"

"I told my brother about the pirates and he doesn't want me to talk to you anymore. He thinks you are a bad influence."

"He told you this?"

"No, I overheard it."

"Senna."

"I didn't mean to. I was looking for the healer and they were talking."

"And you were invisible."

"Yes."

"Why?"

"It's my brother's ship. All the women are confined to a cabin. I don't like being confined."

"I don't think anyone does."

"We need to get off this ship. My brother told the healer to keep you drugged until he could talk to Father." She stood and pulled him up.

"Sounds like I should talk with your brother."

"It wouldn't do any good."

195

"I can at least try. Come, we'll go together, visibly."

"But you don't have a tunic."

"It can't be helped. My clothes are on the other ship." He paused, remembering. "Did everyone make it all right? How did we get to your brother's ship? Wait, before you let us be seen." He pulled her closer and kissed her. "Thanks for coming to my rescue."

She slowly rang a finger down his chest to the region of his belly button and back up. Owen closed his eyes and shivered.

"Any time." She kissed him again. Someone was coming. Owen gently pulled away, then whispered into her ear, "Later." It was a promise.

"Yes, my husband," she whispered meekly with a big grin.

The healer entered the small room, saw the empty cot, and sighed. Owen and Senna followed him as he turned away. Owen waved his hand indicating Senna should let them be visible. She dropped the shield and Owen spoke, "If you are going to talk to Lady Senna's brother, don't bother. I was just going to speak with him myself."

The healer stopped and turned.

"I was. How did you know?"

"A little bird told me".

"He thinks you are a bad influence."

"Does he?"

"She's not wearing a veil."

"Why does she need to?"

"It's, well, she's a woman."

"And she's a lot prettier than you or I. We are the ones who should be wearing veils."

Senna giggled. The healer snorted in spite of himself.

"May I speak to him, husband?"

"You may."

"I've never been good at wearing a veil. Besides, I don't have one with me."

"It's not me you have to convince," the healer said.

"Let's get this over with," Owen said, taking Senna's hand.

"You shouldn't touch a woman in public," the healer advised.

Owen squeezed Senna's hand before dropping it. "Anything else I should know?"

"It would be good if you dressed respectfully."

"Do you have a tunic that will fit?"

"No, but when you come back, find me and I'll put something on those bruises."

Owen nodded and indicated Senna should go ahead of him. They found her brother speaking on deck with one of his sailors. He frowned when he turned and found Senna and Owen behind him.

"Senna, Sir Owen. Glad to see you are awake."

"No you're not," Senna said.

"Senna," Owen said gently. She bit her lip.

"Prince Yusri, would it be possible for Senna and I to go back to our own ship? As you can see, I am not fully attired and neither is Senna. I'm sure you and your men would be more comfortable if we were not here."

Yusri glanced at the bruises on Owen's torso then said, "You, Sir Owen, are welcome to leave but I'm afraid I cannot let Senna go back with you."

"Might I ask why?"

"You put her in a position where she felt she must take a life. My father would never have given her to you if he knew there was a chance that would happen."

"I never would have brought her on this trip if I knew that was going to happen. You cannot think I wanted her to be in that situation. I honor and respect women as much as you do. More so, I dare say. It happened. I am very thankful for her help and proud of her for being so brave. I also hope she is never ever in a situation like that again."

"What about Queen Rabiah?"

"What about her?"

"I see how she dresses, how she acts. It is not appropriate for a woman yet King Tristan does nothing to dissuade her."

"Queen Rabiah is not from Ibirann. She is of the Clan and they treat their women differently. King Tristan respects their traditions. I

197

do not expect Senna to be like Queen Rabiah. I would not want her to be."

Senna's brother was silent for a minute, "She does seem to like you."

He looked at Senna, "And I've never seen her stay visible for so long."

Senna tried hard not to glare but failed.

"All right, you may both go, but take the other women and the boy with you."

"Of course," Owen said, trying to remember what boy Yusri was talking about.

"Go back below deck. I'll let you know when we've pulled beside your ship."

"Thank you Prince Yusri, and thank you for rescuing us."

Senna's brother nodded politely and turned to speak with another sailor. Owen waited until they were below deck before he asked, "What boy?"

"You don't remember?"

"I vaguely remember punching someone."

Senna took his hand, "Let me introduce you."

Owen stayed outside the women's quarters with the sailor who was on guard duty until someone came to say they could transfer. Lydia was still feverish and unsteady on her feet. The healer brought a stretcher. Kaawa and Senna moved Lydia onto it and Owen and the healer carried her onto the deck. The boats had been temporarily tied together and a plank bridge with rope rails stretched across the gap. Senna went first with Kaawa and the boy. Owen and the male healer followed with Lydia. Rabiah and Tristan were waiting for them. Rabiah hugged Senna as she stepped onto the ship, relieved that she and Owen were all right.

Senna gratefully hugged her back, then turned to indicate the people behind her. "Queen Rabiah, this is Kaawa, a healer whom we found on the pirate's ship, and the boy Ice." In the presence of her brother's healer Senna thought it best not to speak with any other males even though King Tristan was present.

The boy looked at Rabiah in her pants and short tunic and said, "You're a queen?" He then turned and said something to Kaawa. Kaawa immediately dropped into a deep curtsy. She said something to Ice and he bowed too. Rabiah thought she recognized the words.

"Are you from the land west of the Unega River?" she tried in the language of that people.

"No, but my people speak the same language," Kaawa replied with a surprised smile as she stood. "How is it that you know my language?"

Rabiah gave her a brief explanation. She broke off when she saw Lydia, "What is wrong with her?" she asked Kaawa.

"I gave her snare weed but we didn't have any soil. It took its life from her. It poisoned her as well. I gave her a potion to combat it. She should be fine in a few days."

"Did you know the weed would do that?"

"I've heard rumors that snare weed could be dangerous, but I've never seen it harm anyone."

"She has a powerful gift."

"Yes. The one who controls the wind will not be happy with her. He does not take defeat lightly."

"Do you think he will come after us?"

"Oh yes. He's on his way if they've figured out how to tame the plant."

"We will depart as soon as the sailors finish inspecting and making repairs."

"You should leave now."

Rabiah repeated the message to Tristan and the captain. They set sail within the hour.

Chapter 16

They sailed for three days nonstop. The wind was not strong, but at least they were moving. Rabiah woke a couple of times each night and climbed to the crow's nest to make sure the pirate ship wasn't sneaking up behind them. Lydia's vines bloomed and fruit grew. Lydia, however, did not get better. Kaawa and Marion tried everything they had on hand. They could get her fever down but the sores in her arm remained puffy with dark shadows around them and now it looked almost like little vines where crawling under her skin and up her arm. Lydia tossed and turned and was only occasionally lucid. Rabiah served as translator while Marion and Kaawa discussed what should be done. Rabiah grew impatient and pressed down on the vine-like things in Lydia's arm. It felt like something was under the skin.

"Why don't you just cut one open and see what's there?" she asked Marion.

"We are not to harm the patient and cutting it open might make her worse."

"She's not getting better. If you are careful, it probably won't harm her. I think we need to see what it is."

Kaawa agreed. She took a small surgical tool and carefully cut the skin lengthwise down the top of one of the smaller dark streaks. Pulling the skin back, they could see it was, indeed, a little branch. It moved. Kaawa jumped and dropped the knife. Rabiah had one of her throwing knives in her hand within a second and gave the black thing a little poke. It wrapped around the blade and started climbing toward her hand. She jerked the knife up and the whole thing slipped

200

out of Lydia's arm. She dropped the knife before the branch could touch her fingers. The blood-covered branch continued to wrap around the knife. When it reached the top, the tip of the branch raised up off the surface and waved around as if it were searching for another place to climb.

"How do we kill it?" Rabiah asked, stepping well away.

"Fire, I'd guess," Marion said.

"I'll be right back. Keep an eye on it."

She hurried out and returned shortly with a sword. She stabbed the middle of the branch. It wiggled as if it were in pain. It remained impaled on the sword tip when she lifted it, so she headed for the galley, holding the sword carefully upright in front of her. The cook stepped out of her way as she charged in and stabbed the sword into the stove. The branch hissed as it caught fire and finally exploded. Relieved, Rabiah shut the stove door, nodded to the cook, and returned to Lydia's cabin.

"Fire seems to work. Shall we remove the rest?"

"Yes. I wonder if we can pull them out by gripping them from the base at the sores. See, the dark is gone around the cut where the branch was."

Kaawa saw where Marion pointed and understood. She grabbed a large pair of tweezers and tried to grab something inside one of the sores. She tugged. The dark line under Lydia's arm wiggled, clearly resisting. Kaawa pulled harder. The branch slid out and bent back as if to grab her. Kaawa dropped the tweezers and the branch. Rabiah stabbed it. She took it to the galley as she had before. The cook eyed her as she opened the stove and put the tip of her sword in again. She watched to make sure the branch burned.

"Are you going to come back Your Highness?" he asked finally.

"Yes."

"This might be easier." He grabbed a pan with a handle and scooped some coals in.

"Thank you," Rabiah said as he gave it to her.

"What are you burning?"

"The things in Miss Lydia's arm."

He made a face. "Hurry then while the coals are nice and hot."

201

They pulled seven branches out in total. Bruises quickly formed where the branches had wiggled and fought and scraped as they were removed. Marion smeared a thick paste on Lydia's arm and wrapped it well. The only sign that they might have stumbled across the source of her malady was that Lydia slept peacefully instead of tossing about.

They stopped at Port Gresado that evening. It was a large port with docks for many different sizes of ships. People along the docks and in other boats gawked at their vine-covered ships. Some of the other ships at the port belonged to members of Senna's family. Prince Yusri went to talk to them in the hopes that they could travel with them back to their home port.

The next morning Senna stayed behind to care for Lydia while Kaawa, Marion and Rabiah went shopping for information and medicines that might help Lydia. Four heavily armed guards traveled with them. Since she was serving as a translator, Rabiah didn't see the point in dressing like a queen. She wore her leather tunic and strapped a short sword to her body. Tristan smiled when he saw her. "You look dangerous."

"That's because I am."

"Don't I know it. I could go with you," he said, grabbing her around the waist.

"You'd get bored. Go meet with the governor. We can go out together later."

"Will you wear that?"

"If you wish."

"You could be my bodyguard."

"Always."

He had to kiss her. He was feeling much better now that they were no longer on the open ocean.

"Hurry back," he said when he finally let her go.

Rabiah enjoyed the outing. She liked exploring the different potion shops and learned a lot just by listening and translating what the different vendors said about their goods. The thing she found the most pleasing was that few people seemed to think it odd that she was wearing pants or carrying a sword. If anyone looked at her too long, she just put her hand on the hilt and stared them down.

They visited five different shops before they found one whose proprietor had any useful information on snare weed. She directed them to a dusty back room with several chairs, then disappeared down into a cellar. She returned with a small bottle.

"The snare weed has gotten a taste of her blood. It won't give up easily. You can either try to burn it away or convince it to leave. The sticks you removed are just the first stage. If she is still feverish, then the weed has spread and will begin growing in places you can't easily reach."

"How do you burn it out?" Marion asked.

"It's dangerous. You must make her very hot for at least an hour. Hot enough to soften wax. This potion will do it, but you must be very careful with how much you give her. Too little won't work and too much will kill her."

"How do we convince it to leave then?" Marion asked.

"You must find someone with richer, more gifted blood than hers. If you place their blood over her wounds, the weed will come out. The blood must be fresh, no more than an hour old and you may need to apply the blood several times. From what you've told me, her gift is strong. It will be hard to find someone with richer blood than hers."

Rabiah repeated everything to Kaawa.

"Ask her how much of the potion we should try," Kaawa said.

"Start with one drop under her tongue," the old woman replied.

"How do you know so much about the weed?" Rabiah asked.

"Do you doubt me?"

"No. You seem to have firsthand knowledge. I was wondering how you acquired it, if you don't mind me asking."

"I don't mind." She took a deep breath that was part sigh before beginning. "My husband was a fisherman. My three boys would help him. Snare weed got into our traps. My husband dealt with snare weed all the time so he thought nothing of pulling it out and cutting it away. This weed was different. It wrapped around his arm and wouldn't let go. My sons cut him free and brought him home. I saw the wounds you described on his arm. I pulled the branches out and burned them but he stayed feverish. Two weeks later, more branches appeared under his skin. They were everywhere. They grew through his chest. I tried removing them again but there were too many. He died.

My sons would not leave the traps there. They tried not to touch the weed but they were still infected. I knew now what would happen. I pulled the branches out and tried different ways to kill them. Heat worked but it took a long time. I raised my eldest son's temperature as far as I dared. He recovered but was never the same. I tried it on my middle son but I went too far. He died. I was cutting the branches out of my younger son and accidentally sliced my hand open. My blood dripped into his cut. My youngest son did not yet have a strong gift. I noticed little black branches begin to bobble up where my blood had mixed with his. I pulled them out. They stopped coming after a while, so I mixed more of my blood with his. More came. I kept adding my blood until no more came. His fever left and he recovered. We left the traps there and moved. I later discovered that stretch of waterway had been cursed. Your seeds must have come from the same area."

"The pirates gave me those seeds and told me they were supposed to be extremely potent. I didn't realize they were cursed," Kaawa said after Rabiah had translated.

"What is done is done," Rabiah said to her.

Marion bought the little bottle of potion and they left, very subdued.

"We will have to try and burn it out," Marion concluded after walking silently for several blocks. "We have something she didn't have. We have you," she said to Rabiah.

"But the older son was damaged by the heat," Rabiah said after she had translated for Kaawa.

"What choice do we have?"

"We know of one person who might have richer blood," Rabiah said, "Perhaps there are more."

"Not that we know of."

"Maybe if we mixed blood from different people?"

"Compared to her blood, all our blood together would just be like water."

"Perhaps there's a way to un-enhance her. Surely the bull priests could reverse what they created."

"Your Highness, there is a temple of the Bull in this port," one of the guards said.

"Do you know where?" Rabiah asked.

"It's this way."

The women followed him out of the working-class neighborhood into one with much nicer buildings of polished stones and spacious walks. A black stone temple arose in the midst of the lighter buildings. The paving stones around the temple were black too. Rabiah's ring heated. She stopped short of stepping on the stones.

"I will wait here."

"What's wrong?" Marion asked.

Rabiah per her hand to her chest over the ring. Marion had seen the ring protect Rabiah before and understood.

"It should be safe. Many people go to the temple," Marion said.

"Perhaps it is just me. I don't like the way the temple feels."

"You do not want to see the temple?" Kaawa asked in her own language, "I have heard it is quite spectacular inside."

"No."

"I will wait with you then."

"There is no need. Go ahead. You can tell me what it looks like."

Two of the guards stayed with Rabiah. She sent two with Kaawa and Marion. The group proceeded to walk across the paving stones and into the temple. Rabiah watched them with her second sight. She couldn't see anything different, but her ring hadn't been wrong yet. The two women were greeted at the door and ushered in. Their guards followed. The large door shut behind them.

The sun was hot. Rabiah retreated to a bench placed under one of the many trees surrounding the temple and waited.

Several minutes later the two healers emerged. Rabiah viewed them again. Their souls looked untarnished. She stood as they approached.

"They were completely unhelpful. First, they denied that they could enhance anything, then they said that even if they could, it could not be reversed. I asked if they knew of anyone else who had been enhanced or might have a gift that was helpful and they couldn't think of a single person. Although, if we make the appropriate sacrifice, they will pray for a miracle," Marion said.

"We can pray ourselves," Rabiah frowned.

"They wanted to know why the rest of our party did not approach."

"What did you tell them?"

"I said you were standing guard out here."

Rabiah nodded, "Good. Let's go back to the ship."

They went back a different way than they had come. Large buildings with impressive facades behind tall fences lined the broad road. Rabiah noticed many of the women in this neighborhood were veiled. Most women seemed to come in pairs and all had at least two guards with them. They put their heads together and whispered as the healers and Rabiah walked by.

They had almost reached what looked like the border of the neighborhood when one of the bull priests caught up with them.

"Healers, I might have the solution," he said breathlessly. He opened his palm to display the black stone that lay within. An evil feeling assaulted her. Rabiah had to force herself not to step back. "If you put this over her wounds it might be powerful enough to call out the weed."

"She's wearing one already," Marion said.

"Ah, but this one has been recently blessed. It is very powerful."

"You are giving it to us?" Marion asked in surprise.

"No. I'm coming with you, if you would like to try it, that is."

"That would be," Marion flashed a glance at Rabiah who gave a small nod, "That would be very kind of you."

The priest joined their group. He walked next to Marion and pelleted her with questions about Lydia and where they had traveled. Marion was very good at not answering questions Rabiah thought.

The docks had been built at different levels so it was easy for them to board their craft. Several of the sailors bowed when they saw

Rabiah, but she put her finger to her lips so they wouldn't call her by her title. She didn't trust the little priest. The priest didn't realize the sailors were bowing to her. He thought they were bowing to him.

"Your crew appears to be very devout. Where did you say you were from?"

"Arles."

"Ah, yes. We have several temples there. We received word recently that the King and Queen were assassinated. My condolences," he said to Marion.

"They are received."

"And their son is now King?"

"Yes."

"And he was recently married?"

"Yes."

"And his wife was cured miraculously?"

"Yes."

"Were you there? Did you see it?"

"I was not there for the healing, no."

"Was it a gift from the Bull? The news we received wasn't clear on that."

"How could you tell if it were from the Bull?"

"If she was wearing a stone of his, it would have cracked because the power would have been used."

"I have no information for you," Marion said. They had arrived at Lydia's cabin. Senna stood to move outside as they entered the small room.

"Any change?" Marion asked.

"She has begun tossing about again."

Rabiah peered at Lydia with her soul sight as Marion removed the bandages from her arm. Her soul was still encased in pink but instead of swirling about, it appeared to be focusing on different areas in her body. The spots weren't just pink. Rabiah peered closer and realized she could actually see the cursed seeds beginning to grow. They were a bright green and clustered around Lydia's chest and abdomen.

The priest put the stone near Lydia's arm. Nothing happened at the surface, but Rabiah could see the pink cloud begin to swirl and increase. The seeds shone brighter. She was afraid they were growing bigger. She cleared her throat. The priest didn't notice but Marion did. Marion looked up. Rabiah shook her head and mouthed the word 'stop'.

Marion gave a little nod and placed her hands over Lydia's body. "It doesn't appear to be working."

"You can tell?"

"Nothing's changing."

"Perhaps I should touch the skin."

Rabiah shook her head violently.

"Her skin is very tender. Your stone is so powerful I'm afraid it would hurt her further. I appreciate your help in this matter though."

The priest nodded, "Might I ask who she is?"

"She is a ward of the King and Queen of Arles."

"The new ones?"

"Yes."

"Are they here? Is this their ship?"

"It is one of them."

"I would be honored to meet them. I could give them a blessing."

"Blessings are always welcome but I believed the King is currently not on board."

"And the Queen?"

"Would that be appropriate for you to meet the Queen and not the King?"

"No, I suppose not."

"Thank you again for coming all this way. Would you like an escort back?"

"No. No one bothers us priests. You were wise to travel with guards though."

"We've heard tales about port cities," Marion smiled.

She walked with him back to the dock. Rabiah followed.

"Peace be on you and your shipmates," the priest bowed before stepping off the ship.

"And on you," Marion said politely, bowing.

She watched the priest leave, then turned to Rabiah. "What did you see?"

"The stone made Lydia's power stir. I can see the seeds. It must because of the curse. They're all over her chest and her abdomen. They glowed stronger when the stone was close."

"That you can see them is good. If we try to burn them out you can tell when they are all gone."

"Do you really want to try that?"

"I think we can do it safely. I'm familiar with the potion we purchased and I can make the antidote in case her fever starts to go too high. You can remove or add heat as needed and watch the seeds. I can monitor her body and make sure it isn't becoming damaged. Tell Kaawa. I'll go make the antidote."

Rabiah told Kaawa the plan, then explained to Senna what they had discovered.

"It sounds too dangerous."

"It's either that or ask the wind-mage to help us."

"Tell me what I can do."

Marion came back with another small vial and a bowl of water with a sponge in case they needed to cool Lydia quickly. She got Lydia to drink several sips of water before placing a drop of the potion under her tongue. Lydia's temperature began to go up almost immediately.

"Senna, keep this wax against Lydia's skin. Let me know as soon as it begins to soften. Rabiah, let me know as soon as anything happens, good or bad."

Obediently, Rabiah sat at Lydia's side, held her hand, and gazed at her torso with her second sight. Kaawa sat at the foot of the bed and waited. Marion monitored Lydia's head.

It was only a few minutes before Senna said, "It's soft."

"Rabiah, anything?"

"The pink is swirling faster but the seeds do look a little dimmer. I don't know if they'll stop glowing when they die though."

"We'll have to hope. Are any near enough to the surface that we could test?"

"No."

"It's too late anyway."

"It's getting softer," Senna said.

"She's too hot Rabiah."

Rabiah pulled some heat into her body. Not too much, but she began to sweat.

"That's better. Anything?"

"No."

"She said it would take an hour."

"Rabiah, she's getting too hot. Take more heat," Marion said suddenly.

Rabiah obeyed while Marion sponged Lydia's head. The seeds stubbornly stayed green. Rabiah was uncomfortably warm now. She stood and removed the leather tunic, leaving the cooler thin one underneath.

"Can you take more? Is anything happening?"

Rabiah looked, then pulled more heat onto herself. She saw one light flicker and go out, but many remained strong.

"I think we got one."

"We can't keep this up. You're already sweating and she's getting hotter."

"I can take a bit more."

"No, unless you want to pass it to me."

Rabiah sent some of her heat to Marion then took more from Lydia.

Senna put out her arm, "Now me."

Rabiah kept at it, taking heat, than passing it on. Kaawa put her arm out after she realized what Rabiah was doing. Two more lights went out. Nothing happened for a few more minutes.

"The wax is getting hard," Senna said.

"I'll have to give her another dose or we can try raising her heat by sharing some of our energy. The medicine should still be working. It may be she is just too ill to make any more heat," Marion said.

Rabiah translated for Kaawa who immediately placed her hands on Lydia and shared some of her own energy. Lydia's temperature went back up, but only for a short while. Between the three of them they could only keep it up another ten minutes.

Marion finally pushed back.

"How did we do?" she asked.

"We got a few, but there are many left."

Marian sighed. "I need to think on this. Lady Senna, will you please continue to monitor her temperature. I want to retrieve my book of potions. I'll be back shortly."

"Gladly."

"There's got to be a way to kill a plant without hurting a person," Rabiah heard Marion mumble under her breath as she left the room.

Rabiah explained to Kaawa what was happening, then put back on her tunic and went up on the deck to get some air. Perhaps if she mediated and prayed an answer would come to her. She had planned to go up to the crow's nest. A puff of wind made her look towards the dock. A young man with long hair in a long cape had his hands up as if he had just pushed someone. Twenty feet away a sailor on guard was picking himself up off the dock. There were two older, beefier men behind the cloaked one. Rabiah peered at the cloaked man's soul. It swirled pink. She tapped a nearby sailor's shoulder and whispered "wind-mage" in his ear. Before the sailor had time to respond, she ran and jumped onto the dock in front of the mage, hand on her knife.

"Greetings," she said in Common.

"Out of my way, woman."

"I know who you are. Why are you here?"

"I've come to take your ship."

"With three people? No you haven't."

"I could."

"I've seen your power. I know what you are capable of. Now why are you here?"

"I want that plant off my ship."

Rabiah cocked her head, "What are you willing to do to get it removed?"

He raised his hands, "Kill you if I have to."

211

Rabiah didn't move. "Are you willing to heal?"

He stared at her for a second, "What do you mean?"

"The person who can remove the plant is dying. You might be the only one who can help her."

"What would I have to do?"

"Give her some of your blood."

"Why?"

"We need someone whose blood and power are stronger than hers."

"And if I do this will she come back with me and remove the plant?"

"You are a pirate. Will you return her safely and let us be on our way unmolested?"

"I will, but I cannot speak for everyone else."

"It is your power that gives them an advantage. You can control them if you wish."

"I could."

Rabiah raised an eyebrow.

"And if I don't agree?"

"Then we are done. You may go." She flicked her hand to send him away.

"Your mistress will die."

"Perhaps. Perhaps we will find another cure. Your blood may not even be strong enough."

"There is no stronger."

Rabiah waited. She could hear men whispering and moving about on the ship behind her.

"All right. I will help her if she agrees to remove her plant. If she does so then I and my men will release and not pursue anyone or any of your ships."

"You will not harm or molest or touch her or our people in any way and you must speak for all your people, both men and women."

He gave a nod.

"And you must help without her agreement. She is not lucid. But I will allow you to speak with her if your blood heals her."

"You will allow?" He raised his hands again.

Rabiah nodded. "I will allow and I will repeat our agreement. It is her power and thus her choice."

He lowered his hands. "Deal, but if she chooses not to help, I do not guarantee the safety of anyone aboard your ships."

Rabiah nodded. "You may come with me. Your men can stay here."

"They come with me."

"Are you afraid we will harm you? We will not unless you harm us first. It is the way of my people." She turned and jumped back onto the ship. Several sailors and her two guards were watching warily, hands on their weapons.

"You are from Arles," he said behind her.

"I am of the Clan." She turned and looked at him, waiting. He spoke to his men then leapt onto the deck behind her. The captain approached as if to stop him, but Rabiah raised her hand. "He may be our only hope to heal Miss Lydia. I have asked him on as my guest and I will watch over him. His men are to stay on the dock. Can you please send someone to tell the healer we are coming?"

The captain motioned for one of the sailors to go.

"What may I call you?" Rabiah asked the wind-mage while they gave the sailor time to relay his message.

"Othello, Lord of the Seas," he said grandly.

Rabiah dearly wanted to ask who had made him a lord, but she didn't want to anger him so she held her tongue.

"And what shall I call you?" he asked.

Rabiah did not want him to know anything about her, especially not that she was queen. That could cause problems if the pirate got greedy. "Who do you think I am?" she asked instead.

"How am I to know? Are you supposed to be famous? If so, I haven't heard of you."

She nodded. "That is good." They waited in silence until the sailor appeared a few seconds later.

"They are ready for him Your..."

"Thank you," she cut him off. She led the pirate below deck to Lydia's cabin. Marion was there but Kaawa, the boy, and Senna were

213

nowhere to be seen. Rabiah looked for souls. She found Senna in the corner.

"Healer Marion, this is Othello, Lord of the Seas," she raised an eyebrow that only Marion could see, "Othello, this is Healer Marion. Marion, can you explain to the pirate captain what needs to be done. I'll be right back." Rabiah looked toward Senna and then toward the door. She stepped outside. Senna followed. Rabiah leaned to where she guessed Senna's ear might be and found herself suddenly enveloped by Senna's invisibility.

"Senna," she whispered, "My cabin, my bag, two bracelets. Whatever you do, don't put them on."

"Lydia's?"

"Yes."

Senna hurried away. Rabiah slipped back inside Lydia's room. Her guards made to follow but she stopped them. "It is too crowded. Stay outside." They posted themselves on either side of the doorway and insisted she leave the door open.

"Are you ready?" Marion asked Rabiah.

"Yes." She switched to her second sight and looked for the seeds. There were so many. She didn't see how they could remove them all.

"Tell me if anything happens," Marion said to Rabiah. To the pirate she said, "You may begin."

The pirate took his own knife and sliced a cut across his arm. He let the blood drip onto one of Lydia's wounds.

They waited. Nothing happened.

Rabiah watched. One seed came loose and floated toward the wound.

"I see one."

"Just one?" Marion asked.

"Yes."

"What does that mean?" the pirate asked.

"Your blood may not be strong enough," Marion said.

"How can it not be strong enough? I am stronger than everyone. The priests promised. Do you know how much my power cost?"

"No, but we have an idea." Marion said.

A dark sphere that looked like a swollen seed appeared at the sore. Marion took it with a tweezers and threw it into a bowl.

"I have an idea," Rabiah said. "I will try to pull some of her power into me. Perhaps that will make the pirate's blood look richer."

"Rabiah, be careful." Marion said.

"It won't hurt me and if it affects me, well, you know what to do."

Rabiah grabbed Lydia's ankles and watched with her second sight as she concentrated on pulling it toward her. It was scary how easy it was. Much easier than trying to part it. It flowed up her arms and toward her chest. Her ring heated, then cooled as the pink was absorbed by her mother's stone. The pink kept coming, but it grew dimmer as if she had pulled off the excess. Now she was taking it as fast as it could be made.

"Try it now."

The pirate's arm was no longer bleeding freely. This time he poked the tip of his finger and squeezed out a few drops onto a different sore. Five seeds began moving toward the fresh blood almost immediately.

"It's working. Put some on all the sores," Rabiah said.

The pirate obeyed. Marion began pulling swollen seeds from the sores. A few were beginning to sprout.

"Is this because of what she did to my ship?" the pirate asked.

"No," Rabiah answered.

"How much longer do you think this will take?" he asked.

Rabiah looked. About half of the seeds were gone from Lydia's torso. She could see a line of them leading to her arm.

"We will need more blood after these are removed. There are still many inside."

"Rabiah, we need fire. The seeds are starting to sprout," Marion said, indicating the bowl.

"I cannot let her go. James," she called to one of her guards, "bring us some hot coals, quickly."

"Yes, Your Highness." The guard saluted from the doorway.

215

"Your Highness?" the pirate asked.

"Yes," Rabiah said, resignedly.

"I didn't know the Clan had royalty."

"They don't"

"So you married in."

"Yes."

"So who is she?" the pirate nodded to Lydia.

"She is my ward."

"She looks more like a princess than you, if you don't mind my saying so."

Rabiah shrugged.

"Rabiah!" Marion said as she pulled a long sprout from Lydia's arm. The sprout twisted back trying to wrap itself around Marion's arm.

"Fling it against the wall," Rabiah commanded.

Marion did. With her left hand, Rabiah pulled a knife from her belt and threw it. The impaled sprout wiggled madly against the wall. Rabiah quickly placed her hand back on Lydia's ankle so she could pull off as much power as possible.

"Impressive," the pirate said. "Were you the archer who targeted so many of my pirates?"

"There were several."

"How did they see them?"

"How did you hide them?" Rabiah gave the pirate her raised eyebrow look. He grinned savagely.

"I think I like you," he said.

."Rabiah."

Marion pulled out another sprout. Rabiah pulled the knife from the holder around her right arm. "Fling."

The second sprout wiggled next to the first.

"I hope James gets back soon," Marion commented.

"I have more knives."

"I'm not bad myself," the pirate said.

"Here, Your Highness," the guard said, appearing with a bucket of coals.

"Place it by the bowl and dump in the seeds," Marion instructed, "then pull the sprouts from the wall. You might need to use your sword. Don't let them touch you."

"Yes, healer."

"And give the knives back to the Queen."

"Queen?" the pirate said, "Here I was thinking you were the wife of the second son or something. Are you Queen of Arles?"

Rabiah nodded.

"How did a Clan girl become Queen?"

"It's a long story," Rabiah said.

"Please, entertain me. Looks like we will be here awhile."

"I must concentrate," she said.

"Well then, I will tell my story."

Rabiah nodded to tell him to go on. She did like stories.

"I was not always a pirate. My father was a merchant, a trader. He wasn't the best but he wasn't the worst either. When I reached the age of eight he began taking me on trips so I would learn the trade. We occasionally met pirates but we always managed to escape thanks to my father's gift. He could call a fog so thick that no one but he could see through it. It was hard on him though. He always had to recover for a couple of days afterwards. When I was twelve we escaped from one group of pirates only to run into another group the next day. My father could not defend us. We were captured. My father was slain. They kept me as a cabin boy. I hated it at first but then I got to know some of the men. One was a former Navy man who couldn't find a job after he was released. He'd seen a lot of battle and it changed him. Another became a pirate because he had no other way to feed his family. In his land taxes were very high. He was just taking back what they had taken from him, he said.

They took me under their wing. I found I liked being a pirate. Nothing is more exhilarating then swinging onto a ship amidst a storm of arrows. Sure, there are some slow times, but being a pirate is much more exciting than haggling over the price of things.

"When did you learn to control the wind?" Rabiah asked.

"I don't remember. My mother used to complain that my room always looked like a windstorm had swept through and there has always been a breeze around me. I must have been pretty young because I remember making the leaves flutter so I could chase them."

"So you've always had a strong power?"

"Oh, no. I could control the wind enough to fill the sails of one ship but no more. Our pirate ship flourished because we could outrun all the other ships, but I realized it would be even better if we could work as a team. I heard rumors that it might be possible to enhance one's natural gift. I greased a few palms and learned how it could be done. I became a devout follower of the Bull." He showed Rabiah the black stone around his neck. "I gave them money and slaves. Then, I began to hint how many more gifts I could give if I just had a little more power. It took several visits and months of hinting before the head priest finally spoke to me privately. I had to donate three male children and several chests of gold for the enhancement. It was the most painful thing I've ever felt, but it was worth it. The other pirates flocked to me when they realized what I could do. With my control of the wind and our ability to cloak ourselves, we've rarely lost a boat. That is, until we ran across you."

"That's the last of them for now Marion," Rabiah said. To Othello she said, "Are you ready to try again?"

"I am, but I should speak with my men. They will be wondering what is taking so long."

"I will escort you as soon as the healer is finished," Rabiah said.

Marion pulled the last three seeds from Lydia's arm and wiped off the blood. The seeds gave off an odor of burning cabbage mixed with a faint hint of skunk.

"I will get some fresh coals," Marion said.

Rabiah picked up her knives from the table where the guard had laid them and dipped the tips into the coals. She hoped the fire didn't hurt the blades, but she didn't want the juice from the cursed plant to poison them.

"Let's go," she told the pirate, sheathing her knives.

He stepped out ahead of her and she followed with her guards behind. On deck, a row of sailors with weapons drawn lined the edge of the boat facing the two other pirates who stood on the dock, their faces angry. Othello walked past the sailors as if nothing was amiss, his coat flapping. Rabiah waited onboard as Othello stepped onto the dock and conferred with his two men. He flipped the bigger man a coin. As the pirate turned to reboard, Rabiah saw Tristan approaching with a grandly dressed, portly man. Owen walked behind them. They were about a hundred yards away. Tristan caught her eye and she smiled, then turned her focus on the pirate as he boarded again.

"After you," she told the pirate and followed him below deck.

'Rabiah, who's that.'

'The wind-mage. He's the only one who can heal Lydia.'

'The wind-mage! How did that happen?'

'He wants Lydia to remove the plant from his ship but she can't get well without him, so we made a deal. He's under my protection while we are onboard.'

'And who's protecting you?'

'Senna. He's behaved so far. He told us his story.'

'Does he know who you are?'

'Yes.'

'Be careful then, I'm sure he's not above taking a few hostages.'

'Who's that with you?'

'The governor. He was most impressed that we escaped the pirates and wanted to see our vines.'

'Best keep him away from Lydia's quarters.'

'Indeed.'

The pirate sauntered to the cabin and plopped down on the stool. Marion was waiting. With her soul vision, Rabiah could see Senna still standing in the corner. Rabiah gave her a discreet nod. She took Lydia's ankles again and waited for the pink swirling around Lydia to thin. It didn't take as long. After their attempt to raise her temperature and the release of so much magical energy, she hoped Lydia would not become too weak.

The pirate poked another finger and dripped the blood onto Lydia's wounds. More of the seeds broke loose. There were only a few remaining now. The seeds began to pop up out of the wounds.

"How long have you had your enhanced power," Rabiah asked, wanting to fill the silence.

"A couple of years. At first there were just a few ships that joined us, but we were so successful that the merchant ships began traveling in larger and larger fleets. Some even hired navy ships to escort them through our territory. More pirates joined us because they couldn't win against those large numbers. We've also begun expanding our territory. That is why, I suppose, you were only three ships strong. You weren't expecting us."

"We are not merchant ships, just travelers."

"Bounty can be more rewarding than plunder."

"Surely you can't expand your territory too far. You are only one man. How much water can you cover?"

"I am one, but I don't have to be there all the time. Many of the pirates have been doing this much longer than I. If they use oars, they can handle things without me."

"You must get tired."

He smiled proudly, "My power is not infinite but I can last much longer than a normal person. I will not say how long though. I'm insulted you tried to sneak it out of me."

"I'm worried about Lydia. I've been pulling power off of her for some time and it seems to be lessening."

"How can you tell?"

She looked at him, her soul sight still on. In the dim light he noticed her eyes seemed to shine with a light of their own, "We both have our secrets."

Rabiah, we're coming down.'

"Shut the door," she ordered the guards.

"Why?" the pirate tensed.

"The governor is on board. He's coming below decks. I don't think Lydia would appreciate meeting him in this state."

"How do you know he's coming?"

"I saw him on the dock. You can crack the door and look out yourself if you don't believe me."

The pirate smoothly stood and did just that. He could see a large man just coming downstairs. The younger, neatly dressed, man in front of him addressed the large man as governor. He watched a few seconds more then slid back to his seat.

220

"That taller, younger man. I remember seeing him before, with you, after we captured your ship. Is that your husband? Is that the King of Arles?"

"Yes."

"He was the one you smiled at on the dock."

"Yes."

"You knew he had gone to speak with the governor and guessed he was bringing him for a tour."

Rabiah said nothing.

"You probably heard them coming."

Rabiah gave a little smile. The pirate took that as affirmation.

"You could have just said so."

"You still would have checked."

"True."

They could hear them talking as they passed by Lydia's door. The governor asked who was behind the door and Tristan explained his wife was a healer and she was helping the ship's healer treat someone who was very ill.

"Why the guards?" the governor asked. "Don't you have enough on deck?"

"There was an attempt on her life," they heard Tristan answer. Their voices faded.

"You're a healer?!" the pirate asked, sounding surprised.

"An untrained one, but I have a few skills."

"Like pulling power away from someone."

"Apparently. I've never tried it before."

"Why did someone try to kill you?"

"I assume it's because they didn't like my husband's choice of wife."

"And here I thought the guards were there because of me."

"I'm sure they would have been if they weren't already," Rabiah said soothingly.

They lapsed into silence. They heard voices pass by again.

We're going on deck,' Tristan sent.

"You can open the door again if you wish," she told the pirate.

221

"I do. Those seeds smell worse than some of the pirates." He opened the door and stepped out. Rabiah kept her eyes on him. He didn't move out of her sight.

"Do you mind if I freshen the air a bit?"

"Be my guest," she smiled.

A light breeze blew through the room. After a few seconds it did smell better.

"Your Highness, I think I'm done. How many more?" Marion asked.

"Just a few."

"These coals will do then. Can you spare a little more blood?" Marion asked the pirate.

"Of course," he said generously and poked his finger again, "Would it be too much to ask that you heal me when you are done?" he asked Rabiah.

"I do not know how to heal cuts, but I'm sure Healer Marion could help you."

"I'd be glad to," Marion agreed.

The pirate squeezed some blood on Lydia's arm again. All but one was released. Rabiah released an expletive in her language.

"What was that?" Marion asked, thinking she had misunderstood something.

"There's one left. Othello, come, stand by me."

"Lord Othello."

"Othello, Lord of the Sea, please come and stand by me," Rabiah said impatiently.

Immediately he stood up and slid over by her. "I like the way you said that."

Rabiah ignored his attempt at flirtation and instructed him to hold his freshly cut finger over one of Lydia's cuts.

"I'm going to try and send some of Lydia's power to you. Maybe it will be enough to dislodge that last seed."

She grabbed his right wrist with her left hand and concentrated on forcing the pink mist across her chest, down her left arm and into the pirate. His own pink cloud swirled and became denser. She transferred power for a full minute before she said, "Try now."

222

He squeezed. A couple of drops of blood sluggishly fell onto the open wound. Rabiah watched in relief as the last seed wavered and finally broke loose. It had already sprouted, Rabiah realized, and was almost as big as the ones they had pulled from her arms. She let go of the pirate's wrist.

"That did it."

Othello flexed his fingers and sent a puff of wind to extinguish the lamp.

"Wow. I feel charged."

"Charged enough that you can relight the lamp so I can see?" Marion asked in an irritated voice.

"Oh, pardon," the pirate said. He relit the lamp and sat back on his stool. "How long until she wakes up?"

"There's no telling. She's been like this for several days and she's probably very weak," Marion said.

The pirate leaned forward and studied Lydia's pale face. Marion had braided her hair so it wouldn't get tangled but small strands had come undone around her face. As ill as she was, she still looked beautiful, Rabiah thought. The pirate stroked a finger down her cheek.

"No. None of that. You promised you wouldn't touch her," Rabiah said sternly.

He shrugged, "I'm a pirate. We're not known for keeping our word."

"Back away or I'll take your power the way I did hers."

He stood up quickly, his hands in front of him. The stool went flying. "You'd have to catch me first."

"True. And I don't want to take your power. It is your gift. You have helped us as we asked and I am grateful. She is my ward, however, and I know she would not want a strange man touching her as she slept," Rabiah said calmly.

"What if she were awake?"

Rabiah shrugged. "Perhaps, but you'll have to wait until she's awake to ask her."

The pirate picked up the stool and sat back down. He gazed tenderly on Lydia's face as Marion finished pulling the seeds from her arms. Rabiah double checked to make sure they were all gone. She even had Marion roll Lydia over. Othello was quiet. Perhaps sharing some of Lydia's power with him had not been the best idea. He was looking as love-sick as Owen had. Blocking the connection with copper had worked before. She walked to Senna's corner and put out her hand. The two bracelets appeared in them. Discretely she showed them to Marion and together they rolled Lydia on her side so that her back was to the pirate. Rabiah leaned over and slid the bracelets onto each of Lydia's wrists.

They shrank to fit. They pulled the blanket up to cover her arms and let her roll onto her back. Rabiah watched Othello carefully. He still had that odd, sappy expression on his face. Why hadn't it worked? She gazed deeper within him. The pink around his soul was dense and looked to swirl in two different directions.

"Othello, Lord of the Sea, will you please rise and follow me?" Rabiah said softly.

He tore his gaze off of Lydia and looked at her blearily.

"What is this? Why do I feel this way?"

"How do you feel?"

"Lost. There's something missing. It hurts," he tapped his chest, "here."

"Can you take the power back out of him?" Marion asked.

"I will try."

Rabiah squatted in front of the pirate, "Othello, may I hold your hands?"

"Why?"

"I want to try and help you."

He thrust them toward her.

She took his wrists and looked deep within him again, searching for a pattern. The pink swirl closest to his soul went a different direction than the one outside. Rabiah looked at Lydia. Hers went the same direction as the one outside. She concentrated on that portion of the pink. It spun and flowed up and around her arms and was absorbed by her mother's stone. She stopped when she thought she had it all.

"Better?" she asked, still gripping his hands.

224

"Yes."

She didn't like the way he was looking into her eyes. Hastily, she let go and stood. "Lydia is weak. She'll need a day or more to recover even if she wakes. I will escort you off the ship. Come back tomorrow morning and I'll inform you of her progress.

"I have kept my side of the bargain," he said.

"Yes, but's she's still unconscious. She can't do anything if she's sleeping."

"I will stay here and wait."

Rabiah shook her head. "No, it is dangerous for you. She is not just an enchanter of plants. She can enchant people too. I had forgotten and I was upset that the last seedling would not release. I should have been more patient. By sharing her power with you I put you under her spell. It takes a couple of days to wear off. It's better if you are separate."

"Then you must come with me as a hostage."

"That wasn't our agreement. You want her to remove the plant. I agreed to let you ask her. I will stick to my word. You can ask her now if you like or you can ask her when she wakes up."

"I will take her then."

Rabiah shook her head. "She needs the healer still, as do you. Marion, will you heal him please?"

Marion reached for his hand. The pirate snatched it out of her reach like a spoiled child.

"That's fine. It will heal on its own. I was just doing it as a courtesy," Marion said evenly.

Othello stuck his hand out. Marion took it, put a little leaf from her pouch over his fingertips and concentrated. The wounds sealed. She then saw to the cut on his arm. As soon as she was done, the pirate grabbed Marion and put a dagger to her neck. Marion yelped. The guards appeared at the door, hands on their weapons. Rabiah raised her hand to stop them.

"If you won't come as a hostage, I'll take her."

"Why don't you stab yourself in the foot while you're at it? Lydia needs her," Rabiah said.

"It's your choice," the pirate said. "You or her."

225

Rabiah heard something. She switched to her soul sight. Senna was right behind the pirate. Rabiah shook her head to indicate Senna should stop.

"Fine, I'll come with you, but I have to release Lydia's power first so she can heal. Let Marion go. You can stay and watch."

"I will not release her."

"You will regret your choice," Rabiah said after a pause.

She turned, reached under the blanket, and removed the bracelets from Lydia's arms. Lydia felt cool, almost too cool. She left the bracelets on Lydia's stomach. Lydia's power swirled but she looked weak and pale. Rabiah put her left hand on her mother's stone. It was so full of energy it felt hot. It had absorbed Lydia's energy, could she pull from it back out? She tried pulling a small amount. She watched as it flowed easily into her hand around the stone. It was no longer pink. It was bright white like the energy of the souls she could see. She touched Lydia's shoulder and let the energy flow into her. Lydia's skin warmed. She could see the pink swirling and thickening. Rabiah stopped when she realized the pink had begun to flow down Lydia's other arm and onto the floor. Thankfully, it flowed towards the pirate and not Marion or Senna. She pulled a little power off so that the pink stopped flowing. It only Lydia would wake, she could speak with the pirate and they'd be done.

"Lydia. Will you wake?" Rabiah asked, shaking her a little. There was no response. Rabiah said a little prayer, quickly stuck her hands back under the blanket to palm the bracelets, and turned.

"Her power is unbound. She felt cold. I sent her a little energy," she told Marion.

"Release her. I will go with you," she said to the pirate.

"Don't do it," Marion said.

"You first," the pirate said. "Tell the guards to stand down." He kept the knife at Marion's throat.

Apparently unbinding Lydia's power was not going to have any effect on him. "They will never let you take me or Marion," she told him. "You need to put down the knife. I will keep my word. You must be patient."

"I will take you if I want. They can't stop me."

"You can't start a windstorm in here. It's too small."

"No, but I can blow them away from the door." He was holding Marion to him with one hand and the knife in the other. He pointed the hand with the knife toward the guards at the door. Marion took the opportunity to drop out of his hold and rolled out of the way. That was all the opening Rabiah needed.

"Get back!" she yelled to Senna, and dove at Othello. The pirate slammed against the door frame. His knife went flying. He raised his hands to call up the wind but she was too quick. She slammed his head into the wood again.

"You crossed the line. You threatened Marion. I claim my right to defend her," she whispered fiercely in his ear. She felt his arm move and slammed his head into the wall again. It knocked him out. She let him fall into a heap.

Senna appeared beside her, "Wow. Remind me not to get you mad." The two guards came into the room and pulled him up.

"To bind or not to bind?" she said, holding the bracelets in her hand.

"What are you going to do with him?" Marion asked, rubbing her neck.

"Throw him off our ship. He broke our agreement."

"He'll take his revenge. Bind him so he can't destroy the ship," Marion said.

"What do you think, Senna?"

"He'll really be mad if you take his power, but he is a pirate. He and his men are causing all kinds of problems in the shipping lanes. We have captured him. We should turn him in. They will put him to death."

"He may have broken his word, but I don't wish to break mine."

"Bind him then."

"Two of us should do it, I think."

"I will," said Marion and Senna at the same time.

"He will try to get them off. If he figures out how to do it he will come after us. Senna and I will do it. Senna is hard to find and I have my own protection."

"Your Highness, you should let us do it," the guards said.

"It is a grave responsibility, taking away a man's gift."

"He will target you."

"He will target me anyway."

"We should just arrest him," the guard said.

"He did help Lydia," Rabiah argued.

"You should ask the King," said the guard.

The pirate moaned. Rabiah handed a bracelet to Senna and they slipped them on the pirate's wrists at the same time.

"Hide," Rabiah told Senna. Senna disappeared.

Othello moved his head.

"Take him on deck. Perhaps the King is there," Rabiah said to the guards.

'Tristan, where are you?'

'Escorting the governor to his carriage. What's wrong? Did the pirate try something?'

'Yes. He got impatient. He had Marion at knifepoint. I gave him Lydia's bracelets. I'm going to release him to his friends. Are they still on the dock?"

'No. They are watching from a bar near the end of the dock. Are you sure that's wise? Why don't you just arrest him? He did try to capture us.'

'He helped Lydia. He is under my protection. I cannot turn on him like that.'

'What is he like?'

'Young. Rash. Proud.'

'How did you get the bracelets on him?'

'I banged his head against the wall first.'

He chuckled through their link.

'If you insist on freeing him, the bracelets are probably the way to go, but don't tell Uncle. He paid a lot for those.'

'Thank you.'

'For what?'

'For agreeing with me.'

'Wait until I get back to bring him out.'

'Why?'

'I want to see what happens,' he sent, but she knew it was because he was worried about what might happen.

She had followed the guards onto the deck while she was communicating with Tristan. The pirate was now standing half-awake between them. He focused on Rabiah as consciousness slowly came to him. He tried to lift his arm to rub his head, but then realized his arm was being held by a guard.

"You! You will pay!" He lifted his hand at his waist and pointed his finger at her. The gentle breeze stayed gentle. He shook his hand and tried again.

"What have you done?" he cried.

"I bound your power. You should not have grabbed Marion."

"Unbind it."

"No. You will use it against our ships."

"This was not our agreement."

"It was. I gave my word as a woman of the Clan that I would not harm you if you did not harm any of us. You put a knife to Marion's neck. Be glad that I am not having you arrested. I am letting you go because you helped Lydia."

He glared at her for a minute, then asked, "What about my ship?"

"Does it matter now?"

"Yes. It's still a good ship. I helped her. She should at least remove her plant. You said you would let me speak to her."

"Come back tomorrow. If she is awake I will let you speak to her. You healed her. I will honor our deal but if you attempt to harm anyone else I will have you arrested."

They waited until Tristan boarded the ship, then Rabiah instructed the guards to follow her with the pirate. Several sailors lined up with bows and arrows. She stood on the dock and waited, apparently unarmed, for Othello's lumbering guards to approach.

"What is this?" one of them asked. "What did you do to him?"

"I am returning him to you. He threatened our healer at knifepoint so I claimed the right to protect her. He'll have a sore head."

"That's nothing new," the shorter one chuckled.

"And I bound his powers so he can't retaliate."

His companions looked at her in shock and then each other. Their faces turned ugly. They pulled out their knives. "You had better just unbind his powers, miss."

"Can you guarantee the safety of our ships if I do?"

"No, but you made a deal. He helps you, you help us. He helped you. I saw the cut."

"I will still allow him to talk to the one who can control the plants when she wakes. She is still recovering. I asked him to come back later and he got pushy."

"Why should we trust you? You could have soldiers waiting to arrest us in the morning."

"The governor was on our ship. I hid your friend. I could have had him arrested but instead I'm returning him to you. I made a deal and I will honor my bargain. I am not a pirate who goes back on his word."

She motioned for the guards to bring Othello closer.

"Put your hands up as you walk to them so I know you're not going for the knife in your belt. I wouldn't twitch if I were you. There are at least ten arrows aimed your way," she told Othello.

He scowled at her but did as he was told. He put his arms down when he was out of range. She watched as his two friends fell into step behind him as they left the dock.

Tristan came up beside her and put his arm around her. "You certainly know how to make life interesting."

Chapter 17

They set an extra guard that night. Lydia had not awaken by the time the three pirates arrived the next morning. They did not come from land. They just suddenly appeared at the end of the dock. Rabiah assumed they had a boat somewhere near. She was waiting with Tristan on the deck. He stayed there as she jumped down on the dock to greet the pirates. Senna and Owen were already on the dock, invisible.

"Good morning," she said, walking smoothly up to them. She knew the sailors behind had their bows ready.

"Your Highness," the larger pirate bowed his head.

"She is not yet awake."

"May I see her?" Othello asked plaintively.

Rabiah thought for a minute, then nodded, "You may. But your guards stay behind."

"No," said the shorter pirate. "I don't trust you. You've done something to him."

"Why do you say that?"

"He's not thinking right. He doesn't even care that he's lost his powers. He was talking all evening about the girl and about you when he was asleep."

"Me?"

"It must have been you. You're the only one we know with hair like that."

She must not have removed all of Lydia's power, although it didn't explain why he was dreaming of her. She looked at him with her soul sight. She could see a faint trace of pink swirling in the opposite direction around his core.

"He is under her spell," she told them. "I don't know if it will wear off. I can try and remove it."

"What do you mean, under her spell?" the smaller pirate growled.

"She can enchant more than plants."

"And you can remove it?"

"Yes, I can try."

"Do it." He pushed Othello toward her. He stumbled to a stop in front of her.

Rabiah spoke to him, "Othello, I'm going to try and help you. May I have your wrists?"

He nodded trustingly and held them out to her. His wrists were bloody with cuts all around the bracelets.

"What happened?" she asked.

"We tried to have the bracelets removed," the taller pirate said.

"You can't cut them off," Rabiah stated.

"We found that out," the pirate said wryly.

Rabiah grasped the pirate's arm above the cuts. She tried pulling off the pink but she couldn't. The bracelets must be stopping her. She moved to let go but Othello grabbed her arms. She looked up at him. "Othello, what are you doing?"

"You're mine. I'm not letting you go."

"Let go Othello or I will have to hurt you," Rabiah said firmly.

The two other pirates pulled out their knives. Rabiah whipped her hands free and sent Othello flying backwards towards them. She had her own daggers unsheathed and ready by the time the pirates had untangled themselves.

"Go. I will hang a scarf when she awakes and can speak. Stay away until then and teach him some manners."

"What did you do to him?"

"Nothing. I could not remove the enchantment."

"You can't leave him like this."

"I'll try again when he returns, but only if he behaves."

They disappeared over the side of the dock as she watched, her knives ready. Tristan joined her.

"What was that all about? Why did you take his wrists?"

"He's enchanted by Lydia. I tried to remove the enchantment. I couldn't. For some reason he also wants me."

"Well, he can't have you." He put his arm around her.

"I'm sorry Tristan. I was trying to help Lydia. I didn't realize this would become so complicated."

"You've done well. No one has been hurt, except maybe the pirate. Lydia is on the mend. We'll just have to be prepared. They probably would've tried to sneak on board and take over the ship if you hadn't made that deal. Come. We'll go explore the city like we planned to yesterday. Then we can attend the party the governor has invited us to."

"Let me change first."

"You don't want to wear your fighting gear?"

"No, I just want to be your wife for a while."

He gave her a little squeeze. "Go change. I'll tell Owen the plan. Where is he anyway?" he asked, looking around.

"They're over by those crates," Rabiah said. "You could just tell him mentally."

"He got married so I could make a treaty. I thought I'd go easy on him for a while."

Rabiah changed into a tunic with light, flowing fabric. She didn't wear a veil, but she did put on a scarf with a single jewel dangling down her forehead the way she'd seen some of the women wear them the day before. She couldn't bring herself to leave her belt or her knives behind. She stopped to check on Lydia before they left. Lydia was still sleeping peacefully. Marion was with her.

"Any change?"

"No. No fever. No tossing. I was finally able to heal her arm. I think she's just really worn out."

Rabiah explained what had happened and where she was going.

"Be careful, Your Highness. I'll bet those pirates are keeping a close eye on you."

233

"You be careful too. Have some night berry ready. Othello's still enchanted and he is impatient."

"I've got it right here." She pulled a little package from her pocket.

Tristan met her as she left Lydia's cabin. He stopped and just gazed at her, a smile playing around his face.

"What?"

"You look completely different from the way you did a few minutes ago. And yet, if I kiss you," he pulled her close and did just that, "I know you truly are my Warrior Queen."

"Tristan, you're going to mess up my scarf."

"Am I?" He started nuzzling her neck.

She laughed, "Later. Owen is waiting."

"So I'll tell him we are delayed. He won't mind."

"No, I suppose he won't."

"Besides, if you're going to look like that, I need to change too or everyone will think I'm just one of your servants."

"You could be my bodyguard."

"No. I want everyone to know we are together."

They left the ship an hour later and spent an enjoyable day with Owen and Senna. Everyone treated them like royalty which, Rabiah supposed, they were. The four guards with them only enforced the image. They returned to the ship an hour before sunset to prepare for the party. Lydia still slept. There had been no sign of the pirates. Senna helped her dress as she had more of an idea of what was expected than Rabiah. Senna insisted Tristan and Rabiah wear their crowns. Rabiah compromised and wore the tiara that her Father-in-law had given her. The governor sent a carriage for them and their guards. Snuggled close to Tristan where she could see around him through the window, Rabiah felt relaxed and at peace with the world. She thanked the Spirit for such a beautiful day and a lovely night.

The governor's house was large, beautiful, and very richly decorated. At least two hundred guests wandered about the cool marble rooms. The food was delicious. Rabiah ate her fill, finding herself very hungry. Due to his position as King, Tristan was seated next to the governor as guest of honor. Rabiah was seated next to the governor's wife. The governor's wife was large like her husband and very talkative. She kept asking Rabiah questions but then guessing the answers before Rabiah had a chance to finish chewing to answer them herself.

After the meal, the tables were pushed aside and a band began to play. Tristan pulled Rabiah onto the floor as the first dance began. Lydia was not there to tell them it was inappropriate to dance so soon after his parent's death and Rabiah was glad. It was the first time they'd danced together at an actual dance. Tristan's enthusiasm for dancing made it even more enjoyable for her.

They got in two dances together before a mixed-couples dance was called. The partners switched after every couple of turns around the dance floor. Tristan taught her the steps the first time around and then she was on her own. She danced with a sweaty man, then a smelly man, then a tall one who kept stepping on her toes, then finally found herself back in Tristan's arms again.

"So how did you do?" he asked.

"You are the best partner I've had all night," she said.

He laughed. The next dance was very slow. They left the floor to get a drink. Tristan left her sitting with a couple of their guards while he went to speak to the musicians. He came back ginning.

"Are you ready to dance the spider dance?"

"Are you ready to get sick?"

"I'm feeling great."

She shook her head and took a sip of punch. Senna and Owen walked up to them, drinks in hand.

"Are you enjoying the dancing?" Rabiah asked Senna.

"It's very different. I've never seen this kind of dancing except when you and King Tristan did it for my father. Owen said he would teach me later when he's not acting as bodyguard."

"Owen, you should dance with her. You'll be close to us if you're on the floor."

"You'll probably want to wait out the next dance though," Tristan grinned.

"Let me guess, the spider dance?"

Rabiah sighed loudly.

"I'll have a bucket ready," Owen said.

The dance started. Only five couples were confident enough to try it. Senna thought Tristan and Rabiah were the best. "I want to learn that one," she told Owen.

"You'll have to ask the King. I was never any good at it."

"Maybe we can learn together," she said hopefully. Owen didn't dissuade her. She was only sixteen to his twenty-two and in some ways still very young. He enjoyed being around her though. She had a quirky sense of humor yet could also be very wise. He was also strongly attracted to her. A single touch from her or sometimes just a look made him feel as if his insides were melting. In his wildest dreams he had never envisioned a wife like her for himself. He had thanked Rabiah's Spirit a few times that Senna was his.

The dance ended. Two of the couples completely botched the ending. One of the women landed on her rear. The King and Queen had the best finish yet, Owen thought. Several people applauded. Tristan looked pale. Owen wasn't surprised when Rabiah kissed him. Owen had to look away.

"You don't like to see them kiss?" Senna asked.

"It's not that. Sometimes it's too bright to watch."

They were leaving the dance floor and heading right for them. Several people congratulated them as they went by. Rabiah smiled and thanked them. Tristan tried to smile but it came out more as a grimace.

"He's going to be sick Senna. Let's clear a path for them to the gardens," Owen said.

There were several doors on each side of the room open to the cool night air outside. As quickly as they could, but trying not to noticeably hurry, they pushed through the crowd to the fresh air beyond the first door. Tristan promptly went to a bush and threw up. Owen handed him his glass of wine to rinse out his mouth.

"Does he always get sick when he dances that dance? He wasn't even spinning," Senna asked quietly as Tristan went to spit the wine in the grass.

"He's not sick. The Queen is. It's only temporary, I hope."

"Queen Rabiah? But she looks fine."

"I'll let them explain," he said as Tristan and Rabiah rejoined them.

"Let who explain what?" Rabiah asked.

"You, explain why King Tristan is sick yet you were the one spinning."

"Oh." Rabiah looked around. Even with her soul sight they appeared to be alone.

In a low voice she said, "I'm expecting but for some reason Tristan has the morning sickness. We think it's due to our shared gift."

"Really?! That's amazing. Would you do that for me Owen?"

"Yes Owen, would you do that for your wife?" Tristan asked, taking a sip of wine.

"Not if I can help it," Owen said honestly.

Senna sighed, "Well, I guess I can't have everything. When is the baby due?"

"Babies. Sometime in the summer," Rabiah said with a happy smile.

"Babies?" Senna bit her lip, "Oh."

"What's wrong Senna?" Owen asked.

"Nothing. Sounds like another dance has started. Do you want to go back inside?"

"I think I'll stay out in the fresh air a little longer," Tristan said, offering Rabiah his arm. There was a path of white gravel that led deeper into the garden. Tristan took it. Owen and Senna followed behind.

"What's wrong Senna," Owen asked quietly so that Tristan and Rabiah could not hear.

"One of my sisters had twins. She was in labor for three days. They all died."

Owen squeezed her hand. "She will be all right. Her god has saved her once. I can't believe he would send her twins just to take them all away. We must pray to her Great Spirit to watch over them."

After a peaceful walk through the garden, they went back inside. They had just acquired fresh drinks when their host came by and claimed Rabiah for a dance. Tristan politely returned the favor by asking the governor's wife to dance. Rabiah was relieved to find it was a step she remembered. Another gentleman soon cut in. He wasn't talkative like the governor. He didn't say a word to her, but bowed at the end of the dance and stayed with her to wait for the next dance. The music started. She didn't know the steps.

"I'm sorry. I don't know this one," she said starting to back away.

He smiled and proceeded to guide her, still without saying a word.

'Rabiah, keep your eyes open. Owen says the governor looks guilty and he and his wife are leaving the room,' Tristan sent.

On the side opposite the dance floor, near the exits to the gardens on the other side of the room, another man cut in. Her ring heated and she felt a sharp point at her back.

"Othello?"

"Hello my Queen. Surprised to see me?"

"Yes."

'Othello is here. Dancing with me. He has a knife,' she sent to Tristan and Owen.

'Can you get away?'

'Yes, but let me find out what he is up to.'

"Aren't you going to ask why I am here?"

"No, but I'm sure you'll tell me."

"You know me so well already," he smiled.

He smelled odd. She followed the smell to the hand grasping her own. The cuts under his bracelet looked swollen and red.

"Othello, your wrists are infected. You need a healer."

"You can be my healer," he said, "but we'll have plenty of time for that later." He was steering her toward the door.

She planted her feet. "What do you want Othello?"

"You, of course. What is one ship compared to you?"

"Me?" He prodded her to move.

"I've never met a woman like you. You can fight, you can transfer power, you're beautiful, and you were even strong enough to bind my powers."

"Othello, stop this. I told you I would let you know when Lydia is awake."

"How could you tell? You haven't been on the ship all day. You've been gallivanting around the city with your pansy of a husband."

"She's been unconscious all day. I checked before we left for the party."

"No matter. As soon as we're done here we're going to take the ship anyway."

"We?"

"Yes. You, me, and twenty of my closest pirate pals."

"What makes you think I'm coming with you?"

"Because if you don't they'll kill everyone here, including your husband. You wouldn't want that on your conscious, would you?"

Rabiah looked out the open door with her soul sight on. She saw several stationary souls spread throughout the garden.

'He's got men stationed in the gardens,' she sent to Tristan and Owen.

'Owen sees them.'

'He says if I don't go with him they will attack.'

'Since the governor and his wife have disappeared, I assume they will attack anyway. Senna found us some swords. I'll send her to you. Owen has warned the guards.'

'Keep Senna with you. I have something in mind.'

Rabiah spun suddenly out of Othello's grasp and ended up behind him. She kicked him in the center of his back, making him stumble forward, then turned and ran. Angrily, he signaled the waiting pirates before giving chase. As she danced, Rabiah had noticed several weapons hung in decoration along the wall up the grand set of stairs. She ran for them now, taking the stairs two at a time. She reached a bow and quiver first and ripped them off the wall. There were five arrows. She spun, the bow ready in her hands. Othello was coming up the stairs behind her. She pulled back to fire an arrow toward his chest. The old string broke under the strain. She threw the bow at him and ran higher. There was a sword on display further up. She quickly lifted it from the wall and turned to face him. He raised his hands and dropped his knife.

239

"You wouldn't hurt an unarmed man would you?"

"Call them off."

"Come with me."

"No. I have a husband."

"You did."

"And still do."

He advanced a step. She did not back up. "Othello, I don't wish to kill you. I will keep our original bargain but you must stop this now."

"No deal. I want you."

He advanced another step. She made a threatening slash. He pulled a multi-pronged knife from behind his back and tried to catch her blade. She twisted the knife out of his hand and kicked. He flew backwards down the stairs. She hopped up onto the stair rail and slid down. She landed next to his prone body. His soul was still present but he wasn't moving.

Another pirate attacked. She went beneath his blade and he fell. She looked around. There had to be more than twenty attackers. Several were trying to herd the women into a mass while others were fighting the guards that the various lords had brought with them. Rabiah ran for the women. She saw a pirate fall to an invisible opponent and gave a silent cheer for Senna.

Rabiah slid between the females and the pirate closest to them who was poking at them with a crusty blade. He fell. Two more came. They were not skilled. She beat them easily, one after another. Her ring heated and she passed her own blade in front of her face. It knocked a knife away before it hit her eye. She threw one of her own knives in return. The knife-throwing pirate fell, clutching his throat. Another pirate stepped in front of her. He was dressed in dark, close-fitting material that was tailored to allow freedom of movement. It quickly became apparent that he was well-trained. She didn't have time to play. She pretended to be weaker than she was, then attacked with such fury, he honored her by blowing her a kiss as he fell. On and on they came. It was like fighting the Arles army all over again. She acquired a second short sword and stopped them all. Finally, there was no one left to fight. She lowered her arms. The floor and her clothes were covered in blood. She looked out at the dance floor. Bodies were strewn everywhere. For a second, she wanted to sink to her knees and cry. There were others standing and looking around as she was. Tristan and Owen were not far. They had worked their way closer during the fighting. Tristan was holding his upper arm. Owen's tunic was slashed but he wasn't bleeding.

"Tristan, are you and Owen all right?" she asked as they came up to her.

"Fine. Just a couple of nicks. Looks like you were busy," Tristan commented, looking at the circle of bodies before her.

"A little."

"Senna?" Owen asked, looking around.

Senna stepped from behind a curtain, "I'm here." She ran to Owen and he scooped her up into his arms.

Tristan put his uninjured arm around Rabiah and squeezed her close, planting a kiss on her head. The guards came up to talk to him. Rabiah turned to the women she had been protecting. "Is everyone all right."

She received a disjointed chorus of "Yes, Your Highness." As they passed by her to search for their husbands and escorts, many curtsied or bowed respectfully. Others completely ignored her, so intent were they on finding their escorts and escaping. An older woman curtsied then stepped close.

"Thank you for you protection. That was some fighting. Who taught you to yield a sword so well?"

"My brothers."

"They must be formidable indeed."

Rabiah gave a sad little smile. The woman leaned closer. "I have the gift of precognition. Unfortunately, I only see small pieces of bigger events. You will need this." She slipped off her bracelet. It was silver with a large black stone inset into the middle. Rabiah stepped back but her ring did not heat. She did not sense anything evil coming from it.

"It's not like those other stones," the woman said, noticing Rabiah's reaction. "It's not from the Bull temple. It is older than

241

that. It was my great-great-grandmother's. Something told me to wear it tonight and now something is telling me to give it to you. "

"I can't take this," Rabiah said.

"My great-great-grandmother had many pieces. This is one of my least favorite. Please, take it."

Rabiah put out her hand. Her ring gave no warning, so she accepted the bracelet gracefully. The woman curtsied again and walked away.

"Let me, Your Highness." Senna took the bracelet and put it on her own wrist. "It doesn't seem to have any magical properties. I'll wear it for you unless you want to wear it."

"Thanks Senna. I'll take it. She seemed trustworthy."

Senna handed it back to her. Rabiah held the bracelet to her ring. Nothing happened so she put it on.

A group of uniformed men poured through the doors. They posted themselves along the exits. The governor entered after them through the main door. He looked around, his face emotionless. When he spied Tristan and Owen his face lit up with a big smile and he hurried across the room to join them.

"He's truly relieved to see you," Owen mumbled to Tristan, "but worried too."

"King Tristan, Sir Owen, I'm so glad to see that you and your wives are safe." He got distracted by all the bodies lying around them. "Did you two defeat all these pirates?"

"No, my wife did," Tristan said proudly, "with some help from Lady Senna."

"She did?" the governor said in disbelief, noticing for the first time the two bloody swords Rabiah held.

"Yes. It's best not to make her mad," Tristan continued. "Did you not see her in action?"

"No, no. I sensed something was amiss and went to call the guard."

"Why didn't you warn us?"

"I didn't want to cause a panic. Besides, it appears you were quite able to defend yourselves." The governor was looking around as he talked as if searching for someone.

"Who are you looking for?" Tristan asked.

"Just seeing if I recognize anyone."

"You know the pirates?"

"It has been my misfortune to meet that wind-mage a few times."

"There was no wind. Why would you think he was here?"

"No reason, no reason." He looked at them again. "I guess the party is over. I'll call one of my carriages for you."

"Thank you."

The governor walked away. "Are we going to use his carriage?" Rabiah asked.

"It's probably safer than walking the streets at night dressed as we are. If there are any other pirates, at least we'll be moving faster than they. What *did* happen to the wind-mage?"

Rabiah looked toward the bottom of the stairs. The pirate was not there. "He fell down the stairs. He was still alive when I passed him."

"Where did you find that sword?" Owen asked.

Rabiah looked down at the sword in the hand Owen was pointing to. The hilt was beautifully decorated yet comfortable. The blade was thinner than she was used to but therefore lighter. After the extensive use she had made of it, she knew it was well made.

"I pulled it off the wall." She thought to put it back, but decided she'd hang on to it until they got back to the ship. She could leave it in the carriage if they made it safely.

They made their way over to the bottom of the stairs while they waited for their carriage. Tristan was curious as to where the pirate could have gone. There was blood where the pirate had fallen. A broad streak indicated someone had dragged the body away.

All around them the governor's guards and the servants were beginning to clean up. A few of the pirates were still alive. She prayed for all of them. The guests were all clustered by the main exit waiting to leave. The governor stood near the door, speaking to each of them as they passed. Some of the men shook his hand, others were quite irate and made sure the governor knew it. More than a few

243

of the ladies sobbed quietly and sought comfort on their husband's arms.

After a few minutes a servant approached to inform them that their carriage was ready. The line to exit was much reduced.

"King Tristan, please don't let this episode cloud your view of our peaceful city," the governor said when they finally reached him.

"These things happen. I hope none of the guests or their people were seriously injured."

"I'm not aware of any serious injuries among the guests. I think one of the guards was killed though."

"We thank you for your hospitality."

"How soon do you think you will depart from our fine port?"

"I'm not sure. I must speak with the captains and see how the repairs are progressing."

The governor bowed. Tristan walked past him. Rabiah was behind him and stopped in front of the governor. "Governor," she said, holding up the fancy sword, "Do you mind if I borrow this sword for the ride home? I'll leave it in the carriage when we get to the dock. It's a very nice sword."

"Ah, that. That was my predecessor's sword. I hear he was a good fighter. You may keep it."

A bright smile lit up her face, "Really? Thank you."

"You're welcome. It's the least I can do."

"It was a nice party," Rabiah said, seeking to calm him. Even without Owen's gift she could tell he was upset.

"Thank you, I'm sorry it turned into such a disaster."

"I've been at worse." She politely gave him a small nod and followed after Tristan.

A servant opened the door to the carriage. One of the guards climbed in and inspected it before Tristan and Rabiah got in. Rabiah noticed the guard had a scratch along his side. Another guard was limping slightly. He did not seem to be seriously injured. Rabiah took a seat next to the window facing backwards so she could see behind the carriage. Senna sat next to her and Tristan sat in front of her. A couple of guards climbed in. Owen sat next to the driver. More guards climbed on back. Rabiah felt very claustrophobic.

The ride was uneventful. Rabiah thought she saw a few people disappear as they drove by, but no one followed. They stopped at the end of the dock. They could just see the silhouette of the ship against the starry sky. One of the guards went with Owen to make sure the dock was clear and that all was well aboard the ship. Rabiah didn't like sitting in the cramped carriage. She was sure pirates would attack any second. She was about to insist the guards open the door and let her out when Owen came back to say all was clear. Rabiah had never been so relieved to get out of a carriage. She took a deep breath of night air and let out a small sigh.

"Are you all right?" Tristan asked.

"I am now."

Rabiah and Senna stopped to check on Lydia as soon as they boarded the ship. Kaawa was with her.

"How is she?" Rabiah asked in Kaawa's language.

"Still sleeping but no fever and no tossing. How was the party?"

"Nice until the pirates came."

"Are you hurt?" Kaawa asked noticing the blood on her clothes for the first time in the dim light.

"No, I'm unharmed, although some of the men have some scratch wounds. Is Marion awake?" Rabiah asked.

"I thought she was. She said she was going up for a bit of fresh air about a half-hour ago but would be back down to take my place. You didn't see her on deck?"

"No. I'll go look for her."

"If she's sleeping, I can heal them. I just need to go somewhere with more light."

"Thank you Kaawa."

Rabiah couldn't find Marion on deck, in her cabin, or anywhere else on the ship. Tristan and Senna helped her look. She could tell Tristan's cut was bothering him, so Rabiah ordered all the injured men, including Tristan to line up so Kaawa could fix their wounds. Senna took Kaawa's place at Lydia's side. Owen went with Rabiah to see if Marion was on one of the other ships. They couldn't find her anywhere and no one had seen her. Truly worried now, Rabiah climbed into the crow's nest and felt for souls. She was surprised

245

how many were along the docks and on the dark ships but there were none that felt remotely like Marion. She felt as far as she could but with the houses and ships in the way, she could only see so far.

'I can't feel her,' she told Tristan, *'Do you think something happened? Could she have fallen overboard?'*

'I don't see how, but we can look.'

The sailors lowered a row boat with several lanterns and searched around the ships. It was hard to wait. She was beginning to think they wouldn't find anything, which could be good or bad, she wasn't sure which, when there was a yell. She ran to the sound to see what they had discovered. The sailors in the boat were pulling something that looked like a body out of the water. Rabiah could see that whatever it was had no soul. They flipped the dark shape over. There was a face. It was Marion. No. It was a man. Rabiah felt relief it wasn't Marion and sadness that yet another person was dead. Owen went down to talk with the sailors.

"He was on guard earlier. Looks like his throat was slit," he said when he came back.

"Is anyone else missing?" Rabiah asked.

"I'll check," Owen said.

"The pirates must have her. We need to find her," Rabiah said, "Quickly, before the pirates hurt her, if they haven't already. Do any of your men have gifts that might help?" she asked the three captains who had gathered to confer. When no one else stepped forward, Senna's brother finally spoke.

"I have one with an excellent sense of smell, better than any hound. He might be able to track her." He sent a sailor to retrieve the man. The sailor came back in a few minutes with a man of average height, average weight, but an above average nose.

"Let me smell something of hers," the man said to Tristan.

Rabiah quickly retrieved a tunic from Marion's cabin. The man took it, bunched it under his nose and breathed deeply. He exhaled and breathed deeply again. Then he nodded and handed the tunic back to Rabiah.

"He's got the scent," Senna's brother said.

The man started wandering the deck of their ship, sniffing the air occasionally. He looked over the edge of the boat, then exited onto the dock. Several sailors followed him. Rabiah wanted to go but Tristan stopped her.

"They'll find her. You've done enough for one night. I can feel how tired you are and I'm tired too. Someone needs to be awake in the morning."

He was right. The only thing that was keeping her going was the serge that always came when she had to fight or there was danger. She buried her face in his shoulder as she allowed the emotions that she had pushed away until now to finally catch up to her. She did not like to kill and she knew she had done so. There had been no other way to ensure the pirates didn't get back up to hurt the women after she had brought them down. He held her tight, feeling her sorrow and regret along with his own. Finally he said gently, "Come on, let's get you cleaned up."

She woke late in the morning. The ship was rocking underneath her as if they were at sea. Was there a storm? Tristan wasn't in the cabin. She dressed quickly and went to find him. He was on deck, standing near Owen, looking out behind the ship. Land was only a thin strip on the horizon.

"Tristan! Why are we at sea? What about Marion?"

He turned to her with a smile. "Good morning sleepy head." She let him kiss her on the cheek then started at him pointedly. He laughed. "She's fine. They found her. She rescued herself. I would have awakened you when she returned but she wouldn't let me. She's still sleeping I think."

Rabiah was so overcome with emotion, she had to hang her head for a few seconds to collect herself. She finally raised her head to ask, "And why are we at sea?"

"Repairs are complete and I was tired of those pirates. Hopefully it will be clear all the way back. Some wedding trip, eh?"

"Would have been rather boring otherwise," Rabiah said, standing close so he could put his arm around her.

"Boring would have been fine with me," Owen commented, "I think I'll go see if Senna is awake."

Rabiah stood looking out at the water for a few minutes then asked, "What shall we do today?"

Tristan was looking pale, "First, you are going to eat. I've noticed I feel better after you eat."

"Sorry, my husband. I'll go right now. I love you," she said, kissing him on the cheek. She left him in the fresh air and went down to the galley in search of food.

Chapter 18

Lydia still slept. After breakfast, Rabiah took Kaawa's place at Lydia's side. Marion woke around noon and came to change places with Rabiah.

Rabiah hugged Marion tightly. "What happened? How did you escape?"

Marion shrugged. "They surprised me when I was walking around the deck. One of them climbed over the side and grabbed me. He put his hand over my mouth so I couldn't scream. I don't think he must have ever washed his hands as bad as they smelled. He jumped with me in his arms. I thought we would surely die, but he landed easily. That must have been his gift. They rowed me away to a filthy, smelly tavern and took me to a back room. The wind-mage was there. They wanted me to heal him but I didn't have any of my supplies except for the sleeping powder. I told them that. They found a few supplies and brought them, but it was too late. He died. I noticed because the bracelets on his wrists suddenly became loose. I grabbed his wrists and pretended to be healing him. His wrists were awful. I don't know that I could have saved his arms even with my supplies. They were watching me closely so I couldn't remove the bracelets, but I angled them so they didn't look loose. I turned my back on them to get a cup of water, or so I let them believe. One of the pirates, I think it was one of the ones who came with him when he visited us, realized Othello was dead. I turned to find them all looking at me like they were going to kill me. I blew some sleeping dust into the air and put my dusty hand into the face of anyone who tried to grab me. There were only a five pirates in the room with me so it didn't take long. I slipped the bracelets off and walked as calmly as I could out of the room. I didn't want to walk through the bar area so I looked for a back door. I found one, then I regretted it. The alleyway was scarier than the tavern. Have you ever felt like someone was watching you? It felt like at least ten sets of eyes were on me. I didn't run though. Fear makes predators hungrier. I could hear several voices in front of the tavern so I stopped at the edge of the building to figure out how I could get around them. I almost jumped out of my skin when one of them, an Ibirannian, stepped in front of me and bowed. He was part of my rescue party. I've never been so happy to see a bunch of men in my life."

She reached into her pocket and pulled out the bracelets. "I cleaned them."

"I almost wish I had never seen these things," Rabiah said, taking them from her.

"You warned him and tried to be fair. You protected all of us by using those."

"Why must I take so many lives to protect the ones I love," Rabiah sighed.

Marion pulled her into another hug. "You've saved more than you've harmed. Without you it would have been much worse."

Lydia awoke later that afternoon. Ice was sent around the ship with the good news. Rabiah immediately put down her book and went with Tristan to see her. Lydia was propped up with pillows and looked like a pale, golden angle. Rabiah surprised herself by feeling a surge of affection for Lydia. She took her limp hand and greeted her with a big smile.

"Hello Lydia. I'm glad you are finally awake."

"You are?" Lydia said skeptically.

"We both are," Tristan said firmly.

"We were afraid we would lose you for a while," Rabiah added. "How are you feeling?"

"Sore. Especially my arm, but it feels better than it did. Was it infected?"

"Not in the way you would think," Marion said.

"May I see?"

"I'll show you later when I change the bandage. Your Highnesses, would you mind sitting with Lydia while I go find her something to eat?"

"Not at all," Rabiah said. She sat down on the stool near the bed. Tristan found one near the wall.

"So tell me what happened while I've been sleeping. How many days have passed?"

"You were asleep for five days," Rabiah said.

"Five days! What happened?"

"The seeds were cursed," Tristan said.

"So the healer we rescued was trying to kill me?" Lydia asked.

"No. Kaawa didn't know they were bad," Rabiah said.

"So how did you break the curse?"

"The Queen made a deal with the wind-mage," Tristan said.

"What deal?"

"He wanted your plant off his ship. I told him if he helped us, I'd let him ask you for help," Rabiah said.

"Is he here then?"

"No, he's dead," Rabiah said.

"Did you kill him?"

"Yes."

"Not directly," Tristan cut in.

"No, but the result was the same," Rabiah said.

"Tell me what happened," Lydia said.

Rabiah did. Killing strangers was easy. Killing someone whose story you knew was harder. For some reason, she had liked the wind-mage. If he had just trusted her a little more, or maybe if she had just gone as his hostage he would still be alive. Would things have turned out better? Perhaps not for the people the pirates preyed upon.

Marion arrived just as Rabiah finished the story. Rabiah stood to get out of the way. "We'll go so you can eat."

"Queen Rabiah," Lydia said.

"Yes, Lydia?" Rabiah stopped at the door and looked back.

"Thank you for saving me. Don't blame yourself for his death. It was his own fault."

Rabiah didn't agree with her but she nodded before she left.

Chapter 19

It took another week to reach Ibirann. They had been gone a little over a month from Arles. Reports from the North described a winter colder and stormier than anyone could remember. It was even a little cooler than normal in Ibirann. No one was eager to get back to the cold. King Abbus encouraged them to stay a while longer and take a tour of his beautiful country. Several of his sons and grandsons were planning an extensive hunting and camping trip inland. There were many beautiful lakes and waterfalls to see. King Abbus' second wife, Niyaf, and her daughter, Iris seemed pleased when Rabiah agreed to accompany them. Senna, Kaawa, and Ice went too. Most of the advisors who hadn't already returned to Arles stayed behind. Lydia, who was still recovering, stayed behind as well.

When they returned three weeks later, a change had come over the palace. Whereas the gardens had looked beautiful before, now they were outstanding with lush, green leaves and vibrant blooms everywhere.

"I see Lydia has enjoyed herself," Tristan commented.

"It's beautiful," Rabiah agreed.

Kaawa and Ice had not returned with them. They had met a group of traders heading in the direction of Kaawa's home country. The traders had agreed to take Kaawa and Ice there if Kaawa would serve as their healer.

That night, they shared stories of their travels. As before, the men and women ate separately. After the meal there was entertainment. The servants wheeled out a large wooden frame painted gold with many strings strung within it. Rabiah was at a loss to guess what it was.

'What is that Tristan?' she sent across the room.

'It is a harp.'

'That's what Lydia can play?'

'Yes.'

'I wonder if she played it while we were gone.'

Lydia stood and glided over to the harp. Gracefully she sat down. As if completely unaware of the rest of the people in the room, she began to pluck the strings. Rabiah had never heard anything like it. The music was so peaceful and soothing. It made her feel closer to the Great Spirit somehow. She sat quietly and closed her eyes so she could listen without distraction from her other senses.

Lydia finished to much applause and returned to her pillow. Everyone else seemed to like her playing but she couldn't help looking Rabiah's way to see her reaction. The room divider had been removed so the women were all veiled. All she could see of Rabiah was her closed eyes. Niyaf noticed Lydia looking and nudged Rabiah. Rabiah's eyes flew open and landed on Lydia. Lydia could tell she was smiling. Had Rabiah been doing whatever it was she and Tristan did because of their shared gift? So the Queen didn't like her music. No matter. Everyone else did. Lydia looked away. She didn't realize Rabiah had moved from her place at the table to squat behind her until Rabiah spoke.

"That was beautiful Lydia."

Lydia felt a little thrill at the compliment. "Thank you, Your Highness. I thought you had fallen asleep."

"No. I was enjoying your music with the Great Spirit."

"You were praying?"

"More like listening. Where did you find the harp?"

"It was in the music room. Some of the women play."

"I wonder if there's one in our castle. I'd love to hear you play again when we get back."

Rabiah went back to her seat as some male dancers ran out.

King Abbus leaned over to Tristan as the dancers performed.

"That girl, Lydia, who speaks for her?"

"She speaks for herself."

"She has no male guardian?"

"That would be me I suppose."

"Tell me more about her. What is her history? She is obviously well brought-up."

Tristan took a sip of his drink before beginning. "Her father planned for her to marry me. He brought her up to be a queen, but he also dabbled in demons. We suspect it was he who paid the assassin to kill my parents and Rabiah. He traded his soul to a demon so the demon would take control of Arles and put Lydia on the throne. The demon did not succeed. He even paid a large sum to have Lydia's powers enhanced so they would be more worthy of a queen."

"Enhanced?"

"Yes. She told us her gift was to make flowers bloom. Now she can make a full plant sprout from seed in just a few minutes."

"So her father was ambitious."

"Yes."

"Her mother?"

"Died when she was young."

"What do you plan to do with her?"

"Rabiah has hired her as an assistant of sorts. She has a home in the castle. Beyond that I cannot say."

"She is very gifted."

"Yes."

"She needs a husband who will appreciate her gifts."

"I suppose."

"And a position of limited power."

"That would be best I think."

"I'd like to ask her hand in marriage."

"To whom?" Tristan asked, surprised.

"To me."

Tristan opened his mouth but nothing came out. Finally, he said the first thing, well the second thing he could think of, "but you have daughters older than she."

255

"It is not unheard of for an older man to take a younger wife."

"No, I suppose not," Tristan said after a few seconds. "I will speak to her and see if she wishes to accept your proposal."

Lydia was still sleeping in the women's room connected to the guest bedroom where Tristan and Rabiah slept. Tristan stopped her before she retired for the night. Rabiah was already in bed but still awake.

"Lydia, King Abbus asked for your hand in marriage. How do you want me to respond?"

"He did?" She sounded pleased Tristan thought.

"Yes."

Lydia dropped down to sit on the end of the bed. "I don't know what to say."

"Are you interested in him as a husband?" Tristan asked.

"He's very nice. He let me try things in his gardens. He even made suggestions. He heard me practicing the harp and said I should play tonight."

"How does he talk to you if he's not supposed to speak to you?"

"He doesn't. His daughters or one of his wives walk with us and he talks to them where I can hear."

"There are other considerations when it comes to a husband," Rabiah said. "He's old enough to be your father."

"He doesn't seem that old."

"He has three other wives," Tristan said.

"I know. They all have their own beds. They don't have to sleep with their husband every night. They take turns. I wouldn't mind."

"You'd have to wear a veil for the rest of your life," Rabiah said.

"I rather like them."

"And while you are always welcome in Arles, Ibirann would be your home," Tristan said.

"I don't have a home in Arles anymore and the only family I have is as good as dead. This is a beautiful place where plants grow year round. I could be happy here."

"Sleep on it Lydia before you make your decision. It is not one to make lightly," Tristan said.

"Like you did?" she asked, not quite innocently.

"That was different."

Lydia gave him a skeptical look and turned to Rabiah. "What would you do?"

"Pray for guidance."

"And then?"

"If I truly thought I could be happy here for the rest of my life I'd say yes, but so many things can happen. You are still young Lydia. You could find a husband without other wives who is closer to your age."

"Who would have me? I have no dowry, or very little anyway."

"But you have some remarkable gifts."

"Lydia, I will find you a husband in Arles if you desire," Tristan said.

"Do you not want me to marry King Abbus?"

"I don't want you to marry him and then regret it."

"I will think on what you have said." Lydia pushed herself up and walked to the women's room. At the door she turned and said, "If I say yes I'll finally be a Queen."

"But at what price Lydia?" Rabiah asked.

Lydia gave her answer first thing the next morning. Tristan waited all day to speak to King Abbus in case she changed her mind but she remained firm. As soon as the entertainment began after the evening meal, King Abbus turned to Tristan and eagerly asked, "Did you have a chance to speak with Lydia?"

"She said yes, but," Tristan continued quickly before King Abbus got too excited, "I was wondering, would it not be better to have her as a daughter? You'd still be able to enjoy her talents but she'd have a husband closer to her own age."

"You are suggesting she marry one of my sons?"

"If you didn't mind either way, then yes."

"No. I want her for myself. I have not felt such interest in a woman for a long time."

"She is young enough to be your daughter."

"It doesn't seem that way."

"That's the same thing she said."

"Did she?" King Abbus smiled and gazed Lydia's way. Lydia raised her head as if she could feel the King's gaze upon her. Heart sinking, Tristan suddenly realized what might be going on.

'Rabiah, look at King Abbus. Has Lydia extended her influence again?'

There was a pause before she answered. *'Not that I can see from here. Does Owen see anything?'*

Tristan silently asked Owen to look. Owen shook his head. It was a concern though. Tristan cleared his throat to get King Abbus' attention. "There is something we must speak about concerning Lydia." He paused and waited for King Abbus' full attention. "Her power doesn't just affect plants. She can influence people too."

"You don't think she's using her powers on me do you?"

"No. Sir Owen can see it. It does not appear to be affecting you, but that doesn't mean she won't use it unintentionally or otherwise in the future."

"So you are saying I shouldn't marry her?"

"No. Just be careful. Her powers can be blocked with copper bracelets."

"On me or her?"

"Her, although it might work if they are on you, but the bracelets would block your gift too."

"Do you know what my gift is?" King Abbus asked with amusement.

"No."

"I can control dogs. I don't like dogs. They slobber and they smell. They are worse than babies. I'll wear the bracelets and I'll have my advisors keep an eye on me."

"One other thing," Tristan said, "What happens if she outlives you?"

"A good question since that is likely. All of my wives will have the option to retire to the smaller palace or return to the homes of their fathers. Or, if they have sons, the sons may choose to provide them a house. They will all receive enough money to support them for the remainder of their lives. We can let the lawyers decide a proper sum for Lydia tomorrow."

The wedding took place a week later. Lydia made a wedding tunic out of the fabric she had purchased on their trip. Rabiah thought she looked absolutely beautiful, even under a veil. Only a few people worshiped the bull in Ibirann but there was a priest of the bull there as well as the leader of King Abbus' religion. A wedding was one of the only times an Ibirannian man was allowed to sit with a woman in public. Lydia sat proudly next to her new husband as the celebration went deep into the night. She seemed happy. Rabiah didn't feel much like celebrating.

The women around Rabiah all began to stand.

"What's going on?" Rabiah asked Niyaf.

"We're going to get the bride ready. She was your handmaiden, you are the closest she has to a mother here. You must go get her and bring her to us."

Rabiah did as instructed. It seemed as if every eye was on her as she crossed the open space between the men and the women. Lydia was expecting her. She rose gracefully from the pillow beside her new husband and took Rabiah's outstretched hand. Lydia's hand was clammy. Rabiah gave Lydia's hand a little squeeze before dropping it as they began walking back across the floor.

"Nervous?"

"A little."

"I was too."

"You were?"

"Yes, but only when I thought about it. When I was with him, before we became fully man and wife, I wasn't nervous at all."

"I thought he married you on the battlefield."

"He did, but I was injured, then he was ill. It was several weeks before anything happened."

"What is it like?"

They had reached the women's side. The other women crowded around them. It suddenly dawned on Rabiah to wonder how much Lydia knew about what happened between men and women. Lydia had no mother and no female friends. Rabiah had only known

259

because her sister-in-law had explained it. She walked with the group as the other women, talking happily, led them on. They took Lydia to a large room with many beds. They helped her removed her jewels and veils and bridal tunic, then they wrapped her in a traditional red bridal robe that Rabiah had found for her. The other women didn't seem too impressed.

"What is traditional here?" Rabiah asked Niyaf. Rabiah had practiced speaking Ibirannian during their long camping trip. They could now communicate much more easily.

"It's a long, flowing garment that's almost see-through. I didn't wear it on my wedding night either. Our traditional garment is more of a very long wrap. The man has to work to get to us," she smiled.

"I'm not sure she knows what's coming."

"We will escort her to the King's room. You can speak with her then. I won't let King Abbus in until you are done."

The women put long veils over Lydias' head and face. The colors went well with the red of the robe. Lydia looked very mysterious. Led by the first wife, the women escorted Lydia down a long hallway in the direction of the men's sleeping quarters. They entered a spacious bedroom with a large bed in the middle. The women had Lydia climb into the bed, then they arranged her veils and the robe around her. She looked beautiful. Rabiah thought it a bit disturbing that she was to be presented so obviously, but she was not Lydia.

The other women left back down the hallway. Niyaf went out the door that led to the men's side. "I will be right here," she said as she shut the door, leaving Rabiah and Lydia alone. Rabiah sat on the edge of the bed. "You look very lovely."

"I feel very strange. What happens next?"

"Has anyone explained to you what happens between a man and a woman?"

"I know they kiss. You and King Tristan certainly do it a lot."

"Do you know how babies are made?"

"I know a woman must be married first, or should be."

Rabiah bit her lip as she looked at Lydia, trying to decide what to say. She didn't want to make her more nervous than she already was.

However, she should have some idea of what to expect. She finally said, "He will touch you. All of you. I don't know if they do things differently in this country, but there might be no clothes between you. And you can touch him. All of him. And at some point he will join with you. The first time there will be pain, but that only happens once."

"What do you mean, join with me?"

"You'll see. Men and women have different parts for a reason. Don't be nervous. I'm sure King Abbus knows just what to do. I'll bet he will enjoy teaching you. Your body will know what to do. Just follow his lead."

"I can't do this."

"Remember when I asked you to kiss Owen and you said the same thing?"

"Yes. And I didn't kiss him."

"But did you want to?"

"Not really."

"Do you want to kiss King Abbus?"

Lydia thought a little, then nodded. "Yes. I have wanted to for a while."

"Then don't worry about the rest. Start with the kiss. That's the hardest part."

"Really?" Lydia asked half skeptical, half hopeful.

"Really."

Lydia took a deep breath. "I can do this. I can kiss him. I want to kiss him."

"Good." Rabiah could hear male voices approaching, "He will be here shortly." Rabiah stood and walked over to the door where Niyaf waited.

"Queen Rabiah?" Lydia said.

"Yes?" Rabiah turned, her hand on the door.

"Will I like it?"

Rabiah studied her for a moment. Other than Tristan, Lydia hadn't shown any interest in men before, and she had been irritated with any signs of physical affection on their wedding trip. "I don't

261

know," Rabiah answered honestly, "but you might enjoy it more than you ever imagined."

Rabiah pulled open the door. Men were lining the hallway. True to her word, Niyaf was blocking the door. Tristan was with the group of men behind King Abbus.

"Let's go," she told Niyaf. Together, they crossed the room and departed through the women's entrance. Rabiah looked back as she shut the door. King Abbus was crossing the room heading towards Lydia, a big smile on his face. She could just see Tristan in the other doorway. He raised his eyebrow at her. She gave him a little wave, then closed the door.

'Why was Niyaf blocking the door?' Tristan sent a few seconds later.

'Someone had to tell Lydia what was coming.'

'She didn't know.'

'No.'

'Wish I'd thought to ask her before she agreed to the marriage.'

'I think she'll be all right. She was looking forward to kissing him.'

'Stop. I don't want to know any more.'

'What? You don't think it's sweet that they've found each other?'

'Very sweet. I just don't want to envision it.'

After the rather challenging talk with Lydia, Rabiah was feeling ornery. *'Do you think King Abbus has kissed her yet? I wonder if his lips are dry or soft.'*

'Rabiah! Stop that.'

'Do you think he's started undressing her yet? I got her a bridal robe.'

'Rabiah!'

'Remember when you started undressing me?' She suddenly wasn't interested in teasing him.

'I remember.' He felt her want and shared it, *'Where are you?'*

'Almost back to the women's quarters.'

'Can you slip away? I'll meet you in the dining hall.'

'What about my guard?'

'I'll bring mine.'

"Rabiah!"

Belatedly, Rabiah realized Niyaf had been talking to her.

"Sorry Niyaf. What did you say?" Niyaf shook her head. She'd noticed that Rabiah often seemed to get lost in her thoughts. She should caution her about that.

"Did it go well with Lydia?"

"I think so. I didn't tell her everything, just enough, I hope, that she wouldn't be shocked. I didn't want to make her even more nervous. Does everyone just go to bed now that the bride and groom have left?"

"Oh, no. The party is only just beginning. The men will drink for an hour, then go and serenade the couple."

"What?"

"Don't worry, they won't go in the room. Afterwards, they will come out and drink some more. Most end up sleeping it off in the dining room."

"What do the women do?"

"We party in our rooms, those of us who don't have children to care for in the morning. You can join us."

"Would you mind if I didn't?"

"Why?"

"My husband..." Rabiah felt a blush creeping up her cheeks.

"Ah. Did he indicate he wanted you? You should go then, but not through the main room. The men are in there and the women's guard are not. I'll show you another way to the guest rooms."

Rabiah let Tristan know she would meet them in their room and followed Niyaf. Niyaf led her outside into one of the gardens and around the back of the palace. Above the palace wall Rabiah could see the starry night stretching high above the trees. "It is so lovely here."

"Don't you have skies in Arles?" Niyaf asked.

"Yes, but no trees with flowers that smell so good."

"It is not time for these to bloom yet. It will be interesting with our new fourth wife around."

"Does it bother you that there is another?"

"What is one more? My husband has much love to give. I don't mind sharing."

"I like having my husband all to myself."

263

"You are young and do not yet have children to take away your time."

"We will," Rabiah said, putting her hand to her slightly swollen belly.

"I thought so." They shared a smile.

"Come, the door we seek is down this way. You must not keep your husband waiting." Rabiah followed. It was dark, but the stars and the sliver of moon gave enough light to walk safely on the path. Rabiah's ring suddenly grew hot. Instinctively, she grabbed Niyaf's arm to pull her closer and drew one of the knives from her arm holders. Dark shapes surrounded them. One of them grabbed Niyaf. One tried to grab Rabiah but she stabbed him in the face with her knife and elbowed another in the throat before stabbing him in the belly.

"Stop!" a man yelled, "or I will kill this one."

"What do you want?" Rabiah asked with her knives up, ready for more. She switched to her soul sight. At least ten. Two were already injured. She could take on eight. If only she had two more knives!

"Are you Queen Rabiah?"

"Yes."

"We want you."

"Why?"

Niyaf yelped, "No questions or I stab her again. You are to come with us."

Rabiah looked at the dark shape that held Niyaf. It was too dark to safely target him. Niyaf would fight him if she could but Rabiah didn't know how badly injured she was. "I will go with you if you set her free."

"No, Rabiah," Niyaf said in her language. She yelped again.

"If you kill her I will fight you and you will all die." Rabiah looked around. "All ten of you. I've already injured two."

A couple of the souls moved a step back. With her veils on, her face was shrouded in dark. All they could see were her eyes and they were glowing.

"You will come peacefully?"

"You have my word, I will come peacefully, but I will not move until she is released and safely through the door."

She quickly sent a message telling Tristan and Owen where they were and what was going on. Hopefully she could delay her would-be kidnappers until help came.

The man pushed Niyaf toward the door. "Go!"

Niyaf was holding her side, "I will not."

The man kicked Niyaf hard, in the chest, knocking her to the ground. Rabiah ran and attacked him from the side with a running kick. It was like hitting a tree. She bounced off but managed to land on her feet. She knew how to take a tree down. She dropped and swept his legs out from under him. He fell but grabbed at her. She scooted away. He kept coming. She rolled backwards. Her veils got in her way. She couldn't see. She ripped them off.

"Do it!" one of the men yelled.

Her ring heated. She looked around but didn't see anything flying at her. Several of the souls around her fell to the ground. She was still squatting close to the ground. The man who had kicked Niyaf had stopped after the yell but now he lunged at her and tried to grab her arm. Her ring heated. A light like a lightning spark shot out from her wrist to his hand. His hand was thrown away. She took advantage of his distraction to stab at his neck with her knife. It was like trying to stab a piece of petrified wood.

"Seems like we are at an impasse. I can't grab you and you can't stab me."

"So leave then."

"Not without you." He yelled to the men around them, "Grab the other one."

There were three left standing. Rabiah threw the knives she held at the souls who moved toward Niyaf. One fell. The other stopped. She pulled the knives from the holders around her calves.

"You're down to two," she said.

"And there's only one of you."

Her ring heated. She moved to the side as a knife went flying by. She flung one of hers back at the source. The soul moved as if the body were staggering back. She had been wrong about the two. The one who had stopped when she'd thrown her first set of knives moved towards Niyaf again. Rabiah sprang up suddenly and charged him. The man on the ground tried to grab her as she went over him but she avoided his hands and used his back as a springboard to tackle the other one. He went down. Rabiah made sure he'd stay down by punching him in the throat. She rolled back in front of Niyaf and crouched with her knife ready. With her normal sight, she could just see Niyaf lying on the ground behind her holding her side.

"You're down to one."

"Look again little Queen. Your friend is injured. If you don't come with me we will kill her."

She switched back to her soul sight. There were at least ten more.

"You'll have to get through me first."

"They have bows. It shouldn't be hard."

It was dark. She couldn't see to block them and her ring only protected her. But she only had to hold him off for a minute or so more.

"Niyaf, can you get up?" she asked in Ibirann, hoping the man would not be able to understand.

"Not without help," Niyaf squeezed out.

"I just need you to crouch behind me. I can protect you if you are right behind me. Hold on to me and pull yourself up."

Niyaf attempted to rise. Rabiah placed herself in front of Niyaf's head and torso. Niyaf made it to a sitting position but couldn't go any further. She leaned her head and shoulder onto Rabiah's back. She heard the twang of a bow. Rabiah's ring heated and it missed to her right. The second one passed her on the left.

"This is your last chance little Queen. The archers have you surrounded. You can't block her entire body with yours. Surrender or I will attack. Your friend will not survive."

What would happen if she had Niyaf lay down and she lay on top of her? Would the ring do all the work? It had protected her directly on occasion, but usually the ring warned her or helped direct her movements so she could defend herself. A well placed arrow would be able to reach Niyaf.

'Tristan, where are you?'

'Coming. We're almost to the door. We went the wrong way.'

"Tell me why you want me so badly." she said to the man.

"I don't. The bull priests want you."

"Why?"

"Who knows?

"Are they paying you?"

"No. It was part of the deal."

Rabiah suddenly placed the voice. It was one of Othello's friends.

"What deal?"

"Doesn't matter. Are you coming with me or shall I kill your friend?"

'Tristan?'

'Wrong door.'

'If I surrender they'll let Niyaf live. They have us surrounded. I'll try to slow them down so you can rescue me.'

'Rabiah, wait!'

'I'm out of time.'

"I will go with you but you must promise none of your people will touch her or injure her any further."

"Deal."

"Rabiah, no."

"It's all right Niyaf. My husband will be here soon," she said in Ibirann.

"Move. Now." The man barked.

Rabiah squeezed Niyaf's shoulder and stood up. She just had to give Tristan time. She would go with them but she didn't promise she'd stay with them.

She put her knife into the holder on her arm and walked away as slowly as she dared.

'Rabiah I'm almost there. I know we're close. I can feel you.'

"Seal the door," the man ordered.

One of the archers ran up and touched the door. The crack around the door disappeared as the wood of the frame and the wood of the door merged.

267

Tristan, they've sealed the door somehow. You'll have to come another way.'

'You're still there?'

'Yes, they're collecting all the injured.'

The man was behind her, supervising.

"Let's move." He indicated Rabiah should start walking. She did so, slowly. There was a loud thump as something hit the sealed door.

"Move faster or she dies."

Rabiah looked back. There was no one near Niyaf. The man saw her looking.

"There's an archer in the tree. He'll wait for my signal before he leaves. If we don't get to the ship within the designated time he'll kill her."

"How will he know when you've reached the ship?"

"We have our ways."

"You made a deal."

"I didn't promise I wouldn't kill her."

Tristan, the man says Niyaf is covered by an archer. They're taking me to a ship. I think he's one of the pirates.'

'Can you get away?'

'Not yet. He says they have a way of communicating with the archer. If we don't reach the ship the archer will kill her. I can't tell if he's bluffing. There are too many branches and trees.'

'Why do they want you?'

'He said the bull priests want me. Something about a deal.'

"One more thing little Queen," the man said. "You must put these on." He showed her a pair of locking copper bracelets.

"That wasn't part of the deal."

"It is now." He nodded towards one of the archers helping another man along. "Watch your friend."

Rabiah turned to look. A flaming arrow landed near Niyaf. It went out in the moist dirt. "Put them on or the next one hits her heart."

'He's not bluffing.'

"Now!"

She put her wrists out. He tried to slam them on but they flew off.

"Pick them up and put them on," he growled.

"I may not be able to."

"You better or she dies."

She did as he asked. They stayed on. He locked them and put the string the key was on around his neck.

"How did you know we'd be here? We didn't even know we'd be here."

"One of the pirates has the gift of premonition. Very unpredictable but sometimes it works out. Now start walking or I'll test and see how well those bracelets work."

She started walking.

'Tristan, they made me put copper bracelets on.'

There was no response. *'Tristan? Please answer me.'*

Still no response. She followed their link and ran into a copper-colored wall sitting right across it. Uncle had been wrong. Their powers could be blocked by copper. Desperately, she search for her link to Owen. It was completely gone. Why was Tristan's link still there? She switched back to her soul sight. She couldn't see anything but the dark shapes around her. She tried feeling for souls. She could feel the two little ones in her belly but no others. She stumbled on something in the dark.

"Copper's working eh?" the pirate heckled. "Can't see in the dark anymore can you? No need to worry. The wagon is right here. Climb in."

In the dark she could just make out the rectangular shape of a wagon with low sides. She climbed in and sat in the corner. The pirates piled their downed comrades in and sat around the edges. The wagon was crowded. It started moving rapidly downhill. Rabiah closed her eyes. *'Great Spirit, please guide me. I don't know what to do.'*

She felt a sense of peace wash over her. *'Patience.'* She felt. *'Patience.'*

The Spirit was with her. She would wait. She tried to calm her mind but it was racing too fast. She could try to reach Tristan again. She followed the link. There was the copper. She touched it in her mind. It was flat and smooth like copper should be. She tried pushing against it, but it wouldn't move. Could she go around it? She looked it every direction but it stretched as far as she could see all around. The link looked like it was going through the copper, but was it? She sent a pulse of heat along the line. It flowed like a bead until it reached the metal, then stopped. Rabiah concentrated on pushing the bead through the copper. It didn't move. She wanted to scream in frustration. She took deep breaths to calm herself. They were soul mates. She hadn't had a gift until she met Tristan. Her gift was still working, it was just limited to her own body. Didn't that mean their souls were still joined? It had happened when he kissed her. They had gone somewhere else. It was a place very different from here. There were clouds, not earth, not metal. Their link had been forged there. That was where she needed to go. She imagined kissing him. She imagined the way the kiss had felt. She focused on him and shut out everything else. There were the clouds and that feeling of peace and joy, but where was he?

Tristan? she asked quietly, then louder and longer *'TRISTAN!'*

Something was pulling her away. *'TRISTAN!'*

She opened her eyes to find the pirate shaking her. Her eyes were glowing so much he took a step back.

"Get out of the wagon."

She complied.

"Go. In front of me to that ship, there."

She did as he instructed. She thought of diving off the other side but she couldn't be sure Niyaf was safe yet. She looked around as she walked on the ship. There were many men busily preparing to set sail. She felt a breeze ruffle her hair and turned to look. A thin man in a long cloak and long hair stood at the helm watching them board. His cloak seemed to move on its own accord. Othello? But he was dead. A shorter man whom she recognized as Othello's other friend met them.

"I see you had a few casualties.

"We got lucky. She was with another woman. If she hadn't been trying to protect the other woman we probably wouldn't have made it back."

"She's just a girl."

"Her eyes glow. She can see in the dark. She knew how many of us there were. She stabbed John in the cheek, Marcos in the stomach, and got Mac in the throat. She would have gotten me if it weren't for my gift."

"What happened to the rest?"

"The wind must have changed when we tried to use the night berry. They all went down."

"Yet you got the bracelets on her."

"She put them on herself to protect her friend."

"Ralphy was very pleased when he saw you had her. It was the first time I've seen him smile since he came back."

"Maybe he'll finally go back to normal."

"He wants her in the captain's cabin."

"That's not a good idea."

"I know. Let's put her downstairs for now. We can fetch her when he's free. I'll keep an eye on her. You go keep Ralphy in check. He knows the faster he can get away the faster he can see her and I'm afraid he's going to make us fly, literally."

The shorter pirate led her below deck and showed her to a very small room with a couple of bunks built into one wall and not much else. There was no window and only one door. It was very dark. She did not want to go in. What would happen if she fought now?

'Now?' she asked.

'Patience.'

She went into the small room and sat on the bottom bunk. The pirate shut and looked the door. It was pitch black. There was nothing to do but lay back. She would try to reach Tristan again. She was sure she'd been close. The ship started to move. She imagined kissing Tristan again and the feeling she got. It was easier to get there this time. Tristan was probably worried about her and wondering why he couldn't reach her. Her heart felt like it would overflow with love for him. Where was he? She couldn't see him. She could only see clouds and something that looked like trees in the distance. She closed her eyes and listened the way she listened for the Spirit. The Spirit was there, all around. It loved her. It encircled her and held

271

her as she cried tears of joy to be there and tears of sadness that Tristan wasn't with her. Then she felt a tug. She could feel him, her husband. Laughing, she ran and dove toward him. It was like slipping down a mud slide except without the mud.

'Tristan!'

He was there. His joy at her presence washed over her. She took his hand, or his equivalent of a hand and pulled him back up into the clouds with her.

'Rabiah! Thank the Spirit. You are all right?'

'Yes.'

'Why couldn't I reach you?'

'They bound me with copper. Our link is still there, but I had to find another way around.'

'Where are you?'

'On a ship. I think we just left the docks. How is Niyaf? Is she alive?'

'Yes. She's with the healers. I think she'll be all right. She was stabbed in the side and might have a couple of cracked ribs.'

'I'm sorry I couldn't wait anymore.'

'Niyaf told us what you did to protect her. I would have done the same. Are they treating you all right?'

'They've locked me in a very small cabin with no window and no light.'

'So no way to escape.'

'Not that I can see.'

'We're coming. We're on our way to the ships as we speak. I'd better go so we can board.'

'I love you Tristan.'

'I love you too.'

Chapter 20

'*What should I do now, Great Spirit?*' she asked. She suddenly felt very tired. Sleep would be good. She closed her eyes. At some point she found her way back up to the clouds. Tristan was already there. She ran to him joyfully. He picked her up and swung her around.

'*How did you know I would come?*' she asked him.

'*I didn't. I can feel you from here. Owen said when you contacted me before he had to grab me or I would have fallen off my horse. He's watching me. Whichever way I try to go, that's the way we're heading. Are you still in the little cabin?*'

'*Yes. The Spirit told me to sleep.*'

'*I wish I could just pull you to me.*'

'*I wish you could too.*'

'*Sleep here, with me. I'll watch over you.*'

'*There's no danger here. You can sleep too.*'

'*I don't want to sleep. I want to hold you.*'

She lay down on the soft cloud and he lay beside her, wrapping his arms around her and pulling her close. She slept. It was perhaps the most comfortable sleep she'd ever had.

She awoke to something brushing her face. She flinched but didn't open her eyes. She could smell something familiar. It smelled like ocean air on the wind at the front of a storm. It smelled like Othello.

"Wake up my Warrior Queen. I've been waiting all night to see you. I've been patient. Isn't that what you asked of me? Now it's time to wake up."

It was Othello's voice. Rabiah opened her eyes. It *was* Othello. He had a lantern with him so it wasn't as dark.

"Othello?! How are you here?"

"You mean how am I alive?"

Rabiah nodded.

"I got a miracle."

"How?" she asked.

He pulled a black stone on a chain from under his shirt. There was a large crack across it. "All that money I gave to the priests finally paid off. After your healer disappeared, leaving me dead, my friends took me to the priests. They restored my life and healed me." He held up his wrists. In the dim light she could see faint scars where he had tried to remove the bracelets.

"I am glad they were able to help you."

"Are you?"

"Yes. I never wanted you dead."

He smiled at her and extended his hand. "Come with me out of this little room. I told them to put you in my cabin but they didn't listen. You are my queen, not my prisoner."

She pushed herself up. "But..." A surge of nausea hit her. She quickly lay back down. It was too late. She was going to be sick. She leaned over the side of the bed and heaved. There wasn't much in her stomach. Othello jumped back.

"Sorry," she said, wiping her mouth with the back of her hand and laying back on the bunk. Her eyes were watering.

"You're sick."

"I just need a couple of crackers or some bread and I'll be fine."

"I thought we could eat breakfast together," he said, sounding unsure.

She was hungry and nauseous at the same time. Is this what Tristan felt every morning? "I just need a little something to settle my stomach. Can you bring me some bread or crackers and a little water?"

"Sure. Yes. I'll be right back." He shut the door and locked it, taking the light with him.

It seemed to take forever for him to return. The smell of her own stomach juices in the small room did nothing to ease the nausea. She knew if she moved she'd just be sick again.

He finally returned. Stepping carefully and reaching as far as he could, he handed her a piece of bread. She took a few bites and lay still for a minute before sitting up to take a sip from the canteen he offered. She put her head on the wall behind her and concentrated on breathing instead of her overly-watering mouth.

"Thank you. That's much better," she finally said.

"Would you like to eat with me?"

She was wary of going with him, but she could not stay in the little room anymore, not with the smell. She nodded and carefully stood. She felt much better once they were above deck and she could breathe the fresh air. She followed him across the deck to the captain's cabin. His taller friend stopped him.

"Ralphy, I told you to leave her down there."

Othello waved him off, "She needs to eat."

"We can just take her some food."

"She was sick."

"If she has motion sickness she won't keep it down anyway."

"She is a queen. She should be treated as such."

"She is a girl with dangerous powers. Leave her be."

"I'm going to eat breakfast with her."

"You're going to be sorry."

"She is bound and I am not. She cannot hurt me."

"I wouldn't be so sure of that. I will guard you as you eat."

"There is no need."

"Humor me."

Othello sighed and marched on. Rabiah followed him. The pirate followed them both.

There was already food laid out on the small table in the cabin. Rabiah wondered if all the beautiful wooden furniture was Othello's or if had belonged to the former captain. She guessed the latter. Along with the small table which had two chairs, there was a chest, a built-in bed, a bookshelf with doors, and a desk with many small

275

drawers. The walls were decorated with an assortment of sailing apparatus and knives of various lengths and sizes.

She caught a whiff of the food. She was hungry. No, she wasn't. She was queasy. The smell was going to make her sick. Sweat broke out on her brow. She stepped back. The pirate behind her pushed her back into the room.

"Othello, can we eat on the deck please?"

"It will be quieter here," he turned to say. Then he caught a look at her pale face. "Yes. Michael, can you bring the food?"

"I am not your servant." Michael stated. Othello didn't seem to hear him. He indicated Rabiah should go before him back to the deck where he bade her sit on a barrel next to a crate on the deck. Michael followed without the food.

"Better?" Othello asked.

"Yes. The fresh air helps."

"I'll get the food. I'll be right back."

Michael waited until Othello was in the cabin then said, "It's not going to work."

"What's not going to work?"

"Whatever it is you're doing."

"I'm not doing anything other than trying not to be sick." She closed her eyes and took deep breaths. Michael studied her. She did look a bit pasty. The waves weren't even that big. How could she be such a good fighter and such a weakling when it came to waves? Surely she hadn't been this sick all the time on her husband's boat.

Othello returned with the tray of food. He placed it on the crate and sat opposite Rabiah. It looked good. There was bread and eggs and ham and slices of orange. She picked up an orange slice and tried it. It made her think of Tristan and the oranges he had shared with her. She looked out over the water so Othello wouldn't see the tear that rolled down her cheek.

It was a slow start, but once she'd begun her appetite overcame her nausea and she ate heartily. Othello noticed. "You seem to be feeling better."

"Yes." Her mind was now able to focus. She looked at him. "Where are we going?"

"Back to Port Gresado. The priests want to speak with you."

"Why?"

"They want to know how you have both fighting and healing powers."

"There are priests in Arles. They can talk to me there."

"The ones in Arles aren't the ones who healed me or made the deal."

"What deal?"

"They agreed to heal me if my friends brought you."

"So you will take me back to my husband after we have spoken?"

"We can talk about the details later." He took a bite of food then said, "Tell me something. I've been wondering this since I met you. How did a Clangirl become a queen?"

"I married a prince."

He gave her an exasperated look, "Obviously, but how did you meet?"

She closed her eyes, remembering. "Fighting. I was the last of my people on the field. He challenged me. I was tired. He defeated me. I thought he was going to kill me but he kissed me instead." She smiled, remembering that kiss. "It was magical. He felt it too. I was injured. My leg was broken. He married me on the field to protect me."

"He defeated you?"

She opened her eyes. "Yes. He was fresh and I'd been fighting all day."

"So you're not invincible."

"Invincibility is not my gift."

He grabbed her wrist, or tried to. Her ring heated and his hand flew back.

"You're pretty close to it."

She shrugged.

Othello pushed his plate away and stretched. "I need to rest. I'll escort you back downstairs unless you want to come with me."

"Can I have something to clean the floor with or some sand?"

"A queen should not clean. I'll put you in a different room."

"Thank you, Othello."

Michael stepped back so Rabiah could rise. He'd been standing behind her with his arms crossed the entire meal.

She hated to ask, but she realized she had another problem, "Othello, is there some place I can go to relieve myself?"

"Oh. Yes. I'll take you to one of the passenger rooms. There's probably a pot in there."

She stood. The ship hit a larger wave. Nausea hit her again. She put her hand over her mouth and quickly sat back down again. Closing her eyes, she breathed in the fresh ocean air slowly and deeply.

"I think I'd better sit still for a while."

"Are you always like this when you're on a ship?" Othello asked.

"No."

"What's wrong with you then?"

She held up one wrist to display the copper bracelet.

"So that's where this is going," Michael said. "She's trying to get you to take the bracelets off. She's not really sick," he said as Rabiah made a sudden move towards the railing and threw up everything she'd just eaten.

She felt better. She hung over the rail and watched the waves, letting the mist splash on her face. What if she just jumped in? How far away was Tristan?

"Don't even think about it. The water is full of sharks," Michael said behind her.

She spit, to get the taste out of her mouth, then stood and turned. Othello was still seated behind her, watching her.

"Why would the bracelets make you sick?"

"They are blocking my husband's gift."

"And what is that?"

"He's been taking my sickness on himself so I don't feel as bad."

"He's been sick for you?"

"Yes."

"How close does he have to be?"

"I don't know. We haven't been this far apart since we've been married."

Othello pushed himself up. "Come on, I'll show you to the passenger quarters."

"She'll probably just mess it up," Michael said.

"So find her a bucket."

The passenger quarters were beneath the quarterdeck in the middle of the ship with a door to a short hallway that led to the lowest deck level. The room Othello showed her was small, but bigger than the dark little room she had stayed in the night before. There was a square window above the bed, a small, built in table beside the head of the bed, and a chair. There was also a chamber pot beneath the bed.

"My lady, your room," Othello said grandly, stepping aside so she could enter.

"Thank you."

"Is there anything I can get you?"

"Can I have another orange? Oranges seem to help."

"Of course. I'll get it myself."

"Thank you."

Michael shut the door firmly behind Othello, leaving her alone. She noticed the door could be locked from the inside with a hook. She left it unhooked and sat on the bed to wait for Othello. He returned in just a couple of minutes with an orange and a piece of bread. He handed them to her with a tender smile.

"I've got to get some rest so I can power the ship if the wind dies. I'll talk to you later."

"Thank you Othello."

He left, leaving a whiff of breeze behind him. Michael pulled the door shut again with a frown. She hooked the door shut on her side and finally had a chance to relieve herself. She dumped the pot out the window. The window was bigger than she had realized at first. She might be able to climb out. She stuck her head out and looked up. The rail was only a few feet above her. If she escaped, what then?

She needed to tell Tristan what she'd learned. She sat back on the bed with her knees out to the side and her feet crossed in front of her. She said a little prayer to the Spirit, then concentrated on reaching their special place. He was there, waiting for her. He hugged her tightly.

'*Are they treating you all right? I wanted to go down and check on you but I didn't want to pull you away at a bad time.*'

'*Yes. Othello had breakfast with me on the deck then I threw it all up. They took me to a room with a window because I threw up in the little dark one they had me in.*'

'*Othello? I thought he was dead.*'

'*He got a miracle. I was part of the deal. He's taking me to the priests in Port Gresado.*'

'*Why do they want you?*'

'*To talk to me he said.*'

'*Why go to all this trouble? You could talk to the priests in Arles.*'

'*I don't know.*'

'*What are they going to do with you after they take you to the priests?*'

'*I don't know. Othello said we could discuss that later.*'

'*Does Othello still have his powers?*'

'*Yes. He was using them all night I think.*'

'*Then we are farther behind you than I'd hoped.*'

'*I might be able to escape. The window to this room is small but I might fit. I'm only a few feet below deck.*'

'*There's nowhere to go. You'd still be on a boat full of pirates.*'

'*Perhaps I can find a way to slow down the ship.*'

'*Then you'd be on a boat full of angry pirates. If they're not hurting you, perhaps it would be better to wait. I will follow you no matter where they take you.*'

He kissed her then. How long it lasted she couldn't say. It was a kiss of longing and promise and rejuvenation. She could feel him taking her sickness upon himself. It wouldn't last she knew, but the fact that he did it made her love him all the more.

'*I have an idea,*' he said after he had finally pulled away. '*The sailor who can speak to dolphins is on board. Dolphins can travel faster than our ships and if he can talk to them, I bet they talk to each other. I will ask him if he can have a few dolphins follow the ship. If things get bad you can take to the water. Don't do it unless you're sure they are there though. There are a lot of sharks.*'

'*So I've heard. How will I know they're there?*'

'I'll ask him to make two jump at the same time.'

Something was pulling her away.

'I'll look for them. I have to go.'

'I love you always. Come back when you can.'

She opened her eyes. Othello was sitting on the bed right in front of her. Michael glared at her from the doorway.

"What are you doing here?"

"When you didn't open the door, I used a knife to raise the hook. What were you doing?"

"Sitting on the bed."

"I could see that. You were smiling so much you were almost glowing."

"Was I?" She smiled, thinking of Owen grousing at Tristan back on their ship.

"What were you thinking about?"

"My husband."

He frowned a little, then pulled something from behind his back. It was a little dark bottle with a stopper.

"I got this for you. It should help with your motion sickness."

"What is it?"

"I had our healer mix up a potion for you."

"That's very considerate." She pulled off the stopper and sniffed. She recognized the smell. It was the same potion Marion had given Tristan.

"Do you want to take some now? I brought some water."

"I'm feeling a little better right now, but I would like some water."

"He said you should take it every couple of hours even when you feel fine so you don't get sick again."

He clearly expected her to take the potion now. She sighed and handed the bottle back to Othello. "I appreciate you giving this to me but I can't take this."

"Why not?"

"One of the main ingredients is maiden weed. I can't take that right now."

"Why?"

"Because it can make a woman lose her baby. I don't want to lose mine."

It took a second for her words to sink in. "You're pregnant?"

"Yes."

"That's why you're sick?"

"Yes."

Othello stood, his face a mask, and stormed out of the room. A violent breeze blew her hair around her face as he pushed past Michael. Michael raised his eyebrow at her and shut the door. She stood and locked it again. It gave her a little privacy, although not much if it was that easy to open. She wondered if the copper bracelets could be unlocked with a knife. She reached for the knife in her arm holder. It was gone. They must have taken it when she was sleeping earlier. The ones hidden in her belt were still there. She poked the end of one knife in the lock and moved it around. Nothing happened at first. She kept wiggling and twisting, then finally heard a click. She kept turning the knife until the lock sprang open and fell off. She quickly started working on the other hand. It was easier this time and only took a minute to open. The door banged as something hit it from the other side. She hurriedly slid the knife back in her belt and stuffed the bracelets down the crack between the mattress and the wall. She was tugging her sleeves down when the door slammed opened violently and Othello came in. He shut the door behind him and locked it with the hook.

"Hi Othello. I thought you were going to rest."

"I couldn't rest. I keep thinking of you."

"Of me? Why?"

He took a step so he could stand over her on the bed. "Why is it I can't touch you and yet your husband managed to impregnate you? What did he do differently?"

"He is my husband."

"Not any more. I have bound you and claim you as my slave. You are no longer his wife."

"You didn't bind me. I bound myself. Doesn't that mean I'm my own slave?"

"You did it on the command of my first mate who told you to do it on my command, therefore, you are mine."

"That is some clever reasoning but I am not now, nor will I ever be yours," Rabiah said firmly.

The air started to swirl. Except for the orange, the bread, and the sheets on the bed, there wasn't much to blow around. She grabbed the orange before it rolled onto the floor.

"Othello, what are you doing?"

The wind died down. Rabiah pushed her hair back out of her face. Othello suddenly dropped onto the bed with her. "You said the kiss was magical. Maybe mine would be even more so."

"I suppose it's possible, but it's too late. I've already married Tristan."

"It's never too late." He pulled a knife out and pointed it at her. "Kiss me or die."

"That's not going to work."

"It will. I've bound your powers."

"You don't know what my gift is."

"You are a healer."

"That's only part of it."

"And a fighter."

"That's not my gift, at least, it's not the kind you are thinking of."

"Kiss me."

"No."

He slashed angrily at her with the knife. She leaned back quickly so that he completely missed her, then sprang off the bed. "Don't do this Othello."

Her back was to the door. She felt the air stir as it opened. An arm snaked around her from behind. Before it could touch her, Rabiah dropped and spun so that she was in the hallway behind Michael. She punched him in the kidneys and lower back. He turned towards her to fight back and she kneed him hard in the groin. He grunted and bent in pain. So he wasn't impervious to punches, just knives. She pushed him as hard as she could into the wall behind him. His arm hit the edge of the doorframe painfully and he fell.

Rubbing his arm, he made a sound like a growl before starting to stand back up. She looked quickly back at Othello. He was coming her way with the knife in his hand. Perhaps it was time to run. She slipped past Michael as he tried to grab her toward and ran for the door to the deck.

"I wouldn't do that if I were you." Michael said behind her.

Ignoring him, she ran out into the sunlight to the great surprise of three pirates working on the lower deck.

She couldn't get away from the ship. They would probably catch her, but while she was free she could do as much damage as possible. She took advantage of the pirates' surprise and grabbed the swords off the belts of two of them. The swords where long and curved. She'd seen some like them before but had never had a chance to use them. She ran up the steps to the foredeck and reached over the rail of the ship where the first large bottom sail was tied. She hacked at the cable holding the corner of the sail down. The sword was sharp. It sliced easily through the cable. Encouraged, she leapt up on the rail and ran back towards the back of the boat, hacking the cables for the middle and back-most sails. The rest of the pirates were starting to take notice. She managed to cut the second cable of the back-most sail before her forward path was blocked. She leaped and climbed up the net-like shroud that went up to the crow's nest.

The ship had three masts and each mast had three sails. There were also a couple of sails attached to the bowsprit in the front. The tops of the sails were stretched along wooden bars that were perpendicular to the masts. The bottom corners of each sail were tied to the top bar of the sail below. She climbed out on the first bar and cut the cable holding the middle sail. She repeated the process on the other side. Pirates were coming up after her. She climbed higher and slashed at the corners of the top sail. There was a cable from the rear mast to the mainmast. She cut the cable and swung to the bottom of the second sail on the mainmast. She was cutting the first corner when the first arrow whizzed by. She cut the second corner and climbed ahead of the advancing pirates. She freed the top sail. There was a cable tying the foremast to the mainmast but there were already pirates waiting for her. She didn't hesitate. If she could just cut one more sail, the ship would be that much slower. She cut the cable between the masts and swung, aiming directly at one of the pirates. He fell down a few feet but caught himself in the shroud. She didn't have time to get out on the bar to cut the second sail and get back so she climbed until she could reach the cables holding the sails tied to the bowsprit. The sails fell gracefully, their tips landing in the water. A gust of wind lifted her hair from her face. She looked down to see Othello standing in the middle of the lower deck, his hands pointed in her direction. She was not going to be caught at the top of a mast again in a windstorm. There was only one more big sail to take down and it was beneath her, billowing beautifully. It might be fun to jump on. She stuck the two swords in her belt on either side of her hips. If she fell, well, she just wouldn't fall. She reached into her belt with one hand for one of her throwing knives, grabbed onto the horizontal bar on top of the sail, and swung into the sail. It *was* fun hitting the puffy cloth. She stabbed the knife into the cloth. The sail started to rip as her weight bore it down. It was hard holding it in the cloth, even with two hands. The knife hit a seam and popped out. She fell, arms and legs flailing for a moment before her reflexes took over and she flipped so she could see beneath her. The bottom sail, whose bottom cables she'd already cut, billowed right below her. She fell into its white folds and grabbed hold. She slid down and was deposited on her feet neatly at the base of the bowsprit. The sail momentarily blocked her view of the rest of the ship, but once it blew back up, the view was not encouraging. A crowd of angry pirates with swords drawn stared back at her. Othello stood in the midst of them, his cloak and hair blowing in his ever-present breeze. Should she take to the water? How long would it take the sharks to find her? She could try to swim, but if the pirates could catch Owen, they could surely catch her. *'Great Spirit, what should I do?'*

She suddenly remembered she could talk to Tristan the way they normally did again.

'Tristan?'

'Rabiah! I can hear you again. How did you get the bracelets off?'

'With my knife.'

'What are you doing now? Your heart is racing.'

285

'I stopped the ship.'

'How?'

'I cut the ropes tying the sails down.'

'And the pirates didn't notice?'

'No. They noticed. They haven't caught me yet though.'

'Rabiah! I can't...We won't get there in time!' She could hear the panic in his thoughts.

'The Spirit is helping me. Don't worry. Are the dolphins on their way?'

'Yes.'

'Good.'

'What happened to waiting?'

'Othello tried to kiss me. I ran away and found some swords so I thought I'd use them. They're curved. I've never used curved ones before.'

'Be careful.'

'I will.'

Othello was advancing with his hands clenched by his side and his cloak swirling violently. The pirates moved out of his way. He climbed the steps to the foredeck and stopped in front of her. She pulled the curved swords from her belt.

"Come with me and I'll see that no harm comes to you."

"Will you try to kiss me again?"

"No." He unclenched and clenched his hands again.

"I don't want to be locked up again. I want to stay here."

"It is not safe for you here."

"I'm on a pirate ship. It's not safe for me anywhere."

"Come. With. Me."

"Stay here with me. You can rest and I'll sit right here. You can't use your power to sail the ship right now anyway."

The reminder made his cape flare higher.

"Come with me now or you will feel the full fury of my power."

"Where are you going to take me?"

"Back to your room."

It would be foolish to risk her life and those of her babes if she didn't have to. Perhaps she should go with him.

"Will you let me be?"

He gave a terse nod.

"All right. Lead the way."

"Put your weapons down."

"No. I won't hurt you if you don't try to hurt me."

"You have my word I won't try to hurt you."

"But not the word of the other pirates."

"I will protect you."

"I like them. They're curved," Rabiah said, holding up one of the swords and admiring the edge. "I won't use them unless someone tries to attack me."

"You are trying my patience. Put the swords down or I will turn the wind on you."

"Here, catch." Rabiah tossed him one of the swords. "I want to see what it's like to fight with one."

"I am not going to fight you."

"If you beat me I'll go with you."

"I can't beat you. It's your gift."

"No it's not. I've just had a lot of practice."

He was tempted, she could tell. She swung the sword around a few times to see how it felt, trying to entice him. Fighting or wrestling had always put her brothers in a better mood. She figured it would work on Othello too.

"All right. I'll fight you. But if I win you have to put the sword down when you come with me."

"If I win I get to stay here and keep the sword. Deal?"

"How are we going to decide who wins?" She noticed he hadn't agreed to her deal. No matter. Perhaps she could drag the duel out long enough for the dolphins to arrive.

"First person to yield or fall down."

"Not first blood?"

"You may not be able to cut me."

He nodded and raised his sword. She raised hers. He made a slicing motion. She countered. Fighting with a curved sword was more challenging than she had expected. It seemed to be meant for slicing rather than stabbing. Othello was good and obviously used to a curved sword. She had difficulty defending herself at first. He was pressing her closer and closer to the ship's railing. He was winning and he knew it. But she was learning. It took her a couple of minutes, then she seemed to become one with the blade. She liked the sound of them rubbing against each other. He was on the defensive now. The wind picked up.

"No using your gift. That's cheating," Rabiah protested.

"You're using yours."

"No I'm not."

"You can't be this good naturally."

"My brothers taught me. I was the Clan Champion for several years. I trained all the time."

Now that she knew how to use the blade, she could speed up. She had to work hard not to injure him.

"Yield Othello. Stay up here with me. I cannot be your wife but I'll gladly be your friend."

"I'm the captain. I can't lose in front of everyone."

"We could just call it a draw."

He was getting sloppy. She wasn't trying to hurt him, but she made a cut across his arm. He slapped his other hand over the cut.

"Sorry Othello. I didn't mean to do that."

The wind picked up again. "I can't lose. Yield to me."

"Can we stay up here on the deck?"

"Why? Why can't you just cooperate?"

"I like the fresh air and I did cooperate until you tried to kiss me."

They fought a couple of seconds more. Rabiah could have knocked him down, but she let the opportunity pass.

"All right. Yield to me and you can stay here."

She gave him a little smile and held the sword in front of her face and gave a little bow.

"But you have to give me the sword."

She tossed it to him. "Thank you for sparring with me."

"About time. Get her out of here," Michael ordered, storming up the steps.

"She's staying here," Othello said.

"She can't stay here. We have to fix the sails."

"I'll stay out of the way," Rabiah said.

"It's not going to work," said Michael.

"Why not?" Rabiah asked. "There's plenty of room on deck."

"No. Whatever you've done to Ralphy won't work on me."

"I haven't done anything."

"No? You bound his powers, you killed him, you sabotaged his ship, again, and yet he still seems to like you."

"I was only defending myself."

"How is sabotaging the ship going to help you?" Michael growled.

"You can't take me to the priests if the boat can't move."

"Why don't you want to speak with the priests?" Othello asked.

"The stones feel wrong. They feel evil. I don't like getting close to them."

"Perhaps the priests will agree to speak with you outside of the temple."

"Do they know who I am? Do they know I am the Queen of Arles?"

"Yes."

"Then why did they ask you to capture me? They could have just waited until I got back to Arles. I don't trust them."

"It doesn't matter what you think," Michael said. "You are our prisoner. You have cost us valuable time and therefore money. Get below or I will find a way to force you. Othello is not the only talented pirate on this ship."

"I will not. Othello made a deal with me and he is the captain."

"The last time he made a deal with you he ended up dead. I am overriding him on this one."

Rabiah looked at Othello. He shrugged.

"The reason our deal fell through the last time was because you didn't keep your word. Are you going to repeat the mistake again?" she asked him.

"I'll put you in the passenger quarters. You'll still have fresh air."

She heard something. Was it a dolphin call? She glanced behind the ship. Two bodies leapt from the water, their wet skin shining in the sun. Her rescuers! She could just run to the side and jump in, although it would be a long dive. There was still Othello. He would put up a fight when the other ships got here. It would be safer for all if he was incapacitated. Would that be against the Clan law if she put him to sleep although he wasn't fighting her? It wouldn't hurt him and they had kidnapped her.

She nodded. "Lead the way."

"Really?" He looked at her suspiciously.

She shrugged.

"You go in front of me." He pointed with one of the swords.

They walked down the steps. The pirates parted before them, staring at her menacingly. She smiled heartily at them. A whiff of something cooking floated her way from the galley. Her stomach rumbled. She hoped the orange and the bread were still in the room. She headed for the door under the quarterdeck.

"Not there."

She stopped and looked back at him. "Why not?"

"I still need to rest and I'll have to keep an eye on you for your own safety. Michael will be busy directing the repairs."

"Where then?"

"To my quarters."

"Othello," she said, a warning in her voice.

"I won't try anything. I promise."

"Why bother even saying it if you don't mean it?"

"I do mean it when I say it."

"Can I get the food you brought me first?"

"You're hungry?"

"Yes."

"All right."

He let her go ahead of him and grab the food, then he directed her up the steps to the quarterdeck. The captain's quarters where at the very back of the boat. He let her go ahead of him, then shut the door and locked it with a skeleton key which he took with him. He directed her to sit in one of the chairs near the small table, then lay down on his bed with the swords between him and the wall. Rabiah tore open the orange and savored it, then she ate the bread. She looked at him. Othello's eyes were closed. He probably wasn't asleep, but he was doing a good job faking it. She stood and went to look out the wide set of windows along the back of the ship. It was as if she was on the water with no ship beneath her. The dolphins were behind them.

'Tristan, I see the dolphins.'

'What's happening? Can you get to them?'

'I'm in Othello's quarters. He's sleeping, or pretending to.'

'You're where?'

'Othello's room. We have an understanding. I sparred with him using the curved swords. I think it put him in a better mood, but the other pirates were still angry. He brought me here so he could keep an eye on me while they fixed the ship.'

'He didn't try to touch you?'

'He can't. The ring won't let him. I'm going to try and put him into a deeper sleep so when you get here he won't be able to fight back.'

'Take care my love. We'll be there as soon as we can. The dolphins say we're only a couple of hours away.'

'Dolphins can tell time?'

'Not exactly. That's just the way the sailor interpreted it.'

"It's a nice view, isn't it?" Othello said from the bed.

"I thought you were sleeping," she said, turning away from the window to look at him.

"I can't with you in here."

"Am I making too much noise?"

"No. You are just distracting."

"Sorry."

"Come sit next to me and talk."

She obliged him, grabbing a chair from the table as she passed. "What do you want to talk about?"

"You. You've never told me your story, just bits and pieces."

"What do you want to know?"

"Tell me about your family. About your brothers."

"I have four. Three older and one younger." She told him a little about each one and about her niece and nephew. Othello was lying with one hand on his forehead and one hand dangling down over the side of the bed near her. His eyes were closed but he kept asking questions whenever she stopped talking. If she was going to put him to sleep, now would be a good time. She took his hand and started rubbing it. He lifted his hand off his eyes and looked at her in surprise.

"It used to help my little brother sleep, especially after my mother died."

"How did she die?"

"There was a flood. My little brother fell in. My mother jumped in to save him. She got him to the side, but a big tree swept her away. She was pulled out farther downstream, still alive. There was water in her lungs. She got sick and died a few days later. My husband almost died the same way."

"What happened?"

She told him while slowly pulling energy from him. He was very drowsy when she finished the story, but still had enough energy to talk.

"You're using your gift aren't you?"

"Yes."

"Why?"

"It will help you sleep."

"How long?"

"A couple of hours."

"If I had met you first, do you think you would be mine now?"

"No."

"Why?"

"First, you are a pirate. There is very little chance we would have ever met. Second, you steal from people. That is not the Clan way."

"You married your enemy on the battlefield. He was killing your friends. How is that better than a pirate?"

"I told you the kiss was magical. I could tell who he was from the kiss. Well, I didn't know he was a prince, but I knew the important parts."

"Maybe if you kissed me it would be magical."

"No. Tristan and I were made for each other. It's our gift."

"What do you mean?"

"We share a gift. Neither of us had one before we met. It was only when we found each other that we discovered it."

"What is your gift?"

"Each other."

He could barely keep his eyes open now.

"He's coming isn't he?"

"Yes."

"He's..." Othello's voice tapered off.

"Good night, Othello." She pulled enough energy off to keep him asleep for several hours.

There was a noise at the door. She put Othello's hand on his chest just as Michael opened the door.

"What did you do to him? Did you kill him again?"

"He's sleeping."

The pirate strode straight to Othello's side. Rabiah quickly scooted out of his way. He put his hand on Othello's chest to make sure he was still breathing, then tried to shake him awake.

"Why won't he wake?"

"I helped him sleep."

"How long will he be out?"

"A couple of hours maybe."

Michael let go of Othello's shoulder and turned to her. She did not like the look on his face.

"That's it. I am going to throw you in that smelly little room and lock the door until we get to land." He advanced on her. She felt the wall behind her. Perfect. She pretended to be scared.

"You can't touch me, remember?"

He stopped with a disturbing grin on his face. "I can't but I wonder if my friend can. Hugh, get in here."

Othello's other friend came into the room carrying a coil of rope.

"Let's see what you can do against him." Michael stepped back with his arms crossed across his chest.

The two ends of the rope started to snake toward her. How could one fight rope? He was using his gift, she would use hers. She ran lightly across the room, slipping between the loops of rope he

293

tried to stop her with, and put her hands on his shoulders. The rope ends followed her and wrapped around her arms and neck. Her ring heated. It kept the rope from getting tight while she pulled off his energy. Her neck and arms were almost completely covered by the time he collapsed in front of her. She shook the rope off her arms, and quickly unwrapped the rope from around her neck while keeping an eye on Michael. He noticed her eyes were now a brilliant green.

"Impressive." He went to the door and called to someone. "But useless against Chanthou. Other people's gifts don't work against him and he is an excellent fighter."

"We'll need more room then," Rabiah said.

"After you," Michael said, gesturing toward the door.

Rabiah went ahead of him as he indicated. She was feeling energized, almost too energized. She took the opportunity to release some of the energy into her mother's stone when Michael couldn't see. The pirate waiting for her was young, wiry, and looked fast. She was dismayed to see over half of the sails were already repaired.

"Here." Michael tossed her a curved sword and another to Chanthou.

"Before we begin, can I change into something a little easier to move in?" She was still wearing the long tunic she had worn to Lydia's wedding.

"It didn't appear to slow you down before."

"You don't know how fast I can move."

"Be my guest. You can wear something of Othello's."

She put the sword down on the deck and went back into Othello's room. Michael watched her from the door. She found a tunic in the chest and turned her back to put it on. She had pants and her wrap on under her long tunics so she didn't expose anything to him other than her still fading scars. Belt back on, she reemerged onto the deck with Michael following. She picked up the sword and swung it a few times before facing her opponent. He bowed then attacked her immediately, trying to catch her off-guard. She slid out of the way, watching him so she could get an idea of his skill.

Michael was smug, watching the odd girl avoid the pirate's knife. He had told him not to kill, but maiming would be appreciated.

Chanthou was going after her with enthusiasm. After a minute though, he had yet to touch her with the knife. Then she started fighting back. She *was* fast. Faster than Chanthou and she handled the blade like a master. Chanthou was now backing away. Somehow she got inside his blade. Chanthou went flying backward. His head hit the corner of the small boat stored on deck. Michael waited for the pirate to get up, but he didn't stir. He looked back at the girl but she was already gone. Where? Of course. She had already cut the corners of two of the sails they had just repaired. Why had Chanthou's gift not worked against her? In fact, how had she managed to put both Othello and Hugh to sleep with the bracelets on? She was at the bow now, cutting the jib sails loose again. It was going to be a lot harder to make repairs with Hugh asleep. She slid down the shroud to land on the foredeck. The pirates had only just realized what had happened. He watched as she tucked the sword into her belt and ran out onto the bowsprit. She turned to look directly at him, gave what must be a salute, then took hold of one of the fallen jib sails and slid down into the water.

Foolish girl. But maybe the sharks wouldn't be able to touch her either. He was loath to rescue her, but he didn't have a choice, not if he wanted to keep Othello alive. He yelled at his best swimmer to go after her. The swimmer ran to the rail, preparing to enter the water, but then stopped.

"I can't catch her."

"What do you mean? Don't tell me she has a swimming gift too."

"No. Dolphins. I can't catch a dolphin."

Michael raced over to the side of the boat. A small pod of dolphins swam by. The girl was in the center, holding on to the fin of one of the animals. He clenched his jaw and turned away. Why had he ever mentioned her to those priests?

"Fix the sails. Send the healer to the captain's quarters." Maybe the healer could wake Hugh.

Chapter 21

They traveled for at least half an hour. The dolphins took turns pulling her. They were very playful, leaping over her occasionally. She was so relieved to be off the ship, she couldn't help laughing at their antics. She sent a message to Tristan telling him she was on her way. The relief he felt on her behalf brought tears to her eyes.

Finally, they came to three ships under full sail heading directly toward them. Two of the dolphins leapt over her. A change came over the middle ship's sails. The ship slowed, then stopped. A dolphin dragged her near a ladder on the side.

"Thank you," Rabiah told all the dolphins surrounding her. She put out her hand and rubbed the skin of those who offered their sides to her. Her arms felt a little shaky after holding onto the fins for so long, but she held on as the long ladder was pulled up. Tristan was waiting. He took her hands and pulled her inside the ship, then hugged her close. He didn't let go for a long time and neither did she. When he finally pulled back there was a big smile on his wet cheeks. His front was all wet too from hugging her.

"I let you out of my sight for five minutes and you go and get kidnapped by pirates! Woman, what will I do with you?"

"Just hold me." He did. She was shaking. Someone put a blanket over her shoulders. Tristan pulled the blanket down to cover her more thoroughly. Then put his arm around her again. He kept it there even as they got underway again and as he spoke with the captain. She was glad.

They continued on their course. The pirates still had to be dealt with. Tristan escorted her to their cabin so she could change.

"That is a wicked-looking sword." She still had the curved blade stuck in her belt. "You fought with that?"

"Yes." She pulled it out and handed it to him so he could look at it.

"Where did you get that tunic?" he asked.

"I found it in Othello's chest. I couldn't fight in my long tunic."

"What happened to your neck?" Tristan approached her to look more closely

She felt it. "What's wrong with it?"

"It looks like a rope burn," he touched it gently.

"One of Othello's friends can control ropes. The ring kept it from getting too tight and I outlasted him."

"Oh, Rabiah." He took her into his arms again. She rested her head against his shoulder. Something warm and wet dripped onto her cheek. "When I couldn't feel you I thought you were dead. I could see our link but I couldn't follow it. That has got to be the worst, the worst night of my life. I couldn't concentrate. We were riding toward the dock with some of the princes when you reached me. Owen said I called your name then tried to dive off the horse. He had to grab my tunic so I wouldn't fall off. I was so happy that you'd reached me, that after I went back to my body I think I kissed him."

"Not on the lips I hope."

He laughed and kissed her with so much love and passion she forgot everything but him for a few minutes.

"Wow," she said between breaths when he finally pulled away, "maybe I should be kidnapped more often."

"Don't you dare."

It took less than an hour to reach the pirate ship. Tristan brought her a large plate of food and insisted she stay in their cabin and rest. Rabiah didn't argue. The ship Rabiah was on hung back while the other two disgorged sailors and soldiers who quickly subdued the pirates. The prisoners were split between the other boat from Arles and Yusri's boat. Tristan didn't want any of the pirates on the same ship as Rabiah lest they escape. Several of the sailors stayed behind to finish making repairs on the pirate's boat.

They arrived back at Ibirann's port city the next day. Rabiah and Tristan stepped off their boat as the first prisoners were being unloaded.

"What will become of them?" she asked Tristan.

"King Abbus will decide. They are his prisoners. I will ask that they be executed. I am tired of that pirate. He went too far."

"Tristan that is not our way. We cannot kill captured people."

"Rabiah, I can't go through that again. I must make sure it will never happen again."

"Let me talk to them."

"Rabiah."

"Please?"

He couldn't say no to her. They walked over to where Owen stood. He was overseeing the unloading of the prisoners from his ship.

"Good morning, Owen."

Mindful of where they were, Owen bowed deeply to her instead of hugging her but decided speaking to her would be appropriate since there was no one close enough to hear them. "Good morning, Warrior Queen. Nice work disabling the ship."

"Is Senna here?"

"No. I made her stay behind. She was quite upset with me." He sounded a little worried.

"I'm sure she'll be happy when she sees you arrive all in one piece."

"Owen," Tristan said, "Were the wind-mage and his cronies on your ship?"

"One is." He nodded to a line of prisoners tied together with rope. The one who had tried to capture her with ropes was in the middle of the line.

"He can control ropes. I'm not sure about chains," Rabiah commented.

Owen nodded and called to one of the sailors.

Rabiah and Tristan walked over to Yusri's ship. Yusri saw them and bowed politely.

"King Tristan, I am glad to see that your wife is safely with us again."

"Thank you for coming to her rescue."

"It has been very exciting since you arrived. I would like to hear how she escaped."

"Perhaps I can tell you later," Tristan said politely. "We are looking for the wind-mage and his close associate."

"The wind-mage is over there. I'm not sure who the other is."

"I am," Rabiah said.

Rabiah walked over to the men laid out on the ground. One was the fighter, Chanthou. A couple had stab wounds. There were several who appeared to be sleeping with no injuries at all. Then there was Othello and the pirate called Michael. Othello watched her approach. His hands were tied behind him.

"Is the wind-mage bound with copper?" she asked.

"We have taken the precaution of binding the man with copper," Yusri said to Tristan.

Michael was sleeping peacefully.

"This man here," she indicated Michael, "Told me he is impervious to metal. How did you capture him?"

Speaking to Tristan, Yusri said, "One of my sailors has the gift of singing people to sleep. His wife finds it a very useful gift when their children are fussy. The longer he sings, the longer people stay asleep."

"Queen Rabiah?" Othello said.

She looked back at him. "Othello." She could see the cracked black stone, and a second, whole stone hanging around his neck.

"Your husband came."

"Yes."

"How did he know where you were? Wait. I know. It is part of your gift."

"Yes."

"Some of the men told me what you did. You beat Chanthou."

She smiled, "Yes."

"And then swam away with the dolphins."

Her smile grew bigger.

"How many gifts do you have?"

"Just one in the sense you mean, but many from others."

Tristan cleared his throat.

"Othello, will you promise that you and your friends will not come after me again if I ask them to spare your lives?"

"Yes," he said, looking at her with sincerity. "Since I will be dead I may be able to keep this promise."

"What do you mean?"

"If we don't bring you to the temple I will lose my life again."

"How?"

"The priests will take it."

"How?"

Othello thought for a second, then looked down at the stones around his neck.

"That's a good question."

Rabiah remembered how eager the priest at one of the ports had been to question her about her miracle. She was curious too.

"Othello, what did you see when you died?"

"Nothing. Blackness. It was cold and dark."

"And when you were coming back?"

"There was a flash of light and I was suddenly back in my body."

"Is that when the stone cracked?"

"It must have been."

"When I died I saw my mother. There were clouds and a light farther off."

"You died?"

"I was stabbed in the heart. My husband and many others prayed for me. The Great Spirit let me and my children live." Subconsciously she put her hand on her belly.

"Who stabbed you?"

"A demon. I exiled him."

"You fight demons?"

"Only when they fight me. Goodbye Othello. May the Great Spirit watch over and guide you," she said sincerely.

"Goodbye my Queen." He bowed his head respectfully to her.

She turned to go.

"I don't trust him," Tristan said once they were out of earshot.

"I know, but he will have to escape prison if the priests don't find him first."

Carriages arrived from the palace. Rabiah and Tristan went ahead of everyone else with four guards in tow. No sooner had Rabiah's foot hit the ground at the palace, then an invisible force hit her and she was squeezed in a tight hug. Senna appeared before her.

"You are all right?"

"Yes."

"And Owen?"

"He's worried that you are mad at him."

"He's unharmed?"

"Yes. I don't think he even got to swing his sword."

Senna kissed Rabiah's cheek through her veil and disappeared.

She was greeted next by Niyaf and her daughter. They both hugged her. Rabiah was careful not to hug Niyaf too tightly. "You are unharmed?" Niyaf asked, holding Rabiah at arm's length as she surveyed her.

"Yes"

"But they aren't?"

"Yes."

"Good."

Lydia was standing next to King Abbus. She stepped forward next and hugged Rabiah. Rabiah was surprised to see tears in her eyes.

"I'm glad you made it back."

"Sorry this had to happen on your wedding night," Rabiah said quietly.

"It's all right," Lydia said, "There will be other nights." Lydia gave her another squeeze then whispered, "I liked the kissing."

They stayed another day so Rabiah could tell her story to King Abbus and his advisors. As she was a woman, they were not allowed to speak to her directly, so they asked Tristan the questions and she answered. She could tell they didn't quite believe her when she told how she'd sabotaged the ship and escaped.

They left the next day. They were still three ships strong even though one of the ships from Arles had long ago left for Arles. In honor of Rabiah's selfless action to save Queen Niyaf, King Abbus gave Tristan a ship. Considering King Abbus sent his chosen heir secretly on board by way of Senna and that the ship was built for speed and defense, Rabiah was sure the ship was not just a gift to honor her. Still, it was a beautiful ship. The wood was stained so dark it was almost black and it cut through the water more smoothly than any boat she'd ever seen.

King Abbus also sent the boy's tutor on board. He was an elderly man who had tutored King Abbus himself years ago. King Abbus declared to everyone that the tutor would be the new Arles ambassador and had already sent word ahead that the old ambassador was recalled. King Abbus didn't trust anyone else. The boat did not come with a crew. He'd seen there were enough crewmen on board the other two Arles ships to man a third and so assumed, correctly, that if he gave a ship as a gift, King Tristan would find a way to get it home.

Rabiah ripped off her veils and let the wind blow through her hair as soon as they were out of sight of the port. Tristan touched her hand as he walked by to retrieve something on the other side of the deck. Since they had fewer sailors, he was helping out and couldn't stop to watch the shore disappear, but he kept finding jobs close to where she stood. She grabbed his arm the next time he walked by and leaned back onto his shoulder. Perhaps he could watch for a second. The captain saw and shook his head. Women. This was exactly why they were banned from some ships. He motioned for another sailor to do the job the King was supposed to do. At least if the King was holding on to her, the Queen was less likely to be scampering all over the ship. He looked at them again. The ship seemed to fall away and he saw the Queen shining in white with huge white wings, a silver and crystal crown that reminded him of sparkling ice, and a silver sword. King Tristan stood beside her, resplendent in gold with a gold sword and shield and crown that sparkled in the sun. He closed his eyes and shook his head. When he opened them again, they were just a solitary couple standing on the bow of the boat with

302

the breeze blowing the Queen's tunic around their legs. Now what did that vision represent? That was the problem with his gift. Fifty percent of the time he had no idea what the visions meant. Some of it was obvious. The crowns meant leadership and they were already King and Queen. Wings meant protector which the Queen had already shown she was. He wasn't sure what the gold and white represented, but two people holding swords? There was a fight ahead.

Thank you for reading this book. If you enjoyed it, won't you please take a moment to leave me a review at your favorite retailer? Also, keep an eye out for the next book in the series. More on the next page.

Thanks!
- Lisa

Rabiah

Book 3

DEMON GOD

Lisa Lagaly

LL Publishing

Excerpt from Rabiah: book 3: DEMON GOD

"The evil one… has taken… notice of… your cousin," the old woman gasped suddenly from her bed. Her outburst was followed by violent coughing. The other occupant of the small room, a young woman with long hair dark only at the roots, rushed from the small table where she had been reading to the old woman's side to prop her so that she could breathe more easily. After the coughing subsided, the young woman held a wooden cup to the sick woman's lips. The old woman took a few sips, then lay back weakly.

"He doesn't know yet what she is, but he is suspicious. It will only be a matter of time," the old woman said, her eyes closed.

"I can't go now. You are too ill Grandmother," the young woman said.

"My time is nearly up. It will be good to leave this old body behind."

"So I can go?"

The old woman opened her cloudy blue eyes to look at her impatient grandchild. With effort, she managed to cover the girl's youthful hand with her own. "You must wait for the first flowers to bloom. I have seen it. Promise me you won't go until then."

"I will wait. I don't think I'd get very far right now anyway. The snow is too deep."

The old woman patted her hand and gave a weak smile. "You are wise my little one. When you go, take my ring to your cousin."

"But she has her mother's stone."

"It's not for her."

"But she already has three. Is it for the spirited one?"

The old lady smiled and patted her granddaughters hand once more before falling back asleep.

Made in the USA
Middletown, DE
09 October 2021

49964910R00182